CHAPTER 1

"Be careful, you say?" Raz asked, smiling at the man standing over him. "That's good advice for one-legged grasshoppers and worn-out old codgers like you. This young rooster's gonna go home, walk the streets of his hometown and wink at pretty girls 'til one winks back."

"You and your slick talk." Cato stroked his white beard. "You goin' home to kick butts and look for love, but not necessarily in that order."

"What's wrong with a man lookin' for some love? After two years out of the game, a man has to find out if all his important parts are still workin' right. But that'll have to wait. First, I'm gonna put on my jeans and hat, walk around the town square and greet folks. I'll have time to do lots of winkin' before I start kickin'."

"Even if your equipment's workin' as good as your mouth, won't keep the undertaker from finding' out if all *his* equipment work right." Cato leaned down to lace Raz's boxing gloves. "You won't be 'round ta see sundown on the second day if you goes back before your narc friend clean up Northville."

"How can he do that, if I don't give him your item?"

Cato threw a cautious look at others in the prison rec room. "Not suh loud. I ain't givin' you dat item 'cause I ready to die. Cleanin' up towns ain't my specialty, and I shore ain't givin' it to you 'cause I like no cops. I got nothin' for cops. You wanna know how to use it best, ask that narc that talked ya into smackin' that crooked deputy in the jaw so ya end up spendin' time wit me in dis hell hole."

Raz glanced at the convict audience. "Enough talk about the *item*. Too many ears in here. I want to walk out, not be carried out in a pine box. I always admired a man who speaks his mind, though, no matter how big a crook he used to be."

"You get lucky enough ta make it back home, 'member it weren't me messed up your town. Was dirty money and them dat love it. I ain't twisted nobody's arm to make 'em take nothin'. Them same crooked cops took that payoffs still in Northville. Better believe they willin' ta do whatever necessary ta keep you from tearin' up they playhouse."

"Surely you liked them crooked cops more than the honest ones. Otherwise, you would've cooperated with my narc friend, Lassiter. He could've got you a deal when he talked to you at Northville. Or later, when he bench-warranted you out of here. He could've sent those crooked cops and your former friends — the ones who burned you — down here to keep you company."

"Dat item'll take care of them that burned me and them crooked cops, too. I be doin' it for you, though, not them cops. Man's got the right ta change his mind 'bout doin' somethin' good, 'specially if a crazy man come along with the right plan."

"I'll get your sweet revenge, *after* I use the item to scare Tank Zelder and Olin Culpepper into arresting that son-of-a-bitch who murdered my wife. That's the reason I came down here. Remember?"

"Dat, and the pleasure of puttin' Tank Zelder on his butt on the courthouse steps."

"Your item is my life insurance policy 'til Tank delivers the killer and I find a way to get my little girl and my mother out of town. That has to happen before the narcs drop the bomb on Northville."

Cato stopped lacing the glove. "How long'll that take?"

"About three months."

"I ain't givin' you that item ta buy ya time ta chase no loose women."

"Spoil sport. Prison has killed your appreciation of the things that give life sparkle."

Cato nodded at the large man putting on boxing gloves opposite them. "Jus' be shore Loop don't snuff out *your* sparkler."

"Loosen up. The woman chasing can wait 'til I let Tank know I've got leverage. I'll let him know I won't give it to the narcs if he gives me what I want."

"You best tell Lassiter dat idea first time you see 'im."

THE BOYS from the BACK ROOM

CALVIN BOWDEN

PUBLISHED BY FIDELI PUBLISHING, INC.

ISBN: 978-1-60414-928-9

*This book is a work of fiction.
Any resemblance to any actual place, event or person,
living or dead, is purely coincidental.*

PRINTED IN THE UNITED STATES OF AMERICA

"Don't worry about that. After all, I can't wink at pretty girls if I'm dead."

"That what you be, you go back ta Northville."

Cato laced up the second glove. "It take mo' than big talk ta pull off what you got in mind, Mr. Razzle-Dazzle. You think life all fun and games, don't ya? You gonna find nothin' but misery waitin' for ya when ya step off dat bus in Northville, 'less you start seein' things da way they is, 'stead of the way you want 'em ta be."

"If you've got any more pearls of wisdom to lay on me, you'd better do it before our in-house ref clangs that starting bell."

"Greed a contagious disease, my crazy friend. Make sure *you* don't come down wit it when you starts puttin' heat on Tank. Might be ya get some offers ya can't refuse."

"As much as I hate dope and dope dealers? No way."

"Every man have his price. Don't matter how high they up the ante, don't forgets what you sposed ta do wit da little jewel in da heel o' Loop's boot."

Raz looked at the two pairs of prison shoes on the floor near them. "That won't be any harder than deciding which shoes I'm supposed to wear out of here after the fight."

"Ones you sposed to wear is da ones on the *left*. Dat item in the heel o' da right shoe. Note to my nephew in da other."

"Loop's got a foot as long as his arm and as wide as his fat ass. What'll I do when a boss notices my shoes don't fit?"

Cato glanced at Raz's large opponent, who had moved into the middle of the room and was jumping and swinging his large arms in preparation for the match. "Slick talker like you think o' somethin'. Right now ya need be thinkin' 'bout how ta keep Loop from killin' ya. He got long left hooks an' right haymakers."

"You couldn't find a smaller con to work on the shoes?"

"Loop the only one I met who have access shoe shop access. He won't do nothin' 'til I promise a shot at da prison heavyweight title 'fore ya leave. So far, he only been in prison brawls. He improve his image he if he beat ya."

"I could stand the punishment better if I knew for sure he put the item where you told him to."

"Loop a good friend o' my cousin in Dallas. She say ta trust 'im. Be more worried 'bout *you* gettin' it to the narcs 'fore Tank's Dixie Mafia make a corpse out o' ya."

"Easy on the corpse talk, gloomy Gus. Saving the item is the least I can do for you after you gave me part of what I came down here for. I won't keep my life insurance policy too long, but Lassiter can wait for it a little. If word gets out about the item before I get a chance to put it to good use…"

Cato tapped Raz's right glove. "Nothin' in life come wit a guarantee. There ain't nothin' for shore 'cept hurtin' and dyin', with a few good times slipped 'tween 'em, if a man lucky."

Raz eyed giant Loop Jackson. "Right now, it seems like I'm in for a heap of hurtin'. I hope I can still walk to the warden's office when he sends for me."

"Loop ain't any bigger than that deputy you laid out gettin' yourself here."

"It was his turn in the barrel."

"Guess a man wit that kind o' reasonin' entitled ta a trip home to get hisself kilt. I gives ya two days."

Raz gave his friend a concerned look. "You're only givin' me two days before the bad guys whack me?"

"Depend on ya gettin' out o' here first," he said as he took another furtive glance at the audience.

The inmates began booing as Raz stood up. "What're you concerned most about, me or that jewel in Loop's boot?"

"Ya knows by now convicts never do nothin' without gettin' somethin'," Cato replied, ignoring the restless spectators. "Won't deny givin' it to ya so I can gets me some sweet revenge. Saved my life, though, so I owes ya." His brown eyes bored into Raz. "Guess it's a tossup."

"You're all heart," Raz said, slamming his gloves together. "Maybe I should've let that con with the shiv finish you off last year."

Cato grunted. "Never thought I'd care what happen to a smart-ass white boy. Wonders never cease." He moved closer. "'Fore Loop scramble ya brains, wanna clear somethin' up. Yoa take on dat hit man ta save *me*, or for what ya wanna get from me?"

"You'll never know for sure, will you?" Raz smiled.

"Ain't you ever serious? Go on, an' let Loop knock ya fool head off. I don't care."

"Truth is, it all happened so quick, the *why* never entered my mind." He tapped his gloves together. "Satisfied?"

Cato's expression softened. "Sometimes ya slip up an' say somethin' sensible. Cleanin' up Northville an' findin' dat killer gonna be a tough job for anybody, sensible or otherwise. Don't mind ya usin' my tape for a insurance policy for a few days. Ya need all da help ya can get, startin' in the warden's office. They prob'ly be a reception committee waitin' ta pick your brains. Least one of 'em likely be a pipeline to them crooks runnin' Northville."

"Is that fact or just a gut feeling?"

"My gut always tell me fact, friend." When Raz glanced down at Loop's shoes, Cato added, "'Member, a man's shoes always buried with 'im or put in da undertaker's burn pile. That a fact."

"You're beginning to depress me." He waved at the spectators and stepped into the open space in the center of the rec hall. Over his shoulder, he told Cato, "Don't worry about me. I'm gonna give those crooks back home the fast shuffle. They won't even have time to cock their pistols."

"Yeah, if Loop don't kill ya first," Cato called back. "Move in fast. Tie 'im up quick an' wear him out 'fore he knock your block off."

"You gonna stand there all day like a crow eyeing a road kill or come out and let me reshape your ugly face?" Raz taunted Loop.

Raz knew at 5'10" and 175 pounds he was no match for Loop's 6'3", 300 pound powerhouse. Loop's body language announced his eagerness to become the new heavyweight champion of the sprawling Texas prison system, and Raz was counting on that overconfidence to give him an edge. He knew he'd have to use all the boxing skills Zeke Lewis taught him during his junior year at Northville High. Those skills had finally let him beat the older and larger school bully, Tank Zelder, later that school year. Those same skills also won him the unofficial heavyweight championship of the general prison population before he was transferred to the Administrative Protection Unit.

Raz raised his gloves and moved toward Loop, ready to find out how much punishment he would have to suffer to be able to smuggle the Cato's mini cassette tape out of the prison. He was no stranger to physical violence —he'd played football in high school and during his first year at the University of Texas — but nothing could've prepared him for the brutality and depravity he encountered in state prison.

Things weren't much better in the Administrative Protection Unit. He and his cellmate ended up here after Raz saved Cato from a paid convict assassin.

The referee rang the bell and Raz approached his opponent. "Okay, lard butt. Come closer so I can make the birdies sing for you."

Loop moved toward him. "Dat razzle-dazzle won't work on me, funny man. I gonna turn off your lights." Perspiration was already running off Loop's face as he raised his massive left arm and went into a boxer's crouch.

The spectators cheered and clapped. They'd all heard how Loop got his nickname — he had arms as long as the West Loop around Dallas, his hometown. He'd never lost a prison brawl.

Raz began dipping and weaving. A lumbering Loop pursued him, trying to get close enough to land a punch. Soon, he was impatient, and surged forward with a wild right. Raz ducked and slammed two quick left jabs to his rib cage.

Loop dropped his guard with a grunt, allowing Raz to hit his face with a quick left hook. Loop grunted again and shook his head, apparently stunned. He kept moving though, even though he was mumbling incoherently.

Raz continued to duck and weave as he moved quickly around Loop, who maintained his clumsy pursuit, breathing hard. Loop swung a wide left, which Raz ducked under before landing a hard left of his own into Loop's big belly. Loop again dropped his guard and Raz staggered him with a hard right to his jaw, earning both cheersand boos from the audience.

Loop recovered quickly, raised his gloves and moved in again, still mumbling. With a sudden giant step forward, he swung another left hook. Raz stepped aside, allowing the blow to bounce off his left glove, then resumed dancing, egging Loop on with a knowing smile.

"Quit chasin' 'im, dummy!" an inmate yelled. "Cancha see he just wearin' ya down?"

"Yeah, move in an' kill his ass!" another yelled. "Jus' smother him wit a kiss!" Everybody laughed at that.

"Y'all dancin' or fightin'? Pretend he a cop!"

Loop swung another left hook, then a wild right, but Raz sidestepped and ducked, each time returning with a hit to his opponent's big belly. Moments later, the winded Loop threw his arms around Raz in a giant bear hug.

A spectator moaned and shouted, "Why doncha quit rubbin' bellies an' start boxin' for God's sake?"

Ignoring the taunts, Loop rabbit-punched the back of Raz's head and growled, "Stand still an' fight fair. We ain't on no damn race track an' I ain't no quarter horse."

"You won't be the prison boxin' champion, neither, unless I take a dive," Raz snapped.

Loop slammed another blow into the back of his head and Raz landed a right against Loop's left kidney. Loop grunted, tightened his bear hug and said, "Cato show you which shoes ta wear out o' here?"

"Yeah. You delice 'em for me?"

"Little itch ain't as bad as them corns I get from wearin' yo' sissy shoes." Loop slammed a left against the side of Raz's head.

Another wave of groans and shouting came from the audience, causing Raz to glance around him. Six of the cons he saw were ex-narc cops . Some were were in for being on the take, or stealing confiscated drugs. Two were former city detectives who'd brutalized arrestees and lied to the grand jury about it. All ex-law enforcement officers sent to prison were housed in special units for their protection — convicts hated cops.

Raz jerked free and hit Loop's belly, but before he could jump back, Loop connected with his head. Raz staggered and Loop lunged forward to deliver a knockout punch. Raz ducked and slammed a quick left-right combination into Loop's midriff. Still dazed, Raz threw his arms around Loop. The spectators cursed and screamed.

Trying to pull free, Loop grunted, "You ain't my type. Save dat huggin' for one o' them bus station party hoes."

"Just wanted to let you rest a while, lard butt, so you can have enough steam to go at least two rounds before I put you down."

"Ha! You 'fraid I make yore champ ass look bad on you last day inside. Take a fall an' save yore strength for dem party girls."

Straining to keep Loop from breaking free, Raz said, "I hope my shoes make corns on your toes as big as those Caddy hubcaps you used to steal."

Loop jerked his right arm free and hit the back of Raz's head, causing him to stumble and drop his arms. Shaking his head to clear his vision, Raz put up his guard against another wide right, then stepped forward and wrapped his arms around Loop again. Another loud moan came from the crowd.

Raz told Loop, "Think you're pretty cute don't you, lard butt? Catching me with that lucky punch. You told Cato you'd fight by the rules."

"I lie," Loop grunted. "Ya know how all us cons lie."

An inmate jumped up and shouted at Raz, "What kind a damn champ is you? Hell, I can whip you myself! Outta the way, Loop!"

Raz looked at the man, one of the ex-narcs from Dallas. "Sit down, Blues Man. Can't take on but one loser at a time."

The bell sounded to end the round and they walked to a row of empty chairs nearby. Sitting down, Raz leaned over and told Loop, "You're as full of manure as a deer camp outhouse, but I hope I can trust you to to do me a favor. Promise you'll look out after Cato."

"Can't do much for 'im 'less they make us roommate when ya check out."

"If you both request it, they will." He wiped a towel across his face. "I don't know how any man with all his marbles can get tight with a crook like you, Loop, but I'm gonna miss you. Cato, too. How much more time you got in here?"

"Three years, if I good," he replied, shaking his head.

"How can you be any other way if you can't get dope or a wild woman?"

"You know better'n that, 'bout the dope, I mean. Bein' without a woman the tough part. Just ain't natural."

"You're right about something for a change. When a man's bed sheet turns into a teepee every time he sleeps on his back, it's time he was sent home."

"Gonna be borin' as hell in the unit without you ta stir shit up. Sometime, I rather be dead than here."

"Tell the boss to put you back in general population. That gang you you ratted on'll take care of that for ya."

Loop looked at Cato. "Cato already axe for a transfer. He fed up, too. He make it in general, I knows I can."

Surprised by Loop's remark, Raz approached Cato. "Tell me you're not serious about leaving administrative protection."

"They transferrin' me ta the old folks wing at Wynne," Cato said with a nod. "I be in the libary. Safe enough job." He didn't look at Raz.

"That's stupid. You transfer out, the mob'll get you for sure. Refusing to cooperate with Lassiter when he bench-warranted you out right after you got here won't help you neither, 'cause all the cons think you talked. Your old bosses and the ones who tried to get you killed prob'ly think the same thing. That new gang thinks you can hurt them, too."

"I cain't keep you from goin' ta Northville, so you's dumb as me. Look sideways at Tank Zelder, he gonna shoot you dead. He the High Sheriff now."

Raz's mind flashed back to the events that earned him his two-year sentence. "Not goin' back home would be like admittin' I don't wanna live anymore, and you know how much I like living."

"Man have the right ta choose where he gonna die. Savin' me at Ellis put ya on the hit list. 'Member dat when the man call you ta his office an' you find out he not in there by hisself. They be lined up like hungry buzzards waitin' for ya ta spill ya guts 'bout what you learn from me. What you say'll beat ya home ta Northville."

"You never let up on the gloom and doom stuff, do you?"

"Ever'body waitin' for ya in da warden office think you bound by dat deal you make wit Lassiter. They think you tell 'im everythin' ya get from me. 'Fore ya start talkin' ta anybody, 'member dis — gangsters don't stay on top 'cause they stupid, an' dat include Tank Zelder and Chief Olin Culpepper."

Raz touched the scars on the left side of his face and throat, his 'Ellis souvenirs.' "Considering the lists I was on before I came to this stink hole, getting on one more won't really matter. It'll bring the number to at least four. Never did like uneven numbers."

"Never like playin' poker wit jokers like you. Maybe my nephew, Snake, help you out in Northville. After ya give 'im my letter, he spread da word 'bout ya bein' back. Community know what ya do for me; they help you. Still got contacts in Houston. Snake know some of 'em. Jus' don't tell nobody you still workin' wit Lassiter."

The bell rang, but Raz kept his eyes on Cato. "How do I know your nephew hasn't been bought by the ones that had you put away?"

"A man can work for two bosses, long as he only work for one at a time. Snake don't have much pull wit dat Dixie Mafia man overseein' Northville. Dat bunch ain't keen on workin' with the brothas. What he got goin' most likely done on the QT. That don't keep him from lovin' money. Tell him my offer still stand on dat snitch Mazurka — ten grand ta take him out for puttin' me in here. Tell Snake keep an eye on dat Mazurka partner, Smeddish. That Dixie bunch meaner than dat bunch I work for."

"Nothing for the woman that set you up, if I find out who she was?"

Cato looked away as he always did when Raz brought up that particular subject. "Who you know to get in so good with the Mexican dope dealers? You must've done something that really pissed them off."

"Weren't no Mexican woman took me down. Mexican don't turn on folks dat straight wit 'em. Got da right attitude, you do okay ta work for 'em. They walk da straight line; they good."

"Any brothas workin' for the Dixie bunch now?"

"Naw. Snake tell me he do lots o' beggin' and butt kissin' 'fore a friend let 'im have a little action. He do most o' his bidness on da sly through dat Houston friend o' mine."

Loop stood up and called out to Raz, "Didn't ya hear the fuckin' bell? 'Less you turn chicken, come on out an' let me get my title."

As Raz turned toward Loop, a key rattled in the hall door and a young guard entered the room. He called out, "Raz Jester, come with me on the double. Warden's waitin'."

The audience booed loudly.

"What 'bout da fight?" Loop moaned as Cato began unlacing Raz's gloves. "Don't take 'em off, Cato. We ain't through yet. He owe me a fight."

Over his shoulder, Raz told Loop, "Let me know when you get out and I'll come to Dallas to finish it, unless your old pals get to ya first."

Loop shook his head and stamped his foot as Cato slipped off the second glove. "Ain't right, man. Ain't right."

Raz sat down and picked up Loop's big shoes. After tying the laces, he stood up and reached for his shirt with an anxious glance at the guard.

Cato held out his hand, and for the first time since they met, he looked scared. "Good luck, brother."

"Same to you, my friend. And thanks for the… you-know-what."

Raz buttoned his shirt on the way to the door. Stopping there, he turned, clasped his hands over his head in a boxer's victory salute and said, "Still the prison heavyweight champion…"

CHAPTER 2

Walking briskly beside the guard, Raz asked, "What's gonna happen in the warden's office, boss? Anybody in there with him?"

The guard said nothing and didn't slow his pace. They took the elevator to the first floor and walked to the end of a long hall, stopping in front of a huge mahogany door. The guard knocked lightly.

"Come in," a deep voice responded.

Following the guard into the room, Raz saw four somber-faced men sitting in front of a large desk. They all turned their cold eyes on him as he entered. Ill at ease facing so many strangers, Raz stopped just past the line of chairs to look for the one face he hoped would be there. Drew Lassiter was in the last chair.

Raz smiled at the row of grim faces and said, "Who died?"

The men exchanged puzzled looks as Raz added, "I hope it wasn't the warden, because he promised me a one-way ticket out of this five-star hotel."

A tall, gray-haired man entered through another door, sat down in the high-backed leather chair behind the big desk and said in a deep, assertive voice, "I'm Warden Edsel Poag." Pointing to an empty chair, he added, "Have a seat, Jester."

Raz remained standing as the warden told the others, "Boys, I'll take that steak you owe me the next time you're up this way." He looked at Raz. "I had a bet with them about whether the first thing out of your mouth would be a smart-assed comment."

Raz studied the four faces as he walked to the vacant chair. He nodded, but none of them responded except Lassiter. As he sat down, he recalled Cato's warning, and asked himself, *Which one of these guys is Tank Zelder paying off?*

The warden glanced at some papers in front of him and pointed at the middle-aged man with the big belly and bald head sitting on Raz's left. "This is Horace Stalker," he said. "He's with the state attorney general's office. I believe you've met the gentleman next to him, Drew Lassiter, supervisor with the Department of Public Safety, Narcotics Division."

Lassiter leaned forward to offer his hand. "Good to see you again, Raz."

Forty, and tall with grey eyes and thinning brown hair, Lassiter had a sincere expression on his wide face, long-nosed face. "Raz, that homeless-lookin' dude with the greasy hair on your right is Denny Schroeder," Lassiter said. "He's with the DEA. The gentleman on the end is Jim Vandiver, with the FBI."

Both men nodded, but only the slim, mid-twenties DEA agent offered his hand. His handshake was strong, which was surprising considering his bedraggled appearance. He apparently hadn't shaved in over a week, and his shoulder length brown hair hadn't seen a brush for days. His worn-out blue jeans and baggy gray T-shirt with a pot leaf on it didn't give Raz an instant feeling of confidence in the man.

The FBI agent, dressed in a dark blue suit, white shirt and black tie, was older and heavier than Lassiter. He had dark brown hair, brown eyes, and a bored look that told Raz he didn't like convicts.

Lassiter continued, "I'm sure you remember what I told you about the taskforce your old friend Pop Cheever set up before he retired. He had high hopes it would help fight organized crime in Eastman County and the surrounding area. I just told these gentlemen that Pop was the one who recommended you for this gig. Horace Stalker, there, heads up the taskforce now and he's here to listen to your report. He has to bring the governor up to speed now that you're out."

Lassiter's disclosures in the presence of strangers knotted Raz's stomach, but he remained outwardly calm. Nodding, he told Lassiter, "Mr. Stalker can tell the governor I'm looking forward to being a free man again so I can go home and catch up on some *real* living."

A look of disbelief swept over Lassiter's face. "We didn't come here to listen to your jokes. The governor's not interested in your personal affairs, either. He and that committee want a report on what you've found out. We need to get this thing up and running before the gang's contacts in Northville catch on to what we're doing."

"Is that all?" Raz smiled. "I was afraid you got together so you could tell me it's against the law for an ex-con to have sex."

Schroeder laughed, but the others remained stone-faced. Lassiter leaned forward and said bluntly, "Skidding around, Raz. This is important."

"So is getting out of this shit hole. I really appreciate you guys showing up to see me off and all, but a simple wave as the van drives off is good enough for me."

"I said *stop clowning around*," Lassiter snapped. "We're here to get your report and we hope it'll save you from some hard licks down the road. We don't want word to get out that you're going back to Northville tomorrow with your head full of information from Cato."

Has my release date already leaked? he wondered. *Lassiter's thinks I only got heresay from Cato.* "A little ol' statement from me is all you guys want? What a relief. I was beginnin' to suspect you were gonna tell me all outgoin' busses broke down and all the mechanics went home."

Schroeder snickered, but Lassiter's expression told Raz the agent was really aggravated now. "Get real, Raz," Lassiter said. "This is serious business we're involved in."

"So is living," Raz said, suddenly solemn faced. "I've always been dead serious when I say I'm goin' somewhere to enjoy life for a change. In fact, I'm so anxious 'bout that right now my memory just went blank. It always does that when somebody tries ta make me talk 'bout somethin' that'll get in the way of my good livin'."

"This smart ass isn't ready for release, warden," Vandiver said. "There's not a speck of remorse here. I should be working on some important discrimination cases in this redneck county instead of wasting my time listening to him crack jokes."

"Warden," Lassiter said, "do you have a place where I can talk to Raz alone for a minute?"

The warden nodded toward the door behind him. Looking beyond his guests, he said, "You can leave now, Oscar."

Surprised to find the guard had remained in the room to hear what was said, Raz whirled around to see the young man give him a knowing look before leaving.

Raz turned to the warden. "What's that guard's name?"

Lassiter stood up. "He's nobody for you to be concerned with, just one of the correctional officers working in administration. Come with me."

Feeling like a canary surrounded by a room full of hungry cats, Raz followed Lassiter to the next room, determined not to spoil his plans for using Cato's tape for his own benefit before giving it away.

Closing the door, Lassiter said, "What the hell are you trying to pull, Raz? We had an agreement. That agreement is still good, which means you're still working for me."

"Our agreement didn't say a thing 'bout me spillin' my guts in a room full of strangers when I was discharged. You want to get me killed on my first day out?"

"I told you your job would be risky."

"I can stand risky, but not stupid. This would guarantee me a quick funeral. I don't know those guys in there and I don't trust Oscar. Anything I say could immediately get to the wrong people in Northville."

"Who said?"

"Cato said. And I believe him."

"So, Cato *did* give you some good information?"

Raz nodded. "Even if it's what you need, I won't tell you about it here."

"You should tell me while it's fresh in your mind. The warden has a secretary waiting to transcribe your statement, plus we'll have all those witnesses."

"It'll be safe with me for now."

"It's not all in your head? Is it a written statement? Give it to me."

"I can't, not here. It's my life insurance policy 'til I take care of my family and some other business in Northville."

"What're you planning to do, cut some kind of a deal with Tank and Olin? You can't use Cato's statement to make bargains. It belongs to me."

"Wrong. At this point, it belongs to yours truly. I'll get it to you in a few days."

"What about the governor's pardon? You don't want to jeopardize that, do you?"

"Nope. But nothin' is more important than gettin' home in one piece and having a little time for myself before you hit the hornet's nest with a big rock."

"My gut tells me there's something else making you hold back."

"Since I'll be dependin' on you moving in later, I'll tell you this. Remember when I said the only reason I'd take a fall and come down here was the hope of findin' out who butchered my wife? You assured me that the only man who could help me was Cato Hamilton."

"That's right. He wouldn't give us squat in the Northville jail or when we bench-warranted him out. He's a tough old buzzard."

"He talked to me."

"But not before you saved his life, right? Sorry you got hurt doing that, but it was a lucky break."

"Yeah, right. Now back to our agreement. I wanted the name of the killer and you wanted information 'bout drug trade. It seemed like a good plan at the time. The problem is, Cato doesn't know who killed Patti. I didn't get what I came down here for, so why should I put my life on the line upholdin' an agreement that only helps you?"

Lassiter was silent for a moment. "That's it?"

"Isn't that enough? I have to keep what Cato gave me to scare Tank and Olin into givin' me what Cato couldn't. If my plan works, it'll make takin' the fall worthwhile and mean I didn't waste the last two years of my life."

"I see." Lassiter rubbed his chin. "Getting the name of your wife's killer was only *part* of our agreement. You also wanted to clean up your hometown and send Tank Zelder to prison. What about your old friend, Pop Cheever? He helped set up the special taskforce to fight drugs, and he's the one who told us you were the only man for this job. You don't want to let Pop down, do you?"

"No, I don't. I'll explain things to Pop when I get home. I'll help get my town cleaned up, but not 'til I get what I need out of this. I figure I've got first rights, since it's my life on the line."

"I could have the state attorney general call a special grand jury and subpoena you."

"And I'd say Cato didn't tell me a damn thing."

Lassiter's face flushed. "We can't make a move until you give us Cato's statement. The quicker we get it the better. It'll take us a while to decide which parts are admissible evidence. Not having it will put us in a bad position with the governor's commission and my boss. We know the Dixie Mafia put Cato's organization out of business and we know they're selling drugs from Brownsville to Texarkana, but we don't have enough hard evidence to crack down on anything but small-time dealers. That's why we've *got* to move fast. We need to know who the head man is and who's in charge in the Northville area."

"What if you don't get all of that from Cato's statement? I'm not sure what he put in it. It might only be about Northville and Eastman County."

"It'll still work, because when we put the pressure on the locals and get some convictions, the rest of the outfit will fall like a house of cards. We have to come up with some real evidence soon to stop the governor and attorney general from dissolving the taskforce. If they do that, it'll put us back at square one."

"I need three months."

"*Three months?* I'm disappointed. Two years ago I thought I'd finally found the man I needed to make this happen."

"Look at it this way," Raz said, "I'm not lettin' those crooks off the hook. I'm puttin' them on notice and making 'em sweat for a few days before your boys move in."

Lassiter pulled a card from his shirt pocket. "When you get it through that thick Irish head of yours that you can't make deals with crooked cops, give me a call. Stay out of Tank Zelder's way and put your private war with him on hold. He set you up for Tim Barton's murder because you were getting too close to his money-making schemes. He'll set you up again, that is if he doesn't shoot you first."

"You don't think I'm gonna let a Northville tradition die, do you?"

"You'd better, because this time it'll be your turn in the barrel."

Raz followed Drew back into the warden's office where Agent Vandiver was saying, "I don't care if he does have an IQ of 130 and is the hottest lady's man in Northville, we can't take any action on anything he tells us, no matter how good it sounds. He's too much of a flimflam man to be trusted."

When they stopped near the warden's desk, Horace Stalker said, "You have an unusual first name, Jester. Is Raz your real name?"

"Rumor is he was so good at giving everybody the old razzle-dazzle, his everybody started calling him Raz and the name stuck," the warden said. "He excelled in sports under that name, even when he was young. In high school, he was the star quarterback, and also lettered in track, basketball and baseball. He even got a football scholarship to the University of Texas."

"Well, la-dee-da," Vandiver quipped. "Sounds like a real all-American hero to me. From what I've seen here today, though, I think they should've nicknamed him Bozo. Tell us your real name for our records, clown, so we can get out of here and work on something important."

"From what I hear," the warden said, "nobody calls him by his real name unless he wants a bloody nose. It doesn't even show up in official records. He's been called Raz for so long it's become his legal name."

"Raz and I have a disagreement on when he'll fulfill his part of our agreement," Lassiter said. "I'm convinced he has what we need, but he wants some time to get things in order back home before dropping the bomb."

Schroeder nodded, telling Raz, "Take your time and be careful, pal. It's a jungle out there. The DEA might be able to use what you got from Cato. Let me know as soon as you think it's safe to give it up. Don't take too long, though, because without some real evidence, politically powerful people in Northville and Austin won't let Lassiter move in."

"Northville's just the tip of the iceberg," Lassiter said. "The longer we wait, the bigger it grows."

"Nobody up there is more powerful than your ex-father-in-law, right Raz?" the warden asked. Turning to the others, he added, "The record shows that Raz's deceased wife was the daughter of Isham Lawther. He was so upset when she married Raz that he disowned her and vowed to make Raz pay for ruining her life."

Raz resented the warden for revealing details of his personal life, but thought it best not to criticize the man who was about to give him his freedom. *Cato was right. These vultures will pick my bones and throw them to the wolves in Northville.*

Raz watched as everyone but the warden filed out of the office. When Lassiter reached the door, he turned and gave Raz thumbs up. "I'll be waiting for your call, Jester. Just don't get your ass into a crack we can't pull it out of." He closed the door.

Turning to the warden, Raz said, "Right now, I'm more concerned about livin' through the night. You guys have really put me on the spot."

"That's why I'm sending you straight to one of our southern units," the warden said.

"I was hopin' you'd let me call Fran Druman, my business partner in Northville. She could pick me up."

"Lassiter and I agreed we can't risk having anyone in Northville know your release date. I hope you didn't tell her."

"Haven't seen or heard from her in over a year. What about my things?"

"Your shaving gear and some extra clothes are in a box outside the door. You want your old guitar?"

"I gave it to Cato."

The warden approached him. "We'll kill two ducks with one shot by sending you south to Clemens. It'll keep you from having to spend the night here, and it'll keep you away from the shooters waiting for you at the Houston bus station."

"When will I go to the station?"

"After you spend the night down south under an assumed name. There won't be anybody on the bus who's served time in a unit with you or had anything to do with that attack on Cato."

"How 'bout Oscar? Can we trust him?"

The warden nodded. "He's been here for three years. Haven't lost a releasee during that time." He smiled.

"You guys are makin' a lot of fuss over a man who might be dead by sundown day after tomorrow."

"Who told you that?"

"Just convict talk." Raz smiled. "They all found out I was leavin' somehow."

"That won't hurt anything, as long as it doesn't get outside the unit." Raising his voice, the warden said, "Okay, Oscar, you can come back in now."

The guard stepped into the office, giving Raz another knowing look before he stopped in front of the warden's desk. Something about his expression increased Raz's fears of getting out of the unit alive.

CHAPTER 3

Raz kept an eye on his fellow passengers, as he rode on the bus going to Clemens Unit. He kept checking to see if anyone had an extraordinary interest in him. He didn't recognize anyone, but any of them could've been there when he jumped into the fight to save Cato. The paranoia was uncomfortable. On top of that, the strangers from the warden's office as well as Oscar's suspect behavior had him spooked. He wished his trip home had started in a more positive way.

The bus finally arrived at the pre-release unit just after dark. A middle aged man dressed in a blue business suit led Raz down a long hall to an empty cell. "You'll be known as Tom Lysinger while you're here," he said. "You'll remain here, alone, until you're escorted to the prison van in the morning."

Within the hour, a guard brought Raz his evening meal, a bar of soap, washcloth and towel, a change of underwear and a clean grey shirt. He didn't want anyone to find Lassiter's card on him, so he memorized the number, tore it up and flushed the pieces.

After that, he ate, dropped onto the cot and tried to push his personal safety concerns to the back of his mind. He was anxious to see his four-year old daughter, Becky, and his business partner, Fran Druman.

He'd always believed that what is to be, will be. Worrying about what *could* happen was a waste of time. That didn't stop him from worrying about Cato's warnings, the strangers in the Warden's office and Lassiter's angry denunciation of his failure to deliver Cato's statement.

His probable imminent demise and all the people reminding him of it made him wish he'd never taken the important things in his life for granted.

Every time thought like this, he wondered what had triggered such a drastic change in his perspective. Before his life began falling apart three years ago, he'd concentrated solely on things that led to him having a good time.

He'd always dreaded getting to the time in his life when he'd lose his lust for living. He hoped that time wasn't now and became more anxious to be done with finding the murderer and getting rid of the crooked lawmen and dope dealers.

Alone in this quiet room with nothing to do but think, he found it impossible to keep his mind from revisiting the choices he'd made and the uncertainty of his future. Everything was connected to the tragic events that followed his marriage. That's when his perception had changed.

I hope going home will banish all these gloomy notions. I'm tired of being angry at Tank Zelder and Olin Culpepper for not finding Patti's murderer and for arresting me on a trumped-up murder charge when I tried to find him on my own.

He sighed, recalling the additional responsibilities thrust on him immediately following his graduation from NHS. Marrying Patti and becoming a father were the highest points in his life, and gave his life a depth he never would've known otherwise. He had no regrets about either, but the tragedies following these events had rocked his world. The failure of his marriage and his wife's drug addiction and subsequent murder had pulled him down hard. Prior to that, he remembered being a happy-go-lucky person who was able to overcome any setback.

While in high school, he'd dated lots of pretty girls, but Anita McKnight was his only serious girlfriend before he started going seeing the vivacious and beautiful Patti Lawther. He was totally dedicated to Patti, and stayed that way even after their marriage fell apart. He was as equally devoted to their child when she came along. Becoming a father was a sobering but happy experience, and for a short time, life was good. That was before Patti found drugs, before the devastation of divorce, before her death.

Following Patti's death, Raz was beside himself with grief and anger. He couldn't belive Tank and Olin couldn't find the beast who murdered her, mutilated her body and stuffed its severed parts into a garbage bag and dumped it on a country road. Anger ruled his live at that point.

During these dark days, former sheriff Pop Cheever who'd been his mentor during his youth, told him state narcotic agents were looking for someone to plant in the prison system. They wanted this person to act as an informant and gather evidence about local police involvement in drug trafficking. Pop told Raz if he did this, he might get information about Patti's murder from a convicted drug dealer named Cato Hamilton. Hamilton had refused to cooperate with police, but might talk to a fellow con. Pop seemed sure Cato would know the answers to Raz's questions.

Raz agreed, and the two years he spent in prison as the result meant he'd witnessed more human degradation than he thought possible in a civilized world. He'd failed to find out murderer's identity, but hadn't given up hope. His gut told him the murder and the drugs were connected.

Raz sighed and turned over in his bunk. His failures and disappointments mocked him and kept him from sleep. He sat up on the side of the cot and thought, *There's so much to be done before I can get back to living and my little girl.*

He tried to relax, and ended up thinking about how much better things would be if he could find a good woman who'd love him and Becky and make them a family again. With no prospects, though, that part of his life would have to wait. He'd had a short affair with Fran Druman when she tried to comfort him after his divorce, but he needed something more than that now.

These gloomy thoughts just kept circling his brain, chasing away any hope of sleep. He knew the new gang of drug traffickers in his part of the state wanted to eliminate him, and no amount of security could stop them.

He finally went to sleep around 3 a.m., but didn't rest well. He dreamed the guards made him take off his shoes and then they cut them into little pieces right in front of him. Just as the guard was about to find the tape, he woke up with a start, Cato's warnings ringing in his ears. After pacing the floor for a while, he laid back down and finally got back to sleep again, but his dreams were worse than ever. This time, Becky didn't recognize him and ran screaming when he tried to pick her up. When he caught up with her and persuaded her to look at him, it was Patti's cut up, dead face looking back at him.

After that, he got up, showered, shaved, and got dressed. He sat on his bunk waiting for the guard to bring breakfast. About an hour after he finished eating, the guard opened his door and said, "Time to leave." His eyes swept over Raz from head to foot, stopping at his shoes. "How come they let you leave wearing those things? Take 'em off and I'll find you a pair that fits."

Raz felt a sudden tightness in his belly, but managed to reply calmly, "The doc ordered them special-made for me after I broke my foot." He was appalled by how easily lies just came to him now.

The guard shrugged, and held out an envelope. "Ticket, money and discharge papers. Be careful at the bus station. Fifty dollars doesn't go far these days." He gave him a knowing look.

Raz picked up the cardboard box filled with his personal effects and followed the guard down the hall to the front entrance. A Dodge van was waiting outside.

Stopping, he asked his escort, "Anybody else in the van?"

"You're the first victim. The other eight will be here shortly." He glanced down at Raz's feet again and said, "Good luck with those bad feet."

Raz climbed inside the van and went to the back seat so no one could sit behind him. This also gave him a good vantage point to view his fellow passengers. He studied the faces as they boarded and was relieved when he didn't recognize any of them. They were all young, under twenty-five years old, except for one man who was at least sixty. He was pale, gaunt, and skittish. Raz had seen old timers like him before — repeat-offenders-turned-long-termers who knew little about life outside prison. They all left scared.

His fellow parolees were chatting happily about beer, dope and women. They immediately fell silent when a tall, pot-bellied man in gray pants and shirt climbed into the van. He gave them all a look of contempt and announced, "I'm your driver, Bob Harper. You may address as *Mr.* Harper." He attempted a smile that turned into a sneer. "What an *honor* it is for me to chauffeur another load of fine young graduates from Uncle Bud's School of Etiquette and High Morals." His eyes settled on the old man. "And one slow-ass learner."

Raz smothered an urge to shout, "Cut the lecture, big belly, and get us out of here!"

Mr. Harper pulled out his keys and said, "No loud talkin' and no whistlin' or vulgar remarks yelled at women you see along the way. Got that, trash? You'll all be back in your old filthy lives soon enough. You can hold off actin' like human garbage 'til you get there. There'll be whores at the Houston bus station eager to pick you up and take your discharge money. You'd better turn 'em down, though, unless you want the clap. Got that, assholes?"

The driver closed the sliding door and took his seat behind the wheel. After glancing briefly at each face in the rear-view mirror, he started the motor and drove away. That's when Raz noticed the dark, low-hanging clouds over the level landscape. Moments later, he heard the deep rumble of thunder followed shortly by rain beating loudly against the van's roof.

Raz rode in silence, keeping his eyes on his fellow passengers in case one of them had a contract on him. Nobody took special notice of him, not even the old man who quietly moved back to sit beside him. He didn't make eye contact or speak.

Wonder how much a hit man charges for killing a drug syndicate's designated enemy. Probably not more than $500. That was the going rate when I went in. Cato had told him the price for murder on the inside was sometimes no more than some cigarettes, sex, or a steady supply of drugs.

Raz's pulse quickened when he thought about his reunion with Becky. Taking out his battered wallet, he put his discharge money in it and pulled out the photo of his daughter. She was two when the picture was taken. That had been just a few weeks before he evened the score in his ongoing fight with Tank Zelder and bought himself a ticket to prison.

Becky had always looked like her mother: golden hair, dimpled smile, and intense blue eyes. His jaw tightened when he remembered how Patti, drowning in a sea of drugs, had finally abandoned Becky and him despite his frantic pleas and efforts to save her and their marriage.

As the thunder and rain intensified, he lost himself in thoughts of Patti. She'd kept her youthful appearance, great personality and and charm until she found meth, cocaine and heroin. Her habit had reduced her to a slovenly, unloving, defiant person he hardly recognized.

The possibility that his little girl might believe he'd abandoned her, or that he was a criminal in the truest sense, was troubling. He hoped frequent visits would convince her otherwise and show her how much he loved her. When she was mature enough to understand, he'd explain why he went away.

In less than two hours, the bus pulled into the terminal on Fannin Street in downtown Houston. *Mr.* Harper parked at the curb near the entrance and opened the door. The passengers leaped from their seats, yelping wildly, and ran through the pouring rain into the terminal. The old man hesitated, but prodded by Harper's threatening stare, slowly rose and walked forward. He stopped at the door, as if dreading what awaited him, and then stepped outside, oblivious to the rain pounding his bald head.

Concerned that one of the parolees might stop just outside the van, Raz remained seated and counted them as they ran inside. Convinced that none of them were waiting for him, he picked up his box and approached the open door where he stopped to study the area in the downpour.

"What's the matter, scum?" Harper growled. "Was you spectin' a brass band or somethin'? Get your ass off the damn bus so I can get out of this stinkin' town."

When Raz ignored him, the driver snarled, "There's more than just a little rain waitin' for you, jailbird. It's a tough, rotten world out there. Too tough for trash like you an' the rest of them losers. You'll all screw up an' get sent right back to the Texas's boardin' house for deadbeats soon enough. Now, move along."

Raz searched the faces moving around in the rain, hoping Fran would step forward to welcome him at any moment. He'd written her several weeks ago and told her about his impending release. His letter hadn't been returned, so he figured she'd got it.

When he didn't see Fran or anybody else interested in the occupants of the van, he remembered something else Cato told him: "I've never known a woman who'd wait two weeks for a man, let alone two years."

Conditions are right for an assassin: thunder to cover the sound of gunshots and everybody running to get out of the rain. That thought made Raz hesitate. "Your beauty ain't gonna wash off," the driver snarled, revving, the motor. "Get your ass outta the bus."

Seeing no obvious threat, Raz faced the driver and in a sudden impulse, bowed and said with a forced British accent, "Farewell, Prince Charming. Parting is such sweet sorrow. I do hope I haven't kept you too long from your professorial duties at the State School for Higher Learning and Good Manners. Upon your return to that noble institution, please do me a favor, handsome knight of high intellect and possessor of excellent taste in all things. If, while engaged in your noble pursuit of brotherly love and world understanding, you ever solve the mystery of how there can be more horses asses than there are horses, please send me a note so I will no longer be perplexed by such a monstrous burden of mind. For you see, old chap, since I have never seen a horse with multiple anal passages, the matter has perplexed me to no end."

When the officer's jaw dropped, Raz added, in his normal voice, "Will you do that, Count de Lard-ass? Toodle-ee-do." He promptly stepped into the rain.

"You smart-alack bastard! I hope the first whore you top gives you the clap!"

Hunching his shoulders against the deluge, Raz moved away from the bus and stepped onto a sidewalk already under water as another clap of thunder rolled through. Holding his box with one arm, he walked briskly toward the front entrance.

A sudden gust of wind ripped open the lid of the box and blew a pair of his boxers out onto the sidewalk. When he stooped to pick them up, a shirt and some socks fell out, too. During the scramble to recover everything, the rain suddenly stopped hitting his back.

He looked up into the pretty face of a young woman standing under a large pink umbrella. She had long blonde hair and was smiling down at him. "Looks like you need some help."

Quickly retrieving his things, he stood up and said, "Thanks. You, uh, work around here, or just happen to be passing by?"

"You sure are inquisitive, Raz." She moved so close her breast pushed into his arm and sent shockwaves through his body.

Wary because she knew his name, Raz looked around for others who might be with her. Spotting no one, he turned back to those blue eyes. "Did Fran send you?"

No, I—"

"Then, how'd you know my name?"

Her smile faded, but quickly reappeared as she nodded toward the entrance. "One of your fellow passengers told me, honey."

"Try again, sweetheart. None of them knew name."

"My, you're a suspicious hunk. Doncha wanna come with me and party?"

"How did you know my name?"

"Good contacts in the right places, honey." Her eyes teased him. "The driver and I have a little arrangement. He and my contact at pre-release can really pick 'em. Big brown eyes, wavy red hair, shoulders like a pro quarterback. Mmmm."

Raz let his eyes to meet hers briefly before looking down at her full figure. She was wearing white high-heeled shoes, a painted-on white dress that showed off her assets, and she smelled good.

He felt a sudden urge to grab her and go someplace to play catch-up. His suspicious nature wouldn't allow it, though. "You don't look like a bus station hooker to me. Who are you?"

She pressed her breast against him so hard it almost spilled out of her dress, causing an increased reaction below his belt that threatened his good judgment. Sensing this, the blonde said sweetly, "Honey, since you've never been released from the joint before, how come you know so much about what a bus stationl hooker looks like?"

"I like your class, sweet thing, but seeing as how I already got a good deal waitin' for me at home that I don't want to lose, I'll have to turn ya down. I've gone without for nearly two years; won't hurt me to wait a few more hours. Thanks just the same." He turned to go.

She caught his arm. "Fran said you'd be a tough nut to crack, but I didn't know she meant *this* tough."

"Then Fran *did* send you?" His face brightened. "Why didn't you say so?"

"Can't a girl have a little fun?" she cooed. "I deserve somethin' for takin' you home, don't I?"

"But why didn't Fran come?"

"Oh, uh, she's all tied up in the business. You know, that Armadillo Hole place you were helping her run." She grabbed the umbrella with both hands to stop the wind from jerking it away. "Can't we get out of this storm, honey? My car's parked on the next block."

"What's your connection with the Armadillo Hole, blue eyes?" His lingering suspicions held him back.

"I work there. Now, let's go. You can ask all the questions you want … in the car."

Battling hot urges and cold logic, Raz didn't move.

Her expression suddenly hardened. "You do want to find out who murdered your wife, don't you?"

"You know 'bout that too? How?" he asked, shocked.

"Fran told me all 'bout you. Come on. Maybe on the way you'll change your mind and decide, I'm as good as the one you think's waitin' for you."

As they began walking toward a side street, Raz pulled her close under the umbrella, while keeping an eye out for anyone with more than a passing interest in him. The rain and fading light blurred the faces, but that didn't block his view of the parked cars and the street.

In the middle of the next block, Raz stopped abruptly when he spotted a black sedan parked at the curb up ahead.

"What's wrong now?" the blonde whined.

"That your car?"

"Of course. I mean, it's Fran's. Now, come on, let's get out of this mess."

He continued to study the car. "I will, if you'll tell me who the Merc belongs to. That's not an Eastman County plate."

"How the hell am I supposed to know where Fran bought the damn car? I want to help you. Get you back home so you can prove to your little girl what a great father you are."

She certainly knows how to push my buttons. More than ever, he wanted to believe her, but a gut feeling held him back. "If you're a friend of Fran's, you'll tell me your name and the real reason she didn't come."

At that moment, a sound in the direction of the Mercury diverted his attention. Two men jumped out of it and started running towards them.

Dropping his belongings, Raz whirled and made a dash for the corner. He could hear running footsteps on the wet pavement getting closer. With a fresh burst of speed, he widened the distance between him and his pursuers. As he neared the corner building, a shot rang out, then another and a bullet ripped at his shirtsleeve.

Raz raced down the side street and made a dash for the bus terminal's rear entrance. Glancing over his shoulder, he spotted the gunmen. One was tall and dark, the other short and chubby.

As he got near the loading area, he saw that they'd stopped on the sidewalk. He ran between two busses and their lines of boarding passengers, then went into the building. Once inside, he stopped to catch his breath and look for his pursuers. Relieved to not see them, he wiped water from his eyes and moved into the waiting crowd.

He spotted an empty seat, but decided it safer to remain standing. Looking again at the rear entrance, he was relieved when he saw neither the blonde nor her two associates.

He was shaking from the shock of almost being killed, and the air-conditioning made his wet clothes cold against his skin, adding to his discomfort. *Damn, Cato. You said I'd have at least two days before they killed me.*

A tug on his sleeve brought his attention to a tall black man lifting the side of raincoat to reveal small pouches hanging from his belt. "Want some good stuff?" the man asked, apparently unconcerned about being overheard.

"No, thanks. I'm good."

"It's top grade, man," he persisted. "I got weed and crack."

Raz quickly moved away from him. At the other side of the waiting area he spotted another man talking to two young girls. Judging by the pleased expressions on the girls' faces, the guy was about to make a sale.

Raz was having difficulty blending because people kept moving away after noticing his disheveled appearance and the way he was shaking. He sidled up to another group and folded his arms over his chest in an attempt to trap some body heat. *Who's that blonde working for and where is she now?* he thought as he searched the crowd.

Feeling like he was being too obvious, he decided to head for the bathroom. At least there he'd be less visible. A young policeman with collar-length hair appeared from around the corner and planted himself by the restroom door. When Raz tried to go inside, the cop blocked his way.

"Got a ticket?"

"Didn't know I needed one to take a leak." The uniform made him nervous because it looked like the one Olin Culpepper, Northville Chief of Police, wore.

"Don't get smart with me, jerk," the cop snapped, brandishing his baton. "Are you a bus passenger or not? The restroom is for customers only."

"I'm not a dope dealer, pimp or hired killer, so I must be a customer." He pulled his ticket out of his shirt pocket.

The cop gave him a contemptuous look and examined the ticket. "Should've known it," he said. "Another ignorant East Texas redneck fresh out of the nearest finishing school for thieves and deadbeats." He glanced at Raz's brogans. "You don't even have enough sense to wear a pair of shoes that fit. You won't be out long." He glanced at Raz's wet clothes. "Parole or mandatory release?"

"Either way, I'm legal, so I guess it doesn't matter." He took the ticket and brushed past the cop as he went into the men's room.

The restroom was full of smoke, both regular and pot, and the faint odor of burning crack. Ignoring the suggestive eyes of an effeminate man seated in an open stall with his legs spread apart, Raz urinated and washed his hands. *This isn't much improvement over the prison,* he thought and headed back out to the terminal.

He was relieved when he didn't see the blonde or the two shooters as he scanned the area. He re-examined his state-issued bus ticket and slipped it back in his pocket, thankful the rain hadn't made it illegible. He needed his belongings, but couldn't risk becoming a moving target again. He would dry out on the bus, and pick up some clothes he'd left at long-time friend Boobs Noonan's house. He'd go see Boobs, proprietor of the Soup Kitchen Café, as soon as he got to Northville, then he'd go see Becky.

Wonder who sent the welcoming trio? Was it the guys who took over Cato's business, or Tank Zelder? Regardless, it proves Cato was right: powerful people in Northville are afraid of what I know. Lassiter must think the same thing, or he wouldn't have met me in the warden's office and tried to get what I know before I even left the prison.

When the northbound bus was announced over the intercom, he moved to the door with the other boarding passengers. He scanned outside for the two gunmen, and when he didn't see them, presented his ticket to the driver and boarded. On the way to the back seat opposite the restroom door, he got some inquisitive looks, but pretended not to notice. After checking to make sure the restroom was empty, he sat down and noticed the bus was filled to near capacity.

The driver pulled the bus out from under the covered bay and into the steady downpour, headed toward U.S. Highway 59 North. Peering through the side windows, Raz saw neither the blonde nor her associates. He took a deep breath and exhaled. *I'm safe for the moment, but what about stops along the way? They may try to waylay me in some jerkwater town where they'll have fewer witnesses.*

He leaned back and tried to relax but couldn't because he keep thinking about Cato's dire prediction. He also worried about choosing the right person to safeguard the tape once he took it out of his shoe. Despite those distractions, he was excited about going home, seeing Becky and his invalid 77-year-old mother, and checking with Fran to see if their dance hall was still thriving.

CHAPTER 4

Alone in the back seat as the bus slogged forward in the downpour, Raz flipped on the reading light and took the small photo of Becky from his billfold. Sensing someone watching him, he looked up at an elderly white-haired woman holding onto the back of the next seat to keep from falling. Her left arm was wrapped around a cardboard box like it contained all her worldly goods. She was medium height and chubby, with stooped shoulders. The brightness of her dark eyes behind rimless the spectacles contrasted sharply with her advancing age. He could tell she wanted to speak to him but was reluctant.

"Hello," he said. "May I help you?"

"Mistuh, you mind if I set a spell wit ya?" she asked shyly. "The man settin' by me lit up a cigarette. The smoke jus' tears up this ol' woman's lungs."

"I don't mind at all." He stood and took the box from her, then slid it under the seat. "Please, sit down."

When she didn't move, he realized she needed help and took her arm and helped her until she was safely seated, then took a seat beside her. A pleasant fragrance of soap and clean fabric greeted him.

"Thank you, suh," she said. "You's very kind."

"You're welcome," he said, leaning back to study Becky's photo.

"Your young'un?" she asked.

"Yeah," he replied, holding the picture out for her to see.

She leaned forward and squinted. "Such a pretty chile. I can tell by the way you's lookin' at her; you loves her."

He smiled, nodding.

"Back at the terminal," she said, "I notice how ya didn't have no use for them trash trying ta sell ya dope. Shed 'em like a duck sheddin' water, ya did. That tol' me you was a man I be safe sittin' by."

"You've seen all kinds in your time, I guess."

"Yes-suh. I seen and heard lots in this sinful world I wish I hadn't. That the God's truth. Make a body wonder what to become of us law-abidin' folk."

He smiled. "You're beginnin' ta sound like my Great Aunt Ruth. Since I don't know your name, it okay if I call you Aunt?"

"Name's Beulah."

"Okay, Aunt Beulah. Since you're so much like my home folks, you can call me Raz. That's what folks call me when they're friends. It wouldn't be nice to tell you what they call me when they're not."

"Oh, chile, I can tell you's full o'da devil," she said and chuckled. "You goin' far?"

"As far as my luck will allow."

Puzzled by his repeated attempt at humor, she said, "You gots a kind face, mistuh, and a spark of mischief. Where ya goin' if your luck hold out?"

"Northville."

"Ta see ya fam'ly?" She pointed to the picture.

"You bet. She's all I've got left. Haven't heard from her in nearly two years. She's livin' with her grandparents."

"Where her momma?"

Shaking his head, he pulled out a faded newspaper clipping from his bill-fold. He carefully unfolded it. "Here's an old picture of her mother."

She quietly studied the yellowing clipping. "Purdy lady."

He nodded. "That was taken durin' our senior year in high school at Northville durin' halftime a our district football playoff game in '92. Her name was Patti Lawther before we got married."

She compared the picture to the photo "That little girl the spittin' image of her momma."

"I know. Patti was the prettiest girl at Northville High." He rubbed the jagged scar on his face. "Her rich daddy was sure she'd be the wife of a powerful man one day."

"What he say when she marry you?"

"He said I was the sorriest piece of trash in the county. He said I'd done bad things to his daughter so she'd have to marry me and then I could get to his money."

"That not yo' plan?"

"Nope, but I never could convince him."

"You love her?"

"More than my life. Didn't realize I could ever care that much about anyboyd. She didn't want to marry me at first. Said she'd go to Houston and have an abortion so her parents wouldn't know. When she finally agreed to marry me instead, her daddy disowned her. Said he never wanted to see her again."

"Po' chile. That a heavy burden to put on a girl's shoulder at a time when she need her mama and daddy most. I know it broke prob'ly broke her heart. Why do some folk got to act like that?"

"If you've got a heart of stone and ice water for blood like her dad, you'd know how come. I guess his attitude was probably one of the reasons she changed so much after Becky came along. She started doin' drugs and ran away right after we moved to the country. She went to town to live with drugies and drifters." He stopped.

"What that look for?"

"I'm wondering why I'm telling you my life story. Sorry to bother you with my problems."

"Ain't no bother, young man. Beulah been listenin' ta other folk pro'lems since 'fore you was born."

"Guess it's because I haven't had anybody with a kind face to talk to for a long time."

"I proud to be of use, so talk to this ol' woman all ya want. You was tellin' me 'bout her a-runnin' off." She shook her head. "Shame what losin' fam'ly make a young person do. Her daddy change his mind after his grandbaby born?"

"Nope. He wouldn't even let Patti's mom come to our little place to see Becky. Told me no white trash seed was ever going to be part of his family."

"Jus' show that some folk don't know what real problems is." She suddenly became tense, sliding away from Raz as she spotted his shoes propped against the footrest. "Oh, Lord."

"What's the matter?"

"I seen them kind o' shoes 'fore. How you come by 'em? That pretty lady's rich daddy get you sent up for what you done?"

"He wanted too, but couldn't. I earned that passport myself by punchin' a crooked cop."

"My man done somethin' bad to a mean lawman once an' they give 'im twenty years," she said, tearing up.

"That's rough."

"That the only thing you done?" she asked.

"Besides drinkin' lots of beer, chasin' pretty girls and gettin' in fist fights before I got married? Yes, ma'am." His expression became sober. "But you might not think what I did to that deputy was so bad if you knew what he tried to do to me."

"Sound like there bad blood 'tween you an' dat lawman."

"Bad blood, bad feelings, bad everything. I got crossways with the fat deputy's powerful friends when I tried to save my wife. One of them friends' was the bastard son of Northville's richest citizen. I'd find Patti there and bring her home, but she'd run off again. I couldn't get help from anybody."

"She ever stop runnin' off?"

"Just long enough for me to enroll at the University of Texas and play football a season. After that, I had to make quick trips back to Northville to find her and bring her back to Austin. I quit college when she ran back to Northville the last time to live with her friends. Not long after that, she was murdered." He felt a sudden lump in his throat.

"Oh, Lord! Guess that entitle ya ta bein' mad."

She was silent for a few minutes, but he felt her eyes watch him return the clipping and photo to his billfold. He told her, "Sorry. I really didn't mean to unload on you."

"Trouble ain't no stranger to me, Mr. Raz." She smiled. "Guess that make us kinfolk, don't it? Goin' home mad don't get ya nothin' but trouble, young man."

"Did I say I'm still mad?"

"No need. It wrote all over ya face. Show up all huffy and put-out, them powerful folk gonna send you right back to the pen. Be jus' like wit the men folk in my fam'ly."

He settled back in his seat with her warning and Cato's ringing in his ears. He wondered if Aunt Beulah knew Cato, or if any of his dealers had supplied her kin with drugs. He turned to ask her, but changed his mind, convinced he'd burdened her enough already.

Aunt Beulah also fell silent. Maybe old memories stirred up by their conversation had her attention.

He tried to turn his thoughts to more pleasant things but couldn't dismiss the picture in the yellowed clipping. *Class sweetheart Patti Lawther and class favorite Raz Jester are smiling because Northville leads 14-3 at halftime. Raz Jester, the quarterback with the most wins in Northville football history, has received a football scholarship at University of Texas.*

Raz recalled moving his young bride to his parents' home in the country. Those accommodations in no way resembled the luxurious lifestyle to which Patti was accustomed. As soon as school was out, he went to work on the chicken farm owned by his old friend, Frenchy Patroon. Frenchy let them use one of his small cottages as part of his pay.

By then, Patti's attitude had changed dramatically. Denied her parent's affections during a time when so many changes were happening in her life, she spiraled into depression and took out on him. Her once sparkling personality was gone; she became withdrawn and sad. Her performance during their increasingly rare personal moments became forced and boring, her honey-colored, soft-as-silk hair lost its luster and her crystal blue eyes always looked morose and bloodshot.

When Patti got to the point where she could barely function, he made a thorough search of the house and discovered her stash of pills. She told him she had to have one kind to sleep, and the other to get her going each morning.

She refused to identify her source or stop taking the drugs. She always seemed to be able to get them, and he never found out where they came from. He concentrated on ways to cheer her up, assuring her that things would soon be better for them both. No success. Desperate, he again grilled her about her source, but she remained tightlipped about who supplied the drugs and how she financed her habit.

Caressing his scars, he considered events before and after that game mentioned in the clipping. Patti Lawther was his anchor. He'd made his first full commitment to her. Before that, he hadn't worried about anything other than having fun and playing sports.

Patti's resume was more impressive. She was a straight-A student, head cheerleader, class sweetheart for two years running, and junior year runner-up in the Miss Texas Teen pageant. She was destined to enter Baylor upon graduation. It was hard to believe that her wealthy father, the brother-in-law of Horton Snitker, the richest and most powerful man in the county, could disown her.

The Lawthers had refused to send Raz a more recent photo of Becky, and Mrs. Lawther had stopped writing to him in prison after just one letter. Raz wrote his little girl each week for a while, then it dwindled to once a month, he always hoped for a response. After six months, he quit writing at all; hoping Becky wouldn't think he'd stopped loving her. If that happened, it would be the cruelest blow yet.

He peered through the hard rain, barely able to see the fields beyond the trees that lined the right-of-way. His mind wandered back to Patti's final exit from Austin. After a two-day search, he'd located her in a dilapidated house on the outskirts of Northville. She was living with some some people who had no obvious means of support. He learned later they were some of Punk Hutto's friends and customers. Punk was the town's leading dope advocate and owner of the town's only club. He sold drugs on the side.

After an ugly verbal exchange with Patti and several of her misfit friends, Raz put her and Becky in his pickup and took them to the cottage at Frenchy's place. He called the Lawthers and begged for help with funding rehab for Patti, but they refused to talk to him.

After going back to work for Frenchy, he spent every free minute with Patti and Becky. He didn't want his wife to re-join her addict friends. One day, he came home from work and she was gone.

He immediately went out searching for her and found out she was at Punk Hutto's Rock Shop. She had apparently developed close ties with some of his low-life customers. Raz was furious.

After literarily pulling her out of the Rock Shop and picking up Becky at Gerta Hutto's home where Patti had left her with the maid, they went back to the cottage. That's when he found fresh needle marks on Patti's arm. Enraged, he demanded that she tell him her source. She refused; laughing at him for thinking she would betray her friends. After calming down, he begged her to tell him what he could do to make her happy. She screamed, "You want to make me happy? Get me another fix!"

That's when he called Punk Hutto and told him, "If you ever let my wife back in your place or let any of your meth head friends give her more drugs, I'll mess up your face real good." That threat had come back to bite him at his trial for assaulting Deputy Tank Zelder.

"Cleveland, next stop!"

Raz looked outside and saw neither clouds nor rain, just lots of tall trees and green pastures.

"You get everythin' straight in ya thinkin'?" Beulah asked.

"Sorry I've been such bad company," he said. "You gettin' off here?"

"I get off on up the road a ways."

He was relieved when he saw neither the blonde nor her friends at this bus stop. The passengers getting on posed no threat, either. He leaned back and relaxed as the trip resumed.

Turning to Beulah, he said, "Forgive me, Aunt Beulah. I should've asked you if you needed anythin' back there. You want a soda or a sandwich?"

"I'm fine, thanks. You ain't lookin' so fine, though. Maybe gettin' home make ya calm. You get outta prison da right way, nobody be lookin' for you."

"Any way a man gets out of that zoo is the right way, believe me. I was so wound up in my own thoughts earlier that I forgot to ask about your family. Is your husband doin' okay now?"

"My man pass a long time ago," she said sadly. "All my boys, too, 'cept one. He turn his back on da Lord an' join a Arab religion in Houston. He don't like white people no mo'. New church must'a done somethin' good, 'cause he ain't been to the pen again."

"He a Muslim?"

"I believe that what they called. He don't come ta visit much, just send a few dollars now an' again."

"How many children you have?"

"I birth ten chillun. All 'cept dat one boy an' two girls pass on. One girl, she live up here on the ol' place. The other'n live in the Third Ward in Houston. That where I been, visitin' her. She want me ta stay wit her 'stead of comin' back up here ta my ol' shack."

"Why'd you come back?"

"I rather be snake po', livin' on the ground under a big oak tree eatin' 'possum and armadilla than live in Houston. If a person don't believe there a Hell, he oughta go there for a spell. It Satan's playhouse fo' shore. All that dopin' and killin' and sportin' goin' on. No self-respectin', Lord-lovin' person live there 'less he loss his mind."

"I guess you wouldn't be too crazy about Northville, either."

"Don't tell me dopin' and sportin' done spread to dat town too. I thought all dem little towns still be livin' by the good book."

"'Fraid not. The old been gone a long time." He shook his head. "It's amazing how two people that have never met can be so much alike in their thinking. Sure would like for you to meet my Great Aunt Ruth."

"You reckon she'd be willin' ta put up with an ol' lady like me?"

"She has a friend, who's an ol' lady like you, who's lived with her for years. She's Aunt Ruth's best friend."

"Aunt Ruth sound like a mighty fine person." She hesitated. "Jus' don't know what come over folks, actin' like dat. Need ta read the Good Book.'

"I'm not so sure that'd help."

She gasped. "Mr. Raz, if life sposed to be cute all the time, don't ya reckon the Lord woulda had his disciples write a joke book 'stead of a list of rules?"

"I reckon He would. My guess is you haven't had much time for fun in your life."

She looked out at the passing woodlands, "Mistuh, I was too busy takin' care of my chillun and my man ta think 'bout myself. I ain't complainin', 'cause that what God want me ta do."

"Maybe you should have a talk with some of our country's women's libbers."

"Ha! Who gonna take care of sinnin' men folk an' they babies if us womenfolk don't? Doin' that don't bother me none. No, suh. Make me feel good inside. If feelin' that way's fun, I had lots of it. I tries to love ever'body — good and bad." She paused a moment. "People jus' don't love each other like the Lord intend no mo'. They been listenin' to what the Devil say. Ever'body love money, an' dope an' good times. They too wrapped up in theyselves."

She settled back with a sigh, as if all this talk had made her tired. Raz's thoughts turned back to Northville.

Happenings in his hometown the last ten years or so proved what Aunt Beulah had just said. His life did improve a bit when he went to work for Fran Druman at the Armadillo Hole, a country and western dance hall in Northville. They'd pulled some political strings, and got to sell beer as a private club. Sad and disgusted about his inability to find Patti and his little girl the last time Patti ran away, he'd stopped at the place to get a cold beer. While there, he learned Fran needed a bartender, bouncer and general handyman. Frenchy didn't have much for him to do on the farm, so he'd taken the job.

Business was already good at the Hole, and it got better when his friends found out he was working there. Because of this extra business, and Fran's frequent business trips to Houston, she asked him to become her business partner.

When he wasn't working, he continued looking for Patti and Becky. Friends had reported seeing Patti at various places, mostly Punk's club or the town's only hotel, strangely named God's Hotel.

Tank and Olin Culpepper ignored his pleas for help with the search. He learned later that'd been working for his inlaws and had found Becky. Once they found her, his inlaws set up a custody hearing in the Coldwater district court. They wanted custody of his daughter. Their action surprised him, since they'd had nothing to do with their granddaughter before that.

He wasn't notified about the hearing, and had no money for an attorney to contest the transfer of custody, but he did attend the proceedings. That's when he'd discovered the hearing was for *permanent* legal custody. He pleaded for the order to be temporary until he could establish a suitable home for himself and Becky, but his appeal had no effect because his inlaws had lots of money and political clout.

Raz rationalized that his daughter would be better off with the Lawthers, for a while anyway, in view of Patti's destructive lifestyle. That did not soften the blow of losing her to them, though. What made things worse for him was the ruling that he could only visit Becky once a month.

Determined to regain custody of his daughter, he'd saved some money and hired Harley Ritter, Boobs Noonan's attorney, to file a motion for a re-hearing. The judge denied this request on the grounds that he could not provide full-time care for his daughter and was not married. Sadly, this was true. No one in his family would qualify as a caregiver. His mother was in a nursing home and his only female relative, Great Aunt Ruth McShan, was ninety-five years old.

Unlike his personal life, the Armadillo Hole continued to prosper. It consistently attracted more customers each week than Punk's Hard Rock Club, a fact that did not set well with Northville's leading drug advocate.

Despite Raz's responsibilities at the Hole, he continued looking for Patti. On those rare occasions when he found her, she refused to go home or even talk to him. Out of desperation, he finally forced her into his pickup one day and drove her to his parents' house. Tank arrested him an hour later on a charge of disturbing the peace and disorderly conduct. Fran paid his fine so he could go back to work.

Three months later, Patti's dismembered body was found in a garbage bag on the side of a country road. His fireman friend, Ethan Lewis, warned Raz not to view her remains because the killer had slashed her breasts, stomach and private parts with a sharp knife. The police said he had to view her remains to identify her, so he'd had to see what was left of her.

"Livingston!"

He jumped like he'd been poked by a cattle prod, as the announcement abruptly returned him to the present.

CHAPTER 5

Raz turned to find Beulah calmly studying him. "I been watchin' ya, Mistuh Raz. You got a troubled mind, so I pray for you."

"Why? Was I frothing at the mouth?" He smiled.

"You cain't cover up everythin' with a joke, Mr. Raz. This ol' woman see through that like glass. I pray you turn ta the Lord for help 'stead o' takin' matters in yo' own hands."

"You're sounding more like my Aunt Ruth every time you talk. Can I jump off the bus and get you something at this stop?"

She shook her head. "I get off up the road a ways. You take care of your own self."

There was no sign of the blonde or her two gun-happy friends outside the station. He didn't want to risk running into them getting a sandwich, so he stayed on the bus. After two passengers got off and their suitcases were removed from the luggage compartment, the driver went inside the station. Moments later, he returned and got the bus back on the road.

Raz tried to relax, but was still too shaken by memories of what he saw when he viewed his wife's mutilated body at the Coldwater funeral home. He didn't sleep well for weeks after that. Convinced that Tank and Olin would never find her murderer, he'd started his own investigation. He questioned customers in the Hard Rock Club first, hoping someone had seen or heard something he could use.

During one of his visits to Punk's place, he saw a couple of old friends. One of them, Tim Barton, said he only came there to drink beer and pick up girls. Raz had other beer-drinking friends, and Tank and Olin had used their close association with Bryan Fulton to help Punk get private club status, but didn't frequent the place. They gave their business to the Armadillo Hole, which surprisingly, had been granted a beer license shortly after Fran built the place.

Tim Barton told him he'd seen Patti at the Hard Rock Club once with a couple of long-haired types. "As a matter of fact," he said, "one of 'em's at that table over there." Raz approached the buy, but he refused to talk. So Raz had dragged him outside for a more meaningful conversation. He'd just begun grilling him when Olin Culpepper arrived to arrest him for disturbing the peace again.

After paying his fine the next morning, Raz went to the old hotel. He got nothing from the transients there but dirty looks. Finally, he tried flashing enough money for a week's supply of weed. That loosened the tongue of one of the residents. Beckoning Raz to the side, the man said, "I saw a woman looked like that leavin' the hotel with a guy a few days 'fore she got murdered. Short, fat guy, with long dirty blond hair and a baby face. Hotel manager called him Medic. 'Fore that, on the same night, I saw her wit a well-dressed dude wearin' a back hat. Don't know his name."

Raz pushed more bills into the guy's shirt pocket. "Maybe that'll jog your memory."

"I heard talk he was a banker someplace. Don't know where."

Before he could say more, Shag Shammerhorn, the hotel manager, rushed over with a couple of his tattooed friends and told Raz to leave or get beat up.

Later that night, as Raz was driving to his mother's place, somebody shot at him. He gave chase, but the shooter got away. This was the first of several warnings he'd receive.

More determined than ever to continue his search following his conversation at the hotel, Raz talked to Sonny Irby the next day. He was the only banker Raz knew. Sonny was the chief loan officer at Northville State Bank, owned by Horton Snitker, who was rumored to be Punk Hutto's biological father.

Sonny refused to talk or discuss anything about the banker seen with Patti at the hotel. "If you bother me again," he'd said, "I'll call Olin Culpepper and file charges against you."

Raz continued looking for Medic, but didn't find him or anyone else who would admit to knowing him.

Two weeks later, when it appeared his investigation had reached a dead end, Raz got a call from Tim.

"Raz, you still lookin' to buy some antique knives?"

"What? Tim, you drunk?"

"Just got a lead on one I think you'd be interested in."

"Okay, I'll bite."

"Belongs to a butcher. He still has it."

Raz sat up straight and gripped the phone. "This about Patti's killer?"

"Yeah. I'm over at Punk's joint."

"So, can you give me a name?"

"Not now. Too many people around, if you know what I mean."

"Can you meet me? Name the time and place."

"How could I forget the midnight beer bash we had at the picnic grounds on Town Lake Road? That was some senior year at good ol' NHS. Sure you won't stop by and throw back a few?"

"Midnight at the park?"

"Okay. Talk to you later."

Hoping Tim had spotted Medic, Raz drove to the park. He saw Tim's pickup under the lone security light; the driver's side door was open. He rushed over and found his friend lying in a pool of his own blood, dead. His body had been horribly slashed, and there were several stab wounds in his chest and stomach.

After recovering from the shock of seeing this, Raz pointed his flashlight beam around the area. There was no one else around and there were no other cars. He saw fresh tire tracks leading away from the truck. Upon closer examination of the open door, he found the word "movie" scrawled in blood on the inside panel. Shining his light on Tim's right hand, he saw blood on his finger.

Raz didn't have a cellphone, so he raced toward town to call an ambulance and report his findings to the Sheriff, Obie Peavy. Just inside the city limits, Tank and Olin pulled him over.

He though it was odd that they'd be waiting in that particular location that time of night, but figured it would save him some time in reporting Tim's murder. Instead of going to the scene, however, they'd searched *his* truck and "found" a bloody knife.

The bus slowed down, dragging him back to the present. Puzzled buy the unscheduled stop, he peered out at the highway, half expecting to find the Merc blocking the north lane.

"This here where I get off," Beulah said, sliding forward.

He looked outside. "Where are we?"

"Jus' 'bout to Moscow."

"Russia? We must've made a wrong turn somewhere."

She waved a hand at him and shook her head as the bus rolled to a stop on the shoulder of the highway.

Raz helped her to her feet and picked up her box of belongings, "Be careful now," he cautioned. "Hold on to the back of the seats 'til we get to the door. I'll go ahead and help you down the steps."

By the time he stepped to the ground, the driver had already retrieved an old battered suitcase from the baggage compartment and set it on the grass. Raz put the cardboard box next to it and went back to help his new friend off the bus. He looked around for Beulah's ride, but no one was there.

"Someone supposed to meet you here?" he asked.

"Yes-suh. Elvira always late. She awful forgetful in her old age. Don't you fret. She be here directly."

Raz looked at the driver waiting by the door. "We can't just leave her here like this."

"She'll be okay," the driver said, glancing at his watch. "I've done it before. Let's go. Got a schedule to keep."

Feeling a tug on his arm, Raz turned and found Beulah's dark eyes fixed on him. She said softly, "No matter how heavy da burdens be, young man, they cain't bear down no harder than those dat bore down on the One who died ta save us all. I pray for ya tonight 'fore climbin' 'tween the sheets."

Her statement moved him. "Thanks, Aunt Beulah, but your time might be better spent praying for somebody who shows a lot more promise than this ol' sinner." He patted her shoulder. "Bye now. Be sure you cook all them 'possums and armadillas well done."

Following the driver inside, Raz turned on the landing and waved. Beulah smiled and raised a gnarled hand as the bus moved back onto the highway.

Stopping midway down the isle, Raz leaned over and looked back until the forlorn figure sitting on the old suitcase disappeared from view. Sitting down, he thought about her positive attitude and her parting words. He wished he understood the belief that made such a sweet old woman unafraid to wait alone in a desolate place. When he sat down, he felt a lump in the seat and scooted to one side to see wha it was. There was a pocket-sized New Testament laying there. Opening the worn cover, he gently thumbed through its pages, noting many were dog-eared or marked with heavy underlining to note certain passages. Leaves at the beginning and end had more notes made by the same shaky hand.

He tucked the little Bible in his shirt pocket. *Aunt Beulah must have forgotten this, or it slipped out of her purse. I'll give it to the driver when we get off at Northville and ask him to return it to her on their next trip together.*

Looking at the rolling, wooded countryside, he sighed, glad to be free again. He looked forward to being reunited with Becky and his mother, as well as being back at the old home place in the country. He leaned against the headrest and before long, dozed off.

"Coldwater, next stop!"

He woke with a start and looked around, excited that he was nearly home. *Twenty more miles and I'll be in Northville.* His anticipation had made the 150-mile trip seem longer than usual.

His enthusiasm quickly took a back seat to concerns about who'd be waiting for him in Coldwater. It was a fitting place for the shooters to wipe him out, since it was the place where he was found not guilty of murdering of Tim Barton.

The driver pulled into the small bus depot located in the town's business district and parked under the covered loading bay. He exited the bus and stood by the open door to assist an elderly couple as they got off. After that, he unlocked the luggage compartment without closing the bus door.

Raz peered over the tops of the seats, scanning the surrounding parking area as the driver walked inside the terminal. *No black Merc or shooters — good.* Still apprehensive, he turned back to watch the open bus door, in case someone had found a way to approach that was out of his line of sight.

Moments later, the bus moved slightly and his pulse quickened. *Someone's on the steps.* Sitting up straight, he saw a young black man sporting dreds in a striped polo shirt. He stopped on the top step of the bus, pulled off his sunglasses and studied the passengers.

Raz looked from the young man's dark, angry eyes to his hands. He could see both of them, but the loose shirt was ideal for concealing a weapon. Something in Raz's gut warned him that the stranger was gunning for him.

He steeled himself for an attack as the mysterious figure moved slowly down the isle, examining each passenger. When the man got to Raz, he looked down at him with cold eyes. Studying him a moment, he stepped closer and said in a strained voice, "I need to talk to ya outside, man."

"Why? I don't know you," Raz said, his palms sweating.

"But I know *you*," he said. "Uncle Cato tol' me 'look for the ugliest white dude on the fuckin' bus to Northville.' That you. You gonna get off or not?"

"Snake Hamilton?"

"No, man, Kevin Costner. Now, if you're comin', move it. The driver'll be back any second."

Raz stood up, but remembered the run-in with the blonde and asked, "How do I know for sure you're Cato's nephew?"

"'Cause I tol' you," he snapped. "I come over here as a favor to Uncle Cato, but he warn me you be lippy. Well, I done what he ask, smart ass, so I'm buggin' out. Cain't afford ta be seen wit ya anyway." He turned and started toward the door.

"Okay, Bright Eyes. I'm coming," Raz said and followed him off the bus.

Snake didn't stop until he'd walked about a hundred feet from the bus. "Uncle Cato say last year he try ta talk you out o' comin' back to Northville, but it don't do no good 'cause you so damn bull-headed. He tol' me when you gettin' out an' say I should meet the bus in case you lucky an' make it this far. Spose ta pick ya up an' take ya to Northville so ya get there in one damn piece."

"Cato didn't tell me you were picking me up."

"He tell me ta make sure ya don't take that bus home, 'cause a bunch o' bad-asses is waitin' for ya. You comin' or not?"

"How did you know I'd be on *this* bus?"

"Didn't, man." He stamped his foot.

"Then who tipped you off?"

"Nobody. I been meetin' every fcuckin' bus comin' out o' Houston dis month. Driver seen me so many times I had ta start waitin' 'til he go inside so I don't get my ass run off. Them buses that didn't stop, I beat ta Northville an' wait for 'em there. Any more dumb questions?"

Raz felt more at ease now. "I don't suppose a man would go to that much trouble if he was working for the people who burned his uncle."

"Talk, talk." Snake cast a nervous look around. "Man, can't you see I'm sweatin' blood? Can't afford ta be seen standin' here jawin' with no white dude. 'Specially one who prob'ly be dead by sundown. Now, quit flappin' yo' lips an' make up yo' mind."

"Afraid your *friends* will see you? There's only one set of crooks around here you'd have to be afraid of. You working for them?"

"I do what I gotta do for the bread, man. Who they is ain't none o' your damn bidness."

"But they helped put your uncle away."

"So I do a little bidness with the dudes that put Uncle Cato in da slammer. Not like I can do nothin' ta hurt him where he at. I know what you done for Cato. That why I be draggin' my ass over here again. I help ya any way I can, long as ya don't give me too much sass an' ya don't mess up my connections."

"Some connections. I hear the new gang runs Northville now, just like the one Cato worked for did."

Snake took another quick look around. "Motor mouth. You ever quit talkin' an' turn on ya brain? Either ride the fuckin' bus to Northville an' take a chance on gettin' yo' white ass kilt, or I slips ya in nice and cool-like so ys can live a while longer. Up to you. So, make up ya damn mind, 'cause I'm 'bout ta split."

Recalling the events at the Houston bus station, Raz caught Snake's arm as he turned to walk away. "Why do the crooks in Northville still want to shut me up? It's been nearly two years since I rocked their boat. Is it because of something they've heard?"

"They ain't stupid. They got the word on ya bein' tight wit Uncle Cato."

"That's the only reason? Tell me everything you know, if you want that special something from your uncle."

"You shittin' me? What *special* somethin' that be? Uncle Cato don't say nothin' 'bout sendin' somethin'.'"

"He did and you can't have it until you tell me why they want me dead before they know what I'm going to do now that I'm out."

"Sound like somebody already try to whack you." His dark eyes remained fixed on Raz. "That it?"

Raz told him what happened at the Houston bus terminal. "If you really want to help, tell me who might be behind it, and why."

Snake glanced around again, made more nervous by Raz's disclosure. When he began walking away without answering, Raz fell into step beside him.

Snake stopped. "I don't know nothin' 'bout who try ta whack ya in Houston. Think I know why, though. 'Sides you bein' tight wit Uncle Cato, top dudes know you got somethin' from 'im."

His remark surprised Raz. "You really know how to get a man's attention. How could anybody in Northville find out Cato gave me something to bring home? If he actually did, that is."

"You askin' dumb questions again. How the hell should I know? Somebody in the pen prob'ly shot off his mouth an' it got to the man here or the boss in Houston — Ed somebody. You think they got where they is by bein' brainless?"

"I guess they think I've still got this alleged statement on me, and by getting me they can get it."

"Cato give you somethin', where else it be? You ain't been anyplace to leave it. Has you? Guess they figure they gettin' two quacks with one whack."

"Very poetic. Any more wise observations?"

"Even a red-headed peckerwood like you surely know what they do to ya after ya got tight with Uncle Cato, 'specially if he give you somethin'. Feel me?"

Should I trust him? Maybe the gang bought him, too.

Raz looked around for the black Merc and shooters but saw no threats. *So far, my plan's still good; I just have to live long enough to put it into motion. I need to get that tape someplace safe and then make sure Tank and his associates know I have it. What worries me is how word got out about me having something from Cato. Loop didn't unwrap the tape, so no one's seen it since Cato wrapped it up.*

Did Cato tell somebody else in case something happened to me before I got it delivered? Possibly. I'd bet on one of the men in the warden's office, though. Maybe Oscar.

"'Bout a week ago I hear you bringin' somethin' out wit you. Don't know how long the top dogs knowed 'bout it 'fore that. You some kind of blabbermouth or somethin'?"

Cato's nephew must be close to those at the top to know all this. Maybe he's trying to improve his position with the new gang by taking the tape and delivering it himself.

Sensing Raz's suspicions, Snake snapped, "Man, how come you lookin' at me like a buzzard eyeballin' road kill?"

"I guess the next thing you'll say is that I'm supposed to give Cato's statement to you for safe-keeping. Right?"

"*Hell no!* I ain't stupid. I got lots more livin' ta do."

Snake's spontaneous response told Raz he'd probably jumped to the wrong conclusion.

Snake whirled and walked away, calling back over his shoulder, "I'm splittin', man. I ain't dickin' wit you no more!"

"Where's your car in case I decide to go with you?"

"Wait on the corner," he said, and pointed east without stopping. "I pick your ass up soon as I know you ain't been made. Don't do no lip flappin' wit nobody 'fore I get back."

Raz stood behind a large pine tree on the corner to avoid being seen from the bus station or the street. A couple of minutes later, a red Porsche 911 stopped at the curb. Unable to see inside the darkly tinted windows, Raz stayed put.

The window lowered and Snake yelled, "What you waitin' for? Get in!"

Raz jumped into the Porche, and Snake made a skidding U-turn, got back on the highway and sped away toward Northville.

Raz whistled as he looked at the plush interior. "Nice wheels. You've either been shoveling tons of chicken shit, or selling lots of dope in The Quarters and over in Coldwater."

"There you go again, puttin' ya nose in somebody else's bidness. Ain't you got enough heat on you?"

"How do you expect me to trust you if you won't tell me anything?"

Snake grunted. "You jus' keep pushin', jabbin' and swingin'. You do jus' like wore out ol' Zeke Lewis taught you. This ain't no playground pissin' contest. Feel me?"

Wanting to test Snake's reaction, he asked, "It's obvious you believe what you heard about Cato giving me a statement. You think I still have it on me?'

"You got terminal stupid disease'? Like I already tol' you, can't be nowhere else. My guess, you ain't stopped nowhere but the fuckin' bus station since you got sprung. They most likely got a crooked cop or a pusher watchin' to make sure ya don't ditch it."

"Your intelligence is exceeded only by your good looks, Bright Eyes. If you really want to help me, put out the word that I've already delivered the statement to somebody Cato and I trust, and that as long as Tank and his crowd leave me alone, it'll stay with that third party. If they move on me or I end up dead, it will be delivered it to the narcs. I need some breathing room. I've got lots of living to catch up on."

"I look crazy to you? I ain't getting' my teeth knocked out 'cause I mixed up in anythin' you a part of. I like livin'."

"You seem to know a lot about what *they* believe and what *they* will do."

Snake hit the brakes and the sports car skidded to a stop on the shoulder of the road, thrusting Raz toward the windshield. Recovering, he said, "Why the hell you do that?"

"You think all niggas be liars? I don't lie 'bout nothin' involvin' my uncle."

"Don't go gettin' all offended."

"Smart ass, I tol' ya why I pick ya up — for my uncle. You think I done it for some other reason, get out an' walk."

Snake's reaction convinced Raz that his mistrust of all things and all people was about to screw up a connection with the only person who'd tried to help him since he got out. "Sorry 'bout that, Bright Eyes. Your uncle taught me to be careful. I do appreciate what you're doing for me."

Mumbling, Snake pulled back on the road and drove in silence.

Raz decided he would have to be the one to break the ice. "Cato told me all about his old gang and how they were paying off Tank and Olin before he got set up. Did the new gang keep Cato's dealers running things, or did they get the boot too?"

"What difference it make who runnin' things now? Seem like ya still workin' for the narcs, askin' questions like that."

"Still?"

"There ya go, actin' cute again. Cato's nephew, 'member? I seen him after he nearly got hisself killed 'cause the cops pulled him out on that bench warrant. Ever'body think he goin' ta talk."

"If a man goes out for a walk, he needs to know where he's least likely to step on a snake. Oops, no offense intended."

Snake continued looking ahead, pretending he hadn't heard, so Raz said, "Cato said he suspects the Dixie Mafia runs things now and he thinks they had something to do with him being set up. I thought they might've cleaned house when they took over. That's all. Cato said the Dixie bunch had been trying to move in on him for a long time. He told me one of their men, a guy called Alabama, came to see him a couple of times before it all went down. He tried to get him to help make a case against the Mexican Mafia."

"He tol' ya that?" Snake glanced at Raz, seemingly on the verge of telling him more. He thought better of it and shook his head. "Forget it, man. Play it cool. Slip back into town like a cat burglar, find yo'self a woman an' bury yo'self in the good livin'."

When Raz didn't respond immediately, Snake added, "I hear you quite a hit wit the ladies 'fore you knock Beergut on his ass. Find you 'nother honey an' let this stuff be."

"You think just like Loop Proctor. You related?"

"Who the hell is Loop Proctor?"

"Forget it. I've got a lady friend. At least, I *had* one. I need a woman, bad, but don't know how she feels about me now. What I want more than anything is to keep Tank and his friends off my back so I can go to work and take care of my little girl and my mother."

"You ain't been listenin'. The bad asses an' they friends ain't gonna let ya do nothin' 'til they find that item Cato give you an' put a permanent lock on yo' flappin' lips."

"That shouldn't keep you and me from doing a little business together."

Snake raised his eyebrows and looked over his shades. "Bidness? Depend on how cool you is." He pulled a small metal box out of his shirt pocket. "Have a toke. Let your hair down. Forget 'bout yo' troubles. Be cool wit ol' Snake."

"No, thanks."

"Little crack, then? They a pipe an' a few rocks in the console."

"I'm fine."

Snake picked up speed, settling on seventy-five. "You wanna see dat ol' friend the High Sheriff, you find him in the new courthouse substation on the north side o' town. Jus' don't take 'nother swing at 'im, 'cause he blow you away dis time. He use any half-ass excuse to do it, too. Culpepper's got a hair trigger."

"All through elementary and middle school, Tank beat my ass every chance he got. Especially when I took a girl away from him. He got even madder after he found out Zeke Lewis was teaching me how to box. Even though he was two years older than me and a lot bigger, I finally whupped him when I was in eleventh grade." He laughed. "He was so pissed off he dropped out of school and never came back. Got the job as Northville's resident deputy with the new sheriff, after Pop retired a couple of years later."

"He a lot bigger and meaner since he got ta be sheriff. Best not ta tangle wit him."

"How is Zeke?"

"Still bitchin' an' moanin' 'bout how sorry young folks is these days. You ask me, he been hit in the head too many time." He grinned. "Want me ta drop you at his place? He put you up for the night; you be safe there. Nobody lookin' for ya on that side o' town."

"No. I've got to see my daughter and my mother. Just drop me off at the Armadillo Hole. I really need to check on my business first."

Snake gave him a disbelieving look.

"What?" Raz asked.

"You been gone too long. There ain't no Armadillo Hole no mo'. It the Hard Rock Club now. Punk Hutto took over right after you was busted."

The bad news was a shock. "What happened? Fran's still in town, isn't she?"

"I don't get too deep into that shit," Snake said. "I hear she left town real fast-like."

"Why? Where'd she go?"

"How the hell would I know? I ain't got no direct gossip line."

"Is the drug situation in Northville as bad as it was when I left?"

"Worse. Pot, crack, meth and pills everywhere. Ecstasy and smack on the rise too. Things so bad, folks make Chief Pain-in-the-Ass Culpepper put a cop and a dog at the high school."

"Cato's sources told him the main man in Eastman County now is somebody called Rudy. Ever hear of him?"

Snake turned to him, visibly shaken. "Why you bust right out and axe me somethin' like that? I ain't heard nothin', ain't listened ta nothin', an' I ain't answerin' no more damn questions."

"My chances of staying alive are better if I know who's who. What about Mazurka and Smeddish? They worked for Cato, right? They still in town? Cato said they were the Mexican Mafia's hit men when he was in charge. He told me all about Mazurka getting on the stand to turn state's evidence against him. Cato thought he might've cut a deal with the new bosses for doing that."

Snake didn't respond, so Raz continued. "Cato knows what Mazurka looks like, but he's never seen Smeddish. I figured you might know both of 'em. Cato told me to ask you to find somebody to whack Mazurka."

Snake's eyes widened. "Cato tell you that?"

Raz nodded.

"You talkn' 'bout somethin' too hot ta handle. I seen Mazurka 'round town a time or two. He a big, ugly guy. Don't know no Smeddish."

"How about Alabama?"

Silence

"Now that Punk Hutto owns the Hole," Raz continued, "I need to find out how he fits into the new setup."

When Snake said nothing, Raz decided he'd better stop with the questions. He rode in silence for a while, still shaken by the news about the Hole. *Now I'm gonna have to find a job. Maybe Frenchy has some work for me.*

The news about Fran's disappearance was disturbing. He realized that Cato always clammed up when he mentioned her name, he'd just never thought to ask why. He asked Snake, "You have any idea why Cato wouldn't talk to me about Fran Druman?"

"He not tell you?"

"Obviously not."

"Some no-good, trashy woman set Cato up. He say she hang around him, bein' real sweet, beggin' him to hit the sheets. He started bangin' her and she move in with him. Things was goin' good 'til she tip off the cops 'bout a big shipment of new stuff. That when he busted — him an' a couple of Mexican mules an' that moose, Mazurka. That all I know."

"He tell you the woman's name?"

Snake kept his eyes on the road, ignoring the question.

Raz turned to look out at the scenery speeding by. He spotted landmarks and knew they were just outside the Northville city limits. He turned to Snake again and said, "Two more questions. Okay? I figure a man who's spent nearly two years in the pen for doing the public a favor is entitled to that."

"Can't stop you."

"Fair enough. Here's a little background on the first question. Before Tank and Olin threw that bloody knife in my pickup and I was tried for Tim Barton's murder, a hippie over at the old hotel told me that he saw my wife with a big-butted white man just before she was killed. He was about 5'5", hundred ninety pounds with long blond hair and a boyish-face. You ever seen a man like that around Northville?"

Snake pulled off his sunglasses to give Raz a cautious look. "This strictly 'tween you an' me. Right?"

"Yeah."

"Uncle Cato say you one cool dude, so I guess I'll answer that question for ya, if ya answer one for me. You save Uncle Cato's life 'cause he needed help or 'cause you want ta pick his brain to get at somethin' the cops couldn't?"

"I'll tell you what I told him. It happened so fast, I don't know. When I saw he was about to be killed, I just jumped in. Sure, I wanted information, but I can't say that's the reason I saved his life. After that, I was transferred to his cell and we became good friends."

Snake gave him a skeptical look, allowing the car to drift over on the shoulder. He jerked it back into the lane, telling Raz, "I ain't sayin' I believe ya, but Uncle Cato trust you and say you cool."

"Then how 'bout answering my question?"

"Not sure. There a lot of crappy lookin' white folk comin' and goin' over at that flophouse. I heard 'bout a short, pudgy dude that coulda been the one they call Medic. I ain't seen him myself an' that's okay wit me."

"You hear anything that might help me find him?"

"Only that he a bad mofo. 'Fore he come here, he work at the hospital — nurse or some shit like that."

"Is he a friend of Punk's?"

"That the second question?"

"Nope. A bonus."

"No fuckin' bonuses! Move on."

"Okay. Where are Smeddish and Mazurka headquartered now, and why was Rudy, whoever he is, picked to run things? Is he the one paying off Tank and Olin now?"

Snake hit his palm against the steering wheel. "Hold on! Can't you count? You say *one* more question."

"I'm not just asking for me; it's for Cato too. I've got something that's his and I intend to use it in a way that causes the most damage. Doing this is gonna make more enemies for me. That's why I need to know."

"Like I say, I don't know no Smeddish. Same go for Rudy an' Medic. I already tell you all I know 'bout Mazurka. Squealin' ain't my style. I don't wanna wake up dead." He shrugged his shoulders. "Them on the white side o' the tracks leave me alone long as I jus' push a little pot and crack in The Quarters and Coldwater. I keep things on the QT, don't get nosey and keep my damn mouth shut."

"You keep talking about *them*. Who's that exactly?"

"There you go, losin' count again. You done axed your last damn question."

The city limit sign came into view and Raz tapped Snake's shoulder. "Pull over."

"Why?"

"You heard me, Bright Eyes. Pull over and let me out."

Snake slowed down and pulled off on the shoulder. "You do what Snake say an' slip in, real cool like. Get shed of whatever Cato give you and find yo'self a ol' lady. Don't go gettin' stupid trompin' 'round like you the head rooster comin' to the barnyard to kick big rooster butts."

"Kicking butts and looking for love might be the only games in town for me. Okay, I'll try to be cool for a while if Tank doesn't dig his spurs into me." He reached for the door handle.

"You don't find a woman, head over to Bull Hayter's café. Tell Bull I send you an' he fix you up with a hot number on me."

"Thanks, but no thanks. Right now, I'm gonna walk around the Square, see the sights and look for some friendly faces."

"Not cool, man. Slip in like a shadow, an' stay outta sight."

"Thanks for the lift." Raz stepped out. "If you hear anything that might help me find Fran, give me a holler. I really need my share of that business she sold."

"Yeah, yeah, like that gonna happen," Snake muttered, then burned rubber as he sped away.

When he was gone, Raz looked up ahead at the business district on the left side of the highway to make sure it wasn't a mirage. *I'm really home.* He'd looked forward to greeting the friendly folks while strolling around the town square on his way over to the Lawther home. He was so happy to be back, for a moment he forgot the unpleasant things he had to do.

Reality would come back to smack him in the face all too soon, but for now he was going to concentrate on seeing his family. *I'll go see Boobs, and visit Becky and mom, then I'll get my pickup out of the barn and go see Pop Cheever.* He'd tell Pop about his private talk with Lassiter in the warden's office and maybe get some friendly advice. *After Pop's, I'll go see Frenchy.* Frenchy Patroon was a close friend often had an alcohol-loosened tongue and a need to impress that caused him to blab things he shouldn't.

Raz started walking, and felt generally pleased about coming home, even though he had lots of worries circling in his thoughts. He'd feel much better if Cato's warning would stop interfering with his good mood. *If you go back to Northville, you'll be dead by the time the sun sets on the second day.*

CHAPTER 6

As Raz walked through town, his thoughts wandered. Northville had the dubious distinction of being one of the poorest towns in Texas, even though two of the richest families in the state lived here. That rating never concerned Raz because he didn't believe the size of a man's bank account was a proper gauge of his happiness. Horton Snitker, the richest man in town, never appeared to be happy about anything. Isham Lawther, the second richest, was the most miserable person Raz had ever had the displeasure of knowing.

Horton Snitker had become instantly wealthy when he'd married Eldora North, the only child of the town's founder, Benjamin North. Horton liked to wheel and deal, and ended up expanding that wealth. He now owned land, timber mills, commercial buildings and had established Northville's only bank. He also built a large poultry processing plant on the outskirts of Northville, a feed store to supply the local ranchers, had several oil- and gas-producing wells on various properties, and his latest acquisition was a General Motors dealership in Coldwater. Because of this, everybody called him Ol' Money Bags.

The majority of employees in Horton's various enterprises were illegal immigrants. He liked them because he thought they worked harder for less money and they didn't file complaints about safety, wages or overtime pay.

Those in public office in Northville and Eastman County kowtowed to Ol' Money BAgs, everyone but Tank and Olin, that is. They'd become a power unto themselves, thanks to payoffs from drug trade. However, they still considered Horton's special needs and knew better than to do anything that would truly tick him off. None of them wanted to bring federal or state regulators down on their various profit-making enterprises. That included Drew Lassiter's state narcotics bureau.

The weekly newspaper and the radio station were careful not to invoke Ol' Moneybags' wrath, and only reported local happenings that perpetuated the myth of Northville as an idyllic small-town. Some believed Horton ignored anything negative about the town. Everything was good, as long as it didn't interfere with his business affairs or threaten the welfare of "Punk" Hutto and his mother, Gerta.

Everyone in town thought Punk was Ol' Moneybags' son. He'd never publically acknowledged this, but residents treated Punk like royalty just in case. There'd been a paternity suit at one point, but it was dropped in exchange for bailing Punk out of some legal problems.

Punk was a public nuisance who was deep in the local drug trade. The other line of gossip connected to him that he could do as he pleased because his mother, Gerta Hutto, was Chief Culpepper's long-time secretary and took care of things before they became official.

Crossing the highway during a break in traffic, Raz turned his eyes to the bus station on the far side of the Square. He headed that direction to leave Aunt Beulah's New Testament with the driver, making a conscious effort to steer clear of the sheriff's office.

Raz turned his mind away from the sordid private affairs of the citizens of Northville, and thought about his much-anticipated reunion with Becky. Seeing her would be the highlight of his return, but he didn't look forward to having to go up against Isham Lawther to regain custody.

Isham, who was in his sixties now, was a highly excitable little man with shifty gray eyes glaring out from behind the thick glasses that always rested on his long, thin nose. He was a busybody and often stuck that nose into other people's affairs. He'd been mayor for thirty years, and his close ties with Horton Snitker, plus his generous donations to the town's largest church guaranteed the votes he needed to keep the job as long as he wanted. He liked the un-salaried position because it allowed him to head the city-owned water and gas departments, which gave him authority to make all supply purchases from his own company. Illegal, yes, but nobody dared complain.

Stopping, Raz stared in disgust at the former Armadillo Hole. The sign out front now read, "Hard Rock Club, Punk Hutto, Proprietor."

When Raz had gone to jail, the Armadillo Hole was the top venue in the area for bluegrass and country music. Back then it'd been painted white, now its multicolored swirl paint job made it look like something Punk created while he was high.

Being here again made him think about Fran. His olive-skinned former business associate had black hair, large brown eyes, and a figure that made men drool. She was a warm and caring woman who loved moving around the dance floor to a smooth country western number.

He and Fran had not become intimately involved until Patti rejected him the last time and gone to a place where he couldn't find her. He'd never forget the events leading up to his affair with Fran. Depressed and reeling from being dealt a legal triple whammy: a restraining order, divorce papers and a supervised visitation order saying he couldn't see Becky unless he was accompanied by Olin or Tank, Raz had been devastated. He'd retreated to a dark corner table at the Hole and started drinking beer.

Trying to rescue him from drowning his troubles, Fran had asked him to dance. After the second number, she asked him to join her back in her live-in office. At that time, he and Patti hadn't been intimate for over a year.

He sighed, remembering the happy early months of his marriage. He'd taught his bride to dance the Cotton Eyed Joe and the schottische at the Armadillo Hole. She'd pretended to enjoy it, just to make him happy. *Now she's dead.*

Moving on from that sad thought, he walked a little faster on his way to Boobs' house. He thought of more practical things as he went. *What will I do if Boobs didn't keep my clothes? I've got to get out of these things and into some thing normal. Boobs'll know all the latest gossip, too. She aways keeps up with all the happenings in Northville.*

He also thought about his fun-loving old friend Frenchy Patroon and Pop Cheever, the best mentor a teenage boy ever had.

Traffic was light, and as he walked and reminisced he noticed that little had changed while he'd been gone. At the south ends of the Square, a larger-than-life likeness of a confederate soldier was locked in an eternal stare-down with the concrete statue of town fonder Benjamin North. The latter, marred by mildew and rust was surrounded by a red brick restraining wall spray-painted with phrases like, "John is Mary's stud" "Yay Timber Wolves!" and "Legalize Pot."

The stone soldier, however, remained clean. Rumor said a keeper of the faith in the "Lost Cause" sprayed it with bird repellent and washed it several times a year. This always happened during the night, so no one knew who the mysterious keeper was.

Raz smiled, recalling how he and a few of his buddies had jumped a group of potheads putting a joint in the soldier's outstretched fingers. To his knowledge, that was the last attempted desecration of Johnny Reb.

He studied the far side of the Square where Drake's Cafe served as the local bus station. If anybody, friend or foe, expected him, they'd be waiting for the bus that was just pulling in. Two passengers got off, and a woman and two children climbed aboard. He didn't see the black Merc or anyone taking a special interest in the passengers who'd just got off the bus, so he resumed walking.

The only thing new on the Square was a Ferris wheel. *I'm back in time to enjoy homecoming, it's always on the first Saturday in June.* The festivities would include more rides, concession stands, and a swarm of rowdy boys and giggling girls. There'd be lively country music, and some pressing of hands by aspiring politicians. *Hope I'm still alive at the end of the week to enjoy it all.*

Beyond the buildings at the northern leg of the Square, he saw the white steeple of the Baptist Church. Isham Lawther and Horton Snitker were members there and Olin Culpepper taught Sunday school. The four other churches in town had members with less clout.

He stopped suddenly when an old dusty green Cadillac pulled in from the highway and parked near the bus station. A large Latino was the car's lone occupant. His goatee, mustache, black hat, red shirt and dark sunglasses indicated he was not a local.

Did the blonde and her two friends send him? Or, maybe he works for Tank and Olin. It's safer to check him out when there are witnesses. He headed for the Caddy at a brisk pace, only to see the gas-guzzler pull out and head north on the highway.

Seeing no one else out of place, he continued walking deciding to try to see Becky before going to Boobs' place.

Suddenly, a high-pitched voice behind him called, "Raz! Raz Jester!" The voice belonged to a short, red-faced fat man who was walking quickly his way, grunting and puffing as he went. *God, it's Lard Haskins!* Haskins was the bungling idiot who pleaded with Raz all through high school to fix him up with girls. Like Tank, Lard could never get a date.

"Hello, Lard," Raz said, resuming his walk. "You're rushing me. I haven't been home long enough to know which girls are puttin' out to losers."

Catching up with Raz, Lard lifted his big straw rodeo hat to wipe the sweat off his brow. "Don't want no girl, Raz. I come to fetch you."

"Then where's the brass band? I feel insulted."

"Stop kiddin' around," he said, putting his hat back on and pushing it down to the top of his ears. "I'm serious. When you wasn't on the bus, Tank sent me out lookin' for ya. Said to bring ya over to his office."

Raz pointed at a shining object on Lard's shirt. "What's that?"

"You blind. It's a badge. I'm Tank's—"

"Pimp?"

"That ain't nice." His face reddened. "The sheriff wants to talk to ya 'bout some legal stuff. It's real important."

"Then tell him to call my executive secretary." He resumed walking. "She makes all my appointments with ex-bootleggers, whore mongers and crooked cops."

"Now, cut that out." Lard said as he strained to catch up. "Tank'll be hoppin' mad an' you'll be in deep trouble."

Raz stopped to face Lard again, as two old men at the curb nodded and began eavesdropping. Raz said, "I'm real disappointed in you, Lard. Getting chummy with the man who dealt me so much misery all these years. I thought I was your friend."

"You were … are! You can still fix me up sometimes. I mean. Oh, shit! I don't know what I mean. Are you comin' or not?"

"Nope, but you can deliver a message to Tank for me," he said, and tapped Lard's badge. "It'll give you something to do to earn your pay for a change."

"You ain't gonna give me 'nother riddle ta solve, are ya?"

"It might be a riddle to you, but it won't be to your boss. Tell him I won't give that special package he and his friends are looking for to the narcs if he arrests Patti's killer and keeps the crocodiles off my tail 'til I get my personal affairs in order. Can you remember all that?"

"There you go, speaking in riddles again. What special package?"

"Just tell him. He'll know what I'm talking about." Raz started walking.

"Okay, but do me a favor?" Lard's voice became more high-pitched as he struggled to keep up. "Jus' walk a ways with me so everybody'll think you're doin' what I tol' ya to do. I ain't never been able to do nothin' right. You know that. If all these folks see ya make a monkey out o' me, Tank'll fire me as sure as God put whiskers on catfish."

Raz stopped and turned angry eyes on Lard. "He'd be doing you a favor. Come on. I'll walk with ya 'til we get 'round the corner. Then you can tell Tank what I said 'bout that special package. If he ignores my message and you keep working for him, you'll get scratched by that wildcat I've got stored away, too."

"What in Sam Hill you talkin' 'bout? What wildcat?"

Raz's intentions were to walk the entire length of the west side of the Square on his way to the Lawther home, but since he didn't want to do that accompanied by a fat deputy sheriff, he stepped up the pace and turned west on Pine Street. Lard fell back, finally, shouting at him, "You'll be sorry, Raz."

"Pro'bly," Raz replied. *Good thing Lard happened by. It made my notice to Tank official. Maybe now I can walk the streets unmolested.*

Making sure he'd lost Lard, he walked one block south on First Street, turned left on Magnolia and went back to the Square. *No Cadillac and no sign of the Merc. Good.*

He passed a new clothing store and two vacant buildings. When he met two old men with familiar faces, they spoke politely and shook his hand. "Hi, Raz," one said. "Glad to see you back." Raz returned their greeting and moved on. A bit further on, he met two elderly ladies who also spoke to him and smiled shyly.

There were several other people in town shopping, and three old men sat on the Jaycee-provided courtesy bench. They'd probably come to town to visit and gossip. Near them, two merchants were draping red and blue bunting on their storefronts, getting ready for Saturday's homecoming festivities.

Where Oak Street entered the Square up ahead, he spotted a group of kids standing in front of the old hotel. Most of them wore faded blue jeans, trucker caps and wrinkled shirts. This was where the vagrant said he'd seen the pudgy man with Patti.

Getting closer, he saw the hotel's new name: God's Palace. He'd heard through the grapevine about how a reformed doper-turned-preacher had talked the little old church ladies and some of the social clubs into refurbishing the building and turning it into a home for "God's unfortunate children."

He watched four of the loiterers leering at a young woman walking past them. One apparently said something off-color and she blushed and walked faster. When she'd gone, they turned their attention to Raz as he approached.

Not wanting to delay getting to the Lawther home or get involved in a brawl, for that matter, Raz stepped off the sidewalk with the intention of walking around the somewhat threatening group. He jumped back on the curb, when an old Ford pickup rounded the corner driving dangerously close to the sidewalk. Its bumper sticker read, "Honk If You Love Jesus!"

He resumed walking parallel to the sidewalk, and out of the corner of his eye saw the young men watching him. They'd moved to block his path, mumbling words he couldn't make out. *Is this the reception committee? Wish I'd gone straight to Boobs' place!*

He moved further from the sidewalk, hoping to avoid the group of "God's unfortunate children" coming toward him. That didn't work, and two of them suddenly jumped in front of him, forcing him to stop. One said, "Look at them shoes, Shag. Straight off the line at the state pen."

The name Shag rang a bell, and Raz recognized the manager who'd ordered him out of the hotel when he was there two years ago. This revelation made him suspect Shag and his friends were told to intercept him.

Raz moved further to the side, but they mirrored his movement. "How come you lookin' so sad, shit-kicker?" Shag asked in a mocking tone. "Your horse die while you was gone?"

Another said, "He ain't gonna say nothin', Shag. He one of them strong, silent types that like ta put it to livestock." They all laughed.

Surrounded now, Raz clenched his jaw and waited. "Tell me, man. Is makin' out wit a cow as good as doin' it with a broad?" one asked.

After another round of laughter, Shag Shammerhorn, the tallest and heaviest of them all, asked, "Want a joint, man? Come on in and we fix you up wit some good stuff, right out o' Mexico."

"We ain't got no young heifers in there, though" the first guy said in a sing-song voice, "but we fix you up wit something better if you nice."

Trying to remain outwardly calm, Raz stared into Shag's deep-set eyes, gauging his chances. The man was at least six inches taller than him, and much heavier.

"I axed you a question! Nobody ignores Shag Shammerhorn."

The others circled tighter as Raz calmly said, "Never figured a man who cultivates facial hair 'round his mouth to make it resemble his ass was worthy of my attention."

A hush fell over the group. Shag's jaw dropped. Raz added, "Sure appreciate you lettin' me know that it's Ass Face Day. You're the second guy I've run into like that today. So, ass face, want me to polish my prison shoes with your filthy beard or the seat of your baggy ass britches when I shove my foot up where the sun don't shine?"

Shag clenched his fists and glanced at his friends for support.

Raz went on, "I'm assuming your ass is in the usual place and not actually behind that filthy bush around your mouth?"

"Take 'im, Shag!" one of the men behind Raz said. "Then we'll drag 'im inside an' search 'im."

Shag took a step forward, but stopped when he noticed several people on the street watching. He forced a smile, "He jus' all full of hate ain't he, boys? You got no love in your heart for nobody. Doncha know God love you?"

The others laughed, and pressed so close that Raz nearly choked on their collective stink. "You a preacher, too?" Raz asked. "I thought you were a philosopher who doesn't like soap. Just goes to show how wrong a man can be when he makes snap judgments 'bout vermin."

Shag's forced smile disappeared. "You hostile, man. Ain't he hostile, boys? He ain't no true believer in the new ways. God gonna frown on you, boy," he said, and glanced at the observers on the sidewalk again.

When Raz moved to walk by, Shag slammed his left fist into Raz's ribs, making him to grunt and slump over. Raz recovered his balance just in time to jerk his head away from Shag's sweeping right, aimed at his chin. Raz tried to walk away, but they rushed him. He kicked the closest man in the belly and punched the one grabbing him from behind in the jaw.

Raz assumed a boxer's stance as Shag charged, then a flurry of left jabs and a right cross sent the doper stumbling backward on the sidewalk. Raz whirled toward the others, ready to rumble, but a heavy blow to his head from behind set off a flash of light in his brain and he dropped to the sidewalk.

CHAPTER 7

Raz woke with his naked back pressed against a hard, rough surface. He opened his eyes to a single light bulb hanging from a high ceiling. Rolling his head side to side, he realized he was in a musty-smelling room, where sagging and torn wallpaper covered the walls. A dresser was the only other piece of furniture besides the bed he was laying on.

He was about to get up when he noticed a man sitting on the other side of the bed and quickly closed his eyes. "Tank and his big shot friends should've let us haul 'im out to the country an' finish 'im off," the man said. "That little ol' book he had on 'im ain't big enough ta hide no statement from Cato, an' them underlined words don't mean shit."

A second man, apparently standing outside Raz's field of vision, replied, "Tank an' Olin must've thought it was somethin' since he ain't got nothin' else on 'im. Shag said they tol' 'im they might need the jailbird ta tell 'em what it all means if they's some code in them underlined words. If there ain't, then they'll let us do what it takes to make 'im tell us where it's at."

The first man signed. "Well, hell! I'm tired of sittin' an' waitin'. I'm goin' down for a beer. No need for two of us here anyway."

Raz heard a door open and then shut. When he was sure no one could see him, he felt around to see what he was laying on. It felt like some kind of rug. He relaxed and became still again, but looked toward the man still in the room with him. He was a young, fat man with long black hair and dark eyes. He was leaning against the wall holding a pistol, oblivious to Raz's conscious state.

Raz looked past the man and saw a window covered by a drawn brown shade. He guessed he was in one of the unfurnished rooms of the old hotel.

Get the hell out of here! his brain screamed at him. *How can I do that when I'm laying here naked and there's a guy with a gun just a few feet away?* His head hurt and he wasn't sure how steady he'd be when he stood up. *Take the gun. Find my clothes. Get out of here.*

With his heart pounding, he slowly moved first his left, then his right arm. When he didn't hear a reaction from his guard, he groaned slightly and rolled his head enough to see him better through half-closed eyes.

The man jumped to his feet at the sound, and walked over to him. He pointed the pistol at Raz's chest and muttered, "I coulda swore you moved." He kicked Raz's leg. "Hey, man. You awake? Damn! Where's Shag? He shoulda been back by now."

Appearing to come around, Raz moaned and mumbled some gibberish.

"What's that, man? What you say? You tryin' to tell me where it is?"

Raz mumbled again, ending with two words spoken clearly, "—for Tank."

The man leaned closer, shifting the pistol to one side. "What 'bout Tank? You got somethin' for 'im?"

Raz slammed his right fist into the jaw hovering above him, and the pistol dropped to the floor. As the man slumped over, Raz quipped, "You're not my type, handsome," and shoved him to the floor.

He scooped up the pistol and jumped to his feet, only wobbling a little. He found his clothes and put them on quickly. He picked the old newspaper clipping lying nearby, along with his empty billfold and his little girl's photo. He felt a knot in his belly when he thought about his shoes, but he spotted them near the side of the bed with their heels still intact and let out big sigh of relief.

That done, he turned to the unconscious guard as the man groaned and sat up suddenly. Raz gave him a swift kick to the head and he fell back to the floor, unconscious. "That's one for the road, ass hat."

Raz went to the window and raised the shade. The gravel-covered alley below confirmed that he was on the first floor of the old hotel. He unlocked the window and pulled up hard, but it was stuck. The effort made his head throb, but he pulled again with all his strength. The window finally came loose and he raised it enough to climb outside.

Once outside, he felt a bit woozy but happy to still be alive, fully dressed and in possession of his shoes. He looked both ways and walked south toward

Magnolia Street. He didn't get far before he had to retie his huge shoes to keep them from falling off.

He spotted Cecil Cassidy, owner of a boot and shoe repair shop, who met Raz halfway to the corner. "I've been lookin' for you," Cecil said. "They threatened to beat me up when I tried to keep 'em from takin' you into the hotel. What happened?"

They began walking toward the Square as they talked. "After the dopers got me inside, they stripped me." He touched his head. "I woke up in a stinking room with a headache. You see what happened before that?"

"Part of it," he said, nodding. "Helen Murphy told me how one of 'em made a pass at her, so I come out to see what I could do. That's when I saw you on the ground. When I run up there an' asked them guys what was goin' on, the one with the red beard said you started a fight an' they had to stop you."

"I wish they hadn't stopped me quite so hard." he said, as he rubbed the back of his head with a grimace.

"I run back to my store an' called Olin Culpepper's office, but when I tol' Gerta what I wanted him for, she said he weren't available. Come on to the store an' tell me all about it. I'll give you a cold drink."

When they got to Cecil's shop, Raz sank down on a bench just inside the door. "Think I'll just sit here a minute. I'm still a little groggy."

Cecil returned promptly with a bottle of Dr. Pepper and a wet washcloth. "Wipe your face and arms with this. It'll make ya feel better." Looking at his shoes, he added, "How you walk in them shoes? They ain't even close to your size."

"I was in such a hurry to get home I didn't care what I wore out of that place." At least he didn't tell his old friend a lie.

"It's good to see you back home, Raz. Sorry 'bout the reception committee. Somebody need to clean that hotel up. If Pop was still sheriff, I guarantee he wouldn't put up with that crowd. They all hoodlums an' drug addicts. A disgrace to the town."

"There's more of 'em than when I left, that's for sure. Somebody must be treatin' them real good."

"The do-gooders in our churches donal all that fixin' up with the help of an anonymous donor and a federal grant. Shag Shammerhorn brought in a friend from California he claim was a preacher so they could call it a church. They get free handouts from charities and such and don't have to worry 'bout taxes. They get free gov'ment commodities too. Tank an' Olin don't seem to care what goes on there, neither."

A passing middle-aged woman approached Raz and offered him her hand. "Welcome home, Raz. Glad ta see you back."

"Hi, Miz Mertzel," Raz said, getting to his feet. He also waved at a man walking by outside. "Mr. Wilhoit, how you doin'?" he said, then sat down because his knees were wobbling.

"I want you to know that there ain't a person in town blames you for cold-cockin' Tank like ya did," Cecil said. "Damn shame they sent you to the pen for it too. Folks say if you hadn't pleaded guilty, a jury woulda let ya go."

"Thanks! Someday I'll tell ya why I had to do it."

"Having the people on your side ain't gonna smooth the road for you none. Gossip has it, Tank an' his friends gonna make things mighty tough on you now that he's sheriff."

"So I've heard."

"We all been wonderin' if you gonna let the past be, or start lookin' for your wife's killer again. Might be best ta forget that an' move on. Them that know you best say you never dodge a fight. One thing's for sure. Nobody wants you hurt or sent back to the pen."

"I appreciate that." Turning, he looked through the showcase window and found that the old Caddy had returned to its spot at the bus station. The sight caused the lump on the back of his head to throb worse than ever.

"Them lowlifes at the hotel just a tip of the iceberg. There's dope everywhere now, but mostly down at Punk's new place. We got people comin' from all over 'cause of it too."

"Nobody else got murdered while I was gone, did they?" he asked as he continued to look at the green Caddy.

"Don't know for sure." Cecil followed his gaze to the far side of the Square. "Right after you left, a woman come up missin'. Tank and Olin did a half-ass investigation. Guess the local newspaper was too 'fraid of steppin' on toes ta write much about it."

"Who was she?"

"Don't remember a name, but she the one used to run the Armadillo Hole. Ain't that where—"

"Fran Druman?"

"Yeah, that the one."

"Surely the paper covered something about it."

"Nope. Not a word."

Raz stroked the scar on the side of his face while studying the Caddy. The driver was still behind the wheel, like he was waiting for someone. *Maybe he's waiting for the shooters from Houston. Maybe Shag called him after they didn't find Cato's statement. I gotta go see Becky.* Standing, he patted Cecil's shoulder. "Thanks for the cold drink. Tell the missus I said hello."

"You can't leave. No tellin' what them outlaws will try next. Ain't you gonna at least file a police report?"

He laughed. "You already called Gerta. Remember? Cops around here won't do me any good. I'll make it through somehow. Thanks for the drink."

He wanted to call Tank in case Lard hadn't delivered his message, but didn't want to make Cecil a part of his troubles. *I'll call from the next available phone. I have to make sure my plan's going to work. What I wouldn't give for a prepaid cellphone right now.*

Although shaken by the beating and the bad news about his former business partner, Raz realized there were more important things at stake now. He could get a line on Fran through Snake or Boobs, after he took care of the higher priority things on his list.

With the Caddy still waiting across the way and no sign of Shag and his friends, he decided to buy something for Becky at Ivey's Drug Store. *Oops! No money.*

He entered the store, and after visiting with Seth Ivey for a few moments, explained his predicament. Seth told him his credit was good, so he purchased a stuffed rabbit and was on his way. When he hit the sidewalk, he couldn't stop thinking about Fran. *Did the new gang force her to leave town after she got crossways with their boss?? Did she sell out and take my twenty-five percent to greener pastures? Cato said a man can't expect a healthy woman to sit and watch the rats play while her tomcat is away.*

He looked at the stores along the north side of the Square, particularly the gas and water office next door to Isham Lawther's Hardware. Raz figured Isham was in one of those buildings, greedily rubbing his hands together and anticipating another big order from the city's utility company.

The marquee on the old Texan Theater next to Lawther's Hardware announced the feature in Spanish, another sign of Northville's evolution.

He left the Square at Pine Street, and turned to see if the Caddy had decided to follow. He was alone, so he walked to the end of the block, then turned on Second Avenue. This would take him to the Williamsburg Addition, where Northville's wealthiest families lived.

One block down, he came to Ira McClelland's barbershop. *At least that hasn't changed.* He'd got his first haircut there.

He looked across a vacant lot at the little frame building on First Avenue where Punk Hutto's first club, The Rock Heap, had been. Punk had been the trailblazer pothead in high school, and the first to use speed and cocaine. During his freshman year, he'd grown his hair out and dyed it blue on one side and pink on the other. He'd also begun wearing dirty, mismatched clothes, and acting out at school. His rebelliousness got him recognition from his peers and a strong following among those who shared his tastes in music and contempt for authority. Neither the teachers nor the principal would discipline him because of his connections.

Punk's entourage had grown considerably during his senior year. His friends adopted the mannerisms and vocabulary of movie renegades and rock stars. Acid rock and rap music perpetually blared from their cars as they sped around town.

Raz and his friends, on the other hand, had maintained an interest in country music, beer and regular tobacco. Subsequently, many fights broke between the kickers, their group, and the surfers, Punk's crowd. Eventually, everyone at school had been pretty much forced to choose one group or the other.

An approaching car pulled Raz from his memories, and he glanced over his shoulder to see the old Caddy moving his way. *Only a few more blocks to Becky.* He quickened his step. *Nobody's out on this street. Perfect place for a murder.*

CHAPTER 8

The Caddy pulled up beside Raz, and the window rolled down. "Hey, Jester. My name's Rick Zapata. We need to talk."

Raz kept walking, watching out of the corner of his eye. Over his shoulder he said, "I don't wanna talk to you. Get lost."

"This is the first chance I've had to talk to you in private. I'm a narc, man."

"And I'm a Jewish aviator working for the PLO home guard. Beat it! Tell your friends over at the hotel to lay off, too, unless they want to go to the pen with Tank when the *real* narcs start kickin' butts. And, tell your pal Punk Hutto I'll talk to him later about my share of the Armadillo Hole."

Zapata stopped his car and got out. Soon he fell in step with Raz. "Friends at the hotel? Real narcs? What are you talking about, man? I'm on the level."

Raz stopped to face the man. "If you're a narc, you'd know I've already told Lassiter my deal with him is off for the time being."

"Lassiter? Who's Lassiter?"

"If you don't know Lassiter, then I know you're lying," he said and raised his fists.

"Okay! Okay!" Zapata threw up his hands. "I know you're a boxer. Will you just listen? My supervisor told me to find out if you'd changed your mind about needing some help."

Raz continued walking

Zapata followed, telling him, "I saw what happened back there on the Square. You've got something those guys want and their friends won't stop 'til they get it. You won't live another day if you don't work with me."

Remembering Cato's similar time line, Raz continued walking.

Zapata said, "I heard you're hard headed, but this is *muy loco*. At least hear me out. But not here. Somebody could come by any second."

Raz stopped and watched as the big Mexican got back into his car. "I hope you ain't dead the next time I see you." He shook his head and mumbled something in Spanish before driving off.

Raz arrived at the back corner of a high brick privacy fence on Second Street. It'd been built by residents to keep the "undesirables" from looking into the Williamsburg Addition. Before going to the entrance around the front corner on McShan Road, he stopped to study the new brick building at the end of McShan, where it intersected with the highway. The Texas flag and a tall antenna tower indicated it was Tank's new sub-office. There were two cars parked by the side entrance. The first one had a decal on its door. *Probably Olin Culpepper's ride. They must still be trying to figure out the "code" in Aunt Beulah's Bible. When they figure out I've escaped, they'll forget about that Bible soon enough.*

Across the park on McShan Road, he saw the nursing home where his mother had lived for the last eight years. It was a disturbing reminder of how close he was to losing her. Three years ago, her doctor said she'd never get better. *Mom, I'll come by after seeing Becky,* he promised silently. She didn't know where he'd been for the last two years and he wanted to get it together before seeing her.

Raz admired the oldest, most beautiful residential area of Northville as he strolled through the Williamsburg Addition. As far back as he could remember, there'd only been four houses here: the Drakes two-story frame house, the Lawthers' two-story Cape Cod, Horton Snitker's antebellum, and the town founder's modest bungalow, which was now a museum.

Surprisingly, today he saw fifth home had been added while he was away. It was a long, ranch-style house that looked a little out of place. *Hmmm. Wonder who finally broke into the town's inner circle?*

Walking onto the Lawther's red brick driveway, Raz stopped under the metal arch connecting two white columns and viewed the grounds. *Immaculate as usual. Freshly mowed yard, colorful flowerbeds — the perfect home.* He'd hoped to find Becky outside playing, since it would've spared him a confrontation with her grandparents, but that wasn't to be.

He walked briskly up the winding driveway, crossed the porch, rang the bell and stepped back to wait while his pulse pounded. Hearing approaching footsteps, his sense of anticipation grew stronger.

The door swung open and an elderly maid gave him a surprised look and smiled. "Mr. Raz!"

"Hi, Zonie." Zonie had been with the Lawthers forever. Although some in town labeled her an "Aunt Jemima," she was highly regarded by most and loved by the kid's who'd had her as their nanny.

He smiled. "Is Becky here, ma'am?"

Zonie's smile turned upside when a voice from within asked, "Who is it, Zonie?"

Elizabeth Lawther appeared and gasped. "Oh, my god. It's *you!*"

"And a good afternoon to you, too, Mother Lawther. You're as charming as ever, I see. I've come to see my daughter."

His former mother-in-law hesitated, then replied in a frightened voice, "Since you weren't on the bus, we... that is *I*, thought perhaps..." Her gaze turned to his bruised forehead. "Oh, my! You've already been in a fight?"

"Weren't by choice, ma'am. Becky's all right, isn't she?"

"Oh, yes. She's fine. It's just that we have strict orders from her grandfather about, you know. I do wish Mr. Lawther was here to handle this. He could explain it better."

"Don't be afraid of me, Mrs. Lawther. Explain what?" He pulled out the old photo. "See? I haven't seen her since this was taken. Please don't make me wait any longer to find out how she looks now. She's the main reason I came back to Northville. I hope you'll let me see her often enough to prove to her how much I love her. I want to show her what a good father I can be when we're a family again."

Mrs. Lawther's expression told him she wanted to cooperate, but was too afraid. "Didn't you know?" she asked, nervously blotting her neck with a white lace handkerchief. "Isham had all your visitation privileges terminated after you left. You're not even supposed to see her in our presence now."

Raz's smile faded. "That's a bitter pill to swallow. Why wasn't I notified?"

"I thought Isham told you."

"No, ma'am, he didn't." His voice was shaking. "I'm not upset with you, Mother Lawther. I know none of it was your doin'. And I know you've taken good care of Becky. But try to understand how this hurtsme. I've gotta see my little girl."

Tears appeared in Mrs. Lawther's eyes, and her chin quivered, but she said nothing.

"Please, just let me see her for a few minutes. I won't run off with her. I plan to get her back, but it'll all be done legal and proper."

"Mee-maw?" a small voice echoed in the foyer.

Raz beamed as he moved toward her. "Hi, Becky," he said, waving to her.

She hesitated. "Are you my daddy?"

"Your one and only, honey. Now, come and give me a big hug."

Becky looked to her grandmother for approval, and then told Raz, "Mee-maw and Paw-paw said you went away. Mommy went away first, then you. Paw-paw said you did a bad thing. That's why they locked you up and I'd never see you again."

Shaken by her remarks, Raz forced a smile. "I'm back now, sweetheart. I was hoping you wouldn't think what I did was bad when I told you I did it for Mommy. I loved her, too. Now that I'm home, I'm going to prove to you that I'm a good daddy. We'll be together again real soon."

"Please don't make promises you know you can't keep, Raz," Mrs. Lawther said sharply. "The child has gone through enough already. Now, perhaps you'd better leave before Isham comes home."

Unable to restrain himself, Raz leaned down and pulled Becky into his arms. She didn't draw back, but didn't return the hug either.

Fighting a sudden lump in his throat, Raz moved her out to arm's length to admire her, realizing she looked more like her mother than ever. "What a pretty girl you are. That sweet smile makes your daddy very happy."

"Are you going to leave again, Daddy?"

"No way, I'm stayin' right here in Northville, close to my sweet little girl." He held out the gift, "It's not much, honey, but it's given with lots of love."

"Oh, that's a pretty package." Her eyes lit up. "May I keep it, Mee-maw?"

"We don't want to make your grandfather angry, do we?" She again glanced at the driveway. "Oh, I suppose it'll be all right this one time."

Becky squealed when pulling the rabbit out of the box. "I'll name her Snowball." She turned her intense blue eyes on Raz. "Thank you, Daddy. I love it."

He stroked her long, blonde hair. "You're not to worry any more about Daddy, okay? And don't worry about your granddad either, because I'm going to work things out with him so you and I can be a family again."

"But Paw-paw told me I belong to him and Mee-maw, now that my momma has gone to Heaven."

"You belong to all of us, honey," he said, fighting another lump, "but most of all, you belong to me. Now, give me a big hug before I leave. While you're at it, give me a kiss, too."

She put her arms around his neck and kissed his cheek.

Standing up, Raz told her, "I'll be back as soon as I can, honey. Meanwhile, Snowball will keep you company."

She nodded, pulling her bunny closer. "Bye, Daddy. I'll miss you."

Raz left misty-eyed and the door was immediately closed behind him. He was walking toward the steps when he heard the door re-open. Turning, he saw Mrs. Lawther beckoning to him. She said, barely above a whisper, "I want to give you something."

She disappeared and returned shortly with a picture of Becky. "It was taken earlier this year. But you must never tell Isham I gave it to you."

The three by five color picture of Becky made his heart skip a beat.

She added, "I also wanted to tell you that I wasn't completely indifferent toward Patti's plight before she died. Isham absolutely forbade me to help her in any way. I did call Gerta on the sly trying to find her after you came by that last time."

Why'd she think Gerta would know where Patti's was? He wanted to ask her, but instead said, "What did Gerta say?"

"She said she didn't know if Patti was still in town, but she'd try to find out." She drew a long breath. "She never called me back."

"That doesn't surprise me. Did you call her to find out why?"

"Yes. She said she hadn't found Patti. She sounded nervous and told me it was best if I didn't call her again. The next morning when I came out to get the newspaper, I found our cat lying on the porch with its head cut off. Such an awful sight."

"Did Isham believe your cat's death had anything with the call to Gerta?"

"Oh, he didn't know I called her and I was too afraid to tell him about either incident. Zonie cleaned up the mess before he came home for lunch and I never called Gerta again. What's it all mean, Raz?"

He held his tongue, deciding not to suggest that the one who killed her cat might have been the one who butchered Patti and stabbed Tim Barton. Instead, he said, "You and I will sit down soon and have a long talk. In the meantime, please do Becky and me a favor. Don't ask Gerta to help you with anything else. Also, please remind Becky how much I love her every day, and that I'll be back as soon. Tell Mr. Lawther I hope he's willing to give me another chance."

As he turned to walk away she said, "Raz, forgive me for not doing more to help Patti when she needed me. I wanted to. Isham and I had horrible fights about it. He threatened me with divorce and physical violence if I disobeyed him. Maybe that photo will make partial amends for my sins."

Stopping, he looked at her and saw the pain in her eyes. "Thanks."

"Take care," she said, closing the oversized door.

Walking down the driveway, he smiled thinking about hugging his little girl. It didn't last long as his thoughts turned to the visitation ban. Just thinking about the possibility of never seeing Becky again and not regaining his parental rights made him feel empty and defeated. *I can't let that happen.*

CHAPTER 9

Raz set out for Boobs' café. He needed of a shot of her good humor and inflated optimism. Boobs had always been a pal. Her real name was Gladys, but for as long as Raz could remember, her large breasts had prompted men to call her by her nickname. She believed life should be lived to the fullest as long as it didn't interfere with somebody else's right to do the same.

On his way, he waved at other familiar faces in cars driving by. They all waved back, and one man even shouted, "Kick some butts, Raz!" It gave him a warm feeling to know he still had people on his side.

He passed an abandoned cotton gin, an old warehouse and the town's first school that had been left to rot and termites on West Oak Street. The formerly asphalted street was now full of potholes and in spots red dirt had reclaimed it.

He could see that Boobs' Soup Kitchen hadn't changed much in the time he'd been gone. The porch and weather-beaten siding were still in bad shape, but seeing the familiar building stirred up fond memories. Some of the best times during his teens were spent in the Back Room here. He and his buddies had passed from boyhood to manhood flirting with the pretty girls that worked there. Always a looker, with her trademark chest, long blond hair and shapely legs, Boobs was the queen of the come-ons. She always flirted with the guys, making them all feel special.

Two old men with familiar faces were sitting on a wooden bench on the front porch as Raz walked up the steps. They got up to shake his hand, and he said, "Hi, Mr. John, Mr. Link. Gettin' plenty?"

John grinned sheepishly. "Yeah, plenty of butt sores from sittin' here so much. I'm relieved to see bein' out of circulation hasn't dampened your sass. You're still as full of devilment as ever. You filled your pleasure cup yet?"

"Not yet, but I've got high hopes. Boobs here?"

Link smiled. "Bigger'n sin and twice as feisty. She'll fill up your cup and then some."

Raz swung open the squeaky screen door and let it to bang shut behind him as he went in. The woman behind the cash register turned at the noise and exclaimed, "Why you letting my door slam shut?" When she saw who'd come in, her face broke into a big smile. "Raz Jester!" Her three customers turned to look at him.

She rushed around the counter holding out her arms. "You sexy hunk! Come here and let me give that hot bod a squeeze!"

"Great. I'm starving for some attention, but don't squeeze too tight. Ya might pop my cork." He met her halfway across the room and they exchanged hugs and kisses. He stepped back to admire her at arm's length. "You've still got it, Boobs," he said, trying not to let his eyes rest on her enticing cleavage for too long.

"I've still got it and a whole lot more, honey. It just keeps spreadin'!" She framed his face with her hands. "You look exactly the same. I can see visitin' Huntsville didn't dim your spark any." Her expression became sober when she felt the scar. "What happened here?"

He touched the scar. "Just a minor misunderstandin' between friends. It's okay."

"What about this bruise on your forehead, and that bump I felt on the back of your head? Friends do that, too?"

"Northville reception committee."

"Tank and Olin?"

"Some of their associates."

"That's a crappy reception for a young stud the girls used to line up for. Too bad Joe's not still around, he might've prevented it. He was a good guy, but Olin fired him."

He patted her hand. "Good to see you, Boobs."

"You too. Before we get too cozy, I need to clean your face up and put something on those bruises."

"It's okay. Don't worry about it. Got a minute to talk?"

"I've got two, love. When did you blow in?"

"An hour or so ago, I think." He rubbed his head. "Lost track of time there for a while." Seeing no strangers present, he followed Boobs to a back table.

After they sat down, she said, "You're edgier than a virgin bride. There ain't nobody in here for you to fret about."

She caught his gaze drifting to her chest and snapped her fingers. "Still got them rovin' eyes, I see. I still look good enough for a tumble? Or you forget how to do it?"

"How could I? I had the best teacher in the county."

"You know what they say 'bout teachers." She winked. "Everyone of 'em has a pet."

"Same ol' Boobs. Hot chili and hot to trot. When are you gonna settle down and start acting like a respectable woman?"

"When I'm dead, love." She lowered her voice. "You know, Raz, I've seen my share of men in their birthday suits, but not many that look like you. Ya got one big hammer there." She laughed, slapping the table. "You oughta be proud, boy. And more generous now that you're back."

He smiled and looked around at the square tables covered with checkered oilcloth and their accompanying straight-backed wooden chairs. "How's business?"

"Lousy!" Her brow wrinkled. "Tank and Olin won't let the liquor board give me a special permit for a private club license so I can sell alcohol. Wish the high moguls in this county would let us vote on legalizin' the sale of beer at least. There are enough admitted drinkers and backslidin' Baptists to pull it off. But Tank and Olin keep convincin' voters to leave it off the ballot. Those crooks don't want any competition for Punk's private club and Tank's bootleggers."

Her remarks made him to wonder how Fran was able to get a beer license so easily, but he had too much on his plate to explore that right now. His expression sober, he said, "Boobs, do you know how Punk got his hands on the Hole? What happened to Fran?"

"Throwin' ice water on a poor girl's fire don't bother you at all, huh love? Well, since you had to ask, I don't know what happened to Fran. She just got lonesome and left town, I guess. Regarding Punk, the sorry little weasel, I wish it had been him that left. How'd he get the Hole? His ol' daddy's rich. How else?"

"Horton Snitker wouldn't do that, because it'd be admittin' he's Punk's daddy. He has to know Punk is into drugs. He wouldn't put himself crossways with the Feds 'cause they might take a closer look at his business practices. He already lost that last battle with 'em over wages. Remember?"

"Now that you mention it, I do remember him refusing to finance Punk's first joint. Punk had to sell enough grass and pills to do it hisself." She put her hand on his. "Can we change the subject, honey? Talkin' about bad stuff'll put a damper on your passions and spoil our reunion."

Her hand felt soft and warm, but he made himself stay focused on other things. "I can party after I figure out what happened to my interest in the Hole. I was banking on working there to make a living for Becky and me. Don't know what I'm gonna do now."

She pulled her hand back. "I was hopin' you'd come home and turn over a new leaf after what being nosey got you last time. First thing you do, though, is start diggin' and snoopin'."

"Boobs, I'm broke. That reception committee took my discharge money. If Fran bought another place, she probably put my share of the Hole in a bank somewhere. I've got to find her and get it."

"I'm more concerned about you and Tank comin' face to face. I'll give you some money, for cryin' out loud."

"Beer Belly and I have been fightin' so long that one more scuffle won't matter much."

"Is that what you thought when you socked him on the courthouse steps two years ago?"

"Partly. I had to keep the tradition alive. I put the time it got me to good use."

"Yeah, lettin' your juices dry up like honey in a cold crock pot. Don't think about givin' Tank any more knuckle sandwiches without engagin' your brain first. Next time they might put you away so long you'll never get your juices to boilin' again. That happens, I'll die an unloved, lonesome ol' hag."

"I've already sent Tank word through Lard that I won't do anything that'll get him sent to the pen if he'll give me what I want. Should've called him myself, I guess."

"I've got a phone. Call him now."

He followed her to the counter where she produced an old style phonebook and a landline phone. He was pleased that other customers were out of earshot.

"I'll look up his number at our new courthouse extension," she said. "Here it is." She called out the number and he dialed it and waited.

After ten rings, he hung up. "Nobody there. Mind if I use your facilities to clean up? I want to visit Mom."

"Sure, if you think Tank will stay off your back for a while. You already been by to see your little girl?"

He nodded, pulling out the new picture. "Ain't she a beauty?"

"That she is, love." She took the picture. "But I heard ol' Chisel Nose Lawther got Bryan Fulton to—"

"Mrs. Lawther told me. After settling in, I'll call a lawyer about getting her back. But first, I need him for something else."

"Well, you'll have to retrieve your share of the Hole to get Harley Ritter to hitch his high-horse to your wagon. He don't work cheap no more."

"I'll give him a call and try to work something out." He leaned forward. "Think hard and try to remember if you heard something about Fran selling out. Anything that might give me a clue about where to find her would be great."

"My memory is real clear about one thing." She gave him a teasing look. "There was talk 'round town that you and Fran had something goin' on over there besides runnin' a dance hall. I've already told you, I don't know the details about her selling the place. Don't think Punk could've got his filthy hands on the Hole if she hadn't wanted him to have it." She smiled. "You know us women. It's that way with everything we've got."

"That doesn't sound like Fran, unless something big happened to change her mind."

"Like what, love?"

"I won't know for sure until I find her. How's business there now, compared to when we owned it?"

"Honey, Punk takes in more money than the IRS. His joint is the biggest thing in this part of the state these days. He books hot rock groups that pull in young folks from all over."

"That means he's still selling what they think they can't live without." He added, as if to himself, "I can't believe she'd just up and run off, and leave our business with somebody like Punk."

"Well, she did, just a few weeks after Tank and his friends brushed you out of their hair."

She returned Becky's photo and said, "I see your little sweetheart 'round town every once in a while with that weak-minded grandmother of hers or Aunt Zonie. She's a darling, all right. Looks just like—" She gave him a pained look.

"I know. Just like her mother."

Boobs put her hand on his. "Honey, I still grieve over what happened to Patti. She was such a bright, pretty girl. Still carrying the torch for her, are you?"

"She's the mother of my child. And yes, it did take a while after I lost her to realize I still have lots of living to do."

"That's the spirit! I just hope Tank and his friends don't stop you."

Remembering Cato's tape, he glanced down the hall. "Still use the Back Room?"

"Naah. All of the customers who used to use it got married, moved or found religion." She nudged him with her elbow. "Remember how it used to be, love?"

"Of course! Can we go in there now? I need a place with a little privacy. You still got my old clothes?"

"I said I'd keep 'em, didn't I?" She stood up. "I'll lay 'em out for you, and maybe take your mind off the bird that got away." She told her customers, "Leave your money on the counter, boys. If you cheat me, I'll tell your wives you was with me in the Back Room."

The men looked sheepishly at her, nodding. One of them said, "It might be worth a divorce. I'd at least find out if you're as hot as your chili was today."

She waved him off. "Anything hotter than that chili would kill you, Giles."

Passing through a door near the dining area, she hooked her arm around Raz's as they headed down the hall. "I'll make you a job offer you can't refuse if you can't find Fran."

"Frenchy might have work for me, I'm going out to talk to him later."

"Shovel chicken shit for peanuts? I'll give you a better deal."

He stopped in front of a side room and pointed to a sign over the door that read: DOMINO HALL. "Where are the domino customers?"

"In the cemetery or one of them God-awful nursing homes. Not many young people play. They consider it an old fogies' game. If you'll partner with me, we'll turn that into a poker room. Texas hold 'em would bring in some cash."

At the end of the hall, they stopped under a sign on the left side of the hall that read: THE BACK ROOM. Pulling keys from her apron pocket, Boobs unlocked the door and they went in the musty-smelling room.

Looking around in subdued light from the one window, Raz saw the bar — a couple of boards laid across two wooden barrels. There were straight-backed chairs pushed under dusty tables and the center of the room where they'd danced was still clear of furniture as if Boobs hoped her old customers would be returning soon.

She flipped on the overhead light and asked, "Does this stir up your blood, love?"

"It really takes me back. Why don't you air it out and use it?"

"I'm gettin' too old to run it and the café by myself. It needs a young stud like you to breathe new life into it. Believe me, young folks who like bluegrass and real country 'n' western music would pack this place every Saturday night."

He spotted a coke cooler behind the bar and detected the faint odor of cigarette smoke. Since Boobs didn't smoke, he suspected the place hadn't been completely abandoned. "It has possibilities, all right."

"I hate seeing it stand idle. This room was the liveliest spot in town back in the day. Used to be the only place young men could get a beer, dance and enjoy the company of pretty young gals without a lot of hassle."

"That's because you only gave door keys to the ones you liked." He glanced at the peephole in the door.

"I had to let some in that I didn't like at all, honey. It had something to do with facin' up to the realities of the world in a small town. I didn't dare tell Punk he couldn't come in, or Tank and Olin. They usually snuck in when you and your friends weren't around. You may recall Olin was always the smart-aleck, and Tank was the bully. But I saw to it they didn't get anything but beer. Even that was illegal, but Olin wouldn't arrest himself." She laughed. "In the early days, Pop Cheever didn't bother us as long as we kept it private."

"Yeah." he said absently while mentally reopening the pink door behind the bar. He remembered sliding between silk sheets on the sweet-smelling, king-sized bed in that room. There was always a vase of fresh flowers in there too. All of his close friends knew about that special room, because Boobs liked football players. Some of those who used it weren't his friends, like Pencil McKnight, Bryan Fulton and Sonny Irby. Bryan, a wannabe politician and Snitker butt-kisser, catered to Punk and his friends, and was rewarded with a four-year scholarship at the University of Texas Law School courtesy of Horton Snitker. Shortly after graduation, Ol' Money Bags backed him in his race for Eastman County District Attorney, the office he'd held when Raz was tried on the trumped-up murder charge.

Bryan had also handled the prosecution when Raz knocked out Tank, until the state attorney general sent one of their lawyers to preside over the trial and sentencing. Raz had learned through the grapevine that Bryan was elected to the state senate after he left. *Senator Bryan Fulton. Give me a break.*

To everybody's surprise, Sonny Irby had managed to get a job at Horton Snitker's bank, but he was no barrel of laughs in the Back Room. Like Tank, Sonny could never attract a pretty girl. Short and overweight, he had a broad, pockmarked face and a large red nose that earned him the nickname "Rudolph." He came to the Back Room to buy female companionship.

He remembered the music from the jukebox and the excited voices rising up in a room full of cigarette smoke. That, and the aroma of spilled beer…

"Have a seat, love," Boobs said, jerking him back to the present.

"Okay, just a minute." He walked to the old Wurlitzer jukebox and leaned down to read the song titles across the front. "This thing still work?"

"Everything I've got still works, love." She flipped a switch and it lit up.

He put a quarter in the slot, pushed #7 and the rich, sultry voice of Marlena Dietrich filled the room with a the song, "The Boys in the Back Room." It was a little scratchy, but the lyrics were still clear.

Raz watched the disc spin and listened to the words until the song ended and the mechanical arm returned it to its allotted slot. Turning to Boobs, he said, "Wasn't that great? Really brings back good memories. Got a beer in that old cooler?"

"Sure do. For a minute there, I was afraid you weren't gonna come back to earth and ask for one."

She returned with two brown, longneck bottles. "Raz, I'm serious about you bein' my business partner. Like I said, you still have lots of friends here, and a bunch of locals don't like that crap they play over at Punk's place. We can put some new records on the jukebox or hire us a band every Friday and Saturday night. We'd make a mint."

"You really think so?"

"Shoot! With Northville's star quarterback to bring in the business, we could get this room goin' again just like before. The rest of the place, too. I saw that look on your face. You miss those good ol' days. We had lots of cold beer on the sly, good music and pretty girls to smooth out the rough spots in a man's day. Yes, siree. We could do that again."

"Bring back the party girls and give all the guys STDs? Everybody would love us for that."

"I ain't denying that party girls ain't like they used to be, love. But if we looked in the right places, we could find something besides thieves, dopers and streetwalkers. We could run a safe, clean business."

"You're forgetting one important point, sweet thing. Guys don't have to lay out lots of money for a good time with girls anymore."

"Sounds like you fell for that ol' line that says it's stupid to buy a garage when you already own a screwdriver?" She gave him a teasing look. "Sounds like you've shot your pistol at some little filly you ran into down at the Houston bus station."

"Haven't fired my pistol at a thing in over two years."

"You must've done something for relief, 'cause you sure as hell ain't treatin' me like the always-cocked-and-ready Raz I used to know." Her expression turned somber. "What's the matter, love? Did I say a dirty word?"

"A woman really did meet me at the bus terminal." He described the blonde. "Have you seen anybody in Northville that fits that description?"

"Nope. But she could be working out of Punk's club." She raised one eyebrow. "Why do I get this gut feeling there's something about her you don't want to tell me?"

He glanced at the door to make sure it was still closed. "A couple of guys with that woman tried to kill me."

"Oh, my God!" Her eyes widened. "Why? Who were they?"

He told her about Cato, and how he clammed up every time he asked about Patti's murder. Then, he told her about the tape.

She listened to everything without interrupting, then asked, "Who were the ones who tried to kill you?" he said.

"Somebody who wants that tape, and me dead, apparently. Cato's nephew, Snake, picked me up in Coldwater and drove me home. He said word was out about me getting some kinda statement out of Cato. They must've planned to get it *and* me with one whack."

"You talking about a regular cassette tape?"

"A mini tape. Cato and I recorded a couple of songs on the first part of it so it wouldn't seem important if someone tried to play it."

"I've heard of rotten songs, love, but nothin' awful enough to get killed over."

"It's not the songs I'm worried about losin'. Cato said he recorded information that'll send people to prison. He explained how his drug business worked when he was riding high, named his contacts and who he paid off. It's hot stuff, apparently."

"What was Cato tryin' to do, get you killed?"

He gave her a surprised look. He'd never thought of that. "What would he gain by gettin' me killed? He gave me the tape after I saved his life. He told me he wanted to get even with the ones who shafted him. He certainly didn't do it 'cause he likes the law."

"Never met Cato, but I knew what kind of business he was in. I heard he was sly and more crooked than a barrel of greased earthworms. Honey, I wouldn't bet my life on anything he said."

Not wanting to further fuel her skepticism about his choices, he decided he wouldn't mention the fight at the hotel, or his confrontation with Zapata. "I was counting on the tape as life insurance. Thought all I had to do was get it to a third party I could trust before they whacked me and everything would be good." He flashed back to the two shooters in Houston. "I didn't count on them jumping me before I got a chance to talk to Tank and explain my plan. I sent him word but looks like his deputy forgot to deliver it."

"You told Lard Haskins? That dumbbell never did anything right."

"Guess I'll call Tank as soon as I find a safe place to hide my insurance policy. He'll spread the word, 'cause he knows his fat will be the first to hit the fire if that tape gets into the wrong hands."

"You mean you haven't already dropped it off somewhere? Please don't say it's still on you."

He nodded and she slapped her palms against the table. "Of all the lame-brained things I've ever heard, Raz Jester, this takes the cake! First, you cold-cock a deputy sheriff in front of a courthouse full of witnesses, and now this. Coming this far with that thing in your pocket is beyond crazy — it's plumb insane."

"Who would I leave it with, the bus driver? He's the only person I've met besides an old lady on the bus. I had to wait 'til I got home."

"Fork it over." She held out her hand. "I'll put it where they can't find it."

"You're the only one in town besides Pop Cheever I'd trust with it, but I don't want that bunch of killers gunning for either of you."

"Pop ain't here. Remember what I always told you about a bird in the hand?"

"Too risky." He shook his head. "Call Harley. I want to leave it with him."

"That rascal won't take it unless you put some green in his greedy little hand. Where you gonna find that kind of money?"

"Possibly a loan from Frenchy Patroon."

"How long would that take? You need to ditch that hot potato now."

"Maybe Harley'll take it on *promise* of payment."

She laughed. "This ain't no time to crack jokes, love. Tell you what. If you're dead set on havin' Harley keep your insurance policy, I'll handle the finances and deliver it to him first thing in the morning. You can pay me back when you get your share of the Hole." She winked. "Or you can pay it in trade."

"Find him for me and I'll get my pickup and deliver it to him tonight."

"Man, you just won't give a poor girl a chance to play catch-up, will you? Okay, I'll call him." She walked to the landline phone and dialed a number. "The things a desperate girl won't do for a tumble."

When the call was answered, she said, "Boobs Noonan here, darlin'. I've got ta talk to Harley."

She paused, then said sharply, "Tell Harley to call me the minute he gets back, got that?" She hung up, telling Raz, "Harley's out of town on a case. Won't be back 'til the first of next week. That means you'll have to put that little item in my hot little hands after all."

In view of what had already happened, he knew there was no other option. Zapata, the hotel thugs, the shooters — any of them could reappear any time. He'd be an easy target walking to the nursing home or the old Jester place. "Since Tank and his friends didn't see me come in here, I guess it'll be safe if you hold it 'til tomorrow morning. By then I'll figure out a way to take it if off your hands 'til Harley gets back."

"What will you do between now and then?"

"Get my truck and visit friends. Can I have my clothes now? These duds make me stand out like black warts on a pretty woman's nose."

"Follow me, love."

In her living quarters at the end of the hall, she took an armful of his clothes out of a chest-of-drawers and laid them on her bed. "Your boots and hat are in the closet." She made no move to leave the room.

As Boobs watched, he pulled out a soft, short-sleeved denim shirt and a pair of old jeans from the pile on the bed. He unbuttoned his prison shirt, took it off, and put on the denim one. Then he sat down on the bed to take off the brogans. When he stood up to take off his trousers, he hesitated.

"You mean I don't get to stay for the main event? What a gyp!" She sighed and said, "I'll be in the Back Room." She left, closing the door.

Pulling on his jeans, he hooked his leather belt together behind a large silver buckle with a Texas emblem on it and went to the closet to retrieve his soft Southwestern style Resistol and his old Luchese boots that Boobs had kept clean and polished. Pulling on the low-heeled tan boots, he transferred the pistol and his billfold from the discarded pants and let out a loud "Yee-ha!" as he flexed his toes.

He adjusted his hat in front of Boobs' mirror to make sure the brim still had the right amount of roll on the sides, then studied his reflection with a certain degree of satisfaction. "Do I know you?"

Using the Case pocketknife he'd found in the jeans, he got down on his knees and began cutting away the heel of the shoe containing the tape. After cutting through the stitches, he slipped the blade under the cap and pried it off over the nails. Putting his knife on the floor, he pulled a thin, plastic-wrapped object about two inches long from the rectangular hole in the inner side of the heel and examined it for leaks. "Great. Loop did a good job." He dropped it into his shirt pocket.

Under the heel of the other shoe he found a small envelope neatly folded into a flat package about two inches square. Putting it in his back pocket, he picked up his prison brogans and joined Boobs in the Back Room. He felt like a new man.

Boobs gave him a long catcall and whistle. "My, ain't you a handsome devil? What happened to that horny guy I left in my bedroom?"

"He's right here, horns and all." Sitting down opposite her, he handed over the tape. "Here's my insurance policy. Where you gonna put it?"

She turned it over, studying it. "You said you put some songs on it?"

"Yeah, but I'm not too proud of 'em. One's about the Armadillo Hole."

"Son-of-a-gun!" Her face brightened. "I knew you could make up enough lies to steal a poor woman's virtue, but didn't know you could write and sing songs, too. Can I play it if I can find a machine that'll handle it?"

"*No!*" His sudden reaction startled her. "Sorry," he said. "Of course, you can play it, but not yet. Just put it in a safe place for now. As soon as Harley calls you back, tell him to come over and pick it up. If I'm not here when he comes, then call Tank and tell him Harley'ss got it and has instructions to call the U.S. District Attorney in Tyler and Lassiter with the state narcotics office in Austin if something happens to me. I'll call Harley later and make sure he understands everything."

"Unless you tell me you've made other arrangements, I'll hold it 'til Harley gets back, then I'll tell him what you said. Don't worry; I'll keep it in a safe place, like the other side of my bed. There ain't been nobody there for so long, there's no danger of anyone findin' it there." She laughed. "I'd sure like to hear your songs, though, and so would lots of other people." She slapped his arm. "Tell you what. How about I take it out to NEHI so that brainless DJ Uncle Bud can play your music during homecoming this Saturday?"

"That's another no-no," he said. "The minute that hits the air, Tank and all his Dixie Mafia friends will make a bee-line out there. They'd kill anybody who tried to stop 'em. Can't afford to lose that tape and have nothing for the state narcs." He looked at the brogans. "Where can I dump these shoes?"

"I've still got my wood-burning stove in the cafe. I'll put 'em in a sack and fire it up after closing. While I'm up, I'll put this tape in my special hiding place."

She went into her bedroom. A few minutes later, she passed the door on the way to the serving room up front with a sack in her hands. He heard the heater door open and slam shut and hoped there were no witnesses to what she'd done. Moments later, she rejoined him at the table.

"Don't look so worried," she said. Nobody was up there. Now, what say we tiptoe to my room and fill up the lonely side of my bed?"

"I'll settle for another beer. After that, I've got to go see my mother and get my truck."

"Don't you know that it's not nice to hurt a lady's feelings?" She got another beer and pulled her chair closer. "Seeing you in those clothes makes me think you're ready to step out and reclaim your town. If you're saving your bullets for Fran Druman, remember that a bird in the hand is a lot easier to hit than one on the fly."

"I'll keep that in mind."

"Remember this, too, lover boy. It don't take no genius to realize that somebody with lots of clout was behind Punk's taking over your friend's business. Those people might still have a bigger interest in that gal than you do. If you try to find her, you're likely to butt heads with 'em. You might even cross trails again with those two guys that tried to do a number on you in Houston."

"You sure know how to cheer a man up. Sounds like you might've heard something about Fran and Punk's deal that you haven't told me."

"Intuition tells me that any woman who does business with Punk has got to be as rotten as he is, or awfully scared."

"Since you're such a good detective, I'll ask you about a couple of guys Cato told me about. Ever get a look at a man called Mazurka or one named Smeddish?"

She shook her head. "People in the dope business ain't on my list of close acquaintances. What did the ones in Houston look like? Could've been them that came after you."

"I was too busy runnin' to take notes, but one of 'em was tall, and the other short and chubby." He took a swallow of beer. "Could've been sent down by the guy running things here, somebody called Rudy. Ever hear of him?"

"For a man who wants to keep livin', you sure ask lots of questions."

"When you said what you did about Fran, it got me to thinkin'. Maybe she did get crossways with the outfit running things now. If so, the man in charge would've had something to do with it. If I can talk to him, maybe he'll know where I can find her."

"I've never heard of anybody named Rudy." She moved closer. "Can't we forget all this heavy stuff and live a little?"

He began feeling the effects of the alcohol, and the fire within was burning hotter. He glanced at her chest, but dropped his eyes and shook his head. "It wouldn't be right. You're my friend, and I've already asked you to do too much for me." Looking at the beer, he said, "This is good stuff."

"Everything in my place is good stuff, sugar dumplin'. You're welcome to stay here with me the rest of the day and find out for yourself, if you think you're up to it. That would really give the town biddies something to gossip about." She laughed.

"Do you give rain checks?"

"Only if it's rainin'. There ain't a damn cloud in sight. What's the matter? Am I too old for you now, and saggin' in the wrong places or what?" She squeezed his thigh.

"Don't slide your hand up too high. You do, and I'll have to put on a clean pair of shorts."

"Why suffer, love, when relief is so close?"

"Like I said, it wouldn't be right, you being my friend. I'd just be usin' you."

"So? Use me. When did scruples ever keep Raz Jester from gettin' a girl's most prized possessions?" She eased her hand up a little further. "That noble stuff meant something when I was young and full of romantic nonsense. But at my age, it's just empty words, lover boy."

He took a quick swallow of beer as she snuggled closer and pushed one breast against his elbow. Her perfume and the beer suddenly made his problems seem far away and less complicated. He was reaching the point of no return; beer had always made him affectionate.

"Look at it this way," she said. "It's like separatin' little green peas from little brown peas. Sooner or later, they just get all mixed up in the pot and end up all tastin' the same. Don't you ever feel that way is this crazy, screwed-up world?"

"I've been so busy fighting the alligators chomping at my tail of late, I haven't had time to sort out anything. I've got more at stake now than I did as a teenager comin' here to party. I keep tellin' myself I've come back to live like I did then, but things keep gettin' in the way. You know, things like how to stay alive, get my little girl back, find a butcher."

"Oh, my. You *have* changed." She sighed. "They didn't do nothin' to your good parts to put out your fire while you was in the pen, did they, love?"

"The fire's roaring, but I can't get the damper open all the way. Don't know if it's because of guilt or what. Give me a few more minutes with this beer."

He was embarrassed by his reluctance to jump on the roller coaster ride that Boobs was offering. He told himself it wasn't because he was more aware of their age difference now, but that fact had occurred to him. He hoped she wasn't a mind reader.

Her hand moved higher, and his heart pounded faster and the stirring below strengthened. He had never needed a woman as much as he did now, but when he envisioned himself performing the act, he also saw his little girl and his butchered wife. *Loosen up,* he told himself. *It's okay. You're out of prison. You're no longer morally bound by marriage vows. Your wife is dead. Live again.*

Putting the empty bottle on the table, he walked his fingers up Boobs' arm and pulled her dress off her shoulder. He had just pushed his fingers under the strap of her bra when a sudden pounding on the door made them both jump.

"Go away, I'm busy!" Boobs shouted.

"Boobs, it's Olin Culpepper. Unlock this door! I've got a warrant. I'm here to arrest Raz Jester for assault and battery."

Trapped, damn! The alligators had caught up with him again.

CHAPTER 10

"If we ignore him, maybe he'll go away," Boobs whispered.

Olin knocked again, louder. "Open this damn door or I'll arrest you, too! You're harboring a criminal."

Raz jumped to his feet, whispering, "Stall him."

"Olin, if my name's not on your warrant, you can get lost. Raz ain't here," Boobs said toward the door, then moved quickly over to the window, unlocked it and whispered to Raz, "You've had lots of practice jumpin' out of women's bedroom windows, so go. Don't break a leg, because I want to take up where we left off before I die of old age."

"Don't forget to burn those shoes," Raz said as he ducked out the window, as Olin's fist pounded on the door again.

"Raz was seen entering the premises, so I know he's in there. I can hear you whisperin'."

Raz made it out the window, and then pushed the screen back in place. "Re-hook it," he whispered. "Hide my clothes before you let him in. I'll pick 'em up later."

As he rounded the corner of the café, he stopped to see if Tank was waiting out front. The only vehicle in sight was Olin's police cruiser.

He walked briskly over to Magnolia Street, and then circled back to McShan Road. Glancing at the sun through the trees, he guessed it to be about four o'clock. With the effects of the beer and Boobs' caresses banished by Olin's intrusion and his rush to escape, that monster had been shoved back into its cage for the time being. It was probably best; he had more important things to do. The first of which was visiting his mother.

As he approached the nursing home, he saw a sheriff's car parked in front. He stopped short, trying to figure out what to do next. Judging from the silhouette of the driver, Tank Zelder was in that car watching for him. Disgusted, he sat down to wait behind a big tree. An hour later, the car was still there, so he decided to give up and come back when he could get inside without being seen.

He walked away, moving along McShan Road. *Cato must be psychic. He was totally right about everything so far. Guess it was unrealistic to think I could dodge Tank and his friends for long enough to get thigns done. What I need right now is a safe place to relax and think things out.*

A mile out of town, he stopped at Stump Skeeters' little grocery store. After visiting with Stump and his wife for a few minutes and making sure his credit was still good there, he filled a plastic container with gas and left for his parents' house five miles out of Northville.

He'd been walking for an hour when he heard a car approaching. He glanced back to make sure it wasn't the black Merc or Zapata's Caddy. It was a white Chrysler sedan driven by a petite brunette.

"Hello, darlin'," he said when he recognized the driver. Anita McKnight had been his serious girlfriend in high school, before he fell in love with Patti. After graduation, she'd married Pencil Fountain and moved away.

"What a welcome sight you are!"

"Hi, Raz. You're a hard man to find. I've been driving all over this up-tight town lookin' for you. Finally decided you must be out at your folks' old place. Get in."

"What about this?" he said as he held up the gas can.

She pushed a button and the trunk popped open. "It'll be okay back there for a few minutes."

He stowed fuel and slid into the car's air-conditioned comfort. "Thanks for the lift." He quickly noticed her fuller figure, smoother, glowing complexion. "What will Pencil think about this?"

She kept her eyes on him for a moment as if thirsty to see him. "Pencil and I are divorced."

"Too bad," he said, turning to look through the rear window.

Looking closer at his face, she exclaimed "My God, Raz, what happened to you?"

He fingered the scars. "A little souvenir from the slammer. The bruises are courtesy of some local trash. Nothing for you to worry about."

"I haven't had a chance to tell you how sorry I am about Patti. I was sorry to hear about what happened to you, too. Didn't hear 'bout your troubles with Tank 'til you'd already been sent away."

"Thanks. I appreciate your kind thoughts."

"Now that you're back, I hope things will go your way for a change."

"I got home with all my vital parts intact. That's a start. Now you findin' me and givin' me a ride is making me feel better about things. You're lookin' good, Anita."

She rolled her eyes. "As fresh as ever, ain't ya, cowboy?" She gave him a knowing look. "Raz Jester, the shameless bullshiter and legendary lover. What're you gonna do now that you're back?"

"My immediate plans are to get my truck, visit my mom, and find some pretty young thing to take me on a trip where only angels tread."

"I'm glad to see all the bad luck you've had hasn't hurt your macho ego any."

"I wonder about that sometimes. You seein' anybody?"

"It's not easy to do anything bold or interestin' in this town without everybody knowin' about it. Since you're my standard of excellence, I haven't found anybody new who strikes that spark. After Fran sold the Hole, we don't have a good place to drink beer, dance and look over the prospects."

"You know what happened to Fran?"

"Great. *I* pick you up, and right off you ask about another woman." She shrugged. "Don't know. All I heard were rumors."

"Like what?"

"Like something big happened over at the Hole. Something involving out-of-town operators and Punk. I had enough sense not to ask questions. I hope you do too."

"Cecil Cassidy told me some woman was killed. I was afraid it was Fran."

"Don't know much about that. Just that it happened shortly after you left."

"Did the Hole change ownership before or after Fran disappeared?"

She thought a moment. "I wasn't livin' here at then, but I think both happened about the same time."

He pointed. "Turn here." She turned on Cutoff Road and he asked, "What happened to you and Pencil?"

"You should've told me how he got his nickname. I guess it still would've worked out okay if I hadn't had you to compare him to."

"I figured you'd forgotten about me a long time ago." When she didn't say anything, he added, "Besides, I had plenty of time for thinkin' recently, I decided there's more to carin' about somebody than a roll in the hay."

Her jaw dropped. "Are you a pod person? The Raz Jester I used to know would never say something like that. For a minute there, you sounded almost like a serious-minded person."

He continued looking forward, and said nothing for a few moments as the car bounced over the uneven road. "I had it all, you know. For a while at least. For long enough to build a lot of memories and know what I'd lost when it was gone."

"I still think about Patti, too. Like I said, I was heartbroken when I heard what happened to her. Even though she stole my man, I still liked her."

The conversation was getting too deep and depressing, so he changed the subject. "I heard you're an RN now. You working anywhere?"

"Not since I started my family," she said, laughing. "My real goal was to marry a doctor, retire young and live the good life. Instead, I married Pencil and ended up playing doctor." Her voice had a bitter ring to it.

"Doesn't look like it hurt you any."

"Thanks. I needed that." She opened the console. "Care for a cold one?"

He looked at the small cooler between them. "You still know the way to a man's heart." He popped the cap. "Do you always keep this handy when picking up male hitchhikers?"

"Didn't you tell me once it always pays to be ready?"

"Like I used to be?" He laughed. "Those were the days."

He sipped his beer as Anita dodged the rough spots in the dirt road, dust boiling out behind them. He took a deep relaxing breath and said, "Anita, you're my kind of gal — pretty girl, cool car and a console full of cold beer."

"If memory serves me correctly, any pretty girl was your kind of gal, cowboy."

"When I was in high school, sure. I've done a lot of living since then and it's taught me that quality is better than quantity. Seeing you now makes me remember how we used to like some of the same things — smooth country music, dancing late and partying long. We had some great times together."

"I thought maybe you'd forgotten, with your serious talk and all."

"I want to talk about you and me now." He moved closer to her. "Why don't we go to some quiet place and have a real go at getting re-acquainted?"

"Like you said, we're not kids any more."

"Is that a yes or a no?"

"It means I've been there and done that. I know how it feels to be left out in the cold after getting in over my head with no commitment from you. I'm a mother now and have more important things to think about." She flipped down her sun visor, displaying a photo of a toddler. "I can't just take up where we left off as teenagers."

Bleary-eyed, she quickly looked away and he grabbed the wheel to get them back on the road. "Watch it! It's too hot to walk."

She drove in silence for a few moments. "Raz, if we did go someplace to get re-acquainted, would you just windup throwin' me away again when somethin' better comes along?"

"A man with as much heat on him as I have right now can't give any guarantees about anything. Besides, both of us tried the matrimonial, safe route. Remember?"

"All to well. Seems I have a knack for rememberin' the wrong things."

He studied her with a sense of renewed appreciation. "Looks like we have more in common than I thought. Maybe we can help each other in more ways than one."

"Maybe. Just don't hurry the heavy-breathing part."

"If you'll drive us to that quiet place, you wouldn't have to do anything you didn't feel right about. We'll pretend everything's the way it used to be, think about the *now* instead of tomorrow or next week."

"And where would this private place be?"

"The woods. Remember how good it was when we'd spread a blanket under the trees?"

"I remember the chiggers."

"Don't go all negative on me." He pointed. "Up ahead, just before you get to my parents' place, there's an old logging road that runs to the right for about a mile. Turn there."

Following his directions, they were soon moving through an area of cutover pines and hardwoods where underbrush had almost reclaimed the road. A couple of hundred yards off the road, Raz pointed to a gnarled oak tree. She pulled the car under it, stopped and left the engine running.

"Want me to open a beer for you?" he said.

"I guess one wouldn't hurt."

He noticed her hands trembling when she took it. After several swallows, she said, "This puts my mind in a whirl. I keep thinkin' about the way things used to be with us." She smiled. "Those were our best years, don't you think?"

"We had a helluva time, that's for sure. Everythin' was better if you weren't supposed to do it."

"Only some of us thought that. There was always too much dope. I thank God we didn't get into that." Noticing a hurt expression sweep over his face, she put her hand on his. "Forgive me, Raz. I didn't mean to open old wounds. I'm so sorry."

"That's okay," he said. He searched his brain for something to say that would break the heavy silence, but bad memories had a hold on him. Sighing, he took Anita's empty can and offered her another. She shook her head, too embarrassed to speak.

"Better kill the motor," he said. "It might overheat."

"Sorry about spoiling the mood," she said. "I'll turn off the car, but we'd better roll the windows down or it'll get hot in here pretty fast."

"Sitting in a place like this with a pretty girl helps a person get his thinking right." When she said nothing, he opened another beer and took a swallow. "What were we talking about?"

"Teenage stuff. We felt invincible then; thought all of our dreams would come true if we wished hard and waited long enough."

"I wasn't much of a waiter or a wisher. Always believed more in the now."

They talked until he finished his beer. He took her hand and gave it a gentle, conciliatory squeeze. Being with her made him feel a little better about things, and his libido was starting to come back.

He sighed. "It's hard to sit by a jar of cookies and not grab one, you know."

"Control yourself, cowboy. We're just two old friends out here talking. Remember?"

"Yeah, but my urges aren't listening. Are you one of the few?"

"Few what, fools?"

"Of course not. I mean one of the few women that don't sleep around. The kind a man can depend on, even if he doesn't always have sense enough to appreciate her."

"You *have* changed, Raz Jester."

"Well, don't say it like it's a curse or something. I haven't lost my lust for living, I'm hurting like you can't imagine." He grimaced.

"Raz, what's wrong?"

He pointed to his crotch. "Stone ache."

"What's *that?*"

"You really don't know? It happens when a man gets worked up to make a one hundred yard dash and the starter cancels the race."

"Oh." She blushed. "I'm sorry. Please don't be mad at me."

"My brain's tryin', but my other parts aren't gettin' the message."

"Being here with you gets me all mixed up. I want to let my hair down and go wild, but I promised myself I'd never let you hurt me again. Besides, life makes no sense if a person doesn't live by some kind of moral rules."

"This is no time for a morality lecture," he said, and chuckled.

"Give me some more time. Okay?"

He nodded, getting out. "I need a little fresh air and privacy for a minute." He took several deep breaths while finding a private spot to pee.

"Feelin' better?" she asked when he returned.

"I don't think anything going to explode for now."

The ache in his groin had subsided, allowing him the luxury of settling back and relaxing for a few minutes. Eyes closed, tension gone, he was about to doze off when thoughts of Olin's visit to the Back Room and an arrest warrant hanging over his head ruined the moment. He sat up and sighed.

"What were you thinkin' about?" Anita asked.

"Old, unfinished business." He looked at her. "You?"

"The usual, when it's quiet and I'm alone. Do you realize how many times during the last five years I've thought about how great it was between us?"

"I only have eleven toes."

She slapped his leg lightly. "I think about you about that many times every night."

"Sounds like a line to me. I thought only men came up with corny stuff like that."

"Smarty pants. We never should've split up. Why did we?"

"Things happened." He looked out over the hood at the bushes and trees. "We just took different roads. You should've forgotten me."

"Couldn't. You were my first. And the best."

"First?"

"Don't tell me you didn't know."

"I thought you were just scared."

"That, too. While we're on the subject, there's somethin' else you probably won't believe. I've only done it with you and my husband."

"Really? I didn't know such a woman still existed. That makes you good marriage material for sure."

She didn't respond immediately. Finally, she said, "Raz, do you ever think about me?"

"You aren't gettin' serious again, are you? Lots of waves have hit the beach since we were high school kids, and some of them washed up dead fish."

"Do you think we were any good?" There was a hint of sadness in her voice.

"I think *I'm* pretty good, at some things anyway."

"I don't mean that way, silly. One night, back when I was a senior, about a year after you and I broke up, Daddy caught me and a boy necking in front of our house. My date was smokin' a joint and the smell was everywhere. Daddy was furious. He told me young people were just no damned good. All they wanted to do is smoke pot and screw."

"Your dad was half right." He smiled.

"Can't you be serious for even a few seconds?"

"If you remember, we had to be either a kicker or a doper during high school. I think my friends and I chose the better path. Thought you did too. As for being any good, I guess it depends on how you feel about yourself. It helps knowing you tried to play by the rules and not hurt anyone while tiptoein' through your little patch of tulips."

"You always had a way of makin' things seem uncomplicated." She sighed. "Even though I spoiled our little trip down horizontal-bop lane today, I want you to know that you still make me feel good in other ways. You always did. We should've gotten married instead of splittin' up."

"I remember a certain young woman being a party animal on and off campus following our getting personal out at her parent's lake house. *She* was too wild to be considered the marrying kind."

"I was tryin' to push your jealousy button and force you to make a commitment, dummy. Too bad my scheme didn't work." After being quiet and thoughtful a moment, she added, "Back then, most of us girls were interested in livin' right. But when I hear teenagers talkin' these days, all they talk about is dope and crack and sex like it's nothing more than having a burger and fries. Guess we weren't so bad after all."

"Never thought we were." Glancing at the dash clock, he said, "I should be gettin' over to mom's place and to get my truck."

"Are you disappointed in me?"

He patted her knee. "You're still at the top of my most wanted list. Don't worry about it."

She drove them out of the woods, turning right on Cutoff Road. They were only a short distance away from the old Jester farm on its clay bank at the top of a hill.

The signs of neglect he saw at his parents' farm disturbed Raz. There were waist high weeds and two winters worth of leaves piled up around the fences and buildings. The seventy year old house had darkened with age and its boards were buckling from harsh weather taking its toll.

Anita drove slowly across the culvert and up the slope into the yard, stopping near the porch. She popped the trunk so Raz could retrieve the gas can. He got out and stood quietly, studying the surroundings. He was happy to see the bulge in the tarp thrown over his prized possession that was parked under the lean-to roof of the barn.

Anita moved up beside him, and said, "Except for the weeds, it's just like I remembered it."

He nodded, kissing her on the cheek. "Thanks for the lift, and the trip down memory lane."

"You're welcome. Can I stick around and help? You got groceries?"

"You can give me a jump start." He smiled. "My pickup, I mean. Let me clear out the weeds, then you can pull up in front of the truck."

He slowly cleared a path as she watched. When he finished, he came back to the porch, reached under the sill and retrieved a set of keys. Unlocking the front door, he went in and headed to his bedroom. Once there, he rolled two mounted tires out of the closet.

"Need some help?" Anita asked.

"Thanks. No need for you to get dirty. I'd appreciate another cold beer though."

She went to the cooler in the car and grabbed cold can, then went back to the bedroom, popping the cap as she walked. "You hungry?"

"Starving, but I can wait 'til I get the truck up and running."

They went back outside, and he pulled the tarp off his red '87 Chevy. He stood and admired it a before leaning the wheels against a fender, then he got to work. By the time he'd removed the jack blocks after mounting the wheels, he was covered with dirt and sweat. "Anita, if you can stand the smell of me long enough to get close, I'd appreciate another beer."

She returned shortly with the beer in a foam coozy.

"You know the way to a man's heart," he said. "Thanks. Now, can you jump me?" When she blushed, he smiled and added, "I seem to keep saying all he wrong things. Guess that means I've got a one-track mind, huh?"

He raised the hood and checked the oil and the water in the radiator while Anita went to get her car. The water was low and the battery was low on fluid, too. That meant he'd have head down the hill to the creek after getting it started, because there would be no water from the well until he got the electricity turned on.

He poured the gas into the tank, grabbed jumper cables from behind the seat and helped guide Anita's car into place. As he connected the cable to his battery terminals, he heard a car coming up the drive.

Rushing over to Anita, he shouted, "Get down, somebody's coming!"

"So what? You're not ashamed of me, are you?"

He pulled her down and peeked over the trunk as Rick Zapata pulled up in his green Caddy. He drove by slowly, moving out of sight as he went down the hill.

Raz stood up. "I'd like to know who that guy's working for. I don't think he's a cop."

"Who says he's a cop?" Anita asked as she brushed herself off.

"He did when he stopped me earlier."

"I don't know who he's working for either, but he's probably one of Punk's friends. He hangs out at the Hard Rock Club all the time. I've seen him there."

When she saw the look on his face, she shrugged and said, "Northville's a dull town and there's nothin' else to do."

He turned to his truck, and said gruffly, "You don't owe me any explanations about what you do for fun." He raised the hood on her car and clamped the cables to the battery.

"Just because I went there a few times doesn't mean I did anythin' bad."

"Start your car." The hurt expression on her face made him regret his sudden gruffness.

He climbed behind the wheel of his truck, and after several attempts and much pumping of the gas, the motor roared to life. It was rough at first, then slowly smoothed out. He climbed out and disconnected the cables, avoiding Anita's gaze.

He lowered her hood, and finally looked at her. "Thanks again. I'm sorry I hurt your feelings. They didn't offer sensitivity trainin' in the joint."

"It's okay. Prison must've been awful for you. You were always so independent and proud."

"For a while there, under the oak tree with you, I almost forgot all the bad stuff. Thanks for that."

"Are you goin' to tell me why you're afraid of that guy who just drove by?"

"I don't you mixed up in my troubles, but I think he's workin' with the gang that's tryin' to take what I got. They've already shot at me and rolled me."

"Shot at you? Did you go to the police?"

He laughed. "They're part of the problem."

"What? What's really going on, Raz?"

He wanted to trust in her and explain everything like he did with Boobs, but knowing she'd been going to Punk's place made him hold back. *Was I just being stupid thinking I could rekindle this old flame?*

Sensing his mistrust, she said, "When you figure out that you can trust me, I'll be there for you."

"I'm havin' trouble trustin' anybody right now. Seems like the only time real trouble finds me is when I get serious about a woman. My wife ended up dead, and now I don't know what's happened to Fran."

A hurt expression returned to her face, making him wish he hadn't spoken so bluntly. Never one to conceal true feelings, he couldn't back away now. "Anita, if you're smart, you'll stay as far away from me as you can. At least for a while."

"Let your guard down, Raz. Haven't you heard the third time's the charm?"

He'd forgotten how persistent she could be. *I better quit while I'm ahead here. I don't want to do or say something that ends up driving her away for good. I really need someone I can trust.* "I would ask you to come in while I run the truck down to the creek, but the place is a mess."

"That's no problem. I'll help you clean up."

"Thanks, but after I take care of my truck, I have to see somebody. I'll do it myself tomorrow."

"What time tomorrow?"

"Like I already said, it's too dangerous for you to hang out with me right now. I don't want to be the reason something bad happens to you."

She smiled nervously. "What a nice thing to say, Raz. I appreciate your concern for my safety. It proves what I've always known — you're a descent guy who cares about other people. That's why I went all the way with you in high school, and the reason I hoped we could get somethin' started again today. I'll keep on helpin' you if you'll let me, no strings attached."

He kissed her cheek. "How could any guy with half a brain turn down an offer like that? Have you ever seen a fence I couldn't jump by myself?"

"Besides the one you tried to jump over two years ago that cost you two years of your life?" She groaned, then said, "There I go again, puttin' my foot in my mouth. Forgive me?"

"Just say you're not mad at me for bein' so blunt and we'll call it even. You'd better get goin'. I've got things to do."

"I'm not mad at you, Raz. Just disappointed with myself for expectin' too much too soon."

"Never apologize for tryin' to get what you want. After I clear up some things, we'll get together and have another go at kickin' up our heels and gettin' re-acquainted. Bein' with you today opened doors to good places for me. Guess you could say we're in the same boat — we both need to make a new start. Hope I live long enough to get out of the startin' gate. Okay?"

"Okay."

"Where can I find you?"

"At my mother's. You know where she lives."

"I even remember your number." He gave her a peck on the lips. "Now, back up. I've got to drive my truck down the hill to get some water before she blows up."

She watched him walk to his truck. "You'll call then?"

He climbed into the cab, waving to her. "Sure will, if the bad guys don't get me."

She made a three-point turn and headed for the road. When he moved up behind her Chrysler, he saw her wipe away a tear as she turned toward town. A wave of guilt rushed over him. *I shouldn't have been so blunt. Hell, I didn't even sound excited to call her.*

Smelling hot radiator fumes, he drove quickly down the hill. At Chinquapin Creek, he jumped out and removed the hot radiator cap with an old rag. Steam hissed out. Two buckets of cool creek water quenched the hissing machine. He fetched more for the battery.

When he was finished, he turned the truck around and spun out, sending a shower of gravel and dirt flying, as he raced up the hill. It felt good to be in control of his life for the few minutes he was behind the wheel of his truck.

He drove on past the house a few miles to charge the battery, and thought about Anita as he went. Just being with her had made him feel better than he'd felt in years —and with no sex involved. This was puzzling but satisfying and conflicted with the old Raz's way of thinking. He was usually all about instant gratification. That principal had worked well for him until his life became so complicated.

Maybe he secretly yearned for an end to the cynicism and anger in his life. Being with Anita could be interesting. She gave him hope. *Maybe she'll be the wife I need and a mother for Becky.*

He parked in the front yard but left the motor running so it would keep charging the battery. There'd been no sign of Zapata during his drive. *If he comes by again, I can outrun him on the country roads; he won't know where he's going.*

The sun was setting by the time he swept the house and straightened up his bedroom. Since there was no electricity for a fan, he pulled his mother's rocker out on the front porch and sat there to cool off and contemplate where he'd go to get dinner and gas up. The pickup was still running smoothly with no signs of overheating, but he knew it was about out of gas.

He listened as the katydids made their music and a whippoorwill across the road let out a few plaintive calls. The gentle breeze felt cool against his wet shirt. He sat back and enjoyed the twilight as he considered how long he'd been searching for Patti's killer. He didn't regret the time spent, but wondered if he would ever be able to make up for everything he'd missed or ever be able to get closure.

Other sobering realities circled his mind, too. *I've got no money, no job, and no guarantee of ever getting my share of the money from the Hole. How long before Zapata and the two shooters catch up with me again? Olin and Tank might also arrest me before Harley Ritter can take charge of the tape and put them on notice.*

I shouldn't have trusted my message to that bungling Lard Haskins. I guess I need to call Tank and tell him myself so they lay off. I'll take the tape to Pop and have him tell Tank he's got it, that way Boobs will be out of it. Maybe that will buy me the time I need. He sighed, hating to dwell on such heavy matters while in this peaceful setting.

As he was getting up to head over to the truck, a set of headlights flipped on just above the driveway and a motor roared. With no time to run inside, he dove off the porch and lay flat on the ground as a spotlight lit up the front of the house. Bullets from an automatic weapon ripped into the rocker, porch and both front windows, then the car sped away.

He remained hidden until he was convinced the gunmen hadn't turned around to give it another try. He scrambled into his truck and drove onto Shortcut Road. He went less than a hundred yards before he saw the dim outline of a grown-over cut in the bank that led to his grandfather's old log cabin. He flipped off his lights and drove up the incline to where he couldn't be seen from the road, then stopped and jumped out of the truck. He quickly walked across his mother's old garden, which linked the house and cabin. Walking to a spot that gave him a good view of the front yard, he took cover under the hedge and settled down to wait.

The shooters appearance apparently meant Tank still hadn't received his message. That, or Tank and his associates had figured out that Cato's statement wasn't in Aunt Beulah's Bible and figured it was still with him; so killing him would eliminate their problem. Either option meant Tank was in deep trouble with his bosses, especially now that the assassins had failed to accomplish their mission once again. *At least that will make him more cooperative when I call him about my insurance policy.*

If the shooters came back to search the house as he thought they would, he'd be able to see who they were. *Maybe I'll luck out and it'll be Mazurka and Smeddish.*

Moments later, headlights topped the hill. The vehicle moved slowly to the driveway and stopped. A spotlight flashed on and moved across the front and side yards, then the house. Raz tried to see the make and model of the car, but the glare from the lights was too bright. He couldn't even tell how many people were in the vehicle.

The car suddenly swung into the driveway, flooding the yard and house with more light as it rolled to a stop near the front steps. When the driver killed the spotlight, Raz recognized the black Merc from Houston.

The left back door of the car swung open, causing the dome light to come on. The man getting out was the tall guy who'd chased him at the Houston bus station. *That must be Mazurka,* Raz surmised. He squinted and craned his neck but couldn't identify he driver as the other Houston gunman. *That's not Zapata. Maybe Smeddish?*

Mazurka, holding what appeared to be an Uzi, flipped on the spotlight and found the trail of mashed-down weeds across the front yard. He studied this while the driver opened his door and got out. Raz noted his loose-fitting white pants and multi-colored shirt covering an overweight, 5' 8" frame. His round, boyish face made the man appear much younger than his partner. *Damn, that's the second shooter from Houston.*

"See that trail in the weeds, Smeddish?" Mazurka said in a coarse voice. "I tol' you I saw him drive away. Shit! That's our second screw up tryin' to get him. We'll really catch hell this time."

He called him Smeddish. That really is Smeddish.

"Tank said since the jailbird didn't have it on him when the boys rolled him, he must've left it out here before Snake brought him into town," Smeddish said in a soft voice.

"Too bad them notes in the Bible Shag had weren't what they thought."

"If Shag hadn't thought he had the goods, he would've dumped Jester's ass out in the sticks somewhere after he beat the shit out of him, and we wouldn't be havin' to chase him all over the county. Olin claims to be the Bible expert, an' he said he can't find no message 'bout Northville in them underlined words. Tank said it was the redneck tryin' to con the parole board into releasin' him."

"Maybe Jester got jailhouse religion. Prison does that to some guys."

"Maybe. For sure, it saved his life at the hotel. Now Shag's ass is in a sling after his boys let Jester get away."

"How come that smart ass Snake Hamilton brought him home? Didn't he know that would get his black ass in trouble?"

"He does now," Smeddish said and laughed. "Shag and Alabama roughed him up real good, then searched his car and his place. Shag said he claimed he didn't know shit 'bout Cato's statement, but Rudy and the Houston boss are convinced Cato told him to pick Jester up somewhere down the line to keep us from grabbin' what he was carryin'."

Mazurka swept the beam of light to the barn and back. "If the statement is out here, Jester had to have it on him when the boys rolled him on the Square. They just missed it. Who knows? He coulda pushed it up his ass."

"The boys checked to make sure he didn't. He sure as hell didn't leave it on that prison van. The cop at the bus station told our men he didn't put nothin' in a locker there neither. Olin didn't turn up nothin' at the Soup Kitchen neither. That statement got to be on this property."

"If it's here and we find it, we still won't have Jester."

"That'll be the easy part." Smeddish said. "He can't dodge us much longer in this hick town." He moved toward the porch. "Let's search this place."

Raz got a better look at Smeddish as he walked to the steps. His short, neatly groomed, light brown hair covered his head in shiny waves, and his clothes seemed out of place in this rustic setting.

Mazurka stopped on the porch. "Before we search this shack, why don't we chase him down an' search him ourselves. If he ain't got it, we'll make him tell us where it's at, then whack him and dump his body out in the sticks." He laughed. "He'll end up just like his whore wife."

Raz's anger made it nearly impossible to stay hidden. *Cool it,* he coached himself. *You can hurt them and their bosses more by staying alive.*

"We'll follow orders is what we'll do," Smeddish said. "Alabama is mad as hell and he's in town. He said everybody's headed for the slammer if we don't find that statement before Jester delivers it to the narcs."

"Maybe he already did, an' that's why we can't find it."

"He told Lard he had, but Tank and Rudy think he's lyin' so they won't come after him. He's good at that. Tank said if he'd already given it to the narcs, they'd be makin' their moves. Tank'd give his right nut to find it and put himself back in good with the bosses. Sheriff don't have the final say-so on what's to be done now."

Following the light, Raz monitored their slow, deliberate search of every room. They pulled out drawers, turned over furniture and knocked down shelves. After about 30 minutes, they came back out on the front porch. "There's an old barn out there," Smeddish said. "We've got to check that out, too."

"Let's look under the house first. I don't think he'd leave it in the barn, there's rats."

"I'm not crawling under there," Smeddish said in a voice that went a little high pitched. "Let's walk around to see if he went under anywhere. Ain't no use goin' under otherwise."

Smeddish got two flashlights from the car and began circling the house behind Mazurka. They moved slowly, inspecting the ground under the eaves and between piers. Their lights probed the weeds and tall grass near the outer walls, stopping at the back porch. Raz guessed they'd spotted the mashed-down weeds where he'd retrieved his keys. He heard Smeddish say, "He went under right here. Get down and see what you can find."

Moments later, Raz heard the big man slapping his clothes while reporting, "Nothing under there but spider webs and dust. Ain't no crawl marks past that pier. Looks like he had something hid on it. Could've been the statement, or his keys. Whatever it was, it's gone now."

The gunmen came around the house with their lights bobbing and weaving. At the front steps, Smeddish said, "Alabama told me the Houston boss is really gonna be pissed if Rudy and Tank let the Jester thing get out of control again. He's never let them off the hook for Jester's ol' lady." He sighed. "I was hopin' we'd get lucky this time and take the heat of 'em. Too late to catch that jailbird now. No tellin' where he's at."

"Why don't we go lookin' for him? We can whack him and be done with it. You can tell Tank and Rudy there ain't no damn statement — it's all in Jester's head. With him dead, they won't have to worry 'bout what Cato told him or the statement neither."

"We do that and it shows up later, we'd be dead. I'm not ready to die. Come on."

They took the path Raz had cleared to the barn and began poking around under the side shed, pointing their lights at old plows and barrels. Raz watched them move around inside the storage room and saw them rushing out a few minutes later coughing and sneezing.

"Let's get out of this shit," Smeddish said. "His old pickup will be easy to spot if it's the one Tank tol' us about."

Remembering what Cato told him about finding someone to hit Mazurka, Raz realized this would be the ideal setting. *Nighttime burglary of a residence ... attempted murder would make it legal.* He shook his head. Having the gun in his back pocket gave him some comfort, but didn't make him want to kill anyone unless he was forced to. He watched the intruders drive away.

After waiting several minutes to make sure they hadn't stopped up the road and walked back, Raz returned to his truck and drove to the creek. Parking in the middle of the bridge, he left the motor idling with the lights off and got out. He sat down on the bridge's thick boards and hung his feet over the stream.

Pulse pounding and mind whirling, he listened to the gurgling water just like he used to do when he was a teenager. He'd never told anyone about this private spot, except his mom. During some of those daytime visits to the bridge, he'd fished for perch, but mostly he'd just sat and sorted things out. He hoped being in this spot again would help him re-think his strategy and solve his immediate problems.

Even though he had growing concerns about his personal safety, one thing was certain. To accomplish what he'd set out to do almost three years ago, as well as finish what he'd started with Lassiter and Cato, he had to stick to his original plan. He'd just have to make it work without involving anyone else. Depending on others during his troubles with Patti had failed miserably, and he wouldn't make that mistake again.

I'm not going to hide like a scared rabbit, or tuck tail and run. I've never dodged a fight before and won't start now, he pledged. *I've got too many responsibilities.*

He couldn't fully test his plan until he talked to Tank. That should buy him at least a couple of days to get the tape to someone else and get Boobs out of danger.

After calling Tank, he'd visit Pop to see when he could transfer the tape. Maybe Pops could call Tank before the statement was delivered to him. That call and the subsequent transfer of the tape to Harley Ritter would double the strength of his insurance. More importantly, it would give him time to find a safe place to hide Becky and his mom.

He started feeling a little better, but realized he'd forgotten about Fran. *What's happened to her?*

Another chilling question suddenly occurred to him, *Did Mazurka and Smeddish go to Boobs' place looking for me?* Raz jumped into his truck and headed for town. *I'll check on Boobs first, then get gas and something to eat. After that, I'll go visit Mom.*

CHAPTER 11

S-tump Skeeter's little store was closed, but Stump lived in the back of the building and was always willing to serve his regular customers after hours. Going to the lighted side entrance to his living quarters, Raz knocked and stepped back to wait in the shadows. Moments later, Stump peered cautiously through the screen door and asked gruffly, "Who is it?"

"Raz Jester, Mr. Skeeter." He stepped into the light.

Stump smiled and unlatched the screen door. "Hi, Raz. You okay?"

"Yes, sir, but I need some gas if my credit's still good."

"A Jester's credit is always good with me, son. I'll unlock the front door and turn on the pumps."

"Thanks, but I'd appreciate it if you'd leave the lights off." He glanced toward the road.

After pumping fifteen gallons, Raz found Stump standing under a dim light near the cash register. "Got my ticket ready?" Raz asked.

Stump waved a hand at him. "Don't worry 'bout it. Consider it a comin' home present. Need anythin' else?"

"Yes, sir. Can I use your phone? Got to call a friend."

"Sure. I'll be down the hall if you need me."

Raz dialed Boobs' number, drumming his fingers on the counter as he waited. She announced loud and clear, "Boobs' fun house. Home of fools, soft tools and hard stools."

"Boobs, is everything all right there or are you just drunk enough to make it sound that way?"

"Hello, love. Ready to come back and put out that fire you started? Of course, everything's all right. Why'd you ask?"

"You haven't had any obnoxious visitors since I left?" He looked through the window at McShan Road for signs of other cars.

"Wasn't Olin obnoxious enough to last the rest of the week, honey? He nearly had a stroke when I tol' him you weren't here. Almost tore my place up lookin' for somethin' he said you left here."

"Did he find it?"

"Nope, not after I raised hell and threatened to call my lawyer an' sue him for searchin' my place without a warrant. I thought he was gonna pop off all his shiny buttons. If you're callin' to say you're comin' by for supper, to get the rest of your clothes or to make whoopee, don't do it. One of my customers just tol' me the chief's parked right up the street watchin' the place like a starvin' hawk watches a hen house."

"Did Harley Ritter call you back?"

"Nope. That means the little worm really is out of town. Don't get in a tizzy 'bout that, 'cause the world won't end 'fore he gets back. You're soundin' like you're wound a little tight. Did somethin' bad happen since you left here?"

"Enough to make me know I've I to get that item out of your place."

"With Chief Shiny Buttons on my front step? No way. I wouldn't give it to you if you came by, 'cause that would give those two shooters from Houston another excuse to kill you so they could get it. Don't waste your time tryin' to sneak in the back way and take it away from me neither, unless you got somethin' more excitin' in mind. Don't worry 'bout me. After Olin, nobody's gonna bother me."

"Don't bet your life on it. I'd planned on visiting Pop Cheever first thing in the morning, but I can call him tonight and see if he can come by and pick up that hot potato. I know you'd give it to *him*."

"Okay. If you think he can roll over here in his wheelchair."

"What wheelchair?"

"He had a heart attack and a stroke 'bout a year after you left town, love."

"You waited 'til now to tell me that? How come you didn't tell me sooner?"

"'Cause I was havin' enough trouble keepin' your mind on somethin' besides gloom and doom. Makes no difference, 'cause you wouldn't have involved him in your troubles when you found out. Don't fret. That item is safe with me 'til Harley gets back an' picks it up."

"Can't take that chance. If Pop feels well enough to talk to me, we'll come up with a plan. Keep your doors locked and your eyes peeled for two goons who might pay you a visit before we get things worked out."

"You mean Olin an' Tank?"

"No, worse. They're driving a black Merc. Names are Smeddish and Mazurka."

"I can still give it to that lame-brained Uncle Bud out at the radio station if you want. He'd guard it with his life for the privilege of bein' known as the first to broadcast your singin' talents to the home folks." She laughed.

"You do and I'll break your leg. What about Ethan Lewis? If I can find him and he agrees to come by, will you give it to him?"

"'Nother bad choice, love. He works for the city. That means your ex-father-in-law is his boss. You think he'd do something ol' Chisel Nose wouldn't approve of?"

"Not likely. Just don't give my insurance policy to *anybody* unless I call first. Got that?"

"Love, I've got it. Where are you gonna eat since you can't come to town?"

"I'll manage. Talk to you later and thanks."

He hung up with Boobs' protests ringing in his ears and dialed Tank's new office number. A deep, gruff voice answered, "Yeah?"

"Congratulations, Tank. I've come home to play kick butt and you're number one on my list."

Raz heard Tank speak in muffled tones to someone nearby. Seconds later, he said, "Where the hell are you, jailbird? My deputy gave you strict orders to report to me when you got to town and you didn't do it. That's a violation of the law."

"Whose law?"

"Don't matter. Every ex-convict's got to report to the sheriff's office as soon he gets out. I might be lenient if you come in now."

"As lenient as your friend, Shag, and his friends at the hotel? Get real and listen to me if you're interested in staying out of prison. You must be, otherwise you wouldn't be in your office this time of night waiting for another report from the goons you sent out lookin' for me."

"Don't know what you're talkin' 'bout."

"Then put Olin on the line so I can tell him how to save both your sorry butts."

"I'm by myself."

Raz heard the click of another receiver being lifted off the hook. "Were you by yourself when Lard brought you my message?"

"What message?"

"In case it was too complicated for you to understand the first time, I'll repeat it so Olin will know what it is too. That item you and your pals are lookin' for has already been delivered to a third party. He'll hold onto it and keep his mouth shut as long as you and Olin don't arrest me or have your goons kill me. Anythin' happens to me, he'll deliver it to the state narcs and federal district attorney in Tyler."

"That's pretty bold talk for a man on the run from the law. I've got new warrants on you an' I'm duty-bound to execute 'em."

"Like you were duty bound to find my wife's killer? Tell Shag, Alabama, Smeddish and Mazurka to cool it so I can take care of some personal business. If you do that and arrest the one who butchered Pattie, Cato's statement stays buried. If you haven't left town for parts unknown by then, I might even be willing to negotiate another deal with you and Olin about who I give it to. If you refuse, I'll find the butcher myself after the statement is delivered to the proper authorities and you're arrested. If you'd used your brain for somethin' besides a cash register two years ago, you would've known that was all I ever really wanted."

"You still got that killin' stuck in your craw, jailbird? Hell, that's old news. Nobody'll ever find out which one of your whore wife's johns done that. Who the hell's Smeddish, Mazurka and that other guy?"

"You knew Cato Hamilton, and—"

"I ought to. I'm the one that put him away."

"Then you know Mazurka, 'cause he turned state's evidence. So how 'bout it? We got a deal?"

Heavy breathing reflected Tank's concern. He finally said, "I don't make deals with troublemaking law breakers. Even if I was so inclined, you couldn't deliver. I ain't seen nor heard nothin' yet that proves you've got anythin' but what's in your head." He laughed. "From what I hear, that ain't a safe place to keep nothin'."

"How 'bout you, Olin? You gonna let your fat buddy kill your chance of making a deal? If he does get lucky and get his hands on the statement, he'll use it to save his own ass and leave you out in the cold."

"I'm chief law enforcement officer in this county and I'll decide what's gonna be done," Tank said. "Even if I was interested in anything that lyin' Cato Hamilton tol' you 'bout me and Olin, we — that is, I — wouldn't believe you're holdin' anythin' at all unless I got a call from a third party I trust. If you come on in, we'll talk about it."

"Can I laugh now? If you and Olin let things get screwed up again in Northville like you did two years ago, Ed will send Alabama and some of his boys gunnin' for you."

There was a longer pause, which made Raz wonder if maybe Tank didn't have the authority to make a deal for Cato's tape. If Ed and Rudy knew about the tape, they could've ordered him to use whatever means necessary to get it for them. "Tank? You still there?"

Raz heard muffled voices exchanging comments. Finally, Tank said, "Well, uh... even if I did know what you're talkin' 'bout — which I don't — I couldn't speak for anybody outside my jurisdiction who might be interested. That means I'd have to have time to contact them first."

I was right! Tank can't make a deal without new orders from the gang's leaders.

"My offer is only good if it's between you, me and Olin," Raz said. "You're the only ones who can give me what I want."

"It don't really matter what you want, or who decides what, 'cause either way I win and you lose."

"Don't count on it, Tank, 'cause it's your turn in the barrel."

"Nope. It's your turn, 'cause Olin'll have you in jail by mornin'. I'm sure we can find a way to make you tell us the truth 'bout what you got and where you got it hid. That is, if you don't have a fatal accident first." He laughed. "Everybody knows what a reckless guy you are."

"Tank, talking to you erases all doubt I ever had about whether I did the right thing when I knocked you on your ass two years ago." Raz hung up, disappointed that his plan to provoke Tank hadn't worked. That didn't take away the power of the tape though. Now he needed to get it to Lassiter as soon as he could figure out a way to get out of Boob's place without getting either one of them killed.

He expected to find Stump watching from the hall when he'd finished his call. When he didn't, he called out, "Thanks, Mr. Mr. Skeeter. I'm leaving now. See you later."

He sat in his pickup, thoughts churning. He realized he might never find out who killed Patti, or live long enough to regain custody of Becky and see her grow into a beautiful young woman. All the good times that come with normal living might be lost to him forever. *If I can't get that tape to the right people, my alliance with Lassiter serves no purpose.*

He wanted to go by Boobs' place and get the tape now, but remembered her warning about Olin being parked outside. The chief or one of his friends would watch her place all night. Getting arrested would be the final blow. *Boobs will be safe until morning. The two shooters are most likely still driving around town looking for me.*

Guess I'll at least achieve one of my goals for the day, he thought. *I'll go visit Mom. It'll be good to see her.*

CHAPTER 12

Raz parked in the shadows of a defunct carwash, and killed the motor. From there, he walked two blocks to Arbor Place Assisted Living. He didn't see a police car or the black Merc in front, so he crossed McShan and stopped near the front entrance. When he looked inside, he saw two old people in wheelchairs sitting in the entrance hall, apparently asleep.

There was a fat nurse in a white uniform sitting behind the counter, and when he stepped inside, she recognized him. "What do *you* want?" she asked in a less than friendly way.

"A cup of sugar, honey," he said. "But before you kill me with kindness, I want you to take me back to see Minnie Jester."

"Visitin' hours is over. It's quarter to nine."

"Yeah, and it'll probably be quarter to nine this time tomorrow night too, but I can't come back then."

"You're her son, right?" Her eyes were cold.

"In the flesh, sunshine."

She stood up. "She's expecting you. Otherwise, I wouldn't let you go back. Wait here. I'll make sure she's still up."

"How is she?"

"'Bout the same, I reckon. Memory comes and goes. There ain't no cure for what she got."

"How'd she know I was in town?"

"Don't know who told her. Word's all over town 'bout you bein' back."

He waited by the front door, watching the parking area. He stole a glance at the old couple who were now staring at him with half-dead eyes. He felt sorry for them being locked away in this depressing environment. *It's like a prison for old people. There must be a better way to spend your final days.*

He remembered something his dad told him a long time ago: "I'd rather die while I'm still in charge of the parts God gave me. If I live long enough to get helpless, don't put me in one of them God-awful dyin' homes." *That's one one of the few things we ever agreed on,* he thought.

His father, Robert E. Lee Jester, was fifty when Raz was born, and he'd died by the time Raz was twelve. A self-ordained, Bible-thumping Baptist preacher, he'd choked to death on a chicken bone while eating Sunday dinner at a believer's home. Raz had lots of fights in school over jokes spawned by that incident.

His dad told everybody God had called him to preach when he was in a hay field one hot August day. That revelation came following a three-year absence from his family, spent working in Fort Worth at the only meaningful job he'd ever held. Smiling about local rumors of young Robert E. Lee Jester's romantic escapades, Raz had difficulty visualizing his skinny, homely father as a successful skirt-chaser. Maybe what he told him once about women was the key to his success: Never ask and never take no for a final answer on nothin'.

The nurse finally reappeared, and said, "She'll see you now. Don't stay but a few minutes. It's time all these old folks went to sleep. They've already had their meds."

When he walked in her room, his mother was sitting in her recliner, eyes fixed on the door. She was bent and pale, and her frail appearance shocked him. He smiled and walked to her as tears welled up in her eyes.

"Raz," she said. "You finally come back home."

"Hi, Mama." He wrapped his arms around her and asked, "How's my favorite girl?"

She leaned back to adjust her glasses and fixed hungry eyes on him.

"You're lookin' awfully feisty, young lady. I'll bet every bachelor in this place has his sights on you."

"You always were such a kidder, son. Just like your father."

"How do you feel?"

"Better, now that you're home. I was afraid I'd never see you again. You must've really liked California."

He kissed her cheek. "I told you I'd come back as soon as I could. Remember?" he asked, continuing the ruse his Great Aunt Ruth had told her when he went to prison.

"How's your sister Fannie?" she asked. "She say when she's comin' to see me?"

"Everybody's all right out there. Question is, are they treatin' you okay in here?"

He could see her mind had wandered. She said, barely above a whisper, "I love all my children. But you're my baby. The first and the last are always special, you know."

"Yes, Mama."

"You knew Les was killed in Vietnam, didn't you?"

"Yes, Mama." Les was his only brother. It had been more than forty years, but she always talked about it as if it happened yesterday.

"Fannie's my middle child, you know," she rambled on. "She went away a long time ago and didn't come back. I don't know why. I loved her, too."

"She's still in California, Mama. Guess she's busy with her own family. But I love you enough for all three of us."

"I know you do, son," she said and patted his hand. "You always make that clear. You're a good child. You get married again while you was in California?"

"No, ma'am."

Her blue eyes were pleading now. "I wish I could see your sweet little girl, but they won't bring her here. You know why?"

His jaw muscles rippled, and his scar suddenly began to burn. "You haven't seen her since I left?"

"No, and when I think about it, I cry."

"I'll bring her by as soon as I get some things settled, Mama."

"She didn't go away with her mother, did she?"

"No." He swallowed a lump in his throat. "She's with the Lawthers."

"Why? You're her daddy."

"It's a long story, Mama. I'll explain it some time when you're not so tired."

"Good. Becky needs a momma, and you need a good wife — a virtuous woman, who's not afraid to work and make her husband happy."

"Like you were for dad."

She paused, apparently recalling an earlier time. "Don't be too harsh judgin' your father, son. I know you took lots of teasin' 'cause o' him. He was kind to me when he was around. Whatever his sins, he weren't mean-spirited." She looked at the wall like she could see right through it. "He was 'fraid. It was a fear born out of his weaknesses. He never succeeded as a farmer. Seems like God didn't want him to."

"That's all in the past, Mama. I want you to think about *now*. Think 'bout feelin' better. When you get well enough, I'll take you back home. Won't that be great?"

Her mind was still in the past, apparently, and she'd tuned him out. She always remembered the old times best. "Then God called your daddy to preach. He tried hard to be a true believer, thinkin' it was his last hope. That was after he came back from the airplane factory, you know."

"I remember."

"He was 'fraid of failin' at preachin', too, and if he did that he was 'fraid there'd be no God to take him into eternity." She sighed. "That was his worst fear."

Raz rubbed the scar on his neck. "I understand, Mama."

Returning to the present, she looked at him. "I watch television a lot these days. Seems like ever'body's 'fraid now — don't matter how old they are. Guess he weren't too different from ever'body else."

"No, guess not." He glanced at the door. "The nurse told me I couldn't stay long, so before I go, tell me if you need anythin'."

She shook her head. "Can't think of a thing. Oh, yeah. There *is* somethin'. If you have the time, I'd like to hear some of them old sweet songs again. It would make my last days a lot better."

"Any particular ones?"

"Oh, the Chuck Wagon Gang and the Carter family. John Charles Thomas singin' 'Swing Low, Sweet Chariot,' and 'The Last Rose of Summer.' Them songs have words that tell met God is real an' watchin' over me." She started humming softly.

"Those old records are all broken or worn out, Mama. Don't you remember Aunt Ruth telling you that? I'll see if I can find some of 'em for ya."

A puzzled expression came over her face. "Which one of my children are you? Les, that you back from the war?"

He swallowed hard. "No, Mama. I'm Raz."

"Oh. When did you get back from California?"

The nurse appeared at the door, "You'll have to leave now. She's tired."

Standing up, Raz leaned over and kissed his mother. "Good night, Mama. I love you. I'll be back soon. Okay?"

"Okay, Les," she said, smiling. "I'm happy you're home."

He stopped just outside the door to regain his composure. He hadn't been hit by loss so hard since he'd had to identify his wife's remains.

At the front entrance, he peeked outside to make sure the coast was clear. No cars out front, but there was one he could barely make out in the light from a nearby streetlight. He couldn't tell if it was a police cruiser or not. He couldn't think of a good reason for anyone to park in that particular spot at this time of night, though, unless they were looking for him.

Suspecting the nurse had tipped off whoever was in the car, Raz walked back down the hall looking for a different exit. The only one he found was an emergencies door, and it was locked. Not wanting to set off the alarm and announce his departure route, he walked back up the hall, went into an unoccupied room and picked up the phone. He dialed Boobs' number and closed the door with his toe.

There was no answer after several rings. "Quit yakking with your customers and answer the phone, Boobs," he muttered.

After the tenth ring, a vigorous "Hello!" leaped out at him.

"Boobs, it's Raz."

"I don't know where you are, love, but you'd better stay put. Don't come for that item or anythin' else, 'cause all the sudden you're the hottest number in town. Olin's been back. Wanted to search the place. When I refused, he left an' Tank barged in threatenin' to take me to jail for harborin' a fugitive. He demanded I tell him where you were. When I wouldn't, he left in a huff, then two shabby-lookin' goons showed up an' ordered me to give 'em Cato's statement."

"They hurt you?"

"No, but they would've if a couple of customers hadn't walked in. Said they'd be back after closin'. Not to worry, love. I told 'em I didn't know nothin' 'bout anythin' Cato gave you, but if I ran across it in a bowl of my hash I'd have it broadcast over at NEHI radio."

"I want you to close up and go on a trip. Take that item with you and call Pop Cheever in the morning to let him know where you are so I can pick it up. I'll be going by his place early."

"Me, leave town? Hah! Trash worse than the likes them have tried to push me 'round before, I ain't goin' nowhere. Where are you?"

"At the nursing home, but somebody's waiting for me across the street. I figure it's either Tank or the two goons that came by your place. I'm gonna try to slip out. You don't hear from me in thirty minutes, you'll know I didn't make it. If that happens, I want you to call Drew Lassiter with the Department of Public Safety in Austin. He's their head narc. Call him at home if you have to, or go through the DPS dispatcher. Tell him I'm ready to give him the item, and if he wants to save it *and* yours truly, to call Tank and Olin and lower the boom. He's got to keep them from doin' me in before he gets here. Got that?"

"What do you think I am, a recordin' machine? Let me get a pencil." Moments later she returned to the phone. "Okay, gimme all that stuff again."

He repeated everything, including Lassiter's number from memory. "Don't tell anybody but him, and don't leave with the item unless you're leavin' town."

"You sure throw lots of stuff at a poor, unsuspectin' gal. Too bad it ain't the stuff she was wantin'. Okay, but if you're in such a bind, why not call this Lassiter guy yourself and tell him to come get the damned thing? Seems like that would save ya a lot of trouble."

"He couldn't get here before tomorrow and that'd be too late. I'll call you again in a bit if I can get out of here. I appreciate you, sweet woman. Bye."

He moved back to the door. Peeking up the hall, he saw the nurse's desk was unoccupied and heard nothing but the faint sound of a TV somewhere in the distance. He went back in the room and closed the door. After raising the window and pushing out the screen, he opened the door again and sprinted down the hall to the door emergency exit. He shoved the door open and set off the alarm, then went back to the room. He crawled out the window and closed it behind him.

Walking briskly along the wall of the building while the alarm bell rang, he watched a flashlight beam cut through the darkness as Olin Culpepper ran across the grounds. When he reached the door and didn't see Raz, he let out a loud, "Damn!"

Raz darted from shrub to shrub until he was off the property, then he crossed the street. The back door of the nursing home slammed shut, silencing the alarm. Looking back, he saw another car move up to the door with its spotlight lighting up the grounds at the end of the building.

Raz got to his pickup, started it and slowly zigzagged several blocks to the next available stoplight. He turned on his headlights and headed for his Aunt Ruth's house, 20 miles out of Northville and just over the county line. He didn't want to involve her in this, but her house was the only safe place available to him now. *I need some sleep and a something to eat. I don't think Tank and Olin know where Ruth lives.*

Avoiding arrest at the nursing home was his third escape from the fate Cato said awaited him in Northville, and the day wasn't over yet. *If my luck holds for the rest of the night and all day tomorrow, at least I'll prove Cato's prediction wrong.*

CHAPTER 13

Aunt Ruth McShan at age ninety-six was the only surviving member of Grandfather Jester's family. When Raz had last seen her, she was still mentally alert and able to move around her house and yard without assistance. She told Raz once that the recipe for a long life had four vital ingredients: strong seed, luck, horse sense and good whiskey. She'd outlived her husband and two sons, claiming that both boys sprang from strong seed, but each lacked one or more of the other essential elements.

Aunt Ruth, always strong-willed and outspoken, had recently become particularly critical of "America's shame," a term she used to describe the country's moral decline and hell-bent race for personal gratification and meaningless gadgets. She directed her wrath at all who challenged her views.

Before her marriage, she'd taught the elementary grades in a one-room schoolhouse near her farm. Raz's dad said she was a strict disciplinarian, and was highly respected in the community.

She'd always been supportive of Raz, and he found her practice of drinking an ounce of whiskey each day to "barricade against the chills of the world" an endearing quality. Raz thought she was one of the last of the pioneers who tamed the Texas frontier.

It was almost ten o'clock when Raz turned off a dirt road onto the long lane that ran through the woods to his great aunt's house. He saw the dim glow of light behind a drawn living room shade and knew he wouldn't be waking his aunt and her friend with his visit. Parking in front of the house under some low-hanging limbs, he got out and walked slowly to the door. His aunt wasn't fond of strangers, so he wanted to give her a chance to see who was outside before knocking on the door. She often greeted unwanted visitors by shoving her old double-barreled, twelve-gauge shotgun in their faces.

The quiet, still country night seemed untainted by modern world cruelties. Raz knew, however, that his arrival had not gone unnoticed, so he called out, "Aunt Ruth? It's me, Raz."

He heard a chair slide on the wooden floor and the hushed, excited voices of the two women inside. The shade was pulled back a bit, and someone peeked out. The front porch light snapped on, and a shrill woman's voice called out, "Who you say it is?"

"You can put down your shotgun. It's your hungry great-nephew in the flesh," he shouted. His aunt was hard of hearing, but that didn't affect her marksmanship.

The door swung open, and a tall, thin woman with white hair stepped out, shotgun in hand. She squinted against the glare of the porch light to get a look at him. When she recognized him, she leaned the gun against the wall and clapped her hands. "You're a sight for sore eyes, boy. Come on in. Look who's here, Jennie."

"Thanks for not shootin' me. How are ya, sweetheart?"

She kissed him on both cheeks before stepping back to admire him. "Fine as a swamp frog's hair and you're lookin' pretty fit yourself. Handsome as ever, you devil."

He pinched her cheek. "And you're still as pretty as a red fox sittin' atop the chicken coop."

She waved a hand at him. "If you're through lyin', you can come on in the house."

Inside, he was greeted by his aunt's live-in friend. She was shorter and heavier than his aunt and her short hair was whiter. Extending his hand, he said, "How are ya, Jennie? I'm surprised you're still puttin' up with this cranky ol' woman."

"Hi, Raz," Jennie said. "Good to see ya."

His great aunt pointed to a brown sofa with wooden arms and said, "Park yourself and talk to me. Had supper yet?"

"No, ma'am, but I need to use your phone first."

"You know where it's at. Help yourself. I've waited two years to swap lies with you, so I guess I can wait a few more minutes."

He went to the phone that was sitting on a shelf in the hall and dialed Boobs' number. A slightly grumpy voice answered, "Yeah?"

"Boobs, I made it. You don't have to call Lassiter. Anybody else been by your place?"

"No. I told those two goons if they bothered me again, I'd pour hot chili on their love sticks. Olin's car's still parked down the street, which is too bad for me, 'cause it gets lonesome every night after I close this joint. It's worse tonight, after you came by and got my hopes up. I could kill that ass Olin for interruptin' what was lookin' like the best day I've had in years." She laughed.

"Things will settle down pretty soon and we'll have another cold one and discuss old times. I'll call you in the mornin' after I visit Pop. Sleep tight now, and don't let the love bugs bite. Bye."

He returned to the living room and sat down next to his great-aunt, who asked teasingly, "Does she still love ya, boy?"

"Boobs loves everybody." He smiled and said, "You need a guard dog out here in these woods. Comin' in at night makes me see why townies say only lovers, sick folks, and crazy people come to places this far out in the sticks.

Aunt Ruth leaned forward and asked, "Which one of those you fall under, handsome?" She laughed, slapping her thigh. "Only God comes back here, Razie boy, and that's just so He can say He's been here."

Raz turned to Jennie, who sat near him in a wooden rocker. "It's not safe for two good-lookin' women like you to live here alone. You need a man around. Where's your man, Jennie?"

"Humph! I wouldn't call that pair of britches a man. Your aunt an' me don't need no men folk for nothin'. Our yearnin' days are over, praise the Lord."

Aunt Ruth tapped his arm. "But not yours, eh Raz? You still straight an' strong, an' wearin' a smile on that good-lookin' face..." Her voice trailed off as she noticed his scars. "What in Heaven's name happen to ya, honey?"

"Just a little friendly fracas."

"Friendly, my foot." Her eyes narrowed. "You've had plenty o' fights, but you ain't never came out of one holdin' the short end o' the stick." She touched his face. "Poor baby."

"I'm okay. How're you doin'?"

"Got no complaints. If things were any better, I'd have to start givin' part of myself away."

"Sounds like you've already had your ounce of medicine tonight."

Jennie grunted. "That ounce bidness went out the window like a thief in the night wit her first spell of lumbago ten year ago. It more like four now."

Aunt Ruth waved her hand dismissively at Jennie. "Don't pay no attention to her. I've caught her lots of times gettin' a little snifter for herself. Seriously, I'm so happy you're home, Raz. I'm glad to see prison didn't dampen your spirits none. You get what you went down there for?"

When he gave Jennie a cautious look, Aunt Ruth said, "Don't worry 'bout Jennie knowin' your business. I told her our conversation in the Coldwater jail word for word. We share all our troubles an' concerns. I'd trust her with my life."

He shook his head. "No, I didn't get what I went for. Cato didn't know who killed Patti after all. But it wasn't a totally wasted trip."

"When I came home from visitin' you, Jennie told me she knows Cato Hamilton."

"How well?" he asked Jeanie.

"Well enough ta know I don't want ta know him better. Only saw him a couple times out to Bull Hayter's café when he was visitin' his nephew."

"Snake?"

She nodded and said, "Hear tell he ain't no better'n Cato. Me an' my family never had no dealings wit either one. Never had no use for what they sellin'."

"That's good news." He told them about how Snake picked him up in Coldwater. "Haven't decided if I trust him or not, but I am close friends with Cato."

"Word got out in The Quarters 'bout what you done for Cato," Jennie said. "You always have a lot friends over the tracks, but you got lots more now."

"Since Cato didn't tell ya what you went to find out, I guess you come back more determined than ever to get that killer yourself," Aunt Ruth said.

"You ever seen a hill a Jester couldn't climb?" he asked. "I can't let a couple of kicks in my rump stop me."

"That's my boy," she said. "You got to remember what it was like goin' up against money and power. If you weren't a Jester, I'd tell you to have enough sense to know when you're licked. If I was still a churchgoer, I'd tell ya to give it to God — but I ain't been to church in forty years. I say, you got to do for yourself."

"I've got a few leads," he told her. "I can make some progress if I can keep the wolves off my tail for a while." He told her what happened at his house, and about the new charges filed against him by the men at God's Palace. "Cato warned me about comin' back, but I had to."

"Of course ya did, boy. This your home. This where your roots are, an' ya can't let nobody scare you away." Her expression became grim again. "I'm afraid for you, Raz boy. Ain't there any lawman in Northville can help you?"

"Not since Pop retired."

"Too bad. Pop's an honest man. Can't say the same for the one there now. Jeanie and the Northville newspaper keep me informed 'bout what's goin' on over there."

She sighed, apparently exhausted, and added, "I wonder sometimes if I'm still livin' in the country where I was born."

"No use fretting 'bout what you can't change, Aunt Ruth."

"'Cause I'm old and decrepit? If I was young, I sure as hell would run for congress, by golly. I'd show 'em what for!"

"Calm down, Miss Ruth," Jennie said. "You don't want your blood pressure jumpin' through the roof again."

"I'm too busy fightin' my own war right now to get involved with politics," Raz told his Aunt. "I got so many alligators snapping at my tail right now, I was hoping you'd let me stay here tonight."

She nodded. "I do get a little preachy sometime, honey. Age has certain privileges, like runnin' my mouth. Sure, you can spend the night. You can live here full time if you want to. I'll get ya some supper and some homemade coconut pie to start things off right."

"Great. I'm starving."

"Jennie, would you bring Raz a couple of sandwiches and a piece of pie?" Ruth asked. Turning to Raz, she asked, "Need a little snort to wet your whistle?"

"Thanks. I'm so dirty I'd be an insult to good whiskey. Is it okay if I take a shower after I eat?"

She stood up slowly with a groan. "You know where it is. Help yourself to anythin' ya need. 'Fore that though, I've got somethin' ta give ya. I'm gonna give it to you now 'cause I'll probably be asleep by the time you get through with your supper."

Moments later, Jennie brought in sandwiches, a piece of pie and a glass of milk. Raz had polished off the first sandwich when Aunt Ruth returned with a small box and an old sword in a rusty metal sheath.

She sat down in front of him and said, "'Fore your great-grandfather died, he tol' me ta give these things ta the oldest male Jester livin' 'fore I died. Since you're the *only* male survivor, I'm passin' them on ta ya now. Most young folks don't care for old stuff an' old ways, but ya can at least keep 'em safe an' show 'em the respect they're due. Like 'em or not, they're part of your heritage."

He put his sandwich down beside the pie and milk on the coffee table. "Is that the Civil War sword Granddad Jester showed me when I was a kid?"

She nodded, picking up the box. "Ya came from good seed, boy, handed down mostly from your granddad. He had both good an' bad seed. He was possessed by the devil at times, and inclined to loaf an' fornicate. Your grandpa, who was forty years older than me, was started with one of his good seeds, planted in a good woman. Like I always say, good breedin' shows up in folks, same as in cattle and horses." She looked at the food. "Go ahead and finish. I've seen people eat 'fore."

Raz raised his glass in a toasting nature. Aunt Ruth opened the box and took out a tarnished round medal that was attached to a faded, threadbare red and blue ribbon. "Your great-granddad went in the Confederate Army when he was fourteen — one of the few noble things he ever did. Before the shootin' stopped an' our way of life went away, he got himself this medal. Now it's yours, 'long with this old sword that's 'bout as rusty as I am."

Raz ate the pie as she talked about the heirlooms in a soft, reverent voice. Fingering the medal, he said, "Grandpa never showed me this." He could make out two words on it: Bravery and Honor.

"I've sold everything off ta pay my medical bills, 'cept five acres an' this house. When I die, it goes to Jennie, the best friend God coulda give me. Ya got any objections to that?"

"No, ma'am. Jennie's always been here for you."

She got unsteadily to her feet, telling him in a voice grown weary. "I enjoy your company, boy, but I got to put these ol' bones to bed. If I should die before I wake, Jennie knows where and how I'm ta be buried." She shook her finger at him. "Don't ya ever stop bein' proud of bein' a Jester an' a true son of the south."

He stood and attempted to hug her, but she pushed him away. "Don't go gettin' all mushy on me. I ain't dead yet. Soon will be, though, if I don't get me some rest. 'Night."

"'Night, Aunt Ruth. Love ya."

She didn't respond until she got to the hall door. There, she turned and said, "Love's a precious commodity, not to be spoken of lightly. You never been stingy in that regard, so I never doubt ya love me. Love you too, Raz boy, 'cause you're bone of my bone, and blood of my blood. She paused and smiled. "Keep on bein' who you are, boy." Pointing a gnarled finger at him, she concluded, "Don't ya wait 'til I die ta come back ta see me neither."

She disappeared down the dark hallway, and Raz stared after her for several moments. Turning, he told Jennie "Thanks for the food. If you don't mind, I'll take a shower and get some sleep after I move my truck so no one can see it."

He drove his truck behind the house and parked next to some thick bushes. He put his newly acquired family heirlooms behind the seat. He locked the truck, then went back in the house through the back door, which Jeanie had unlocked for him.

He took a shower and washed his underwear in the sink, then put them on a wire hanger and hooked it over the shower rod. *Guess I'll have to sleep in the nude tonight. Hope these're dry by morning.* He turned down the bed, flipped off the light and lay down.

He was tired, but he couldn't relax. He kept thinking about everything that had happened since he'd left prison. He was also having second thoughts about working for Lassiter. *Guess I've got no other option.*

Hoping to relieve his troubled mind, he thought back to simpler days in Boobs' Back Room. In those days, drinking a few cold ones could relax him and make him feel like all was right with the world. *Wish things were that simple now,* he thought and sighed.

He stretched and rolled his head from side to side as he thought about Anita McKnight. Seeing her again at this point in his life seemed like fate, much like when Fran appeared in his life and made him her business partner.

A little voice told him that the Fran Druman he knew wouldn't have sold the Hole to Punk Hutto — unless she was forced to. *Did Punk blackmail her into selling? I really don't know anything about Fran's past. Maybe the group that took over Cato's outfit sent her here. Now, that's a disturbing thought. Were the first charges against me part of Punk's plan to get the Hole?*

Now that he was questioning everything and feeling paranoid, he wondered about Anita's claim that she was driving around town looking for him. It seemed pretty fishy in hindsight. *Did she really want to see me, or was she hunting me for someone else? Who told her I was going to be here? Snake knew, and so did Shag and his friends, and Lard and Tank.* Realizing that Cecil Cassidy and the other good folks he'd spoken to on the Square also knew he was back eased his concerns a little.

He tossed and turned for quite a while, finally settling on laying his back. He'd slept comfortably on this feather mattress before, but it was better suited for cold winter nights. Despite the heat, he finally drifted off.

CHAPTER 14

Raz got up at first light, used the bathroom, then shaved with an old razor he found in the cabinet under the sink. The blade was dull, but he endured it and the sting from patting his face with rubbing alcohol instead of aftershave. He pulled his almost dry underwear from the hanger, put them on and returned to the bedroom for the rest of his clothes.

He tiptoed through the house so he wouldn't wake the ladies, and went out to his truck through the back door. His plan was to head over to Pop Cheever's farm, twenty-four miles away.

He wished he had a different vehicle, since the shooters, as well as Tank and Olin all knew what his truck looked like. Knowing Frenchy would have an extra vehicle for him, he turned left and went to his house first.

I'll make this visit short and sweet, then heat to Pop's. Frenchy had never fit in well with Raz's other friends because he was gruff, lacked manners, and cussed like a sailor. Their friendship had endured despite this.

Frenchy was Cajun and had shown up in town about twenty years ago with enough cash to buy a two hundred-acre farm on the western edge of the county. Frenchy didn't know much about farming, and would've lost everything if Raz hadn't helped him every day after school and during the summer. Together, they cut enough trees and pulpwood to keep Frenchy and his girlfriend afloat. Later, Raz helped him build two large broiler chicken houses that eventually provided a steady income.

Raz parked on the road about two hundred yards from the house and walked the rest of the way so he could arrive unnoticed. When he rounded a curve and looked for Frenchy's simple little frame house, Raz stopped short, surprised to see a new brick contemporary with a chimney at each end and white posts along its long front porch glistening in the early sun.

He let out a whistle. "What'd ya do, Frenchy, rob Ol' Money Bags Snitker's bank?"

There was a metal barn just behind the house, and there were two white vans and an eighteen-wheeler parked beside it.

No ordinary greeting was ever sufficient for these two, which meant that after two years Raz needed to do something extra special. Walking briskly up the driveway, he rang the doorbell and stepped back to wait. He knew his fat friend, always a late riser, was grumpier than a grizzly when someone woke him early.

No one answered the door, so Raz pushed the bell six times in a row.

Finally, a shy female voice came from inside. *"Quién es?"*

Hmmm, he thought, *Frenchy must've ditched his old girl for someone new.* He'd learned a little Spanish in high school, so he responded, *"¡Inmigración! Abra la puerta ahora mismo!"*

Raz hoped this joke would shake up his friend. He heard shuffling feet and excited whispering in Spanish as the woman ran from the door. He looked toward the end of the house, half expecting his fat friend to appear there holding a shotgun. What he saw instead were mounds of dirt where somebody had been digging. He also noticed the chicken houses were vacant.

A low, gruff voice reverberated through the door, "Who's there?"

Raz disguised his voice. "U.S. Immigration! I've got a warrant here for the arrest of Frenchy Patroon for importing and harboring illegal aliens. I need Mr. Patroon to come outside right now."

"Like hell I will!" Frenchy snapped. "You're at the wrong house."

Raz choked back a laugh, saying in his natural voice, "Open the door and show your ugly, mug so I'll know for sure."

Following a string of curses and the frantic rattling of the safety chain, Frenchy shouted, "Raz Jester, you crazy bastard!"

His friend swung the door open, blinking sleepily in the morning light. Dressed only in his boxers, his bulging, hairy belly and stubble-covered face made him look a whole lot like a gorilla. He threw his arms around Raz's middle in a powerful bear hug and said, "You crazy Irishman! You scared the shit outta my little flower."

Raz slapped his friend's belly. "Serves you right for living in sin and sleepin' when you should be workin'."

"Hell, man, I have to sleep long hours to build my strength so I can keep up with my little flower," he said, pointing at the small woman peeking at him from behind the door. "Ain't she a beauty?"

"She sure is," Raz said. "Up to your same old tricks, huh? Young girls will kill you yet, you old goat."

"There are worse ways to die, my Tex-ass friend," Frenchy said, winking. Looking up the driveway, he asked, "You walk here?"

"My red roadrunner's 'round the bend. Wanted to surprise you and rattle your chain."

"You nearly broke it, by God. Well, come on in." Frenchy said, then slammed the door shut behind them and pointed to a door beyond the vestibule. "Go in and sit down and we'll swap some lies." He slapped the young woman's butt. "This here's Lupé. Lupé, this joker's Raz Jester — the only real friend I got in this lousy world. Get us some coffee, would ya my little cactus flower?"

The woman smiled shyly and left.

"She don't speak no Cajun, and very little Texan, but she sure as hell knows how to make a man happy, by God. You oughta go to Mexico and get yourself a *señorita*. Make ya a happy man!"

When Raz sat down in the recliner opposite him, Frenchy added, "It's good to see your ugly face again. When you get home?"

"Yesterday. Seems like everybody in the county but you knew I was comin'."

"I ain't been to town lately," After studying Raz a moment, he added, "You look good 'cept for them nasty-ass scars. How the hell that happen?"

Raz told him, and Frenchy said, "That Cato must've been one helluva good friend for you to do that. You ready to go to work now that you're back?"

"Where? I saw your chicken houses are empty."

"Don't need 'em no more. I'm makin' more dough bringin' in what the rich bastards in this country have to have to make money — good, cheap labor.

I truck 'em all over the country. Makin' so much damn money, I 'bout gave up tryin' to spend it all."

"You payin' off the law, or just dodgin' 'em?"

"Shit, there ain't no law no more, not where big business is concerned. Them politicians won't never let the law stop 'em from doin' what they want."

"You sound more like a philosopher than the wine-guzzlin' chicken farmer I used to know. You sure you didn't get a brain transplant? What else you bought besides a lover and this house?"

"Everythin', by God!" Frenchy threw out his hands. "Got me a new Continental, satellite TV, new furniture, and a damned spa. But I didn't buy nothin' from them snobs in Northville. I don't spend a damn dime with 'em, 'cept for groceries. I just ride through town in my Continental, smokin' a Cuban cigar and showin' off my little flower, just to spite them homegrown big shots. I even went to the bank one time and tol' Sonny Irby he could stick all of ol' man Snitker's money up his ass 'cause I don't need it no more. Damned near got me arrested, 'cept Ol' Money Bags needs the cheap labor I provide to run his poultry farms."

"If you don't use Snitker's bank, where you keepin' your money?"

Frenchy leaned forward, lowering his voice. "Lots of folks think I bury it. See all them damn holes dug out there? We leave, an' the fuckin' hippie sons-a-bitches from that ol' hotel downtown come out here an' dig up my land. It's makin' my yard look worse than a damn prairie dog town!"

Lupé came in with coffee and some breakfast taquitos and put them on the table between the two men. Raz grabbed one to eat with his coffee. Swallowing the first bite, he told Frenchy, "This is delicious and spicy, too."

"Everything my little flower does is hot," Frenchy bragged. "You still hell-bent on findin' that killer?"

"You know the Irish. We never give up."

Frenchy shook his head. "I already decide I ain't gonna try ta change your mind 'bout that. I never let nobody change mine once it's set on somethin', so I know better than ta try changin' yours. I won't lie to you neither. You start snoopin' 'round again like before, an' you got 'bout as much chance of stayin' alive as a crawfish in a Cajun café."

Raz took another bite of the taquito instead of responding.

Frenchy went on, "Hell, man, even a dumb Irishman ought to know when he's licked. When I was young, I went up again' somethin' like what you got hung on you. I done what the alligator do best, drag ass. You bein' back is gonna make certain people in town jumpier than a fat frog during giggin' season. You better walk soft an' carry a damn big stick, my friend."

"You seem to know a lot 'bout things in Northville for a man who doesn't do business there."

"I ain't seen you in over two years, but I know all 'bout your stupid pride. Pride is an ass's badge an' it can make ya lose your ass if you ain't careful."

"You're talking like a man who knows somethin' I should know."

"Don't let your imagination run away with ya, my friend. What happened to your wife shouldn't happened to a dog, but whoever done it is long gone by now. If by some miracle he still is around, local lawmen ain't gonna find him 'cause it don't benefit them. You sure as hell can't find him by yourself."

"I've got more to go on now."

"It don't matter what you got if ya ain't drawin' breath."

"I came by to ask you a couple of favors. First, I need some runnin' money. Fran Druman sold the Hole and you went out of the chicken business, so I'm jobless."

Frenchy threw up his hands. "Hell, man, you don't got to go to work yet. You can live here wit me and Lupé. You can help manage my business. I ain't no educated man like you, so I need somebody ta cook the books and keep the damn IRS off my ass." He winked. "Lupé's got a sister."

"Thanks, but it wouldn't work. Tank and Olin know we're friends. They'd find a way to mess up your operation for sure." He told him about his confrontation with the men at the hotel. "Olin's usin' that as an excuse to put me in jail. He and Tank would bust up your place lookin' for me if they knew I was even thinkin' of stayin' here. Plus, they'd probably take you and Lupé to jail and call the Feds."

Lupé came in and handed Frenchy a pair of pants. He pulled them on, then picked up his coffee and offered a toast, "To friendship."

"To friendship and good-lookin' women." Raz took a drink and grabbed another taquito. Feeling sentimental, he leaned forward and said, "I'm gonna ask you a question, and I want ya to give me an honest answer."

Frenchy raised his bushy eyebrows. "When'd I ever give you any other kind?"

"When Patti and I lived out here that first time, did Punk or any of his friends come by and hit on her when I wasn't here?"

The Cajun shifted his 300 pounds, obviously disturbed by the question. "That ain't a fair question, Irish."

"Somebody got her hooked. I always wanted to know who her dealer was. Remember? Not long before I was sent up, a man over at the old hotel told me a big man with a soft baby face and shoulder-length hair was with her the day before she was killed. I thought maybe he was her dealer. You ever see a man like that?"

Frenchy emptied his coffee and belched. "I liked Patti. She was a poor, sad little kitten and she suffered enough for both of us. Why don't you let her rest in peace?"

"And let some animal do the same? I couldn't live with myself knowing I didn't finish what I started."

Frenchy glanced down the hall and squirmed some more. "That Punk Hutto a sorry son-of-a-bitch, just like all them seedy bastards he sent out here."

"Any of them look like the man I described?"

"No, but I didn't seem 'em much 'cause they was usually here when I was gone. My neighbor down the road said sometimes three or four of them bastards'd be here at a time. The one he said he saw the most was tall, with red hair and a beard. The woman I had at the time told me they all had dope, but the red-head was the one kept pushin' her to take pills and smoke pot, the sorry piece of shit. She didn't say who got Patti on the hard stuff, but she did tell me all of them bastards went in your house every time they was here. She thought all of 'em was bangin' her." He gave Raz a hangdog look. "Sorry."

This made Raz's stomach drop and he reached for his scars. "Your neighbor didn't say anything about a big man with long hair?"

"He didn't describe none of 'em. Guess there coulda been somebody like that. I come home unexpected one time and run 'em all off. Peppered their asses with bird shot. Them bastards got my woman hooked too. I slapped the crap outta her and made her tell me what was goin' on. She said after the red-head got her hooked, he threatened to cut off her supply if she didn't let him in her pants. He made her work for him down at the hotel when I was out of town, too." He threw up his hands. "She'd swap ass to anybody for a fix."

"Sounds like you and I got shoved over the waterfall in the same leaky barrel."

"Yeah. On top of bein' a junky, my gal got pregnant. So, I sent her sorry ass back to New Orleans."

"Before you did that, did she or your neighbor ever mention seeing Punk out here with that other trash?"

Frenchy mumbled something under his breath that Raz couldn't make out. "She say they were all Punk's friends, but he only come out here when we was gone. Mostly he sent his buddies. Seems like Shag was always lookin' for girls ta work for him."

"Did you talk to Patti after you found out what was going on?"

"Once, when you went to town. She tol' me to mind my own damn business. Said if I tol' you anythin' she'd say I raped her. That's when I realized how bad off she was. Put me in a real bind, you bein' my friend an' all. I felt awful 'bout it, still do. Just 'cause them bastards got her strung out don't mean one of 'em kilt her."

"Maybe not, but getting mixed up with drugs led to her death. Since she was seen with that particular guy at the hotel where the dealers hang out, I did everything I could to find him before I was sent up. And I'll keep doin' it 'til I find him."

"Ever get a name?"

"Just a nickname. Medic."

"Don't ring no chimes for me. Talk to Pop Cheever. 'Fore he got sick, he come by a couple of times ta see if I'd heard from ya. Maybe go visit him."

Raz glanced at the mantle clock. "I was on my way out to his place before I decided to stop here first. Should've been there by now." He looked at Frenchy. "I left a hot item with Boobs down at the café. I've got to get it out of there fast. If Pop can't get it, you think you could pick it up?" Despite Frenchy's inclination to talk too much, he was desperate to keep Boobs out of danger.

"Sure. Anythin' for a friend. What is it, a bullet with Tank's name on it?"

"Evidence that'll put Tank and the chief of police away for a long time. All you got to do is go in real casual like, act like you're a customer, get the item from Boobs and put it in your pocket. Then, bring it to me. I'll call Boobs right now to let her know she might have to give it to you." He walked over to the phone and dialed Boobs' number.

On the fourth ring, a coarse, sleepy voice said, "Who's interruptin' my beauty sleep?"

"Boobs, it's Raz. Shake out the cobwebs and listen to me. You make it through the night without any other problems?"

"No problems, unless you count a padlock on the front door of a woman's business a problem, love."

"Padlock?"

"Shiny Buttons Olin closed me down. He don't want nobody comin' or goin' 'til he finds what you left here. That ass threatened to charge me with aidin' and abettin'. He got one of his friends posted out front to make sure nobody comes in."

"I'm out at Frenchy's and was about to send him in to pick up the item."

"That braggin' womanizer? You *are* desperate. Makes no difference who you send — no one can come in an' I can't leave without bein' followed.

Raz thought a moment. "I'm betting Olin will let Pop in. I'm goin' to his place when I leave here. Sorry for all the trouble I've caused you, sweetheart."

"All the more reason for ya ta feel obligated ta be nice ta me. Ya know your item is safe with me."

"Hope so, sweetheart. I'll call you as soon as I talk to Pop." He hung up, and told Frenchy why he couldn't go by the café.

After talking to Frenchy for a few more minutes, Raz said his goodbyes and headed for the door, anxious to get to Pop's place. He stopped when the phone rang and he heard Lupé say boobs in Spanish.

"Sólo un momento," Lupe said. *¿Tetas? Yo no conozco a nadie llamado Pechos.* She listened a moment, then gave the phone to Frenchy. *"Alguien en busca de una mujer llamada Pechos."*

Frenchy spoke gruffly into the receiver. "Who's this?" He shrugged and gave the receiver back to Lupé. "Nobody on the line now. Before it went dead, all I heard was heavy breathin'."

Raz told Frenchy, "I'm afraid Boobs is in trouble. Gotta go!"

Frenchy pulled a roll of greenbacks from his pocket. "Here's some travelin' money." He counted out ten, $20 bills and reached into his front pocket. "Here's some change so you can call me on a payphone so it won't give your location away."

"Thanks, I still don't have a damn cellphone. I'll pay you back when I collect my share from the Hole."

"Pay back, hell! No you won't. There's plenty more where that came from."

Raz walked out the door. "Thanks for everything."

Frenchy hurried after him. "Let me know if you need anythin' else. Don't forget what I tol' you 'bout Lupé's purty sister, either."

Raz left the front porch running, and was almost to his truck before he remembered he was supposed to borrow one of Frenchy's rides. *No time to go back. I'll take the back streets, park a couple of blocks from the Soup Kitchen and hope I' not spotted.*

CHAPTER 15

He turned off McShan Road at Fourth Street and drove to a location that provided him a good view of Boobs' place a block away. There was no black Merc and no police car in sight. There were also no customers on the front porch, but since the placed was padlocked he hadn't expected any. There were no outward signs of trouble, which had him puzzled and worried.

He didn't hear the car approaching from behind until it rolled over loose gravel. Whirring, he saw the black Merc headed his way. Shifting into gear, he sped away toward McShan Road. In the rearview, he saw the Merc hot on his tail, along with another large car that pulled out from behind the bushes near the Soup Kitchen. *It was a trap! They knew Boobs tell me what happened and I'd come runnin'. Hope they didn't see the number I called from.*

Skidding wildly onto McShan Road, he got a glimpse of two men in the Merc. The one leaning out the passenger window was Mazurka.

Raz hunkered down over the wheel and gunned it, realizing his only hope was to out-run them. Blowing past Stump Skeeter's place, he glanced back again and saw he hadn't put any extra distance between them. The Merc was much faster on a paved highway.

The roaring motor drowned out the sound of the first bullet that struck his truck, but he saw the spider web bloom across his windshield. Another shot glanced off the outside mirror support.

He stomped the pedal to the floorboard. The speedometer was bumping eighty, too fast to make the curves ahead. When he got to where Cutoff Road swung sharply to the left, he braked to fifty to avoid flipping the truck. Gripping the wheel with both hands, he skidded into the turn. Boiling dust blocked his view of the Merc.

Pulling out of the skid, he glanced back and saw Mazurka leaning out to shoot at him again. Two more bullets slammed into the cab. The Merc was gaining on him.

In high school, Raz had made test runs on this road to see how fast he could take each curve. He knew this next curve coming up and he lofted his foot off the gas as another bullet slammed into his truck.

He swung hard left and jammed the clutch, shifting into passing gear. The extra power kept him out of the ditch, but the brush flashed by dangerously close.

The Merc wasn't so lucky. It skidded into the ditch, bounced off the bank and careened wildly back onto the road in a cloud of dust. Even this didn't slow the pursuit much, and they began closing in on him again.

Raz's pickup was doing seventy now, much faster than he'd ever driven on the straight sections of this dirt road. The most dangerous curve was just ahead, an almost ninety-degree turn. He'd never made it doing more than 35. *Slow down that much and that Merc will eat you alive.* Then he remembered the logging road he and Anita had been on the day before. *It leaves the road in a straight line. I can take it without slowing down.* Steeling himself for the plunge across the shallow ditch, he aimed for the barely visible ruts ahead.

"Geronimo!" he screamed as the truck hit the shoulder and became airborne. *Boom!* It hit the ground and went racing through the weed-covered field, narrowly missing a dead tree. He rolled to a stop in a heavy growth of bushes some two hundred feet from the ditch.

Jumping out, he ran back toward the road and saw the black car in the brush resting upside down with the wheels still spinning. From the looks of things, it must've rolled at least once.

Moving closer, he found both sides of the car and the top crushed in. The driver's door was open and imbedded in the soft soil. He heard nothing at first but the sound of turning wheels. Then he heard a pained "Ooh!" from the back seat.

Raz searched the surrounding area for anyone who'd been thrown out but still might be able to shoot him. Convinced that both shooters were inside the car and injured, he got down on his hands and knees and peered through the open door.

So much dust floated inside the car that he couldn't tell which gunman was moaning. Noting that his hands had sunk into wet dirt, he looked down and saw a spreading circle of gasoline.

He jumped to his feet and ran, expecting an explosion any second. His better judgment was shouting, *Get in your truck and leave!*

"Help me!" a pathetic voice pleaded.

So what if both thugs die? They tried to kill me. Then his more pragmatic side advised, *They might help you find Medic.*

He walked back through the mushy soil, knelt at the open door and crawled inside. There was no sign of Smeddish in the car. Mazurka was trapped on the passenger's side and had blood on his arms and face. His right leg was grotesquely twisted and bleeding.

"Help me!" the big man pleaded.

"Why should I? Those weren't blanks you were shootin' at me."

Mazurka rolled his eyes, grimacing. "We just wanted ta talk."

"With bullets? A dead man can't say nothin'. You didn't get talkative last night before you started blasting away, either."

"I'm hurtin' awful bad! This car's gonna blow! Get me outta here."

"Why, so you can try to shoot at me again? Who you workin' for?"

"Get me outta here. I don't wanna die!" he said hysterically.

"I'll get you out if you answer some questions."

"Okay! Okay! Hurry before it catches fire."

After patting down Mazurka the best he could and finding no pistol, Raz tried pulling him off the seat. He wouldn't budge. Bracing his feet against the caved-in dash, he pushed his shoulders against the seat and it moved back far enough to free Mazurka. He dragged him out and away from the wreck, noting the gasoline fumes were getting stronger.

Once he was out of the car, Mazurka looked at his leg and screamed, "Look at my leg! It ain't s'posed to look like that!" Then he saw the blood on his arms and hands and shrieked, "I'm bleedin' to death! Get me to a hospital!"

Raz leaned down over him and said, "Nope. I'm not doin' anythin' else for ya. Ya haven't answered one question yet. Better get to talkin' or I'll let you kick the bucket right here, then dump ya in the Baptist graveyard up the road."

"Okay, okay. Ask."

"How come you're so dead set on killin' me?"

"'We had orders. They said you knew too much and you got what Cato sent out in your head, 'cause they can't find no statement nowhere else."

"Who are *they?* And how did *they* know I had somethin' from Cato?"

"Don't know. I get orders from Smeddish. Now take me to a hospital."

"I haven't got to the sixty-four-thousand dollar question yet, handsome. What was goin' down at Boobs' place? Why was she tryin' to find me?"

He shook his head. "Don't know. Smeddish went to handle her."

"I thought Smeddish was with you. What do you mean, *handle* her?"

"He didn't say. Chief told Smeddish you stopped there. Guess Smeddish wanted to try one more time ta find what Cato sent out."

"Where is Smeddish?"

Mazurka groaned and rubbed his thigh "Who?"

"Your partner, Smeddish."

Mazurka tried to turn and look at the wreck, but fell back, unable to take the pain. "Smeddish's still in town."

"Then who was with you?"

"Alabama. He's hurt, but he crawled out an' ran back to report to Tank. Left me to die, the bastard!"

Raz looked around, half expecting to see Alabama aiming his pistol at him. He saw no one, but did see a trail of blood heading into the weeds headed toward the road.

Mazurka groaned, "My leg! What's wrong with my leg?"

"Unless you've got real crooked bones, I'd say it's broke. Now, I'm gonna throw a couple more questions at ya. If I like the answers, I'll take you someplace and get you patched up. First question. You said you get your orders from Smeddish. Who's he get his from?"

Mazurka groaned, shaking his head. "Don't know. Never told me."

"You're singing off key, little canary. So, strain real hard and pretend you're singin' to the Coldwater district attorney like you did when you helped burn Cato. Give me a name."

"Rudy or Tank, I guess. Rudy runs things in Northville. Honest ta God, I don't know for sure."

"Where's Alabama from? Who tells him what to do?"

Mazurka shook his head. "Ed sent him up from Houston. He gets all his orders from Ed."

"Ed who?"

"Barrow."

"Who's Medic? He a big guy with long blond or light brown hair that hangs out at God's Palace?"

"Never heard of him. Get me to a doctor."

"I think you're lyin'. He's one of Shag Shammerhorn's friends."

"I *don't* know him."

Disappointed, Raz steeled himself for the biggest question of all. Leaning closer, he asked, "Who gave the order to kill my wife?"

"Which one of them party gals was yours?"

"You know my name."

"Smeddish got his orders from Rudy on how to handle the crazy one. He said Rudy got the okay from Ed."

"The crazy one? Who you talkin' 'bout?"

"All I know is Carol somethin'."

"Carol? Who's Carol? My wife's name was Patti."

Mazurka shook his head. "I had nothin' ta do with that one either. I was in Houston with Alabama when that went down. Honest ta God."

Raz kicked Mazurka's bad leg. "Don't lie to me. Even if you were out of town, you would've found out who did it later."

Mazurka grimaced. "Didn't find out... Smeddish told me... not to ask."

"I think you're lyin' again. So, maybe I should leave you here to die and get word back to Cato Hamilton about your passin'. He promised me a handsome sum for puttin' your lights out, fink."

Mazurka shook his head. "I ain't lyin'. I don't know."

"Then tell me Rudy's last name."

"I... don't... know." His voice was getting weaker. "Ain't never met him."

"Try this one. Who killed Tim Barton?"

"Don't know. Smeddish handled it."

"Two more questions Answer them right and we're out o' here. Why was my wife killed?"

Mazurka closed his eyes like he might pass out. Raz shook him and repeated the question, Mazurka said groggily, "Smeddish said... she was too sick to be trusted... wanted to quit the business... couldn't shake the habit. When Shag wouldn't give her no more dope, Smeddish said she... threatened to go to the Feds. She... knew too much... stayin' with Gerta. She had everybody... real... shook up."

"Who killed her? Was it Medic?"

Mazurka closed his eyes again, and this time didn't open them when Raz shook him. He would die from blood loss or infection if his wounds weren't treated and his leg set.

Alabama'll make it back to town soon, and Tank and Rudy will call Ed Barrow for reinforcements. They'll check Coldwater Hospital for Mazurka when they don't find him in the wreck. That means I can't take him to Coldwater, but I have to save him. He might be Lassiter's prime witness.

The way things are going, I'll have to call Lassiter sooner than I wanted. Maybe Mazurka will keep Lassiter busy and give me more time to get things done.

He dragged Mazurka to his truck by his shoulders, then pulled him into the bed. He closed the tailgate and drove back out to the main road, trying to think of somewhere to take Mazurka and get him patched up. *Anita's parents had a lake house that isn't far from here. That may be the only safe place available.* He turned right.

He followed the back roads to Town Lake. He'd lock Mazurka in the Bryant's boathouse and then call Boobs from the phone in the cottage. Once he was sure she was okay, he'd call Anita and ask her if she'd provide some first aid.

The cabin was only twenty miles from Northville, but the drive took longer than usual because of the indirect route Raz took to get there. When he finally turned off Town Lake Road onto the gravel driveway, he saw the cottage was run down, and perhaps unused. *Great. There might not be a working phone in there.*

He drove slowly through the weeds and down the gentle slope to the dock. Twenty feet from the bank, he swung around and backed up. He remembered that the boat shed was enclosed on all four sides down to the water line, except for an opening behind the boat slip. *A man with two good legs would have trouble getting out of there. Since Mazurka has only one, this is a great place to stash him.*

Raz dropped the tailgate and pulled Mazurka out. When the unconscious man's wounded leg hit the ground, he groaned and tried to sit up. Patting his broken limb, he cried out, fell back and began cursing. "This ain't no hospital!"

"You figure that out all by yourself? Now shut up and be thankful I didn't let you blow up with your car."

"I need a hospital and a doctor! I got my rights!"

"Sure you do. That's why I'm offerin' you this proposition. Stay here and let me get you fixed up, or go with me to the emergency room in Coldwater where I'll call in the Feds and have them charge you with everythin' from assault to attempted murder. I'll tell 'em what you told me out there at the wreck. I'm sure they'll get enough DEA agents over to your hospital room to keep Tank's friends from offin' you."

"You're nuts," he growled.

"And you're about to be buzzard meat or a jailbird. Choice is yours." Raz stood up. "You'd get at least twenty years to serve with your old boss Cato, if the gang didn't kill you first to keep you from singin' like you did with Cato. I'll give you ten to one odds you'll never see prison."

"Okay! Okay! You crazy bastard! Fix me up. I'm hurtin' bad."

"Consider it done. Part of the deal will require you to talk to a narc friend of mine. Otherwise, my promise not to prosecute will be null and void."

Mazurka took a labored breath. "No jail?"

"No jail. You'll get immunity and be put into protective custody, like you were when you testified against Cato. My narc friend will even hide you during your pals' trials if you sing real sweet. After Tank and his friends are put away, you can go anywhere your little black heart desires. I'd suggest Siberia."

Mazurka looked around again. "You can't fix me up in this God forsaken place. I'm gonna die."

"You think I'd let that happen to my star witness? I don't think so, my man!"

"You ain't no doctor. How you gonna fix me up?"

"You'll find out soon enough."

Raz pulled the big man across the ramp and into the hot, musty-smelling shed; Mazurka moaning and cursing the whole way. He stretched him out on the wooden platform alongside the boat slip. "Don't move unless you want to fall in the lake and drown. The door will be locked; so don't even try to get out that way. If you're thinkin' you can swim with that busted leg, just remember there are lots of big water moccasins swimmin' 'round just waiting for some fresh meat. Boat sheds are their favorite hangouts."

"Snakes?" Mazurka said, and tried to sit up, panicked. "I can't stand snakes."

Raz untied the anchor rope from the flat aluminum boat in the slip. "Shut up before I forget our deal and push you the water." He gave the boat a hard push with his foot and it drifted through the opening and out of sight "I'm gonna go call somebody to fix you up. Be back soon. Think happy thoughts while I'm gone."

Moving out on the ramp, Raz closed the door and turned the hasp catch crosswise to prevent it from being opened from the inside. Mazurka's string of curses got weaker as he walked away.

Moving up the incline to the cabin some hundred feet from the water, Raz stepped onto the porch to check the front door of the cottage. It was locked, but he could see a phone sitting on a side table as he looked through the front window.

He went to the back door, but it was locked too. He really didn't want to add breaking and entering to his list of sins, so he decided he'd have to drive around 'til he found a phone. First, he'd have to patch up Mazurka until he could get ahold of Anita. He went to the one-car garage behind the cottage. There was an attached storage room there and he started looking for something he could use as a bandage. He found some old shirts in a cardboard box, and pulled out the cleanest two.

He headed back to the boat shed, tearing off narrow strips of cloth from the shirts on the way. Mazurka appeared to be in a lot of pain and was starting to look scared.

He pushed up on one elbow when Raz came in, saying, "Damn you for dumpin' me in this shack."

Pushing him down, Raz pressed a folded piece of cloth against the cut on the gunman's temple. It was a deep wound, and needed a thorough cleaning and stitches.

"Damn!" Mazurka complained. "What you doin' ta me? You ain't no doctor."

"And you ain't my idea of good fish bait, but I'll roll you into that lake if you don't shut up."

Raz tied a strip of cloth around Mazurka's head to help stop the bleeding. He tore off more pieces of the shirt to cover cuts on his shoulder and left arm. The other wounds weren't deep, and the blood had already dried on them. His arms had turned blue with bruises.

"I'll be back with help real soon, as long as I don't run into some of your friends. In the meantime, don't move around unless you want to start bleeding again."

"You can't leave me here. It ain't humane."

Raz walked to the door. "Nobody knows more about such delicate matters than you. I'll try not to cry my eyes out worryin' 'bout ya before I get back."

Raz re-locked the door drove up to the cabin. He hid his antique sword behind a pier under the back wall and sat down on the porch. Taking off his left boot and sock, he put the small envelope meant for Snake next to his foot and slipped his sock over it, then put his boot back on. He concealed the money Frenchy gave him in the other sock. The wad of cash made for a snug fit, but a little discomfort definitely beat being broke.

He thought about breaking in again, but decided against it since he had to go to town to check on Boobs. He'd use the payphone at the Chevron station near the Square. After talking to Anita he'd call Boobs to make sure she was okay. His last call would be to Tank to tell him about his new insurance policy — Mazurka.

Just inside the city limits, he saw an alarming sight. There was a thick plume of black smoke that looked like it was coming from downtown. He sped up, glancing at it through breaks in the trees. Near the Square, his curiosity turned to near panic.

"Oh, my God. The Soup Kitchen!"

CHAPTER 16

When he got there, the Soup Kitchen was completely engulfed in flames. Firemen were frantically spraying it down with water but from what he could see, there was no hope of saving the building. The townspeople had all come out to see what was going on.

Parking half a block away, Raz jumped out and pushed through the crowd, looking for Boobs' face. At the front steps, the intense heat stopped him.

"Stay back, Raz," somebody yelled. "You can't go in there."

Turning, he saw his friend, Ethan Lewis. He was one of the firemen directing the water onto the flames. Ethan pointed to a tight circle of people in the street and Raz ran over. He stopped short, shocked by what he saw.

Boobs lay stretched out on her back, her face pale and drawn, and her chest covered with blood. He knelt beside her and gave her a gentle hug. She tried to return it, but her arms fell back to the ground and she closed her eyes.

"Anybody call an ambulance?" he yelled.

"One's on the way," somebody answered.

Raz pulled his handkerchief out of his back pocket and shoved it under Boobs' dress, pressing it against the ugly wound on her left breast. Leaning closer, he said, "Boobs, can you hear me?"

Her eyes fluttered open. "'Course I can, love. I'm shot, not deaf."

"Hold on. We'll have you on your way to the hospital in a few minutes. You're gonna be okay."

She managed a faint smile. When her lips moved, he leaned closer to hear her above the noise around them. "I wanted you, love, but not bad enough to get shot."

"That is a little drastic, sweety. Who did this to you? Who set your place on fire?"

"Short, dumpy guy and some mangy-looking character with red hair and a beard."

"Smeddish and Shag. I'll see to it they pay for this!" He glanced at the fire. "I'm so sorry, Boobs. I should've done something to keep this from happenin' to ya. I came after ya called Frenchy, but got chased away."

She put her hand on his. "I called around tryin' to find you as soon as they unlocked the front door an' came bustin' in. I'd just got through to Frenchy's house when one of 'em jerked the line out of the wall."

"Since Olin didn't find what I left with you, I was sure they'd leave you alone 'til I got somebody to pick it up. I was on my way ta see Pop when I saw the smoke. What happened after they jerked the phone out of the wall?"

She bit her lip to keep from crying out. "They tore up everythin'. When they didn't find it, the short one left Red an' a couple of his deadbeat friends ta guard me while he went someplace. I couldn't leave an' no customers could get in."

"Don't talk anymore. Try to relax. The ambulance will be here any minute."

She shook her head. "I gotta tell you while I can, love. I might not... make it. When Red's short buddy finally came back, he was madder'n ever, like maybe he just got some bad news. They started lookin' again, yellin' and cussin'. Said you wouldn't come back ta check on me if ya hadn't left it with me."

"Why'd they shoot you and start the fire?"

She coughed, digging her fingers into his arm. Blood ran out the corner of her mouth. "They found your shoes..."

"You were supposed to burn them, remember?"

"I know, love, but I forgot. Anyway, they really went crazy when they saw the heels was cut off. That convinced 'em Cato's statement was here. They ripped everythin' apart again, and when I still refused to tell 'em where it was, they torched my place, the bastards. I grabbed a skillet an' tried ta stop 'em then they shot me. Said they'd burn it up if I wouldn't give it to them. Me too, 'cause I'd probably listened to it."

Overwhelmed by guilt, he squeezed her hand. "It's my fault this happened. Telling you I'm sorry isn't nearly enough. You'll be fine, and I'll build you another café. I promise."

"No, love." She shook her head. "This is it. And you know what? I don't really care. There ain't nothin' I ain't done or tried, an' I ain't afraid ta die. So, don't you feel bad about it. You hear? I'm just makin' my exit a little earlier than planned." She coughed, harder this time.

He kissed her forehead. "Stop talkin' like a crazy woman. Save your energy."

"It ain't been easy, ya know. No steady man ta stand by me. No family. But I ain't got nobody ta blame but myself. I'm the one that screwed it up. Don't you screw up your life, too. Ya hear?"

She coughed again, and he wiped away another trickle of blood and said, "I told ya ta stop yappin'. Lie still an' save your breath."

"You're telling *me* not ta talk, love? You're dumber than I thought." She coughed again. "You ain't no gentleman, Raz Jester."

"Never claimed ta be."

"You ain't, 'cause ya let me die without givin' me none of your good lovin'. Ya know how long it's been since a good man held me the way a woman wants ta be held?"

"Be quiet. You don't want ta be hauled away bitchin', do you?" He glanced at the concerned faces around his, wondering where the ambulance was and when Tank and Olin would get there.

She coughed and her fingernails dug into his arm again. "Ya can't deny me that too, love," she said. "A woman's got certain rights." Tears welled up in her eyes and a look of terror swept across her face. "Don't leave me, Raz. I don't wanna die alone. I never had nothin' ta brag about, but you an' your buddies in that back room and my chili. That ain't much, is it." After gasping for breath, she added, "Them was good times, eh love?"

"The best. You sure got me started off right in the lovin' department."

She looked through the smoke at the sky. "I sure have missed those days, and bein' with you. Reckon there's a back room full of young boys waitin' for me up there?" She coughed and more blood gushed out.

Glancing around him, he called out, "Where's that ambulance?"

Nobody answered, but he could see the grim faces expressing concern about Boobs all around him. There was some mumbling and pointing, but nobody offered to help. A loud crash sent a shower of sparks skyward where the soup kitchen had stood. *The tape's gone,* he thought.

Boobs stirred in his arms, coughed again and tried to speak, but was almost strangled by more fresh blood. He kissed her forehead, and said, "You can't die on me. Hold on."

She moaned

"What did you say, honey?"

Between coughs, she said weakly, "Glad I could do ya a couple o' favors... 'fore I had ta leave on my... long trip."

He kissed her cheek. "You've done me lots of favors. But forgiving me for causing this is the only one that counts now."

She nodded, attempting a smile and closed her eyes.

"Somebody bring me a towel!" he yelled.

He watched her gasp and choke as she writhed in pain. There was nothing he could do but hold her and feel helpless as she breathed her last breath.

When somebody finally tossed him a towel, Raz gently lowered Boobs' lifeless head to the ground and blotted blood and ashes from her face and neck. Oblivious to everything around him, tears welled up in his eyes. Totally consumed by grief, he didn't hear anyone approaching and jumped when a deep male voice called out his name.

"I figured this fire would make you show up, jailbird quarterback," the voice said.

Raz looked up at the contemptuous smirk on a red-faced Tank Zelder towering over him. His right hand was resting on the butt of his holstered pistol, indicating he hoped Raz would make a run for it so he could finalize his victory with a bullet in Raz's back.

Raz stood up and said angrily, "Look at her, Tank! Look at what your thugs did to the best friend any man ever had!"

Tank looked down and grinned. "Frankly, I don't see how a bullet got through that big fat tit."

Raz took a step forward with clenched fists, but stopped when Tank's hand tighten around his pistol. Trying to keep his temper from overriding his better judgment, he rubbed the scars on his face and neck and said nothing.

"You folks can go on about your business now," Tank announced to the bystanders. "Me and Olin'll take care of things here. Go on. Get outta here!"

"We'll move back, but if it's all the same to you, we'll hang around ta make sure Raz don't get falsely accused again," Cecil Cassidy said.

Olin Culpepper, looking official as usual in his freshly pressed black uniform, shiny buttons and leather accessories, pushed through the crowd to give Boobs' body a cautious look. "Raz," he said, "don't you ever learn?" In a more official tone he announced, "You heard the sheriff, folks. Move back. Better still, just go on home. Make room for the ambulance."

The ambulance raced down Pine, siren blaring and lights flashing. It skidded to a stop in the middle of the street and two attendants jumped out. They ran over to Boobs' body and tried to find a pulse.

"Just haul her off, boys," Tank said. "She's as done as last week's chili."

One of them asked, "The J.P. already been here?"

"Don't worry about Obie Peavy," Tank said. "I can handle him. We've got more important things ta think about right now." He looked at Raz.

The two attendants lifted Boobs onto a gurney and rolled her into the ambulance. As they drove away, Tank said, "Don't look so sad, jailbird. Some people won't even miss her. She say who shot her?"

"Yeah, she did." He raised his voice so all could hear, "Shag Shammerhorn and Smeddish. You and Olin both know them. Shag's the leader of those hippies you ordered to jump me yesterday."

Tank gave Olin a concerned look as an excited murmur ran through the crowd. Turning to them, Tank called out, "Any of you hear Boobs say who done it?"

When no one responded, the sheriff told Raz, "What's a jailbird's word worth, anyway? You're under arrest on that assault charge I filed yesterday. Cuff him, Olin."

Olin stepped forward as Tank added, "I'm chargin' ya with suspicion of arson and murder, too."

Another murmur ran through the crowd, and somebody shouted, "Leave Raz alone, Tank! He wouldn't hurt Boobs. They was friends."

"Yeah," Cecil Cassidy said. "He ain't bothered nobody since he got home 'cept that riffraff you an' Olin let take over the hotel, an' they started it. Turn him loose."

Tank and Olin exchanged glances, and Olin took hold of Raz's arm as a woman in the crowd shouted, "Too bad somebody didn't burn down that dopers' hangout 'stead o' the Soup Kitchen."

"Yeah," said another. "Poor ol' Boobs never bothered nobody 'cept jealous wives."

A man called out, "Give Raz a break, Olin."

Lowering his voice, Tank told Olin, "Let's go before things get ugly." Turning to the crowd, he shouted, "Clear out, all o' ya! Go home. It's over. Everything's under control."

As people moved away, Raz had a strong impulse to run, but knew they'd shoot him if he did. Plus, some of his friends might get hurt or killed in the crossfire. So, he remained still and watched the crowd disperse.

After the street cleared, another shocking sight caught his eye. He saw a pale and emaciated Punk Hutto walking up, flanked by two muscular young men with long hair and beards, their arms folded across their bare chests.

"Hello, class favorite," Punk said with a sickening grin. "Which one of us is the loser now?" He laughed and his frail body swayed like he might fall.

He was either ill or strung out on heroin. His pathetic appearance was made even more bizarre by his wrinkled purple shirt and faded jeans that were held up by a pink rope. His long hair was spiked and colored blue on one side and yellow on the other.

Tank and Olin both seemed puzzled by Punk's sudden appearance. Olin told him, "We're taking the town troublemaker to jail, Punk."

"Don't leave yet. Let me savor the moment." He laughed, telling Raz, "I'm disappointed you didn't come by *my* new club when you got back."

Raz glared at him. "You know, been busy fightin' off vermin. It just slipped my mind. I'm glad you dropped by, though; the sight of ya saves me the trouble of having ta puke later."

Punk's smile disappeared and color rushed to his face. "Smart ass. I see bein' in the slammer ain't changed you none. Don't matter though, 'cause what you think an' do don't count in this town. I doubt you'll be around long enough this time ta find that out for yourself."

"I'll be here to wave bye-bye when the honey wagon hauls you an' your friends off ta the state pen."

"Oh, yeah? What gave you that notion?"

"I got an ace in the hole that Tank and your pals don't know about. It's the one the narcs'll use ta put all of ya away for good. That means you'll have ta kick your habit cold turkey."

Punk looked at Tank and Olin. "What the hell's he talkin' about? What ace does he got?" He nodded toward the smoldering the Soup Kitchen. "You tol' me there was only one thing ta worry about 'sides the quarterback."

"That's right, Punk," Tank said, lowering his voice as he glanced at the nearby firemen. "Don't pay no attention ta him. He's just blowin' smoke. You know all about his razzle-dazzle."

"Cato found out the hard way that Blackie Mazurka don't blow smoke," Raz said. "So will you, after he testifies against ya. He's tol' me lots o' good stuff already, and he's ready ta tell all to the state narcs and federal prosecutor so he won't have ta go ta jail with you guys."

Tank and Olin exchanged anxious glances as Punk told Tank, "I hope he's lyin', big man, otherwise you better find a way ta get that bunglin' fool back here 'fore he spills his guts. If Ed hears what you let happen up here—"

"That's the first sensible thing you ever said, pervert," Raz said. "Better listen to him, sheriff."

"He's lyin'!" Tank growled. "He ain't got Mazurka."

"I'm still alive," Raz said. "What better proof you need? Mazurka really screwed up this time. You already know that though, 'cause Alabama headed straight for your office soon as he crawled out o' that wreck."

Olin gave Tank an accusing look. "You talked to Alabama?"

"Yeah, Tank," Punk said. "Where's Alabama?"

"Come up with a good answer, Mr. High Sheriff," Raz taunted, "so they won't figure out you're trying ta cut 'em out and save yourself." He turned to Olin and Punk and said, "I put Mazurka away where none of ya can find him, and he'll stay there 'til I hear whether Tank and Olin are gonna change their minds 'bout that offer I made 'em earlier."

He looked at Olin and said, "If you and Tank do change your minds, we'll negotiate a sweet deal before I tell the narcs where to find Mazurka."

Tank's confidence disappeared, and for a moment he was at a loss for words. Olin and Punk fixed him with an accusing stare as Punk asked, "What deal? What's he talking about, Tank? You tol' me you sent Mazurka someplace with Alabama."

"Punk, you mean our friendly sheriff didn't tell you about Mazurka an' Alabama havin' a little accident while they chased me out of town?" Raz asked. He looked at Olin and said, "He's had plenty o' time ta tell both o' ya since Alabama got back."

Punk staggered across the street, obviously disturbed by Raz's statement. "For the last time, Tank, where the hell's Alabama and Mazurka?"

"Tell him, Tank," Olin said. "I'd like to know, too."

"Maybe you and Punk should find Alabama and talk to him yourselves," Raz told Olin. "He'll tell you what Tank's keeping from ya." He looked at Punk and added, "And he might even tell ya 'bout that first deal I offered him."

"Shut up, smart ass!" Tank snarled. "You'll pay for this. Don't listen to him, guys. You know he's a flimflam man."

Raz smiled. "Oops! Did I throw a stink bomb into your playhouse, Tank? Sorry. I thought you always kept your friends up to date. I'm disappointed in you, too, Olin. I'm surprised ya didn't know Ed sent his hit men in to supervise the latest problems in Northville. He'll make sure ya don't screw up like ya did two years ago."

Punk's voice trembled as he said to Raz, "I told 'em you'd cause all kinds of trouble with your snoopin' around an' trying ta find out who killed your slut wife. They tol' me they'd see to it you never made it back."

Tank glanced around for possible witnesses and put his hand on his pistol. "Go ahead, Punk, tell him all about his whore wife."

Raz saw Tank nod ever so slightly at Punk, and felt Olin's hand fall away when the chief stepped back. Sensing he was being set up, Raz stood still, believing any movement at all on his part would prove fatal.

Punk came closer to Raz, and with a sick grin said, "That's what your wife was, a whore. She'd do anythin' for a fix. One time I saw her crawl around butt-naked on her hands and knees like a damn dog and give a head job to every man in the room just ta get a fix."

Raz took a quick step toward Punk, but stopped when he remembered Tank's pistol. Trembling with rage, he fixed his eyes on Punk's repugnant face. He coudl see how much pleasure Punk took in that revelation.

Spitting on Raz's chest, Punk sneered and said, "You'll never find out who killed your slut wife, or how much head she gave me and my friends. She even took care o' Tank and Olin once, did 'em both at the same time. Tank hurt her so bad she was out o' business for a week."

Raz whirled to charge Tank, but stopped when Tank jerked out his pistol. He quickly shoved it back into its holster when a car approached and stopped.

"What's goin' on, sheriff?" a man asked.

Tank dropped his hand to his side, "Nothin' for you ta worry about, Norm. Go on about your business."

Norm drove away and Tank told Olin, "Put our prisoner in my car. We'll finish our talk in private."

Olin patted Raz down from foot to shoulder, taking his pocketknife and billfold. When he opened the empty wallet, Raz told him, "Sorry I don't have more cash for ya, but I already gave at the old hotel. Since I'm not on the take, pickin's been slim to none. I have some change, if that'll help your cause any. "

"Smart ass." Olin retuned the wallet and grabbed his arm. "Let's go."

Olin shoved him into the back seat of Tank's car, and Punk slammed the door shut, then leaned down to peer in at him. "Patti's papa was right. You're nothin' but trash. You knocked up his daughter so you could marry into a good family and big money. Now look at you." He laughed.

Raz continued looking straight a head, pretending not to hear. *Stay calm. If you survive a trip to jail, there'll be plenty of time to settle up with all of 'em later.*

As they climbed into the front seat, Olin told Tank, "We can't take him to your office or mine. Too many home-comers wandering 'round and a lot of them are his friends."

Tank started the car, telling Punk, "We'll take him ta your place. Go on ahead of us and unlock that special room of yours. Don't talk ta nobody on the way there."

Punk nodded. "Okay, big guy, but you've still got some splainin' ta do."

Raz was still numb from watching Boobs die. Losing one of his oldest and dearest friends as well as the tape made it impossible to be too concerned about his current situation.

Mazurka, his only hope now, would be lost too, if he couldn't get back to him with medical help soon. If Mazurka died, his plans for living the good life would explode in his face like a bad firecracker.

CHAPTER 17

Tank parked near the back door of the Hard Rock Club. Punk and his bodyguards rolled in beside them in a pink Cadillac. Punk unlocked the club's back door and disappeared inside with his entourage as Tank and Olin pulled Raz from the back seat.

Inside, they passed two doors in the hall that had been added since Raz had been there last. They went left and entered a large room that had formerly been Fran's office/bedroom. The walls were various shades of green, yellow, pink, and purple, applied in irregular curved patterns. The ceiling had indirect lighting from recessed fixtures and there was a large mirror above a king-sized bed.

There were small metal boxes, a Turkish pipe, silver roach clips, a small benzene burner and several ash rays on the bedside tables. The walls were lined with pictures of rock singers, rappers and large photos of nude young women engaged in various sexual acts with both men and women.

Tank shoved Raz into a chair in front of a cluttered black desk as Olin locked the door behind them and turned off the rap music. Tank picked up the desk phone and dialed. Because he spoke in hushed tones and covered his mouth, Raz couldn't understand what he said. He saw his expression change, and the conversation ended with a curt, "Okay. Call me back."

Raz noticed Tank had let himself go since he'd seen him last. He looked twice his age, had gained weight and there was a web of broken blood vessels that made his nose and cheeks appear flushed. He looked like a stroke waiting to happen.

Still angry and shocked, Raz realized the handcuffs he was wearing had probably saved his life: they'd kept him from laying into Tank. He was determined to keep a clear head and escape before Tank thought of a way to get rid of him for good.

Tank opened his mouth to speak, but a loud rapping on the door stopped him. He and Olin exchanged glances, and Tank nodded. Olin cautiously opened the door, and without speaking, left the room. Raz could hear muffled, anxious voices, but couldn't understand anything being said. Presently, Olin reappeared, came in and locked the door.

"What was that all about?" Tank asked.

"Punk said Alabama was up front when he got here. He was all skinned up and mad as hell 'cause you wouldn't take him out ta that wreck ta check on Mazurka." He looked at Raz and added, "Which means our prisoner was tellin' the truth 'bout havin' Mazurka, and you knew it all along."

"Not necessarily. Alabama told me he thought Mazurka was dead."

"You don't know for sure, though. Do you?"

"I sure as hell didn't know the jailbird had him," Tank snapped. "How could I? Alabama said Raz wasn't there when he left."

"You should've told me so I could've gone out there. This is no time ta be flyin' solo. Sounds like you might've been tryin' to keep me out o' the loop."

Tank got off the desk. "We can settle everythin' by lockin' up our prize bullshiter and drivin' out ta that wreck."

"Can't," Olin said. "Punk's friends already left to take Alabama to Coldwater Hospital. It would take us too long runnin' all them dirt roads tryin' ta find that wreck. We'll wait 'til Alabama gets back, or..." He looked at Raz.

"Take the jailbird quarterback with us?" Tank asked, shaking his head. "No way! We can't risk runnin' into more o' his friends." Turning to Raz, he said gruffly, "You lied 'bout Mazurka, didn't you?"

"Would've been if I'd said he was dead," Raz replied.

The sheriff and Olin moved over to the corner of the room and talked low so Raz couldn't make out what was said. They kept glancing at him as they talked. When they'd finished, Tank shook out a cigarette from a pack in his shirt pocket and lit it with a lighter on desk. He inhaled deeply, blowing smoke in Raz's face.

"Those cancer sticks will kill you, if your fellow prisoners down in the pen don't do it first," Raz taunted.

Tank blew more smoke at him. "You're pretty cocky for a man whose best hold card just went up in smoke." He nodded. "Yeah, we found them prison shoes with the heels cut off. You hid that tape Cato gave you at the Soup Kitchen and it done went up in smoke." He smiled.

"That right? Your sorry friends find it and toss it in the fire?"

"Didn't have to. All they had ta do was torch the place. It was there unless Boobs gave it to somebody else."

"Boobs wouldn't do that."

"Aha!" Tank exclaimed, wagging his index finger. "Thanks for confirmin' it. Olin, you notice how I tricked him into confessin' to what we suspected all along? Now all we got ta worry 'bout is Mazurka. *If* he's still alive."

Raz remained silent, disappointed at his slip.

"Since Olin an' me don't believe you got Mazurka, you got nothin' ta offer us." Tank laughed. "You didn't really think I'd accept that proposition you gave Lard, did ya? If I did that, I'd give up a chance ta get two birds with one stone. No need for ya ta play games no more."

"You won't know that for sure 'til we go out to that wreck. A man claiming he's smart enough ta find out where Cato's tape was should be able to figure that out."

"I told everybody, including Rudy, that Cato's message wasn't in all them underlined words in that Bible the boys found in your pocket. After Olin an' some other scripture experts decided the same thing, they put me back in charge of findin' it before you gave it ta the wrong people. That's when I knew it had ta be at the Soup Kitchen, 'cause we searched every other place you been since you got out. We even went through your mother's room after the boys didn't find it at your house out in the sticks."

"You bothered my mother? That's another one I owe you, Mr. High Sheriff."

Tank smiled. "You threatenin' a police officer? Hear that, Olin? He threatened me." He blew more smoke.

"Too bad you dirtied our long runnin' contest by fingerin' me for murder, then makin' things worse by not looking for Patti's butcher," Raz said. "Up 'til then, our fight was clean, honest fun."

Tank jumped off the desk and reached for his baton, but Olin caught his hand. "We need him."

Breathing hard, Tank sat down again, livid. "Smart ass. Servin' two years didn't teach you a damn thing. Figured you would've at least learned our fight ain't even a contest no more, you bein' a convicted felon an' all. Since you didn't learn, I'm gonna make sure our feudin' days are over this time."

"Too bad," Raz said. "I was lookin' forward ta bein' around ta see ya serve at least ten years."

"Keep pushin' it, and ya might get ta die slow, like—"

"Shut up, Tank," Olin snapped. "Stop lettin' him rattle your chain. Unless you decide to start makin' deals on your own, everythin's gonna be taken care of. Calm down!"

"Both of you are an embarrassment to law enforcement," Raz said. "When I think of what a fine lawman Pop Cheever was, and how much good he did for the good people of this county—"

"Pop's dyin' on a piece of ground barely big enough to bury him in," Tank said. "Guess how many of our citizens have paid a little somethin' on his doctor bills or taken him groceries?" He formed a zero with his thumb and forefinger. "That's not gonna happen ta me. Them so-called good people don't give a tinker's dam about a good man like that or me for that matter, so why should I worry 'bout them? They want us ta protect 'em, but they don't care whether we live or die doin' it. "

The silence grew heavy in the room before Olin spoke to Raz. "Why didn't you just serve your time, then come home an' mind your own business? You should've known gettin' mixed up with Cato Hamilton would be bad news an' put you in a tight place."

"Like the one you and Tank put me in when I found Tim Barton's body? Stop playin' games and tell me who killed my wife. Then maybe I'll tell you where to find Mazurka. After that, you can file charges against the killer and tell Ed Barrow and his friends to go to hell. Then, you can do the job you were hired ta do."

They all jumped when the phone rang. Olin promptly picked it up. "Yeah?" He listened for a few seconds, then replied, "Okay. Consider it done." He hung up and told Tank, "We got orders ta make sure Mazurka ain't still in that wrecked car. If he is, and somebody else finds him 'fore we do, that would make certain people very unhappy."

"Tank and I can't consider your offer 'til that's done," he told Raz. "Let's go."

Tank got up to follow Olin and, for a moment, took his eyes off Raz. Raz stood, backed up to the desk and pulled the cigarette lighter into his back pocket. *My guess is they just got approval to kill me. I got to get my brain in gear and find a way to escape, save Mazurka and call Lassiter.*

Raz knew Tank was unpredictable when he was stressed. *If Olin wasn't here, Tank would've already killed me. After that phone call, I think my luck's about to run out.*

Tank pushed Raz into the back seat of his car, then got in on the passenger side while Olin got behind the wheel. Turning to look at Raz, the big sheriff said, "Okay, prove to us you ain't lyin'. Tell us where ta find that wreck."

"Drive out to Shortcut Road. I'll tell ya where to stop."

When they crossed Pine, Raz got a glimpse of the burned-out Soup Kitchen. The sight caused his smoldering anger to rise to new heights. His rage was tempered only by a wave of sadness, and the realization that he would soon share Boobs' fate if he didn't escape.

CHAPTER 18

When they passed the wall along the Williamsburg Addition Raz wondered what Becky was doing, and if she'd thought about him after his brief visit. His biggest regret was failing her. *Will she remember me as she grows up or will she just resent me for not being there for her?* The thought of never seeing her again made him even more determined to survive.

When they passed the city limits sign on McShan Road, Tank pulled out his nightstick and turned to face Raz. "Now, jailbird smart ass, I'm gonna do a little attitude adjustment on ya that'll make us even for that lickin' you gave me back in high school *and* for what you did ta me two years ago. There might even be a little somethin' for them bad things you said 'bout me ta all them voters today." He laughed. "I'll be killin' three birds with one swing, you might say, and it'll keep ya from runnin' away after we put ya on the ground at that wreck."

Raz jerked his knees to the side, but couldn't avoid the heavy blow from Tank's nightstick. Choking back a cry of pain, he shoved his knees the other way when he saw the baton coming down again. He jumped and grunted, but refused to give Tank the satisfaction of a scream.

Tank laughed. "You won't do no more college quarterbackin' with them knees, jailbird. You pro'bly won't even be able ta hunker down over a pretty little rich girl ta get their daddy's money."

"Damn you, Tank!" Raz said through clenched teeth. "Take off these handcuffs and make it a fair fight."

Tank jammed the baton into Raz's ribs and then poked him hard in the stomach, "Ever watch a hungry tomcat play with a mouse 'fore killin' it? How's it feel, mouse?"

Tank rose up in the seat and struck Raz's back and his right thigh. Raz almost passed out.

"Don't mess him up too much," Olin cautioned. "The there might be questions 'bout bruises that don't match the wreck."

Olin's remark verified what Raz already suspected — they had no intention of taking him back to town alive.

Tank settled back in the seat, panting. "I reckon that's enough to teach the bastard not to mess with the law."

Raz lay on his side, groaning. Barely conscious, he felt the car slow down, and the baton prodding him. "Get up, smartass," Tank ordered. "Tell us where ta find that damn wreck 'less ya want another go 'round with my knightstick."

Raz was finally able to get to a sitting position after several tires. His head began to clear just as he saw the sharp turn where the Merc left the road. He told himself, *Escape! Escape now!* But his knees hurt so much that he didn't know if he could even walk, let alone run. Plus, there was the added handicap of the handcuffs. Resigned to cooperating, as least a little, he said, "Stop here."

Tank told Olin, "Back up and find a place to get off the road. We can't be seen out here."

Olin turned onto the old logging road. As soon as they were out of sight, he stopped and got out.

Tank opened the back door, reached behind Raz and took hold of the handcuffs, then dragged him out and dropped him in the weeds. "Get up, quarterback. We got a wreck ta investigate. If Mazurka ain't in it, you're gonna take us where you hid him or you'll be gettin' another beatin'."

Raz climbed unsteadily to his feet, but barely had time to stand before Tank shoved him forward, causing him to fall. He struggled to his feet again and looked toward the scene of the wreck. He nodded. "Out there."

"Lead on," Tank snapped.

Raz limped along, almost falling with each step. Neither Tank nor Olin offered to help him. He'd had lots of injuries playing football, but nothing like this. Each faltering step caused stabbing pains in his knees, ribs and stomach. Finally, the wreck came into view and he stopped.

Tank and Olin cautiously inspected the scene, studying the weeds and bushes around it like they expected unfriendly forces to jump out at them. It was hot, still, and quiet except for Tank's labored breathing.

Looking at the overturned Merc, Tank said to Olin, "I don't see Mazurka. You think the jailbird actually tol' the truth 'bout movin' him?"

Pulling Raz closer, Tank leaned down and peered inside the car. "I'll take a closer look." He released Raz's arm. "Mazurka's still in there, ain't he? Rolled up in the back seat, dead as that big-titted chili cooker friend of yours."

Suspecting his last chance to escape was at hand, Raz gave Tank his best whipped-dog look and said, "You're right. I lied. Mazurka's in there, wedged in tight. It'll take both of ya ta pull him out."

Tank's face lit up. "You see, Olin. I tol' you he was lyin'. Let's get the body out quick so we can finish up here and get back to town. We'll call Ed and Rudy and tell 'em Jester ain't got nothin' on 'em 'cept what's in his head, and we've already taken care of that. It'll make ever'body happy."

The fat sheriff leaned down to peer through the shattered glass in the door. "I can't see nothin'. Come on, Olin. Help me pull some stuff out of the way up front. That'll give us a better look. Don't worry 'bout the quarterback. He can't run. Even if he could, he knows I'll shoot him."

Olin joined Tank, who was already down on his knees at the driver's side door. Feeling the soft, gasoline-soaked sand and leaves under his feet, Raz pulled the cigarette lighter out of his back pocket.

"I can't see nothin' in this mess," Olin complained.

"I covered him up with leaves," Raz told him. "You'll have to crawl inside and move the front seat ta get him out."

Tank glanced at Raz. "Watch him, Olin," Grunting and cursing, he crawled through the door.

Raz rolled the strike wheel on the lighter and felt the heat from the flame against his hands. Turning away from the wreck, he dropped the lighter and jumped forward.

The fumes exploded with a loud *whoosh*, shoving Raz forward like a giant invisible hand. He heard Tank and Olin's startled cries as he fell to the ground and rolled toward the protective cover of the surrounding brush. Getting to his feet, he glimpsed Olin rolling around beating at his pants just outside the lake of fire. Tank was screaming and cursing, as a cloud of black smoke engulfed him.

Not knowing why, Raz found himself limping back to the fire. When he saw Tank's legs through the smoke, he turned sideways and grabbed one of his feet. The heat was intense and the smoke so thick he couldn't breathe. He dragged the sheriff out of the fire, then he broke off the tip of a pine branch, backed up to Tank's burning trousers and snuffed out the flames.

Raz dropped the smoking branch and limped into the woods, almost falling. He soldiered on, grinding his teeth against the pain. Finally, unable to go further, he dropped to the ground to catch his breath.

Knowing he was at least three hundred yards from the wreck made him feel safer. *Can't stop,* he thought. *By now, Olin has radioed his friends in town and Tank's main office in Coldwater.*

Raz guessed Tank's burns weren't life-threatening, but hurting Tank had saved him from getting shot. *Why didn't I just let him burn? Well, guess I didn't want that death on my conscious, too.*

He headed for Frenchy's farm, which was about a mile away. Frenchy'd get the handcuffs off and give him a van so he could drive to Town Lake and save his prime witness. Without Mazurka, he'd have nothing left to offer Lassiter. He had to call him, because too many things had gone wrong to depend on Tank and Olin cooperating. After talking to Lassiter, he hoped he'd have time to get Becky and his mother out of harm's way. It would take days, or even weeks before the narcs worked up enough cases to start making arrests.

He looked over his shoulder toward the wreck. *Someone will spot the smoke and call the fire department any time now.* He pushed on, stopping every hundred yards or so to rest when the pain became unbearable. Finally, the open field between the road and Frenchy's house came into view.

Approaching the barbed wire fence, he stopped to rest his legs and study the area. When he saw no additional vehicles, he lay down and rolled under the fence.

His knock on the front door brought an immediate response. *"Quien es?"*

"Raz."

Lupé slowly cracked the door to peek out. Her eyes opened wide. *"¿Qué te ha pasado? Entrar."* She disappeared down the hall as he limped inside.

Moments later his fat friend Frenchy came down the hall, looking anxious. "My little flower said you looked like—" He stopped short as his eyes swept over Raz. "A squashed cockroach 'bout covers it. What the hell happened to ya?" Frenchy asked as he helped Raz to the sofa.

"Boobs is dead. The Soup Kitchen got burned down."

Frenchy stepped back with a frown. "The hell you say. How'd she die?"

"Shot. When I saw the fire and went to check on her, Tank and Olin arrested me." He pulled his cuffed hands into view.

"So, that's why you look like shit and are walkin' like an ol' man."

"Get these damn things off me. I got things to do."

Frenchy looked at the handcuffs and Raz's tattered shirt then stepped closer to gently touch his back. Raz jumped, realizing he'd been burned.

"Your back, it don't look so good," Frenchy said. "Your shirt looks like you been run rolled in live coals. How'd this happen?"

"I'll explain while you use your bolt cutters on these cuffs. Then I need to make a call."

Frenchy beckoned. "Follow me out to the barn. Afterwards, my little flower will see to your back."

Raz followed the barefoot, fast-stepping Cajun through the kitchen and out the back door, giving him a brief account of what happened as they walked.

When Frenchy noted how much difficulty Raz was having keeping up, he fell back and took hold of his arm. "Them sorry bastards," he said. "You won't let 'em get away with this, will you? If it was me, I'd either beat the crap out o' 'em, head right over to the federal prosecutor's office in Tyler and swear out a complaint about them violatin' your civil rights."

Raz headed for the far end of the metal building, through rows of portable toilets, extra tires, two tandem trailers and a large New Holland tractor. "Frenchy, I got ta take care o' my daughter and mother before I can even think about what I'll do ta Tank an' Olin. 'Fore I do that, I got to make a couple o' phone calls. Get these damn things off me so I'll at least feel like a human bein' again."

"I was cuffed once. Don't like it one bit." Frenchy beckoned to Raz as he pulled down a long-handled bolt cutter off a nail on the wall. "Turn your ass towards me and stand still."

"Cut the connecting link. I doubt you can break the steel."

"Jus' stand still. You're prancin' around like an unbred filly in heat!"

Frenchy grunted as he cranked on the long handles, trying to cut through the metal. On the second attempt, the jaws snapped the connecting link. Raz immediately pulled his arms in front of his body, flexing and rubbing them briskly. "Thanks." He pulled off his tattered shirt. "Burn that in case Tank's still able to come by lookin' for me. I don't want him ta know I been here."

"Able? What'd ya do, poke a hole in his belly? Hold out your hands."

"Try the notched parts that slide inside the other half. They're smaller."

Frenchy took a closer look at the stainless steel. "I don't know, Irish. They're on pretty tight. I might cut you."

"Since when're you concerned 'bout digging your spurs into somebody? Start cuttin'."

"Okay, but don't blame me if I draw blood. Put your arm on the workbench."

After several tries, the first bracelet was off. The procedure drew a little blood, and he rubbed the spot, then put his other arm on the bench so Frenchy could repeat the process.

Raz breathed a sigh of relief as he rubbed his freed wrists. "That's another one I owe you, my Cajun friend. If you have any unexpected company, you'd better convince 'em you haven't seen me or you'll be in trouble too. Now, where's your phone?"

Frenchy pointed. "There's an extension right there. I got a police scanner and a two-way radio in the house if you need 'em. There's a phonebook in the drawer at the end of the bench. Give 'em hell, and when you're through, come in the house and we'll take care of your back and give you another shirt." He left, muttering in French and shaking his head.

Anita answered on the third ring. "Raz! Thank God you're okay. Ethan Lewis told me what happened over at the Soup Kitchen. I've been worried sick ever since. You still in jail?"

"Nope, but there's no time to explain now. I need a big favor, Nancy Nurse. Can you to meet me out at your lake house and help me take care of a man with a broken leg and some bad cuts? Before you agree, let me warn you that it's dangerous. You'll be in serious trouble if the wrong people find out."

"Oh. If your friend's hurt, maybe you should take him to Coldwater Hospital."

"He's not my friend and I can't take him to the hospital. I hate askin' you to do this, but you're the only one I know who knows how ta help him. Without him, I'll be in deeper trouble than ever. I'll understand if you don't want to."

"Well," she said, and took a deep then exhaled. "Of course, I'll help. How soon do you want me there?"

Raz glanced at the white van pulled halfway into the barn. "I'll try ta be there in thirty minutes. Don't go through town on your way out. Drive in the opposite direction for a few minutes, then circle around to the lake. You'll need medical supplies ta clean wounds and splint a broken leg. Okay?"

"Okay, but wait. I've got a message for you. Remember Bull Hayter? He called me and said somebody's been comin' by that needs ta see ya real bad."

"Why'd he call you?"

"I don't know. Bull knows ever'body and ever'thing. Remember?'

"Yeah, I guess so. Thanks. See you in a little while."

He disconnected the call, then his mind went blank and he couldn't remember Lassiter's number. Dialing zero, he told the operator his call involved a police emergency and asked to be connected to DPS headquarters in Austin. Several clicks later a woman answered and he asked to speak to Lassiter. She transferred his call, and another woman told him her boss was not in, and to call his cell. He asked her to wait while he found something to write with, then got the number and hung up. He sat down on a stool and dialed, rubbing his sore knees.

What happens if he can't come in on the case right now? What if Mazurka dies? Cato didn't give me enough details to back up criminal indictments.

Finally, Lassiter's deep voice answered. "Who is this?"

"Raz Jester. You told me to call when I decided I couldn't handle the situation up here alone. I need you, bad. I got a witness ready ta talk."

"Witness? You mean Cato's statement, right?"

"No. That burned up in a fire the bad guys started. I got Blackie Mazurka on ice, so to speak." He told him about the wreck and Mazurka's willingness to cooperate.

"Cato's statement's gone? Damn. You should've given it to me in the warden's office like I wanted. I'm glad you got Mazurka but I can't use anyone you're holding prisoner."

"He's legal. I'm gonna get his injuries taken care of right now, but I wanted to make sure you have a crew ready to move into Northville."

"Don't know if my bosses will let me move in before I talk to Mazurka. They may want me to determine his circumstances from a legal point of view. You've opened a real can of worms now. Tell you what. Go by and talk with Pop Cheever. I'll meet you and Mazurka at his place in the morning."

"I don't want Pop involved in this mess. He's had a stroke."

"He's the only man in Northville we both trust, plus he has the experience and connections we need to get the attorney general on our side. If the local politicians get wind of what we're up to, they'll kick up a fuss. As far as I know, Pop's still on the governor's drug taskforce, and he still pulls lots of weight. You think he'll be able to talk to us?"

"Don't know for sure 'til I go see him. That'll be hard to do without Tank and Olin or their friends spottin' me." He told him what Tank and Olin tried to do to him at the wreck scene.

"Damn, Raz. I told you not to go back and get into such a bind when we couldn't help you. Things'll really get complicated if the sheriff and the chief file charges against you."

"What was I supposed to do, let 'em kill me?"

"It was your call, I guess. I just hope this doesn't mess up our plans with the politicians."

"I'm still alive and kickin' with a witness that's hot to trot. I'd say our plans are in good shape."

"I don't know, Raz. Somethin's fishy. You'd better be dealin' straight with me. Tell you what I'll do. I'll make an unofficial visit to Northville in the morning. If I agree that we can use Mazurka and his information, I'll talk to the attorney general. If he gives me the go-ahead, I'll bring in the cavalry. Call me if Pop's not able to talk."

"Okay, but I've got a special favor to ask. When you dig into this case, be on the lookout for somebody who can finger my wife's killer. Regardless of what we accomplish in Northville, solving that puzzle is still my top priority."

"Consider it done."

"I'll see you at Pop's in the mornin' unless another alligator grabs my ass."

He let out a sigh of relief and turned to the next task at hand. As soon as he took care of Mazurka, he'd find out what Bull Hayter wanted. If Bull told him Snake was looking for him, he hoped it was because he had a lead on Fran. Finding her would open lots of doors.

Hopefully it would be obvious to an unbiased person in the prosecutor's office that he'd acted in self-defense at the wreck scene. However, his experience with the legal system convinced him that *intent* meant nothing in a contest between a poor man and big money. He hoped Lassiter could help him reach his goal of finding Patti's killer. He also hoped to be alive when the job was done.

CHAPTER 19

upé had laid out a pair of boxers and a clean shirt on the sofa, and on the coffee table was a meal of refried beans, chopped meat and flour tortillas. Frenchy and Lupé were already eating, but they stopped when he came into the room. Frenchy jumped up to greet him and said, "You'd better let Lupé have a look at your back. Ain't it burnin'?"

Raz nodded. "It can wait. I've got to be somewhere, but I need wheels. Okay if I borrow your van?"

"Hell yes. She's got a souped-up three-fifty under the hood, twin carbs, and enough tint in the windas ta keep out prying eyes. Where's your truck?"

"Downtown. Up the street from the Soup Kitchen."

"If you want, Lupé'll drop me off tonight and I'll get it and hide it in the woods out back. Keys in it?"

"Yeah. I'd appreciate that, but Tank and Olin might have somebody watchin' it."

"Screw 'em. It ain't a violation of the law ta drive a friend's truck. If they try ta follow me, I'll park it at Olin's church and come home from there."

"Okay, but don't take any chances."

Picking up the clothes, he limped down the hall to the bathroom. He relieved himself, and then washed his face, arms and belly. The back of his neck was sensitive, but not as sore as his side and knees, which were now swollen and black and blue.

Get to the lake while you're still able to drive, he told himself.

The boxers were too big, but they were clean and that was more important. He tightened the waist with a safety pin he found in the medicine cabinet.

He put his jeans on, put on the shirt and limped back to the living room. Not taking the time to button the shirt, he picked up a burrito and a cold beer Frenchy had put on the table for him then walked to the back door, thanking them on the way. He stopped when Frenchy asked, "Don't you want the damn keys?"

"Thought they were in the van." He took a bite of the egg and sausage burrito.

"Slow down. Put on your damn thinkin' cap 'fore somebody else grabs your ass. Here." Frenchy tossed him the keys. "She's full o' gas. Consider it yours as long as you need it. If you want some heat, I got a Barretta you can have. It'll hold enough bullets to shoot from now 'til next Tuesday."

"Thanks, but I got enough trouble already. See ya later. Remember, you haven't seen me."

Raz finished the burrito and the rest of the beer on his way to the garage. He climbed behind the wheel of the van and felt better, even though he ached all over.

He surveyed the interior of the van. "Way to go, Frenchy!" He felt safer behind the dark tinted windows.

He took the backroads to Town Lake, and found Anita waiting for him on the porch swing. She came down the steps to greet him as he drove by her Chrysler to the backside of the garage. A shocked expression flitted over her face when he began limping toward her.

"My God. What happened?"

"I'll explain later." He gave her a peck on the cheek. "Thanks for comin'. I didn't wanna get you involved in this, but I had no one else to turn to."

"I told you to call. Remember? Just tell me what you need."

"First, pull your car 'round back, out of sight from the road."

"All right, but when I get back you'll have to explain why I'm hidin' at my own place."

While she was moving her car, Raz pulled the old sword out of its hiding place and leaned it against a kitchen cabinet just inside the back door.

Anita was back in a few minutes, carrying a bag under one arm and two straight boards about eighteen inches long under the other. "Where to now, Hopalong Cassidy?"

"Cover your face."

"What's wrong with my face?"

"Nothing. It's as pretty as a pink peach, and I want to make sure it stays that way. This man knows who I am, but I don't want him to be able to identify you. I don't even want ya speakin' to him while you're in there."

She looked around. "In where?"

"Your boat house."

"You're kidding!" She looked down the hill. "I've been sittin' out here by myself with a dangerous man just a few feet away? Thanks a lot."

"He's hurt and he's not goin' nowhere. Now, cover your face and let's get to it."

"Just a minute." She disappeared inside the cabin and came back moments later with a bandanna covering her face up to her eyes. "I feel like the Lone Ranger's wife, for cryin' out loud. Are you sure this is necessary?"

"Only if you want to keep on livin'."

She followed him down the hill, and said, "You need some medical attention yourself, cowboy. You're barely able to walk, the back of your neck is blistered and your hair's singed. Will you please tell me what happened to you?"

He motioned to her to keep quiet. "Savin' my prime witness is more important than my sore parts right now. No more talkin'."

Mazurka lay where Raz had left him, and he was terribly still. Anita stared in disbelief, whispering, "Is he dead already?"

Raz put his finger across his lips to remind her not to speak. He looked at Mazurka in the subdued light. "Dead men don't breathe." He shook the gunman's shoulder.

Mazurka stirred and opened his eyes. Groggy, and unable to focus, he didn't recognize Raz right away. He tried to get up, but couldn't manage. "You lyin' bastard. You said you'd get me fixed up. I need a doctor. I'm dyin'."

"I brought you a doctor. Now, try not to be your usual obnoxious self so she can tend to ya. If my plan works, it'll save both our necks."

Anita knelt down and began taking things out of her bag. Raz tried to get his knees to cooperate with kneeling, but found it impossible. Instead, he sat down next to Mazurka and removed the crude bandage he'd applied earlier.

Mazurka jumped. "Ouch! That hurt." He turned his dark eyes on Anita. "Why does she have her face covered? Are you sure she's a doctor?"

"If she helps ya, she's a doctor. Be still and let her clean and dress those cuts. Then we'll set your leg."

Anita poured alcohol on a gauze pad and began dabbing the cut near Mazurka's eye. He flinched, cursing loudly, "I should be in a hospital. My leg's killin' me!"

"We'll take care of it in a minute. Stop bitchin'," Raz said sharply.

After cleaning and bandaging the open wounds, Anita stood up, stretched and looked at Raz for further instruction. She got back down on her knees when he pulled up Mazurka's trousers leg. His ankle was swollen and purple, but no bones were poking through the skin. It was a simple fracture and should be fairly easy to deal with.

Anita pulled a white cloth from the bag and wiped the perspiration from her brow. It was hot inside the tin-covered structure, and the air was stale and humid. Breathing through the double bandana didn't help her much either.

Looking at the injured leg, Anita started to speak, but stopped when Raz shook his head. She wrapped each flat board with soft cloth and tore off several strips of what appeared to be a sheet. Looking at the broken leg, she turned her eyes to Raz to silently ask him to assist and nodded. He moved to the killer's feet.

Without warning the patient, Raz pushed one foot against his crotch and jerked the injured leg straight, ignoring the Mazurka's screams and curses. The stream of expletives was cut short when Mazurka passed out. Anita secured the splints with the strips of cloth and made them tighter with wide strips of tape. "The deed is done, and there won't be an extra charge for the foul language endured," she told Raz.

Grimacing, Raz climbed slowly to his feet. "Thanks. For a minute there, I thought I might chime in with a few choice phrases of my own. My knees are screamin'!" He took several deep breaths and his head cleared a little.

Beckoning to Anita to follow him, he walked out on the ramp, locked the door and limped halfway back up the slope before giving up and lying down in the grass. Anita jerked off the bandana and went to kneel beside him, turning his head to examine his neck.

"You need somethin' on that," she said. "Your back, too, most likely. Now, tell me what happened."

After listening to his explanation, she said, "Raz, I'm so afraid for you. Isn't there someone in law enforcement somewhere who can help?"

He told her about calling Lassiter and his plans for Mazurka. "I got to get my mother and Becky out of town before they get here."

"Didn't you tell me you had a great aunt who lives in the next county? Maybe she could take care of your mother for a while. Gettin' Becky won't be as easy. The Lawthers won't let her go anywhere with you."

"I'll think of a way after I talk to Pop. Don't tell your mom about any of this unless you have to. We don't want them comin' out here."

"Let's go in the house so I can have a look at you and get some bandages on those wounds." She took hold of his hand, helped him to his feet, then walked beside him as they went to the house. Inside, they sat down at the dinette table and she said, "Take off your shirt. I'll get somethin' to put on those burns."

By the time he'd removed his shirt, Anita was back with a clean pair of trousers and a tube of something.

"Just as I figured," she said, looking at his back. "You're red all over. This cream will help, but I doubt it'll do your legs any good. You need to see a real doctor."

He stared through the window while gently rubbing his scar. Noting his preoccupation, she asked, "Why the spaced-out look? You get hit in the head?"

When he didn't respond, she began to put the balm on his back and neck. Trying to snap him out of the trance, she asked, "Where's that high-steppin' cowboy I picked up yesterday? You been hurt before and it never slowed you down. Care to tell me what else is buggin' ya?"

"I think it was partially my fault that Patti got killed. Tim Barton, too. Now I have to add Boobs to that list, and maybe Fran, too."

"Now it comes out. You're on a guilt trip, blamin' yourself for what somebody else did. Always figured you were too smart and full of spark ta fall into that trap."

When his mood remained unchanged, she said, "Cowboy, you've never hurt nobody who wasn't trying ta hurt you first. I haven't heard a soul blame you for what happened to Patti and Tim, and no one will blame you for Boobs neither. Only person who ever said anythin' bad 'bout ya with regard ta Patti was her heartless daddy, the money-grubbin' old crab. People I know in Northville know you did your best to find her killer."

"You better get far away from me and stay away. Boobs was the second, maybe third, woman close to me that's been killed. Patti was murdered, then Fran up and disappears. I'm afraid you'll be next."

She leaned over and kissed his temple. "Don't worry 'bout me, cowboy. We all do what we gotta do. Not 'cause of somebody else, but 'cause that's what our little brains and big dumb hearts tell us ta do."

He glanced at her. "I still think I'm right, but thanks for not thinkin' I've gone off my rocker. I want my little girl back more than anythin', but I'm afraid that might not happen. Every day when I was gone, I looked forward to havin' lots of fun with her and gettin' on with my life. That was before I came home and things got so complicated. When I left the animal cage, I had somethin' I thought would make Tank and his thugs leave me alone long enough to do what I needed to do before the bomb fell. I was convinced that after the state narcs cleaned up Northville and all the smoke cleared, it wouldn't take long ta get my life back on track. I thought the bad guys would trade places with me in the pen and that I'd never be kicked around like a dog again."

"Snap out of it. Things'll work out. You'll have lots of time to get your life back on track and catch up on good times after this is over."

"Judgin' by what you showed me down in the boat shed, I'd say that for a guy with two bad knees and a burned back, you've made some good moves toward gettin' back to those good times."

"Every time I move forward a foot, I get shoved back a mile. I'm thinkin' maybe I should transfer my mom to an out of town facility, grab Becky and run away to Alaska, or someplace where we can't be found. Becky would learn to love me in time."

"You mean *kidnap* her? That's crazy talk, Raz. They'd find you for sure, and then you'd have to do another stretch in prison for kidnapping. Then you'd never get Becky back. Of all the hair-brained schemes I've ever heard, that wins the prize."

"For a little bitty woman, you sure throw a hard punch," he said with a devilish twinkle in his eye. "If memory serves, you're as good as any honky-tonk girl between the sheets, too." Realizing his blunder, he added, "Sorry. I was talkin' without thinkin', as usual. I haven't seen that honky-tonk woman in over two years, and probably never will again. If I do, it'll be for business reasons only."

"Drop your pants," she said.

"What? With these sore knees? There's nothing I'd like better, believe me, but I'm in no shape to play around."

"Of all the egotistical... I want to check your knees, lover boy."

"Oh." He stood up, unsnapped his jeans and let them fall to the floor. "It's done, teacher. Will I still get a gold star by my name?"

She leaned down. "Be still."

"Yes, ma'am."

"I'll get some ice for your knees. It'll help with the swelling and pain."

He watched her take cubes from the freezer and wrap them in a towel. Her sensitivity about his relationship with Fran surprised him, but confirmed what she'd said the day before about her feelings for him after their high school fling. When she leaned over him again, he asked, "What are you most upset about, what I said today, or something I said yesterday?"

She continued arranging the ice pack, and didn't answer.

"Sorry I upset you. I didn't think what Fran and I had was a big deal. I figured ever'body'd forgot about that by now, even you. Besides, we both been married."

Her hands began trembling. "I had no claim on you when you decided to marry Patti. Then, I was separated and living in Dallas when you and the honky-tonk woman hooked-up. You're free now and able to choose her again if you can find her." She looked at him. "That's what you wanted me to say, isn't it?"

"Let me tell you something, darlin'," he said as he covered her hand with his. "I've learned more about carin' from you in two days than I learned in years of doin' my thinkin' with my little brain. I only mentioned Fran 'cause I really believe she'd still be around if she hadn't been connected to me.

Like I've already said, the only reason I want to find her is to get my share from the sale of the Hole. Sure, I wonder why she gave up our business. I suspect it might've had somethin' ta do with whoever killed Patti. If that's the case, it'll help me find the killer. The hanky-panky stuff is over between me and the honky-tonk woman."

"That's a line I've heard Raz Jester use lots of times. How can I be sure you're not just giving me more of your famous razzle-dazzle?"

"'Cause the way I feel now tells me my razzle has run out of dazzle."

Her expression softened a bit. "Until you find Fran, how can you be so sure you don't wanna start things up with her again?"

He gently brushed her chin with his index finger, "Women. You're all so practical and to the point. Can't cut a man a bit of slack in the romance department can ya? At least tell me ya won't count me out 'til I find out if Fran's dead or alive."

"I'll give you another chance, but please promise me you'll be honest with me if you find her and still want to be with her."

"I'm positive I don't want to be with her. " He said and looked around. "This little house holds lots of good memories for me, 'specially when I think about the times we came out here during our junior year."

She nodded. "I was scared to death, and over the moon knowing I'd landed the most popular guy in school."

"Yeah, I was something back then wasn't I?" Raz joked.

"Those were great times. We both had big plans, as I recall, though I suspect yours had more to do with the bed in the front room than our future."

He laughed, then grabbed his sore ribs. "You wouldn't drink more than one beer with me. Said it gave you a headache. But you got real close when we danced. So close, in fact, I almost couldn't control myself. I remember, I couldn't stop kissing your pretty face."

"And tryin' to do a few other things I wouldn't let you do."

He smiled. "I was beginnin' to think we'd never make a love connection, but by the time we did, I'd found out that it was just as good being with you for other reasons. Remember the night when you finally let me have my way with you in that little boat down there? We got so carried away we tipped it over in the middle of the lake. Then you laughed so hard, you swallowed water and almost drowned."

"How could I forget?" She blushed. "Or the time we let the boat drift to the bank and stirred up a nest of wasps."

His laugh was cut short again by his sore ribs. "What happened to us? I thought things were going pretty good, but all of a sudden you started datin' just about every boy in school."

"Humph. Not before you started makin' eyes at every pretty girl."

"I was just bein' friendly."

"Friendly? Not according to what I heard."

"What *you* heard? *I* heard you were makin' it with all the good-lookin' guys. You sure acted like it, anyway."

"Boys and their dirty minds. Didn't you have sense enough to know I was just tryin' ta make you jealous? I thought I was losin' you and I wanted a commitment."

"Really?" He shook his head. "And I thought I knew women."

"You knew a lot about *some* women."

He stiffened suddenly. "What time is it?"

Glancing at her watch, she said, "One thirty-five."

The ice pack slid off his knees when he stood up. "Gotta go see Pop Cheever."

She pushed him back into the chair and reached for the ice pack. "You're in no condition to go anywhere, cowboy. What you really need to do is take care of that back and those knees. You're already flushed. That means you have a fever."

"But Pop's part of my plan."

"Call him. The phone's right over there."

"We can't use that phone under any circumstances. Caller ID could lead the wrong people to my prize witness."

"Okay, let's make a deal. If you eat a couple of sandwiches and rest for an hour with those ice packs on your legs, I'll stop naggin' you."

"When I leave, I want you to go back to town and stay there 'til somebody takes that gangster off my hands. Okay?"

She hesitated. "Maybe."

"No maybes."

She nodded. "Okay. I'll leave a key for you under the back steps."

"You drive a hard bargain. Okay, I'll stay one more hour. But I can only lie down on my good side. Can't do anythin' worth braggin' about in that position."

"You might be surprised by what a nurse can do to *you* in that position. Now go to the front bedroom and lie down. I'll get some more ice."

He sat down on the side of the bed in the front room and tried to pull off his boots. When it hurt his ribs, he tried pushing them down as far as he could with his toes. Even then, he still couldn't bend over far enough to get them off. He pulled them back on and lay down on his side with his feet hanging off the bed. *Better to keep them on anyway. There's too much inside them to try to explain right now.*

He didn't know which was worse, the pain in his knees and side or the anxiety of not knowing if Lassiter would bring his men to Northville and take Mazurka off his hands in the morning. If that didn't happen, Tank and his crew could hunt him down at their leisure. When they found him, he wasn't sure he'd be able to find a way to survive the encounter.

CHAPTER 20

After his mandatory one-hour rest, Raz drove behind Anita to the blacktop road that would lead him, in a roundabout way, to Pop's place. He waved and she waved back and she went on her way.

Raz drove on dirt roads until he reached the blacktop that would take him by Horton Snitker's East-Tex Poultry Processing Plant six miles west of Northville. He'd stay on that road until he got to Pop's farm.

I hope Pop feels well enough to talk. I also hope he's all right with Lassiter comin' to his place. I really need his connections to the governor's task force, and his advice on how to help Lassiter make things happen. Surely Pop kept abreast of things, even though he's retired.

Pop lived in a large, ranch-style brick house at the end of a lane two hundred feet from a cattle guard at the fence line. Tall pecan trees growing outside a four-strand wire fence bordered the gravel driveway. It looked just like he remembered it, which was comforting.

Raz took note of a new wooden privacy fence around three sides of the structure. He also saw something else that didn't fit: a black Lincoln and a red Porsche inside the garage. Had the drug lords finally persuaded his old friend that honest law enforcement didn't pay well enough for his services? *It can't be. The only person in the county who can't be bought by big money is Pop.*

He walked across the screened-in side porch to the kitchen door and knocked. While he waited, he looked at the picturesque view of Charolais cattle grazing between the house and the road.

He heard footsteps, and turned to see a woman dressed in a maid's uniform at the door. He wondered if she was one of Frenchy's illegal imports.

"Who's there?" the woman said with a heavy accent.

"Name's Raz Jester." He looked past her into the hall and dining area. "I came to see Pop."

She shook her head. "*Señor* Cheever no live here." She pointed down the road. "Live there."

Raz turned to look across the pasture but couldn't see anything because of the privacy fence. "He built another house?"

She shook her head. "No build. Live in little house."

"The overseer's house?"

She nodded. "*Sí.* You go there."

She tried to close the door but Raz blocked it with his toe. "Wait, just a minute. *This* is my friend's house."

She shook her head. "No more. You go there." She pointed.

"Who lives here now?" he said.

She shook her head, suddenly nervous. "No can talk more. You go." With that, she slammed the door.

Puzzled, Raz returned to the van and headed back to the hardtop. The small frame house a quarter of a mile down the road had previously been the farm overseer's residence. *Maybe Pop is having money issues? I can't believe he'd move out of his house for any other reason.*

A barbed wire fence ran along the sides and back of the overseer's house and separated it from the surrounding pastures. He drove up the short graveled driveway, parked in the yard near the front steps and got out.

He knocked on the screen door and stepped back to wait. When he knocked the second time he heard someone moving around at the back of the house. A thin man with white hair rolled his wheelchair into the connecting doorway. Adjusteing his rimless glasses and he focused on the front door.

For a moment, Raz thought he was looking at a stranger, but when the man came closer and he got a good look at his eyes, lantern chin and high forehead, he realized it was Pop. *Look at him! He looks so old and weak. I can't ask him to get involved in all this.*

When Pop stopped just inside the door, Raz noted how pale and drawn his face had become. He was relieved to see that his eyes looked alert, even though he now appeared to weigh little more than half his former robust 225 pounds. It was a sad sight.

Raz said, as cheerfully as possible, "Hi, Pop. Long time, no see."

Pop squinted at Raz's outline in the door. "That you, Raz?"

"The one and only. Feel like visitin' a while?"

Pop strained against the wheels to move closer and unlatch the door. "I'd have to be dead to not want to see you, son. Come in. I was beginnin' ta think you forgot about me, just like most o' the other folks 'round here."

Raz bent down and embraced his old friend and mentor. "I'd never forget you, Pop." He wanted to tell him how sorry he was to see that his health had failed, but thought better of it. Instead, he stepped back to admire him. "Same ol' Pop. It's good to see you."

Pop pointed to the sofa. "Have a seat. Excuse the mess. Never was much of a housekeeper. The missus always took good care of that when she was alive."

His voice was weaker, and Raz detected a slur in his speech. The left side of his face was slightly pulled back, and he favored his left hand. *He's had a stroke. Maybe I shouldn't have come,* he thought. He sat down on the faded couch, still trying not to stare at the wheelchair or Pop's drawn face.

Pop wheeled his chair close and asked, "How 'bout a shot of Wild Turkey to celebrate this momentous occasion?"

Raz nodded. "Sounds good, if it's okay for you to take a snort."

"Don't worry 'bout me. What the doc don't know won't hurt me." He rolled his chair from the room.

Raz thought, *I'll play it by ear. I can always leave without telling him anything.*

When Pop returned from the kitchen, he took two glasses filled with a small amount of whiskey from the chair's holding tray and gave one to Raz.

They clinked glasses and Raz said, "To the best man I know."

"To the hope that you'll come through your troubles a healthy man, soon return to the good life," Pop responded. He took a sip and returned the glass to the holder, fixing his steady gaze on Raz the way he'd always done. Raz had always thought those eyes could see straight through to his soul. "You don't have to pretend not to notice that I'm a sick old man, son. Not talkin' about it won't make it not so. I could be worse off. The stroke was a mild one, as was the heart attack that came with it. Can't talk too good, and I can't walk at all but I'm not brain dead." His mouth formed a one-sided smile.

"I'm sorry about your health, Pop. I know a man as strong as you is bound to bounce back."

"Thanks, Raz, but I'm afraid my bouncin' back days are over. I fear my time is close at hand. I'm prepared in my mind for what's to come, so don't fret. It's a natural process, you know. Let's not talk about me. It's you I'm concerned about. Didn't you get my message?"

Raz hesitated. "Oh, yeah. Frenchy said you came by or called a couple of times after I left. Sorry I didn't come by sooner."

"I don't mean *that* message. As soon as the chairman of the drug taskforce committee called to tell me you were bein' released, I called the warden an' tol' him to tell you not to come back to Northville just yet."

Knowing he was still active in the taskforce eased Raz's concerns about coming. "I didn't get that message, but the warden did tell me not to come home." Raz leaned forward. "Why didn't you want me here?"

"Scuttlebutt had it you wouldn't last long if you came back before that narc used what you got from Cato Hamilton to clean things up. The criminal element in and around Northville suspected you'd start turnin' over rocks as soon as ya got back. They were afraid you'd find somethin' they don't want found. They'll try to stop you any way they can."

"They've been tryin'. Did Drew Lassiter call? He's supposed to meet me here in the morning." He hadn't meant to be so blunt, but he was tired of waiting and wishing.

"He did. But I'm afraid you won't like what he said."

"He's not coming."

"He said he'll be here eventually, but not right now, unless somethin' really big happens. Said Horace Stalker called him right after you did sayin' the state probably can't use Mazurka as a witness 'cause his detention is most likely illegal. He told Lassiter that some shyster lawyer has filed an injunction against the DPS to keep them from movin' into Northville. It'll take a couple of days in court to have that looked at. Stalker is the attorney general's man, you know."

"We've met. If Stalker already knew I had Mazurka, it could mean he's somebody else's man too."

"Lassiter said he was afraid to tell him 'bout what happened to Cato's statement. That really would've made him clamp the lid shut on things."

"Did Lassiter also tell you how the tape was lost?"

Pop nodded. "I was sad to hear about Boobs. She was a good ol' gal and I'll miss her. Life goes on, though. Any idea who could've tipped off Stalker about Mazurka?"

"Not for sure, but it had to be somebody local. I told Tank and Olin to try to scare 'em into arrestin' Patti's killer. The only person I told outside of Northville was Lassiter. He said he'd take him off my hands tomorrow."

"My guess is, somebody here called Bryan Fulton. Ever since Bryan was elected to the state senate — that was right after you left — he's been a powerful force. He might've called everybody on the taskforce."

"That really ticks me off. How could Stalker make a judgment about Mazurka's situation without talkin' to me first? After he and one of his buddies tried to kill me, I took him to a place where I could set his broken leg and patch him up." He told Pop what Mazurka and Smeddish did at his parents' home, and what Mazurka and Alabama tried to do out on Shortcut Road. He also explained what happened at the lake house and Mazurka's willingness to turn rat.

Pop studied him a moment. "Good work. Hope they'll let you use Mazurka, but even if they agree he's legal, he won't be any good to you dead. That's just what he'll be if Tank or friends find him. I noticed you're limpin'. That happen during all this scufflin'?"

He told him what happened when Tan and Olin took him out to the scene of the wreck, and about the fire. "I pulled Tank out of the flames, but I doubt he'll consider that when he goes to Coldwater to file charges."

Pop shook his head. "Tank committed a serious violation of the law. You gonna file charges against him?"

"Not yet. Too many people want to use me for target practice. I'll have to wait at least 'til Lassiter and his boys start makin' cases. Surely he'll find a way to get around the crooked politicians."

Pop sighed, "Crooked politicians and criminal lawyers are a good cop's nightmare. They come with the territory, though. You've taken on a heavy load comin' back to Northville. Anythin' else happen since you got out that you wanna tell me about?"

Raz was always amazed by Pop's uncanny ability to sense things unsaid. He told him about the blonde and the two shooters at the Houston bus terminal. "One of them was Mazurka. He told me after the wreck that Smeddish was with him down there."

"What are you gonna do? You're in too deep to quit, and you're to vulnerable to hack it alone."

"You're right. The fish are already in the pan and the fire's hot. I've got to keep runnin' to keep from fallin' down and hope Lassiter finds a way to hold up his end of that agreement we made two years ago."

Pop looked at the scars on Raz's face and neck. "Havin' you put in the cell with Cato Hamilton didn't come without a high price, I see." He sighed. "I'm sorry suggestin' you to Lassiter turned out to be so hard on you. I knew it would be dangerous, but thought you could handle it. Hope you don't have no hard feelings over it."

"No, sir. I'm just sorry to have to get you involved at this point."

"I was involved long before you made your deal with Lassiter, so no apologies necessary. Why didn't you give him Cato's statement when you got out?"

"Because Cato didn't know who killed Patti like Lassiter said he would, so I kept it hopin' I could make a deal with Tank and Olin to arrest the murderer. While they were doing that, I was gonna get my little girl and my mother out of town."

Pop took another sip of whiskey. "I'll talk to my contacts on the governor's committee. Maybe I can convince Stalker to let Lassiter go against Bryan Fulton for a change. I'll also update the Texas Sheriff's Association and some other influential people I know. The committee was always anxious to help me clean up our part of the state when I was sheriff, but lately everybody's waitin' to hear what you got from Cato before they do anything."

Pop took another sip. "You need to be more careful 'til things start poppin'. A neighbor called and told me about the fire at the Soup Kitchen and Boobs before Lassiter called. I turned on my radio to listen to Uncle Bud telling all about it. He said folks told him you took it so hard you almost got in a fight with Tank and Punk Hutto before they cuffed you."

Raz leaned back to relieve the pressure on his swollen knees. "Yeah, I know. The next thing I need to do is find my former business partner, Fran Druman. She's my fallback plan if I don't get to use Mazurka. She might know something about Patti's killer. She must've got pretty tight with whoever talked her into selling Armadillo Hole to Punk Hatto."

"Maybe. But my advice is to find another nice safe hole to crawl into 'til Lassiter can bring in his boys. With no tape, he'll have to use Mazurka or back off."

"I don't have the time to hide and wait for somebody else to do something."

Pop's sad face lit up. "Damn. My sick brain got so mixed up by all you've been tellin' me, I forgot to give you the rest of Lassiter's message. Cato's dead."

His statement shook Raz. "Cato's dead?" He leaned forward. "I'm sorry to hear that."

Forgetting such an important fact meant Pop was sicker than he first thought. Raz said, "I talked to him just before I left — he wasn't sick then."

"He didn't get sick. Lassiter said he was being transferred to another unit when the bus was waylaid by some guys with machine guns. They also killed two guards and some other prisoners."

Raz got up and limped to the front window and looked out. The person who predicted he would die by the end of his second day home had died instead. Whoever killed him knew about the tape. The gang running things now benefitted most from his death. *If they could kill Cato when he was under guard on a prison bus, how long can I stay alive working alone with no guarantee of help?*

The shadow cast by the tree in Pop's yard told him the end of his second day was only a few hours away.

CHAPTER 21

Raz wanted to hit somebody hard — Drew Lassiter, Tank Zelder, Olin Culpepper — any or all would do.

Without turning, he said, "Somethin's wrong with this picture, Pop. I'm gettin' shot at and knocked around like a warped bowling pin while the narcs and the state attorney general quibble about how to keep from hurtin' a sleazy politician's feelings."

"An axe that's flown off the handle won't cut wood," Pop said.

Pop had read his thoughts again. "And honest lawmen held back by rules written and passed by lawyers and insurance agents in Austin won't catch criminals. It's the same as putting a steak in front of a hungry man and saying he can't eat 'cause he don't have a starched napkin and silver fork."

"Nothing worth havin' is ever easy."

"Maybe it's time for the good folks to line up every politician and crooked lawman in a bent-over position on the courthouse steps and then kick their butts so hard their ears ring."

"I could add a few options that might straighten out things a lot quicker."

Raz turned. "Damn the politicians and crooked cops. I'm not giving up now."

"Just don't go flyin' off the handle like you used to, son. This ain't some schoolyard fist fight with the campus bully. Lay back and let things simmer a while. I don't want you gettin' dead."

"I'm tired of waitin' for somebody else to do what they're supposed to do to make things work. I've held up my end of the bargain with Lassiter. Okay, so I lost what I got from Cato, but I have Mazurka now. If our politicians won't let the narcs use that killer's testimony... Since no one's said otherwise, guess I'm still an undercover agent."

"That doesn't give you license to do what's not legal or right."

"Found out a long time ago that bein' right gives a man 'bout as much protection as a swimsuit in a tank full of hungry sharks. It's brought me nothin' but trouble."

"Don't be too hard on the law. Justice is slow 'cause it has to make sure it's right. Since I'm partially responsible for gettin' you into this mess, I'll do all I can ta get ya out of it."

"Cato depended on the law to protect him on that bus and look what happened."

"I can't say I don't know how you feel, son. I was young once, and full of piss and vinegar just like you. From where I'm perched now, though, I'd strongly advise against striking out on your own again. I've lived long enough to know, if a man wants to court danger doing something he believes in, the warnings of an old codger won't stop him. I just wish I was whole, and able to do more for ya."

"You can still help me, Pop. Bringin' me up to date on some things will help a lot. For starters, what happened to your farm and the big house? You've owned that place and a herd of cattle for more than twenty years."

Pop sighed, putting his glass on the coffee table. "Me and the *bank* owned it for twenty years, son. Bought it with a thirty-year loan when Horton Snitker's father-in-law was still alive. When I got sick and fell behind on payments, Horton's new bank president foreclosed and Galaxy Enterprises took it over. Horton gave me this house and one acre to live on for the rest of my life."

"He's all heart. So, what is Galaxy Enterprises? Who owns it?"

"Don't know for sure. Can't see nothin' up there for that damned fence. My neighbor, Sam Phillips, tol' me he sees some fancy-lookin' women comin' and goin'. Also said he saw Gerta Hutto and Olin Culpepper leavin' a couple of times, *and* Bryan Fulton. I heard Bryan and Sonny set it up."

"Think they're dealin' drugs?"

"That what Cato told you?"

Raz shook his head. "He never mentioned Galaxy."

"The biggest dope dealer I ever knew was Cato. He was headquartered in Houston, but he had an apartment in Coldwater. His outfit branched out all over."

"He said he was livin' in Coldwater when he got busted. Said he got caught in the middle of a fight between his outfit and the Dixie Mafia when they tried to take over. He said their Houston boss was Ed Barrow."

"Cato was in a position to reveal lots of things but when Lassiter tried to talk to him, he wouldn't tell him a thing. After that, Tank wouldn't let him have visitors, not even Lassiter. Heard through the grapevine that Cato might've refused to talk 'cause he thought he was gonna beat it on appeal."

"Don't know about that. He still refused to talk when the state narcs bench-warranted him. Somebody apparently thought he caved, otherwise they wouldn't have tried to kill him in prison."

"Looks like they almost got you, too." He motioned at Raz's scars.

Raz took a swallow of whiskey to brace him for an all-important question. "No disrespect intended, Pop, but I have to know. How did Cato get around you when you were sheriff? He said you were still in office when he first got in the business. Said you were an old nut too rusty to turn, but that's all he'd say."

"He didn't get around me," he said, and his blue eyes didn't waver. "He sent in dealers for a while when he first tried movin' into the county. They'd come in with their pot, pills, and crack and I'd hear about it and put 'em in jail. The next day, I'd find an envelope full of cash in my mailbox. I sent a deputy to find Cato and give it back to him. But he always refused to take it, saying he hadn't sent it."

Pop paused, and his face formed a crooked smile. "Cato was a cagey bird. He knew if he owned up to sendin' that money, I'd put him in jail for tryin' to bribe me. After the third or fourth time, I didn't find no more money in my mailbox. I just couldn't throw away what he'd already sent me, though, so I gave it to the First Baptist Church to help 'em build a new parsonage." A mischievous twinkle appeared in his eyes. "I've always heard the Lord moves in mysterious ways."

Raz sighed with relief. "Too bad you weren't still sheriff when Cato finally got busted. Tank wouldn't be deputy."

"All sheriffs have to cut corners to get re-elected. Sam Cook was told if he wanted to stay on as sheriff of Eastman County, he had to recommend a courthouse annex for Northville and hire Tank as resident deputy. Most of the county's political power shifted to Northville not too long after that."

Raz limped back to the sofa as he digested Pop's explanation. "That's why the rich people in the Williamsburg Addition let a stranger to build a big house there?"

"That's Sonny Irby's house."

"Bashful, big-nosed Sonny Irby? I didn't know bank clerks made that kind of money."

"They don't. Bank presidents either. That's what he is now."

"Maybe he got in good with Rudy. Cato said this Rudy's the big stud for the Dixie bunch here. Ever heard of him?"

Pop hesitated, like he was suddenly having trouble with his memory. Staring blankly through the window, he remained silent for a few seconds. Then, a knowing expression returned to his face, and he said, "Rudy, you said? Don't know him. Nickname, most likely."

Not wanting to press his sick old friend any further, Raz reached for his hat.

Pop grabbed his arm. "I know you too well not to noticed there's somethin' else on your mind. Out with it. Cato tell you somethin' 'bout me?"

Raz couldn't lie. "It has nothing to do with you, Pop. You probably know the answer to the question that's been burnin' my brain ever since it happened."

"So, ask me."

"If Isham Lawther pulls so much weight in Northville, why didn't he make Tank and Olin find out who killed Patti?"

"I was afraid you'd get around to askin' me that one day." He sighed. "I never intended to repeat what he tol' me but now that you popped the question, I can't lie to you. I might not be around long enough to talk to you again."

Raz leaned forward as Pop folded his hands in his lap and said, "Before I tell you, promise me you won't get all bent out o' shape an' do somethin' rash to your former father-in-law."

"That might not be an easy promise to keep, but I'll try."

"First, a little background to help you understand why Isham said what he did. You went up against one of the richest, most powerful men in town when you stole the daughter he had primed to marry into money and power." He held up his hands. "Now, I'm not sayin' that any of Patti's misfortunes were your fault. I'm just sayin' you made a connected person and his stooges mad. All his friends in the Williamsburg Addition sided with him, even Horton Snitker. If that wasn't enough, then you go an' get crossways with the local law they put in office."

Pop paused, like he'd lost his terrain of thought. Raz waited a couple of long minutes until Pop became alert again and said, "I wondered the same thing 'til I ran into Isham one day up on the Square, back before all this stroke business. I asked him flat out, and he didn't bat an eye when he said as far he was concerned, his daughter died when she got with you. He said he buried her when she went against him by marryin' you. Isham blames you for everythin' bad that happened to Patti. He said he was glad you got sent to the pen, and that he'd do anythin' ta get you put back in if you ever showed up in Northville again."

Raz felt the color rise in his face and his scars tighten, but remembered his promise. "I didn't get her started on drugs. Doesn't he know that? I didn't make her take up with Horton Snitker's bastard son and his friends, either."

"Simmer down now. I'm not the one that did the accusing. I'm just the messenger."

"Sorry," Raz said, rubbing the scar. It was so tight he was afraid his face might distort like Pop's. He told Pop about going by Isham Lawther's to see Becky and how frightened Mrs. Lawther was that her husband would catch him there. He recounted the story about her cat, too. "She told me she called Gerta one time to ask about Patti. Any idea why she did that?"

"Nope. But as Olin's dispatcher and clerk, Gerta is in a position to know everythin' going on in town."

"I might have to pay Gerta a visit. If I can find a way to get her ticked off at Olin and Tank, she might tell me lots of interestin' things."

"My guess is that up to now, Tank and Olin have been too afraid of the gang's hit men to worry 'bout anythin' Gerta might say. They're more afraid of you than anybody right now. They pro'bly suspect you got as much in your head as Cato had on that tape."

"If that was true, I wouldn't need the tape." He glanced at his watch, eager to visit Bull Hayter.

Pop stared blankly around the room as his mind drifted again, then said, "Boobs' Soup Kitchen was a landmark. I got most of my white hair from bein' raked over the coals by the town church ladies for lettin' her sell beer on the sly and keep women in that back room. I finally convinced 'em that her place was a lot safer than the beer joints and whore houses in Dallas."

"You were always like a father to all of us. Too bad Sam Cook got elected instead of Walter Lipscott when you retired. Walter was a good man. How'd Cook pull that off?"

"That's no puzzle. Money. Horton Snitker, your former father-in-law and their pals pulled lots of strings to get Sam elected. Not long after Sam hired Tank, they decided they'd have a freer hand in runnin' things if the resident deputy was made sheriff. So, Isham and Horton made Sam Cook an offer he couldn't refuse, and he resigned. Once that happened, the commissioners' court made Tank the head man. There are enough Snitker employees and Lawther butt-kissers in the county to re-elect Tank as long as he keeps Punk out of jail and he don't get crossways with the town bosses.

Raz took his last swallow of liquid courage and asked, "Did Tank and Olin try to find out what happened to Fran Druman after she disappeared?"

"Not that I know of. Did Cato ask you to lean on her if you could find her?"

"Why would he do that?"

Pop hesitated, as if suddenly realizing he might've said too much. Finally, the old man said, "I didn't realize she was still so important to you. Sorry."

"That's okay. That's all water under the bridge now. But I need to know why Cato would want me or anybody else to lean on Fran."

Pop fidgeted about in his wheelchair and cleared his throat. "Cato didn't tell you who set him up?"

"Are you tellin' me it was Fran?" He felt his stomach tighten.

"Since the cat's already out of the bag, guess I'll come clean. Fran's real name is Francine Hooker. I found that out when my ranger friend, Tom Nations, in

Tyler brought Tank a warrant for her arrest. He served it right after you got sent up. Tom stopped by here after he left it with Tank. Fran disappeared right after that and Punk took over the Armadillo Hole."

Raz remembered how Cato clammed up every time he mentioned Fran's name. He felt betrayed by Fran. *How could she keep her real name from me? Why do I care so much? If all I want is my share of the Hole, why does this bother me so much? Hurt pride? It's not the first time I've been disappointed by a woman. Am I gonna find out something unexpected and sinister about Anita, too?*

"What was the warrant for?"

"Embezzlement. Her boss in Mississippi claimed she stole lots of his money and ran off with it."

"But Cato told me Blackie Mazurka did him in by turnin' state's evidence."

Pop's eyes were steady. "Cato asked you to hit him, too?"

"He did, or get his nephew Snake Hamilton to find somebody to do it. You haven't told me straight out that Fran burned Cato. If she did, what's the how and why of it?"

"I've already said too much," he said and shook his head, "and I'm tired. We'll talk more when you come again." He offered his hand. "You're a good man, Raz — a bit reckless but honest and trustworthy. After I've had a little time to rest, give me a call and I'll tell you if Lassiter got the go-ahead to come to Northville. I'll also tell you what the committee said."

Raz embraced Pop. "Thanks for still bein' here and for tryin' ta help me. I'll check with you in the mornin' about Lassiter. When he calls, tell him I can hold onto Mazurka for another day, but no longer 'cause he needs to see a doctor."

Raz limped to the van with his head still spinning over the news about Cato and Fran. *If Fran did contribute to Cato's fall, what else did Cato forget to tell me about? Damn.*

CHAPTER 22

The clock on the van's dash read 4:35 when Raz pulled out of Pop's driveway. Seeing Pop like that was a sobering experience. It was almost as shocking as being told there would be no immediate help from Lassiter, and that Fran was capable of making a case against Cato.

Lassiter's predicament confirmed what many convicts had told Raz at Huntsville: politicians and lawmen were the servants of the rich and powerful. He'd never believed that before, but recent experiences were making him have second thoughts. *Am I starting to think like an outlaw? Am I letting criminal values dictate my actions?* He didn't think so, but believed he should work on an attitude adjustment or risk falling into a bottomless pit of despair.

He couldn't allow cynicism to destroy his faith in good people. Despite the contradicting evidence, he believed the good guys were still in the majority. To believe otherwise would be devastating.

The most foolhardy thing he'd probably ever done was joining forces with Lassiter. The plan they'd come up with two years ago involved him decking Tank and being sent to prison where he'd be housed with Cato Hamilton. It had seemed like his only option at the time, but in view of what Pop said about his impulsive nature, he wondered if the act was influenced more by the personal satisfaction he thought it would give him rather than a moral obligation to his dead wife. He remained convinced it was the latter. He still believed he'd acted out of love and respect for the mother of his child. If that was true, why was he still plagued by guilt over Patti's death?

Regardless of how and why the alliance with Lassiter came about, he now found himself in a world of hurt because of it. He might have second thoughts about how things were going, but he remained determined to find his wife's murderer.

As for how he felt about Fran, he'd put too much importance on his brief personal relationship with a woman he barely knew. He was more convinced than ever that she had information that would help him accomplish his goal. Finding her might be difficult. In the mean time, he needed to sort out his feelings about her. *Boobs would tell me to never throw away a bird in the hand for the one that flew away.*

No matter how much he loathed Mazurka, he couldn't let him stay in the boat shed much longer or he'd die. His good and bad nature warred. His reckless side advised: *Roll him into the lake and forget him. The creep tried to kill you.* But his good side argued: *Doing that would make you as bad as the gangsters you're trying to put away.*

He sighed, shaking his head at the conflicting thoughts. He looked forward to ending the whole ugly business of playing cop and fighting bad guys.

Following some lesser-traveled dirt roads, he crossed Highway 59 north of town and drove into The Quarters on his way to Bull Hayter's café on Kennedy Drive. This was the main drag of the ghetto and the only paved street on this side of town. He didn't dare to risk driving down it because Olin Culpepper often patrolled there.

The city council, under the direction of Isham Lawther, never saw fit to pave the other streets in The Quarters or supply the homes there with city water, sewer service or natural gas. The majority of the residents had finally got electricity, no thanks to the city of Northville, after the creation of the Rural Electric Administration.

Raz saw few changes in the little frame houses of the area. They all needed various repairs and a coat of paint. Most of these were rental units, owned by Isham Lawther or Horton Snitker. The owner-occupied houses stood out by comparison. They were well maintained, with green, neatly trimmed lawns.

At the approximate center of The Quarters, Raz turned south on another dirt street, then went down an alley to the backyard of the Black Orchard Café, owned and operated by Bull Hayter.

Bull was a cunning man, known to favor quick money deals, clean or otherwise. Some of Bull's moneymaking schemes were illegal, but the city didn't bother him. There'd been little need for law to intervene since Bull took over the establishment. He maintained order with an iron fist. He also kept up with what went on through friends, informers and other connections.

Raz watched the alley and the back door of the Black Orchid for several minutes, hoping he'd see Snake so he wouldn't have to go inside. The only reason he could think of that would prompt Bull to send him word on the other side of the tracks was Snake wanting to see him.

It looked like Bull hadn't done anything to improve the exterior of the Black Orchid other than apply a coat of blue paint with yellow trim. Raz spotted the air conditioning unit in a window next to the alley, and realized it was a major step forward for Bull.

Getting out, Raz peeked around the corner, looking for Tank or Olin's cars parked out front. So far, their injuries were apparently working in his favor. An old Buick and a Ford pickup were the only vehicles in the parking lot. No sounds came from inside, which meant business was slow at the moment.

Going to the side entrance, he stepped inside the darkened interior and stopped to let his eyes adjust. Three young guys standing by the front entrance gave him hostile looks, but said nothing. The delicious aroma of barbecue wafting from the kitchen mixed with the smell of stale cigarette smoke and dirty floors to complete the ombiance of the place.

Moving out of the little hall into the serving room, he spotted three customers sitting at one of the plain wooden tables, and two men standing near the linoleum-covered counter. Smoking a cigar, looking as fierce as ever, Bull Hayter sat on a stool behind the cash register.

Bull flashed even, white teeth in a big smile as Raz approached. "Lordy, Lordy. Heard you was back and was wonderin' if you'd come by. Zeke already come by ten times askin' if you'd come 'roun' yet."

All of the customers watched Bull come from behind the counter to embrace Raz, who winced from having his back patted. "Hello, Bull. I'm glad to find out some good lookin' woman's husband ain't put your lights out yet. How the hell are you?"

"Fine." Bull's best smile reappeared. "Better now. Come over and have a seat at the counter. Hungry? Bertha Mae's got some fine barbecue goin' back there."

Raz glanced at the other customers again but didn't see Snake. A woman's face appeared at the serving window behind the counter, and her expression brightened. "Hi, Mr. Raz. You're a purty sight for these tired ol' eyes."

"Hi, Bertha Mae." Raz waved. "Found yourself another husband yet?"

"No, suh. Don't won't another ol' man fartin' under my covers."

Raz smiled. "Got any warm left-over chicken and dumplin's? I know Bull didn't let you throw 'em out."

"Sho' have," she replied. "One big bowl comin' up."

Bull pointed toward a table. "Let's sit over there where we can talk private."

Raz saw one of the young men from the counter rush out the front door. Bull glanced at him, but made no comment.

They'd barely got seated when Bertha Mae came out of the kitchen carrying a bowl of chicken and dumplings. They smelled delicious.

"Got 'em nice an' hot with that new microwave Bull got me," she said. "I'm outta corn bread though. Sorry." She disappeared, coming back shortly with a pint jar of iced tea.

"Thank you, ma'am," Raz told her. "It's a shame how you're robbin' some man of such good service."

"Humph!" She tossed her head and returned to the kitchen, shaking the floor with each step.

"That young man left like he had a fire under his tail.," Raz said. "He by any chance a friend of Tank or Olin's?"

"You ain't got no reason to be 'fraid of any these boys. They all know what you done for Cato Hamilton. No, he just leavin' to tell Snake you here."

"I figured that's the reason you called Anita."

Bull nodded.

"But how—"

"Bull know everythin', 'member? I knowed 'bout you and Miss Anita in high school, so I figured you pay her a visit since you ain't got no wife now." He shifted his seat. "But I only call her up ta help you, not 'cause I got any use for Snake. I don't handle his shit in my place."

"Course not."

"I don't have no use for his Uncle Cato, neither." Bull's expression became fierce. "Cato use to send his pusher by with all that stuff. No way."

Raz took another bite of dumplings. He'd always heard Bull didn't allow the hard stuff at his place, but customer he considered "safe" could get away with the small stuff.

Lowering his voice, Bull said, "I sorry 'bout Miz Boobs. That lady treat ever'body right, even when it didn't set good with the main man 'cross the tracks. Sorry 'bout all the crap piled on ya since you got back, too." When Raz gave him a questioning look, he added, "Bull know ever'thing, 'member?"

"How the pistol-toters been treatin' you since I left?"

"Cain't complain. They don't bother me long as I don't talk back, smile a lot and always say 'yes-suh' and 'no-suh.'"

"Talking to me gonna cause you any problems?"

Bull's smile disappeared. "You're hotter than a two-dollar pistol on Saturday night, Raz. A man got ta help his friends if he can do it without stirrin' up too much stink. This a mighty small town."

"Don't worry. Nobody saw me come in, and I'll sneak out the same way. Snake took a chance, pickin' me up in Coldwater. Guess it didn't hurt him though."

"You guess wrong. He got his tail in a crack real good for that. Seem somebody at Punk's place saw you get out his car up the highway. Only reason he don't get his lights put out 'cause he convince 'em he did it ta get at what Cato sent out."

"That reason crossed my mind too."

"You didn't give him nothin' he could use again' ya, did ya?"

"Going by what he said, I figured they already knew everything."

"Watch your mouth 'roun' Snake."

"Hope gettin' in a bind didn't change his mind 'bout doing me a favor." He took another bite of dumplings.

Bull's expression remained somber. "He walkin' a mighty tight rope right now, but you can still count on him if he sees it won't cost nothin'."

"Will he come here if that guy finds him?"

"Nope. He cain't risk bein' seen wit you. You gotta meet him in one of his safe houses after he make sure you ain't brought no company. He know you got yourself arrested, so he afraid you make a deal to get sprung."

"Where do I meet him?"

"Wait 'round, but not here. The chief drives by couple time a day when he able. Yeah, I hear 'bout dat fire, too. Even if he ain't able, he might send one of them informers."

"Guess I could wait over at Zeke's."

A relieved expression swept over Bull's face. "Zeke love that. I'll tell Snake's friend where you is."

Raz finished eating as an ill-at-ease Bull watched, apparently eager for him to leave. Raz wiped his mouth and folded the napkin. "Bull, your expression tells me you're thinking 'bout somethin' besides good-lookin' women and today's receipts. Wanna share?"

Bull said sincerely, "I'm too old an' got too many good things goin' for me to mess up now. Don't want no part dat Aryan Brotherhood or them ones dat burn Cato or the crooked law and they killer friends 'cross the tracks."

"You're thinkin' I'm gonna screw up your good life, right? Well, not if I can help it. You just keep Snake in line, and let me know if you think he's about to throw me to the sharks."

"I do dat, but 'member this. Snake don't come by his name from bein' no angel."

Raz said goodbye and stepped out the side door. He decided to walk to Zeke's little house two blocks away. His knees were still in no condition for walking, but he thought the exercise might work out some of the stiffness.

Wow, Zeke must be eighty by now. The last time I saw him, he was startin' to show his age, Raz thought at he walked. In his youth, Zeke was a sparring partner for Floyd Patterson and a few other big names. Later, he'd trained aspiring heavyweights in St. Louis, Dallas and Houston. He'd come home to Northville to take care of his mother, and stayed on after she died.

When Raz arrived at the gate of Zeke's rickety picket fence, he looked up and down the street to make sure he wasn't being watched. Once he was sure he was alone, he moved up the dirt walkway to the front porch. He knocked, and heard nothing but a TV set or a radio playing in a back room. He knocked again.

"Comin', kids," Zeke said from a distance.

Raz's old friend walked into the front room, straining his eyes to see who was at the door. Halfway across the room, his face broke into a big smile. "Raz! I thought you was somebody else. Come on in and put 'em up."

Raz stepped inside and they took up fighting stances, circling, feinting and jabbing. Out of breath moments later, Zeke dropped his fists, and then gave Raz a big hug. "You still got it, boy," he said admiringly. "And you lookin' good, too. That prison food didn't hurt ya none."

Raz slapped him on the shoulder. "Still eyeballin'g all the pretty girls that walk by?"

"Eyeballin' is my callin'. Can't do nothin' else. Come on back and set a spell an' we'll swap some lies."

Raz followed him into the tiny living room. Zeke turned off the TV and pointed to an extra chair.

"Training any young roosters these days?" Raz asked.

Zeke sat down with a sigh. Raz noticed that his hair was now completely white. "Nary a soul. My ol' eyes done quit on me, and my legs is gone, too. I ain't got nothin' left, 'cept arthritis."

"You still look good to me, ol' timer."

"Lookin' ain't feelin'." Zeke leaned forward. "I been hearin' all kind o' things 'bout ya. Brother back from the joint was talkin' 'bout ya. Tol' me you the toughest white man he ever see. Another'un tol' me 'bout how ya saved dat Cato feller."

Zeke went on, "Yep, ya got a tough row to hoe, bein' crossways with the law. One thin' ta 'member, though, no matter how mean they treat ya 'cross da tracks, you still walk tall in The Quarters."

"I hope Snake Hamilton feels that way. I'm lookin' for him."

"You find him, you be travelin' in mighty sorry comp'ny."

"Ya don't think I can trust him?"

"Only if you got what he want. Soon as you run out, look out."

"Been playin' that game since I got out. Guess I can play a little while longer."

"You got dat winner spirit. Never throw in dat towel, no matter what bad folks does to ya. 'Course don't mean dat devil in ya don't need some work. I'm talkin' 'bout that inner devil dat never let you give up on a fight. You needin' the most work there."

"One minute you're braggin' on me, and the next you're tellin' me to cool it." He smiled. "You're beginnin' to sound like Cato Hamilton."

"Best leave it alone."

"Leave what alone?"

"You knows what I's talkin' 'bout." Zeke's dark eyes bored into him. "You still chasin' revenge. Leave it be."

"What would you do if your wife and best friend got murdered on this side of the tracks and the cops and the DA wouldn't do anything?"

Zeke threw up his hands. "There you go, comin' in quick and hittin' below the belt." Zeke leaned back. "When I was young, there weren't nobody ta tell me different. When I got older an' wiser, I quit fightin' the man. Things I can't whup now, I leave ta the Lord. You should too."

"You sound like a lady I met on the bus comin' in. I might think the same way some day if I'm lucky enough to live as long as you."

There was a light knock at the front door, and Raz followed Zeke to see who it was. It was the man Raz had seen rush out of the Black Orchid.

"Follow me, man," the stranger told Raz.

"We ain't finished our visit," Zeke said.

Raz patted his friend's arm. "We'll finish later. The way my luck's been runnin', I can't say when that might be."

The man on the porch motioned for Raz to wait inside as a car came into view. When it drove out of sight, Raz followed him to an old Ford pickup that was parked at Zeke's front gate. Making a U-turn and heading east, his driver asked, "Where your wheels, man?"

Raz told him.

The man's eyes were unfriendly. "We get your wheels and then you follow me. I hit my brakelights twice and my blinker once, that mean you in front of the right house. Don't drive on and come back later or circle the block or none of that shit. Jus' park and go in."

He drove to the Black Orchid and pulled up next to the van. Raz got out, looked inside to make sure there weren't any unwanted passengers hiding in the back, and got in. He backed out and drove north, following the pickup over to

Sycamore, then east on a dirt road. Seeing the truck's lights flash, Raz pulled over at a dilapidated frame house. The weedy lots next to it were vacant, as was the one across the street.

Set back under large sycamores in an unkempt yard, the unpainted structure looked deserted. The front porch and eaves sagged. He saw no number, but figured it should be 817 based on the houses he'd passed on the way.

Snake's friend stopped at the next corner and turned to watch as Raz parked in the weeds alongside the old house. Raz drove into the backyard and stopped near the back steps. He could tell by the trampled grass and weeds that cars had been coming in from the back street. *I don't see any other cars. If Snake's here, somebody dropped him off.*

He approached the back door under a sagging lean-to cover and knocked lightly. No answer. He tested the door and found it unlocked. Stepping inside, he put his back to the wall to avoid being framed by light coming in through the door. He blinked a couple of times letting his eyes adjust to the shadowy interior that was made even darker by pulled shades and the tress outside.

The room he'd entered was the kitchen. There was an old stove, a dusty dinette table and a rusty refrigerator. A strong odor of pot mixed with the musty wet plaster smell and assaulted his nose.

In the next room, he saw two wooden chairs, a rickey cot and an ashtray filled to overflowing. The walls were bare and the floor was covered with trash.

He pulled one of the chairs into a corner and sat down to wait. Soon, he heard two sets of footsteps approaching the door, but only one person entered the kitchen. Raz watched the connecting door until Snake, wearing another brightly colored shirt that hung loosely over his hips, walked in.

"Hello, bright eyes," Raz said

Snake jumped. "You scared the crap outta me, man. You by yourself?"

"Yeah. Bull sent word you wanted to see me. Whatcha got?"

Snake mumbled something under his breath, then said more clearly, "That's before I found out what a hot item you is, man. How you get loose from the High Sheriff and the Chief? You make some kind o' deal?" He sat down.

"A mouse can't make deals with alley cats, but sometimes he gets lucky." He assumed Snake hadn't heard about the fire or the wreck, so he didn't mention it. "What do you want?"

Snake studied him a moment, like he was having second thoughts. "I's in deep enough shit on account o' you. I get my guts cut out jus' like your friend, Tim Barton, if certain people find out I talkin' to you again."

"You know all about Tim Barton, too?"

"Everything but who done it, which I don't wanna know." He cleared his throat and fidgeted in his chair. "Friend down in Houston have a line on your used-to-be ol' lady. You still interested?"

"I am." Raz leaned forward. "But no more favors before leveling with you about something I just found out. Afterwards, I hope you'll still tell me where to find her."

"What you talkin' 'bout?" Snake eyed him suspiciously.

"Cato's dead."

Snake jumped to his feet. "Say what? When?"

"I just got word. He was shot while they were transferring him to another unit."

Snake threw up his hands in frustration. "How that happen? Guards was wit 'im, wasn't they?" He shook his finger at Raz. "That it, ain't it? Damn guards got paid off."

"Yeah, with bullets in their brains."

Snake clenched and unclenched his fists as he paced back and forth across the room, mumbling and shaking his head. "Can't believe it, man. Uncle Cato dead. That mean them dudes that had him busted finally went all the way. Why? He kept quiet, an' he couldn't hurt nobody no more."

"Somebody apparently thought he could. It might be 'cause the wrong people found out about me havin' his statement."

"I ain't sayin' I don't appreciate what you done for my uncle, but somethin' ain't right. You get shipped home with some statement from him, then all of a sudden he dead."

Raz pulled off his left boot and sock and gave Snake the letter Cato wrote. "Maybe this will help." He pulled his sock and boot back on.

"What the hell?"

"Read it. You *can* read. Can't you?"

Stepping over to a window, Snake rolled up the shade and tore open the small white envelope. He read the contents and, when finished, said, "This a will, man. Uncle Cato leave me his money. Where it at?"

Raz's eyebrows rose. "No more questions or tears shed for your dear, departed uncle? You're all heart. Cato put it in a safe place. It's kind of like my insurance right now. As soon as you convince me you're on my side all the way, I'll tell you where you can find it."

Snake stiffened. "It ain't your fuckin' money, man." He thumped the paper. "Say right here, when he die it all mine. Property, too."

"Money, yes. Property has to be split three ways to include his two sisters in California, when you find them. While you're lookin' for 'em and workin' hard to convince me what a trustworthy nephew you are, I'll just keep the name of the bank and the account number in a special place." He tapped his head. "Make sure nothin' happens to the safe."

Snake pulled down the shade and the room went dark. Mumbling under his breath, he returned to the chair and said, "You better start talkin', man. Right now, I gotta know why them cops turn you loose."

"They didn't. My showing up here with Cato's will has nothing to do with that or with your uncle being killed. Cato wanted you to have the will, just in case. He didn't plan on dying for a while yet."

"What I gotta do to convince you I'm cool?"

"For starters, take me to see Fran Druman and keep your mouth shut about it."

"Didn't say for sure my Houston friend have the right woman. I say I had a *line* on somebody who *might* be your ex-ol' lady. That before you tol' me 'bout Uncle Cato. Now he dead, you got to understand this helpin' shit ain't no damn one-way street. 'Fore I do for you, you gotta tell me what you know 'bout Uncle Cato. Stuff you ain't tol' me yet. I gotta know whose toes I be steppin' on."

Raz shifted his aching knees. "How could I refuse such an eloquent appeal? Cato told me he was burned 'cause he got caught in the middle of a fight between two gangs — the Mexican Mafia and the Dixie Mafia. Locals might've had something to do with it. Dixie bunch might've offered them a better deal.

Anyway, the Dixie mob is in charge now. It's run by a bunch of bad-ass Anglos and a few Mexicans they let in from Cato's old gang."

"They shore don't like the brothas. Punk the only one who give me jobs now and then."

"Do you see any tears in my eyes? As I was sayin', you probably already know one of Cato's muscle men, Blackie Mazurka, turned state's evidence against him to keep from going to the pen. He's one of the old gang that transferred over. Cato told me to tell you to find somebody to take care of him."

"That shit ain't exactly news, man. You ain't said nothin' 'bout knowin' who try to kill Uncle Cato in the pen. I wanna know if it was them same ones that finally got him."

"Could've been. Could've been the new bunch, or some of Tank's Northville pals who didn't want to take chances on Cato messing up their business arrangements. We may never find out. All I know is the first time happened right after he was bench-warranted out by the state narcs. I've been told Cato didn't tell them squat, but the harm was already done."

He leaned forward. "Are we gonna sit here and play twenty questions or we gonna find Fran Druman? I don't wanna waste more time tellin' you things you probably already know. I'm still mad as hell over the reception your hippie friends across the tracks gave me, and sore as a butt boil from gettin' beat up by Tank. I'm ready to get on with it."

Snake smiled. "The High Sheriff laid it on you like he do my brothas?" His smile faded. "You pretty cocky for a man dat might get his ass shot."

"Cato'd be disappointed in you if you don't help me."

Snake rubbed his forehead. "Uncle Cato a silly old man. He too old to run a tough bidness." He pulled a joint out of his shirt pocket and lit it, inhaled deeply, then slowly let the smoke out in Raz's face.

Raz waved it away and said, "Cato told me all about how Punk and his new friends wouldn't let you have anything to sell when the Dixie bunch first took over. Since Punk cut you in on a little action later, you must've done him a big favor. Why don't you tell me what that was?"

Snake blew smoke toward Raz again, after holding it as long as he could. He said sharply, "How the hell else I gonna make real money in this hick town? They got issues with da brothas, and I gotta make money somehow."

Raz looked around at the drab surroundings. "I can tell you're rollin' in it."

Snake jumped to his feet. "I be rich now if sorry-ass Punk ain't lied to me. Stupid for thinkin' dat white man keep his word with a nigga!"

Bull had said Snake was unpredictable, but this outburst told Raz a lot. "So, what happened between you and Punk?"

Snake began pacing the floor again. "I knowed Punk all my life, but he act like he don't know me 'less he want a favor. Wouldn't 'cross town after Cato got busted 'less he want somethin' bad. Said he come over ta make me an offer I can't refuse. Tol' me, all polite-like, that 'cause I was Cato's favorite nephew, I know how to get with his bidness associates. You know, suppliers, runners an' bag men."

"That's strange. I would've thought he and Tank would've told the Dixie bunch who they were by then. After all, it was their friends that busted Cato."

"Who know why he don't know already? Maybe Punk tryin' ta start his own operation. New bunch maybe give Tank orders not to take him in 'cause he hooked. My friend, Lobo, in Houston be one of Uncle Cato's runners. Not 'bout to tell Punk that, though. So, I tol' him I don't know none of Cato's contacts.

"What did he say?"

"He get huffy, like he some kind o' big-shot or somethin'. Call me a lyin' nigga. Went on like that a couple of months, him comin' over makin' threats, orderin' me to give up names an' such. He finally say he see to it I get sent to the slammer if I don't tell. When Uncle Cato got sentenced, he come back, all excited, blabberin' 'bout how he find out 'bout the white lady. He say she the one busted Uncle Cato and she know all Uncle Cato's connections. Only trouble, he can't find her."

"A white lady?"

"Yeah. He say if I find her and get he new boss's name, he set me up in bidness real big."

"Sounds like he was trying to set up his own operation. Did he tell you her name?"

Snake took another long drag off the joint for courage and exhaled. "Fran Druman."

A wave of disappointment swept over Raz. *I really hoped it wasn't true.* "Why didn't you tell me all this when I asked yesterday?"

"Snake don't get mix up in white folk shit. Cato's letter change my mind."

Raz gently rubbed the scar on his face and again wondered why the truth about Fran bothered him so much. "What did you do for Punk after that?"

Snake took another long draw off the joint, holding the smoke in his lungs until he had to breathe again. "Figured I give it a shot. Tol' him 'bout Lobo bein' one o' Cato's mules. Lobo tol' me one time he know lots of Mexico suppliers, some in Cato's outfit, too. Lobo be slippin' me a little grass and other stuff on the sly 'fore Punk give me some penny ante shit."

"And?"

"I figure the new outfit need mules and might be usin' Lobo. Maybe he pick up on some names. I take Punk down ta see him. When we there, feel like Lobo don't wanna do business with Punk. Punk keep pesterin' him and tellin' him he gonna turn him in if he don't cut a deal. After that, Punk got tight with Tank and his new friends."

"How come you're still mad at Punk?"

"He a liar. No big setup like he promise. Nothin' but a little grass and some low grade crack and meth. Can't sell any of it outside The Quarters without sneakin' 'roun' like a thief in the night. I ask him 'bout the big cut, and he say, 'Take your black ass back 'cross the tracks and keep your mouth shut if you wanna keep livin'. I don't need Lobo now 'cause I got me a better deal.'"

"That means Tank used his influence after all."

"That my guess. Anyway, Punk don't talk ta me no more. Send over one of his stinkin' friends if he want a favor 'cross the tracks."

"You didn't hear anything else about what part Fran played in getting Tank and Punk set up with the new gang?"

Snake shook his head. "Nope. I ever find her, I ask her."

"If she's active with the new bunch, you couldn't get close enough. She'll have guards three deep. I'll ask, if we find her. That means you can leave your pistol at home when we go."

Snake didn't respond and his angry glare declared his defiance.

Although encouraged by the prospect of finding Fran, Raz's inner turmoil still raged. Finding out the truth about the woman who'd danced so close and was so affectionate that special night during a critical time in his life was not something he could shrug away. He realized more than ever that he shouldn't have expected Fran to stop living while he was away. *How was she involved with Cato Hamilton, though? How could he have misjudged her like that? Something must've compelled her to do something that drastic.*

"Snake, when can Lobo take me by to see the woman who might be Fran?"

"Never. Won't take you nowhere 'less you wit' me. He tol' me where ta find her. But I ain't sure I wanna take you now. Snake ain't goin' ta the pen for killin' the bitch that burned Uncle Cato, an' that's what'll most likely happen if we find her."

"You wouldn't do that, 'cause I need her as much as you need me." He pointed to his head. "Feel me?"

Snake stared daggers at him and sucked on the blunt again. "You think you a cool dude. In my book, you ain't no different. What you want with that woman now she wronged you?"

"She owes me money. But that's none of your business. You'll get what you want from me by just takin' me to her."

"Smartass!" He dropped the roach and ground it out with is heel. "Should have my head examine for doin' anythin' wit you," he said and paused. "Be here tomorrow, six o'clock. She your ex-ol' lady or not, you tell me where ta find what mine an' my debt to you be paid. Agree?"

Raz stood up. "Yeah. Just remember, I'll have terrible memory loss if I hear you talked to Tank and his friends about any of this. Got it?"

Snake nodded. "Yeah, yeah. I feel ya." He pulled out another joint. "To show there ain't no hard feelin's, have a joint. Loosen up. You too uptight, man."

"Don't use the stuff."

"I thought … your wife … you know—"

"You thought wrong."

Raz returned to the van and left by a back street to get to the road he'd come in on. The whole time, he was mulling over what Snake told him. He noticed the old green Cadillac parked next to a vacant house up ahead. When he slowed down to pass it, Zapata wasn't in it.

Relieved, he sped up and turned north at the next corner. That's when he heard something in the back of the van. He turned and found himself looking down the barrel of a pistol. The van swerved dangerously as he saw the face behind the gun. Zapata.

He beckoned with his pistol and said, "Turn right at the next corner and head for the other side of the tracks. You're not getting away from me this time, champ."

CHAPTER 23

az scolded himself for being so careless. He told Zapata, "If you pull that trigger, you and your friends will never find Mazurka."

Zapata put one hand on the headrest of the passenger seat and said, "Do you see any tears in my eyes? Take Kennedy Drive to Camino Real Motor Court. I'm sure you know it — the place where you went to make out when you were a kid."

Raz glanced back at the Zapata. "In that old flophouse? Punk's really hit a new low. Why don't you just put that gun down so we can talk? I'll make you an offer you can't refuse."

Zapata waved the gun in his face. "No use trying to flimflam your way out of this, Jester. Save all your bullshit for my boss and keep your eyes on the road."

Convinced he had no choice, Raz crossed the railroad tracks and turned left onto the highway. When they go to the Square, Raz saw ribbon-studded booths and a Ferris being setup for homecoming.

Raz turned onto Camino Real Motor Court, located on a narrow strip of land next to the railroad. Single, covered carports separated the two rows of small one-room cabins. Zapata directed Raz to stop at the last one in the second row.

"What does Punk keep here, his strung-out whores?"

Zapata waved the pistol toward the door. "Get out."

"Hold your fire. I'm moving as fast as my sore knees will let me."

When Raz hesitated at the door of the cabin, Zapata pushed the pistol against his back, "Go in quick before somebody spots us."

Raz limped inside, stopping when he saw a man sitting on a sofa against the back wall. "What the hell are *you* doing here?"

Denny Schroeder nodded to Zapata who pushed his pistol under his belt. "Lassiter said you put in a call for the cavalry," Schroeder said. "Since the politicians have him on temporary hold, he asked me to stop by and see what you've got."

Raz looked from the DEA agent to Zapata who had calmly taken a seat at a dinette table. Nodding toward Zapata, he asked, "I heard he's Punk's friend. Does that mean you're in with Punk too?" He pointed an accusing finger at the agent. "Shit. You were the gang's man in the warden's office."

"Wrong on all counts," the agent replied. "Punk just *thinks* Zapata's his friend. And he *is*, up to a point. We can't get information about dope deals from enemies."

Raz looked at Zapata, still skeptical. "I guess you being a fed explains why you didn't know Lassiter, but it doesn't tell me why you pulled a gun on me."

"Remember what happened the first time he tried to talk to you?" Schroeder asked. "It was the only way he could bring you in quietly."

Raz's eyes were still on Zapata. "It'll take a while for me to trust anybody that hangs out with the likes of Punk Hutto."

Zapata's dark eyes flashed. "You think I'd find out more about the local dope business over at the First Baptist Church?"

"Rick's a good agent, but all he's seen so far is lots of simple possession cases, strictly state and local stuff. Lassiter and I want you to give us something bigger, something we can use in federal court where the local yokels have no influence."

Raz laughed suddenly, causing the agents to exchange puzzled glances. Schroeder asked, "What's funny?"

"Look at you," Raz said. "Two hot-shot federal narcotics officers, conducting official business in a dump that no self-respecting rat would be caught dead in, and you're asking a wanted ex-con with busted knees for help."

"So?"

"You two supposedly have the legal power of the whole country backing you, yet you're both sneaking around like *you're* the crooks. You guys should be able to just walk into this town and kick butts without having to lick anybody's boots. Wake up, man. The country is on fire and you're worried about hurting some politician's feelings while the thugs are out stealing all the fire hydrants."

Schroeder said soberly, "We have to work with what the politicians give us. It's not efficient, and it fails sometimes, but it's all we've got."

Schroeder motioned Zapata out of the room. As soon as the door was closed, he said, "Rick can't afford to be seen meeting with a stranger like me, so I can't hang around. I'm under subpoena to testify at a big trial in St. Louis."

Raz wondered if he could trust Schroeder. "You said Lassiter called you?"

"Right after he called Pop Cheever. He told me what happened to the tape."

Realizing only someone working with Lassiter would know that, Raz breathed a sigh of relief and sat down, glad to take the weight off his knees.

"Too bad Lassiter couldn't come up and talk to Mazurka, that killer is the kind of witness both of us need. I can't relieve you of him yet because I have to testify at nine in the morning. I've barely got time to get there as it is."

"I think Mazurka will live 'til you get back. If you decide you can't use him, I'll file charges against him for violating my civil rights. You Feds are strong on that kinda stuff."

"But you're not a minority." He smiled.

"I'm an American citizen, by God. Doesn't that qualify me for something?"

"Simmer down. I was pullin' your chain. If Lassiter's not here by then, I'll help you as soon as I get done with that subpoena. Tell me about Mazurka. You're not holding him against his will, are you?"

"Me? No. I gave him his options and he chose staying with me if I'd treat his wounds and guarantee him no jail time for what he tried to do to me."

"Only the U.S. Attorney can give him immunity."

"I didn't promise him immunity, just that I wouldn't file charges against him."

"Where is he?"

"Where his fellow crooks can't find and kill him. I told Tank and Olin Culpepper he's ready to cooperate, hoping they'd cut me some slack. That blew up in my face like a cheap firecracker."

"Is he free to leave the place where you're holding him?"

"If he can swim with a broken leg."

"If you still have him when I get back, I'll get a warrant in Tyler and take custody. What made you change your mind about working with us?"

"Alligators nipping at my butt like it's roasted chicken. I decided I could do more for my family and my town by staying alive."

"In case the U.S. Attorney finds something wrong with the Mazurka thing after I take custody, we'll need more evidence. Think you can find some more before I get back?"

"I'll know as soon as I find Fran Druman."

Schroeder sat erect. "You know Fran?"

He nodded. "How come I get the impression you know her too?"

"Because I not only know her, we want her in the worst way."

"And I thought I knew women. After talking to you, Pop, and Snake Hamilton, it looks like I didn't know squat about her."

"Lassiter and I have been looking for that woman for more than two years. When she testified in state court, we made a deal with her to make federal cases against some big suppliers and in-between guys. Then she up and disappears on us. If we could find her, we'd bust this town wide open. Other places too, if we can get her to talk."

Raz remained silent, trying to digest the fact that the woman who played him for a fool was not only wanted for felony theft in another state but also by the Feds. The good news: Fran most likely had information on Patti's killer.

Shifting his feet to relieve the pressure on his aching knees, Raz told Schroeder about his and Fran's business arrangement, and how she sold the Hole to Punk Hutto about the same time Cato was sentenced.

"Did you have a written partnership agreement?"

"Nope. But she always kept her word on everything else. I trusted her."

"Do you still trust her?"

"I'm curious, I guess. Looks like she's been a naughty little gal. It's hard for me to believe she's involved with drugs."

"Maybe she wasn't, but she knew who was. She met them through Cato."

"If I find her, what can I do to help you that'll get this monkey off my back?"

"Talk her into coming to see me, or give me her address so the nearest DEA agent can talk to her. Tell her I'll get her immunity from federal prosecution and we won't pursue the matter of her ignoring that grand jury subpoena two years ago. What makes you think she'll even talk to you?"

"Because we had a good thing going at one time. At least *I* thought we did. If that's not enough reason, well, she owes me money."

When he clenched his jaw against the pain in his legs, Schroeder snapped on the bedside light and asked, "Are you okay?"

Raz told him what Tank had done and how he escaped. "They probably have every cop in the state looking for me by now."

"Go to your district attorney and file a complaint. That's a big-ass felony."

"I don't trust the DA, or anybody else on the Eastman County payroll. I'd be lucky to live out the day if I did that." He told Schroeder about being mugged and the attempt on his life at his parents' house.

The agent remained silent a moment, obviously concerned. "Now I see why you're so up-tight. Does Lassiter know what a fix you're in?"

"Most of it. But my first priority right now is finding Fran. If she's willing to give a deposition, when would be a good time for you?"

"Not sure. The DA up there expects the trial will last from three to five days, but like I said, I think they'll be through with me by day after tomorrow. I could pick up Lassiter and go see her then."

"How can I find you?"

"Through Pop Cheever. If you find Fran and she agrees to cooperate with Lassiter and me, Pop will pass the word to Lassiter and he'll come running. No politician would dare fight a federal case that big. You're working agreement with Lassiter is still valid, but that won't keep me from making special arrangements for you to work for me too. How about it? Are you willing to go undercover for the DEA? If so, I'd like you to do some snooping before going to check on Fran. It'll be like working as an agent without a badge. We have a liberal policy regarding that sort of thing."

"You want to pay me for doing what I planned on doing anyway? I'm afraid I wouldn't be a very good snitch."

"Stop thinking like an ex-con. A snitch is somebody who informs on his friends. A paid informant gathers stuff about the bad guys and passes it on to the good guys."

"Okay, okay. I'll do it without the schoolboy lecture. But I'm curious. Just how much do you already know about what's goin' on in Northville?"

"Zapata tells us Punk is strung out and selling dope. Lots of people come to his place to use crack, meth and pot. What I need is something we can take to federal court, but Rick hasn't seen anything big go down that he can swear to. He thinks your sheriff and chief of police are involved in the business, but doesn't know how. He knows about Cato Hamilton, but hasn't been able to find out who took his place or who the big cheese in this county is."

Despite his distrust of the legal system and cops in general, Raz was impressed by Schroeder's sincerity. "If the local bad guys don't whack me by the time you get back, I think I know where to get some stuff you can use."

Schroeder nodded. "Sounds good. My guess is the local operation will start falling like a deck of cards with the first case we file. Just don't kill anybody or get too wild. We'll disown you if you go too crazy."

"A man can't box with one hand tied behind his back. If you wanna catch crooks, you gotta play by their rules."

"Just don't do anything I wouldn't do." He got to his feet. "I'll check in with Pop when I get back. In the meantime, you can slip a note under the door here if something hot goes down. Zapata will find it, call Pop and Lassiter and set up a meeting with him, or me when I get back. If Lassiter is able to move in before I do, give him Mazurka and tell him about Fran." He extended his hand. "Good luck."

Schroeder left, and Raz slowly climbed to his feet. He went to the window and pulled up the shade to see if anybody was outside. The sun had set, and the streetlights hadn't come on yet. There was a red Dodge parked in front of a green pickup outside one of the little cabins three doors down. He didn't see Zapata.

He limped out to the van, got in and drove south to avoid going through the Square again. A hundred yards or so down the highway, he turned onto a dirt road that took him over the railroad tracks and back to The Quarters.

He was surprised to find Zapata's Caddy parked on the street a block from where he'd been arrested. Puzzled, he slowed down and looked up and down the street, but didn't see the agent. Moving closer with his headlights trained on the big car, he took a closer look; still no Zapata.

Sensing something was up, he sped up and headed for the back way to McShan Road and his parents' house. If Schroeder and Lassiter wanted more good evidence fast, he knew where to find it before leaving for Houston. He couldn't allow concerns about proper procedure to get in the way. *Gotta fight fire with fire, daddy used to say.*

There'll be plenty of time to file charges against Tank and Olin after it's safe for me to come out of hiding. He savored the thought of the two crooks being sent to prison. *Sweet revenge for the beating Tank gave me and so much more.*

CHAPTER 24

Two drive-bys at his parents' house showed no sign of a hit man waiting for him. So, on his third pass he swerved into the driveway, stopped at the barn and killed the motor and lights. Feeling his way over to the corn crib, he rummaged around until he found his dad's crowbar. He put it on the seat, backed up behind the house and got out again.

The quarter-moon made barely enough light to see as he moved to the front of the house. He crossed the porch and entered his bedroom. In the dark, he moved his hand under the bed and found his flashlight. The batteries were dead, so he went back to the van and drove to Stump Skeeters' store.

Stump was closing up, but he unlocked the front door and asked Raz in. Glancing at the van, then at Raz's legs, Stump said calmly, "Glad to see you're still kickin', Raz. You bein' back has created quite a stir in town."

This quiet, pleasant man never asked about anybody's personal life or took part in idle gossip, but because of what Tank and Olin had done to Raz two years ago, he always made it clear that Raz had his sympathy. The eighty-year-old storekeeper had never been part of the merchant clique in Northville, either.

"So I've noticed," Raz replied. "Thanks for your concern and for stayin' open for me. I need two C batteries and one of them little throwaway cameras."

Stump glanced at the redness along the side of Raz's neck and turned to the shelves for the batteries. "Ain't got one of them cameras."

"I need a camera bad and I don't have enough money for a cellphone. You got somethin' cheap you could sell me on credit?" He didn't want to reveal much or arouse Stump's curiosity.

"Nope." His eyes lit up, suddenly. "But my daughter left her old SKR camera here. You can borrow it, if you're hard pressed for one."

Raz nodded. "I'd appreciate it, if you have film for it."

Stump disappeared into his living quarters, coming back promptly with a small black camera.

Raz examined the 35 mm Fuji. "There's half a roll of film gone on here already. You sure she won't mind?"

Stump shook his head. "She won't. It's been sittin' here forever. Ever'body likes them digital ones on their phones now. You can bring her pictures back after you have 'em developed. Think there's another roll o' film 'round here someplace. Ya want it too?"

"There's ten left on here, so I'm good. Thanks." He paid for the batteries with the change in his pocket.

"Frenchy come by askin' if I seen ya. Seemed real worried about ya." He glanced at the van.

Raz knew he recognized it, because Frenchy bought gas and groceries here. "If he comes by again, tell him his van and me are both okay."

Stump glanced at Raz's legs. "I will, I guess. Whatever you're doin', better be sure it's worth the risk. Folks hereabouts don't want nothin' else bad happenin' to ya."

"I appreciate that, and I'll try to be careful."

Returning to the van, he drove past the city limits sign and turned off at the first street, went a few blocks and parked behind the old cotton gin. He put the new batteries in the flashlight, and put it and the camera in his back pockets. He picked up the crowbar and limped to the alley behind the businesses facing the Square.

Even with the streetlights up front and the quarter moon above, it was dark in the shadows. In familiar territory now, he soon found the back door of the hotel. He stood still for a moment and listened. Nothing. Convinced no one else was in the immediate area, he moved under the pull-down fire escape to listen again. He heard nothing but a car over on the highway. Northville, as usual, had rolled up its sidewalks early. It was so quiet, the crunch of gravel under his boots sounded like thunder.

He studied the iron fire escape's dim outline against the night sky. Raising the crowbar he hooked it over the last step and pulled. Rust had frozen the pivot points, but he was able to pull the steps to the point where the counterbalance took effect by taking hold of the bar with both hands. With it all the way down, he put his foot on the bottom step. Suddenly he heard a man's voice, then a woman's. Holding his breath, he tried to decide if they were coming his way.

The man spoke again, and then two women laughed. He thought they were still on the Square. He started breathing again, and decided he should find out what was going on. Knowing who was out at this time of night might give him an idea of what they were doing. The stores were all closed, so chances were that anyone out and about was up to no good.

Stepping over to the back corner of the hotel, he saw an unusual and puzzling sight. Beneath a streetlight, three attractive, well-dressed young women were standing beside a black Lincoln talking to Shag Shammerhorn and Sonny Irby. Judging from their jerky mannerisms and volume, he guessed they'd just snorted some coke.

A closer look identified the car as the one he'd seen in the garage at Pop's former home. However, that wasn't the most surprising thing about the scene. One of the women, a blond in a white dress, was the one who'd tried to pick him up in Houston. She was holding onto Shag's arm like she was afraid he'd leave her.

Shag patted her butt and said, "See you girls again next week. If I'm out of town, one of my studs will fill in."

"But, honey," the blonde said, "I don't wanna leave. I'm feeling too good."

Shag opened the car's door and pushed the redhead into the passenger's seat, saying, "There's plenty more of the good stuff where that came from, baby. Now, you girls go straight home and stay there 'til we're ready for you the first of the week." He shut the door.

The streetlight gave Raz a good view of Sonny Irby. He was as ugly as ever, but fatter. Wearing a dark suit, white shirt and black tie, he looked like he was dressed up for church. Sonny hugged the girl by his side, squeezed her boob, and then smacked her butt. "It's been fun," he said, with a silly laugh. "I always enjoy meeting Shag's girls."

Sonny's date slid behind the wheel. Waving, she drove away as Shag and Sonny walked out of sight toward the front of the hotel.

Raz got back to the van as fast as his sore knees would allow, started it and tried to catch up with the women. When he couldn't, he turned around and headed back to the business district, turning down a side street after passing Punk's place. He caught the flash of a red taillight out of the corner of his eye when he turned. Stopping, he backed up and turned down Clarenton, moving without lights until he spotted the Lincoln's dome light come on up ahead. He pulled over, rolled down the tinted window and watched.

The giggling women climbed out of the car and walked up the driveway to a carport. Without knocking, they went inside. Looking around, Raz recognized the area. It was where Gerta Hutto used to live.

It had never been a secret that Gerta was well taken care of. Horton Snitker made sure of it after she threatened to sue and publicly acknowledge him as her baby-daddy. Raz assumed the support stopped when Punk came of age, but seeing the women here made him think she had connections with Shag's business at the old hotel. She might even be connected to the ones who ran Tank and Olin.

Driving slowly by the house, he remembered his mother-in-law telling him about calling Gerta about Patti. In view of what he'd just witnessed, he now knew why. It made him nauseous and angry.

He turned right at the first east-west street, flipping on his lights as he headed back to the Square. He thought about his friend's telling him Patti was seen going in and out of Gerta's house and the old hotel. They'd said when she went in the hotel, she didn't come back out for several days, and when she finally left, she was pale and hollow-eyed.

On a hunch, Raz drove back to the Chevron Station on the highway at the end of Market Street and parked behind a hedge near its restrooms. Like all other legitimate businesses in town, the station was closed at this hour. The only place open was Punk's further down the highway. It was brightly lit, and he could hear the music coming from the place even here.

He walked to the payphone near a streetlight on the curb, put in a quarter and asked information for Gerta's number. He dialed and sat down with a low groan. After the fourth ring, a giggling woman said, "Hello?"

"Gerta?"

"No, honey. This is Clarie. Just a minute."

A husky, cautious voice said, "Who's this?"

"Gerta, darlin'," he said. "This is your boss's favorite man to hate, Raz Jester. How's he feelin' tonight? Did you rub down his sore parts before tuckin' him in?"

A moment of silence, then, "Why're you callin' me, Raz?"

"'Cause Mrs. Lawther said you could tell me what happened to Patti before she died. That's all I ever wanted, you know, to find out what she was up to after leavin' me. That, and who killed her. Olin and Tank must've thought they couldn't tell me without spoilin' their cozy arrangement with the dope dealers. I figured you might not feel that way if you thought you could save your worthless son, Punk, from going to prison."

She told the other women to be quiet, then said, "I was hopin' you weren't comin' back to make more trouble."

"Make trouble. Me?" He laughed. "Don't play dumb. After what happened today, you're smart enough to realize your boss and Tank don't plan on lettin' me live. I know you can help me, so why don't you answer some questions and keep yourself and Horton Snitker's bastard son out of jail?"

"What happened today? What are you talkin' about?" Her voice was suddenly more concerned.

"Gerta, don't you know it's not polite to ask questions when you already know the answers? Are you gonna talk to me or not?"

"Why would I?"

"Already told you. You're smarter than Olin and Tank, darlin'. They don't believe I have Blackie Mazurka and that he's ready to start makin' deals. I might even give him to you in exchange for the information I want. How's that sound? Put you in good standing with the law *and* the crooks."

There was a long silence. Raz was thought she'd dropped the phone. Finally, she said, "I'll tell you all I — uh — heard about what happened to Patti if you bring Mazurka to my place. Can you be here in, say, ten minutes?"

He laughed. "Olin and Tank must not be feelin' so good if it takes 'em that long to jerk on their socks and get there."

"Then I'll come to you," she said. "Just tell me where you are."

"You'd do that for me? How sweet. Your precious li'l Punk will love you for it. I'm sittin' in at the payphone at the Chevron station."

"You alone?"

"As alone as an honest man at a Northville city council meetin'."

"Then stay put. I'll be right over."

Hanging up, Raz snapped a branch off a bush near the curb and unbuttoned his shirt. Standing the branch in the corner of the booth, he draped the shirt over the limbs, squaring the shoulders as best he could, and put his hat on top of it, then he got in the van.

He didn't have to wait long. A black Merc came down Market Street and drove to within fifty feet of the booth, then stopped. Both side windows rolled down and Raz saw Smeddish and a large unknown passenger in the car. *Maybe that's Alabama.*

A long gun barrel came out the rear window. Three quick blasts shattered the still night and the payphone. The Merc burned rubber and turned south on the highway.

Raz whistled. "Gerta, you're a naughty girl, up to your baggy eyes in dirty business."

Retrieving his tattered hat and shirt, he drove up Market two blocks, taking care to detour around the burned-out Soup Kitchen. Just being that close to it sent fresh waves of guilt and anger sweeping over him.

Parking by the old cotton gin again, he walked back to the alley and studied the rear entrance to God's Palace. The latest attempt on his life, and his being so near Boobs' old place had given a new sense of urgency to his mission.

He doubted anything else would surprise him more than finding out how much clout Gerta had with the gang paying off Tank and Olin. He needed to know just how she fit into Northville's chain of command. *Is she Rudy? She's cunning and ruthless enough, and being Olin's secretary/dispatcher puts her at the center of everythin' goin' on in town.*

A siren screamed from the courthouse extension toward the Chevron station. It was a good time to check out the vacant building next to the hotel. He'd been arrested the first time he tried it over two years ago.

He climbed up the fire escape as fast as his sore knees would allow, stopping at the second floor to rest and listen. He heard nothing but loud talk over at the service station. *So far so good.*

He pointed the flashlight's beam at the ledge protruding from the first floor and stepped out on it. Shining the light on deep, mortared joints, he moved his other foot from the iron steps. Easing forward, he reached the corner and jumped onto the roof of the adjoining building. The pain in his knees dropped him when he landed, and he lay motionless for several minutes before he could stand again.

He remembered the front wall of the old store extended above the roof by about a foot, and that the side wall became increasingly lower as it sloped gently to the rear.

Enough light came from a streetlight on the Square for him to find the small wooden enclosure at the center that housed the stairs that ran from a closet on the first floor of the vacant store to the roof. During his previous visit, the stairwell door had been locked from the inside. He'd been trying to pry it open in broad daylight when Olin jumped over the side wall and arrested him.

He swung the flashlight around and saw several lounge chairs and a table near the rear wall, plus what appeared to be a wheel and rope hoist. He guessed that was where deliveries were received.

He wedged the flat end of the crowbar in the jamb and pushed hard. A section broke off but the door didn't move. Examining the door more closely, he saw it was made of plywood reinforced with two-by-sixes around the edges and across its middle. He guessed the lock was near the end of the center crosspiece.

He pushed the curved tip of the bar under the bottom edge of the crosspiece and pried. The beam moved away from the plywood about an inch, barely making a sound. He continued prying its opposite end until it was loose enough to pull off by hand.

He put the bar's flat end under the vertical two-by-six and pulled it off in the same manner, then shut off the flashlight. He could still hear excited voices over at the Chevron station. Rock music thumped from the old hotel now, but the building below him was quiet.

Turning his light back on and pointing it at the door, he found a crack in the top of the plywood and began working the flat tip of the crowbar into it.

He snapped off a sliver about three inches long, then continued to dig and pry at the layers until the tips of two screws came into view. Prying away the wood around them, he put the curved end of the bar against them and pushed. The door swung open. Glancing at his watch, he saw he'd been there for half an hour.

The flashlight lit the narrow stairwell down to a landing. Loud rap music from the hotel covered any sounds he made. He limped down the stairs to the ground level, and found himself in a small storage room filled with dusty cardboard boxes and old mannequins. In addition to the strong odor of mildew, there was a garbage can half-filled with foul-smelling food wrappers, used feminine hygiene products and syringes. Moving things around with a coat hanger he'd picked up off the floor, he saw discarded panty hose and several empty cosmetic boxes. He took the camera out of his picked and took a picture of what he found.

He turned off the flashlight and opened the door that led to the vacant first floor, stopping again to listen. He heard nothing but the deep bass rumble coming from next door. He also smelled pot smoke coming from somewhere close by.

The music stopped and he found himself surrounded by an ominous silence, made more threatening by the darkness. His pulse pumped faster as he stood still and listened to make sure no one else was around. He disliked rap, but he wished they'd start playing it again.

Convinced he was alone, he turned on the light and found plywood covered the entire front wall behind the showcases. He directed his flashlight beam along its walls. The old store was about fifty feet wide and one hundred feet long. In the back corner next to the hotel, he found new plywood walls that made a room about twenty feet square. Wooden steps went up the wall near a door at the second floor level, connecting it to the hotel.

He moved to the new room, and decided it wasn't occupied. He pried its door open, and the smell of perfume assaulted him. He swung his light around the room, finding an unmade king-sized bed, a chest-of-drawers, some chairs, a sofa and a TV. He stepped inside and saw a large electrical cord running across the floor. Following the cord, he found two large lights mounted on a horizontal metal rod, and beneath them was a video camera mounted on a tripod.

The sight struck a vaguely familiar chord in his brain. Then he remembered the word his friend Tim Barton had scrawled on his pickup door in blood: MOVIE. A chill rushed through him.

He stared transfixed at the bed and camera, convinced Shag and his friends were filming pornos in this room. A wave of revulsion swept over him when remembered Patti had spent a lot of time at the hotel before she was killed. If Tim had talked to him before he was killed, he probably would've told him he'd seen Patti in a porno over at Punk's place. The thought sickened him.

Anger replaced revulsion as he thought about Punk's other patrons seeing the mother of his child in homemade porno flicks. It was hard to believe Patti's heroin habit had pushed her to doing something so despicable.

Why'd Sonny Irby risk getting involved in such a sordid business? He's a banker for Christ's sake. Maybe he's still so unlucky with women he had to resort to prostitutes. Or maybe the pervert came to watch. Seeing him with Shag also brought other possibilities to mind. *That big-nosed banker could be the financial backer for the local branch of the Dixie Mafia and Shag's film business. He could also be laundering drug money at Horton Snitker's bank.*

Raz rubbed the scar on his face as he raged inside. He thought about Pop's advice and how Zeke and Aunt Beulah urged him to think before acting. *I can't afford to lose control now. There's too much to do. I gotta take some pics and hope the narcs can use 'em.*

He shined the light back on the area near the bed. On the table next to the bed was an ashtray brimming with cigarette butts and roaches. There was also a crack pipe and a spoon with a bent handle. A woman's gown lay on the foot of the bed. On the table on the opposite side, he saw two burned candles and a box of syringes. He looked closer at pieces of tinfoil and saw crack residue.

In the top drawer of the chest-of-drawers he found a box of videotapes, some titled, some unused. Further rummaging produced still pictures of nude women in suggestive poses. He didn't dare look at more than two or three of these for fear of seeing the one he didn't want to find.

There were open boxes of cosmetics, panties, dirty bras and a couple of fast food receipts issued to God's Palace by the surplus commodities office in Coldwater. There were also two books of food stamps.

He took a picture of the open drawer's contents and a close-up of the receipts made out to God's Palace. He also took a picture of the camera on the tripod with the bed and chest in the background, being sure he got the drug paraphernalia on the table.

Stepping outside the room, he walked backward until the corner of the new wall and the stairs coming from the hotel's second story fit into the camera frame, then snapped another picture. He also took one of the boarded-up front walls of the store. He had three shots left on the roll.

Returning to the room, he put two of the titled videotapes in his back pockets and pulled out the next drawer. It contained a box of unused videotapes, light bulbs and more photos.

He jumped suddenly and turned off his flashlight when the door at the top of the new stairs opened, flooding the space with light. He heard voices, then footsteps as someone started down.

Rushing from the makeshift studio, he sprinted toward the closet stairway, and was almost to it when a man called out, "I hear something, Shag. Listen!"

A switch clicked, and the old store lit up even more as Raz stepped into the stairwell. He turned on his flashlight and shined its beam on the first step.

"Somebody's been here!" another man yelled. "The party room door is open."

Two shots rang out and bullets ripped through the wall of the stairwell as Raz bolted up the steps, unconcerned now about how much noise he made or how much his knees hurt.

"He's goin' to the roof!" Shag shouted. "Take a couple of boys out back and head 'im off!"

Raz took the stairs two at a time. When he got to the roof, he ran for the corner where he'd crawled over. He had just stepped out on the ledge when the back door of the hotel opened and two men rushed out, swinging their lights down the alley, then up toward him.

Before he could jump back, a beam found him and a man shouted, "There he is! Come on up, Shag!"

The man fired and a bullet ricocheted off a brick near Raz's head. He turned and stumbled back on the roof. He heard feet climbing the hidden stairs, leaving him no escape but the side wall.

He reached the opposite side of the roof just as someone jumped out onto the roof from the stairwell behind him and fired a shot. Crawling up on the wall, he leaped to the roof of the next building, but his sore knees gave way, causing him to fall as another shot whizzed by. The man behind him shouted, "Whoever you are, stand up with your hands high!" It was Shag.

Raz felt no new pain from a hit, so he climbed to his feet, struggled over to the next wall in a crouch, and begun scrambling over it when another shot rang out. A sharp pain hissed through his left arm above the elbow, but he managed to get over the wall, falling on his back with a grunt. Knowing he couldn't run, he rolled over against the wall and looked up.

Shag's flashlight's beam moved around on the roof beyond Raz. "Damn you, Jester," Shag growled. "I know it's you. I'm gonna finish what the others started!"

Raz held his breath and saw a leg coming over the wall near his head. He grabbed the foot and jerked hard, Shag fell on his back, dropping his flashlight and pistol. Both scrambled to their feet. Shag dived for the gun but the crowbar bashed against his head felled him without a sound. Raz scooped up the pistol and shoved it inside his belt.

"Hey, Shag?" somebody on the ground shouted. "Where are you, man? You get 'im yet?"

Raz heard somebody else running up the stairs as he picked up his flashlight and limped toward the back wall. He realized if the men on the ground moved up the alley, he'd be caught in the middle with nowhere to run. It appeared Cato's prediction was about to come true; he'd just been off by a few hours.

CHAPTER 25

Turning off his flashlight and shoving it into his front pocket, Raz felt for the four-inch metal vent pipe on the brick wall. Most of these old buildings were built before the advent of inside plumbing, so all supply lines and venting systems had to be on the outside of the structures.

"Bingo!" Raz whispered as he swung his sore legs over the edge and slid down the pipe. He lost his grip just before landing and fell to the ground with a grunt.

"Who's that?" asked a voice in the alley. "That you, Shag?"

Raz hurled a handful of gravel beyond them and while they chased the sound he limped away.

Another voice joined those behind him. "What the hell's goin' on?" It was Tank. Raz was surprised to be relieved that the sheriff hadn't died from his burns.

A man shouted back, "We caught somebody breakin' in our party room, but I think Shag got 'im."

"It's that jailbird quarterback," Tank said. "This means he wasn't at the damned payphone like Gerta said. Where the hell is Shag, anyway? Find 'im and make sure he got that asshole this time."

"Shag? You all right up there?" the man called again. "Where's Paco?"

Raz got to his van, climbed in and drove away. Two blocks from the scene, he flipped on the headlights, and crossed the highway on his way to Town Lake.

His knees throbbed so much that raising his right foot to work the brake was next to impossible. He ached all over. He needed sleep, but doubted rest would erase the shock of finding the evidence in the makeshift porn studio. His anger intensified now that he wasn't being chased and shot at. *I had no idea how far she'd go to get a fix. What else could I have done to save Patti?*

To beat back the guilt prompted by the question, he turned his mind to happy thoughts about Becky. It felt like the life he wanted to live with his daughter had been jumping out of reach ever since he got home. Only stubborn pride and the conviction that certain promises must be kept, no matter the price or method required, had prevented him from giving in to superior forces. Aunt Ruth believed the old ways were dying and he was beginning to suspect she was right.

I'm so tired I don't know if I'll make it. He rolled down the window, hoping the night air would refresh him. It helped, but the road ahead still looked fuzzy. *Stay alert,* he coached. *If you don't get there soon, you'll pass out.*

The lake house should still be a safe place to rest. No one knows I've been hiding there. Most fishermen had abandoned this lake now that there was a new bigger one a few miles away. *After a rest, I'll write a note asking for a meeting with Lassiter and Schroeder. Not tonight though. Tank and his cronies will be combing the town for me.*

No lights were on in the cabin, but he still parked and watched it for a few minutes just to be safe. The only sound was croaking frogs. It was a clear night and he could make out the silhouettes of the boat shed and cabin, but knew he wouldn't be able to spot anyone hiding in the shadows.

He entered the driveway with his lights off, drove past the cabin and parked behind the garage, almost falling when he got out. Recovering his balance, he limped to the front porch. Then he remembered Anita telling him the key would be under the *back* steps. He'd just turned around when he heard something move in the shadows near the swing.

Dropping to the ground on his belly, pulse pounding, he looked in the direction of the sound, wishing he had the crowbar. He reached for his flashlight, and his hand bumped against Shag's pistol. He'd stuck it under his belt and forgotten about it. He jerked it out and yelled, "Who's there?"

"Raz, it's me," a woman's voice responded quickly, "Anita."

He stood up. "Are you crazy? I could've shot you. You weren't supposed to come back here."

"I wanted to make sure you were all right," She was just a dark shadow as she moved across the porch. "I figured you'd at least want something to eat."

"Does anybody know you're here?" he asked as he moved closer.

"Nobody you don't trust. Come on in."

Feeling his way up the steps and along the front wall, he followed her inside. She promptly closed the door and flipped on the ceiling light.

The light blinded them both for a moment. When Anita could see, she looked at him in shock, her eyes wide. "What happened to you this time? Your hat and shirt are full of holes, you're stooped over like an old man and there's blood on your arm." Then she saw the pistol in his hand. "What's *that* for?"

He looked at the gun. "It must be for shooting ex-quarterbacks, since it belonged to a man that tried to kill me. Mind if I sit down now?"

When she continued staring at him, he added, "I had a run-in with some guys who liked to shoot at moving targets. I'm okay, but I need to sit down now, before I fall down. My knees are killing me."

She took his arm. "Come in the kitchen. The shades are all down in there too. I'll make coffee and clean you up. You're a mess."

He sat down with a long sigh, and put the gun on the table.

"Have you eaten?"

He shook his head. "First, I need a beer. Feel like I could drink a whole case. How'd you get out here? I didn't see your car." Suddenly remembering his witness, "What if that killer in the boat shed got up here? Did you even think about that?"

"That's why I had Ethan Lewis come out with me." She walked to the refrigerator. "He made sure your killer was still harmless."

"That's good, but now somebody else knows you're out here. An employee of my ex-father-in-law to boot."

"Raz, you've always trusted Ethan."

"Where is he now?"

She gave Raz a can of Miller Lite and said, "In his truck by my car, out in the trees. Any more questions?"

He took a couple of swallows of the cold beer while watching her fill a pan with water. She then got a cloth and soap from a shelf and said over her shoulder, "Take off that ragged shirt and your pants, too, so I can get you cleaned up. I'll check your back and those sore legs while I'm at it. Once that's done, I'll get some of dad's old clothes for you."

He drank the rest of the beer. "Before you do all that, I'd better check on my prize witness. Do you have makings for a couple of sandwiches? I shouldn't starve him before the narcs take him off my hands. I'd take him a cot if I had one."

"Sandwiches coming up. There's an old folding cot in the garage. Daddy used to sleep on it out on the porch. I'll get a quilt and pillow."

"Great. Better give me another jug of water too."

He found the cot hanging on the back wall, and put it on the porch. He walked back into the kitchen and said, "If I make that boat shed any nicer, I'll have to start charging Mazurka rent."

She put four sandwiches in a paper sack and added a quart jar of water. She also put a rolled-up blanket on the table beside the sack. When Raz picked them up, she slipped a key from the top of the refrigerator into his front pocket. "I had Ethan put a lock on the door. I'll help you since you can't carry everything. I'll take the jar and sack if you can handle the blanket and cot."

"You're a darlin'," he said, turning toward the back door. "Think we can get down there without a light? My hands are full."

"I've done it many times."

At the end of the footpath Raz said, "Put your load on the pier. I'll take it the rest of the way. I don't want him to see you. Remember?"

She put the items beside the door. "Are you sure you don't need me?"

"No talking! You're not supposed to say a word around that guy either. Remember? Now scoot. I'll be fine."

He shined his flashlight on the pier and landing beyond until she walked out of sight, then he unlocked the door and pointed the beam at the walkway along the boat slip. "Wake up, handsome. The zookeeper's here." He picked up the food and water.

Mazurka rolled over and held up his hand against the light. "That you, Jester? Get me out of this shack. Don't you know it's against the law to keep me in a place like this?"

"Are you tied up?" Raz asked as he stood near Mazurka's feet. "You're free to go any time you feel like swimming to shore and walking to town. We made a deal. Remember? My part was to board you so your pals won't shoot you before I deliver you to my narc friend. He'll take your sorry hide to a fine hotel. I've told Tank what a great witness you've been already, so I'm sure he and your other former pals are looking for you with their pistols cocked. They all remember what a sweet deal you cut with the DA who prosecuted Cato."

Mazurka mumbled something under his breath that Raz couldn't understand, but there was no mistaking the fear in his eyes. "You could at least bring me a bed. This floor's hard as a rock."

"Keep your shorts on. Relief is on the way." He put the food and water on the boards and returned with the cot and blanket. "This cot's good enough for soldiers and hunters, so it should be good enough for the likes of you. It's a whole lot better than lyin' in a grave." He unfolded the cot and put it against the back wall.

"I still ain't got no bathroom."

"What am I, your nurse? Just roll over and let it fall through the cracks. If you have to do the other, well, improvise." He moved the food and water closer to the gangster and turned the light toward his feet. "How's the leg?"

"Hurts so bad I can hardly turn over."

"You're breaking my heart. At least you won't be tryin' to run off and spoil my plans." He shined the light back on Mazurka's face. "Your friend Gerta tried to have me killed tonight after I offered to swap you for something I'd rather have more."

Mazurka rose to one elbow. "You talked to Gerta? You've really got my ass in a sling now. What did Smeddish say?"

"Who said I talked to Smeddish?"

He didn't answer as he slid his buttocks toward the cot. "Give me a lift, Jester. I got to get on that thing before the snakes find me."

Raz unrolled the blanket on the cot and dropped the pillow at one end. Putting his hands under Mazurka's shoulders, he told him, "I'll get this end. You can use your good leg to raise your other parts."

Mazurka cried out when Raz pulled him up, but managed to shift his buttocks and legs onto the cot. He uttered a few expletives when Raz adjusted his broken leg,

Raz put the water beside the cot and gave him the sandwiches. "Sleep tight and don't let the moccasins bite. I doubt they'll climb up the legs of that cot, but if one does, give him my regards and lie still. It won't bite as long as you don't move. I'll bring you more to eat tomorrow and take you out of here as soon as one of my narc friends shows. If you get real riled about the accommodations, just consider how lucky you are I didn't let you fry in your car."

Walking out and locking the door behind him, Raz limped up the incline realizing he had to give Mazurka to the narcs real soon, or infection from his leg wound would surely kill him. He'd be no good to anybody if he was dead.

He rejoined Anita in the kitchen without meeting her gaze and sat down at the table where another cold beer was waiting for him. Reaching for it, his eyes fell on the pistol, which in turn caused him to remember the party room. Motionless, he stared at the weapon.

Anita put a pan of water on the chair next to him. "Something you want to tell me about?"

He pretended not to hear her at first, but after a long pause, he answered. "Thinking about it is bad enough." His voice sounded strange, not his.

"Okay. But any time you do want to talk about it, I'll be around to listen. Now, let's take off that awful shirt." She unbuttoned the perforated garment, slipped it off his shoulders and exclaimed, "Wow! Your back is still really red."

He took another swallow of beer. "Then I wasn't crazy when I started feeling like I'd been cooked well-done. What a relief."

Ignoring his sarcasm, she soaped the cloth and squeezed it out as he studied the spot where Shag's bullet had nicked his arm. Dried blood trailed down to his hand, but there was no new blood seeping out of the wound.

She gently wiped his arm "As soon as I clean this, I'll put some more salve on your back and neck. How are the knees?"

"Not so good." He stood up. When he dropped his pants, the camera and tapes hit the floor with a loud thud. He sat back down and she moved around to pull off his boots. "I'd kill for a shot of Novocaine in each one. If you don't have any, an ice pack will do."

She glanced at the camera and tapes, but made no comment as she continued cleaning the wound. Raz jumped when he heard footsteps on the back porch but relaxed when Ethan Lewis entered the room.

"Hi, Raz," he said, looking at his naked back.

"Thanks for coming out, Ethan," Raz said, offering his hand. "And for sca-rin' the crap outta me. I got so tied up with my prize in the boat shed, I clean forgot about you sitting out there. Sorry."

"No sweat. Anita gave me a couple of cold ones to pass the time." He looked at Raz's wounded arm. "The vultures are still after you, I see."

"They'll be after you, too, if they find out you been out here."

"What're you gonna do with that guy in the boat shed? He needs to go to the emergency room in Coldwater."

"He wouldn't live out the night there. He's toppin' the local hit list with me. Hope you didn't let him get a good look at you."

"I didn't. You need me for anything else?"

"Not tonight, but thanks. When you leave, take the long way home. If anybody stops you, have a good story ready about where you've been. Tank and his friends will whack anybody stoppin' them from gettin' at me and that killer down there. It makes no difference who they work for."

Ethan gave him a sober look. "I work for the people of Northville. Okay? You know, the town that's been in an uproar ever since you got back, but now..." He stopped, as if wanting to spare Raz some more bad news.

Raz sensed trouble. "Things couldn't get any worse, so let me have it."

"We made a run out to that fire to pick up Tank and Olin. Olin's in pretty good shape, but Tank got second-degree burns on his legs and one hand, and his face and neck are blistered. Olin told my Chief that they've filed felony assault charges against you, two counts."

Raz heard Anita moan, and for a moment forgot how badly his knees hurt. "I guess he figured he had to give me a reward for pullin' him out of the fire. All I need now is for the state of Texas to declare war on me, too."

"What will you do next?" Anita asked him.

"More of the same, only faster."

"Everybody's talking about what Tank and Olin are puttin' you through," Ethan told Raz. "Cecil Cassidy and a couple of his friends even approached Tank at the doctor's office in Coldwater, but he refused to talk unless they brought you in. The rest of your friends are too scared to say anything. It's a damn shame. If you need me, give me a holler. Good night." He nodded to Anita and left through the back door.

The kitchen soon smelled of soap, skin balm and alcohol as Anita went about tending to his wounds and sore back. She hadn't said a thing since Ethan left, and Raz knew she was worried. He wasn't exactly free of concern himself.

Impressed by how much Anita had done for him, he focused on her instead of his problems. Her manner and helpful acts had wiped away any doubt he had about how much she cared for him. He was lucky to have her in his life again.

He watched her small hands moving gently and efficiently. It had always amazed him how the feminine touch could sooth a man during troubled times, it was true now too. Besides taking his mind off his aches and pains, her attentiveness and nearness eased his worries about his survival.

Sensing his eyes on her, she became self-conscious. When she finished bandaging the gunshot wound, she disappeared down the hall, then came back with a faded blue shirt and khaki pants. "You can put these on after I see to your back. Then it's an ice pack for each of those knees after you lie down."

He looked at the camera on the floor, wanting to tell her what he found out about Patti. He decided he'd tell her later, when there wasn't so much to worry about.

He put the camera and videotapes on the table. "I'll hide these out back somewhere. Don't want you to throw them away while you're cleaning up."

She sat down. "That's what you couldn't talk about?"

He nodded.

"What good're they to you? What'll you do with them?"

"I'm hoping the narcs will use them to get search warrants and file charges."

"You're still working for the state?" It sounded more like a reprimand than a question.

"No more than when I went to prison. It started after a state narc came to me and said he and Pop needed someone who wasn't afraid of taking chances to get solid evidence so they could clean up Northville. I needed help finding Patti's killer, so we made a deal. It seemed like a fair swap at the time."

"You hit Tank so you'd be sent to prison? Only a crazy person would do something like that, Raz."

His jaw muscles rippled, "I would've done it for you if you'd been my murdered wife."

"Oh, well..." She seemed at a loss for words. "What a sweet but morbid thing to say, Raz Jester. I still wish you hadn't done it, but I have the greatest respect for you because you did. Am I forgiven?"

He nodded.

Looking at the camera, she asked, "Want me to take the film to WalMart in Coldwater? They have a one-hour developing service."

He shook his head, not wanting her to take any more risks or see the pictures.

"I'll get the ice," she said, and walked to the refrigerator.

He picked up the pistol. It was a Sig-Sauer 9mm with a staggered clip. Ejecting the cartridge from the firing chamber, he pushed six more rounds out of the magazine. He reloaded the gun and put another round in the firing chamber, making sure the safety was on.

The metallic sounds caused Anita to flinch "Please don't do that," she said. "I hate guns. They're made for killing people."

"Or to *prevent* people from killing me." His eye moved away from the gun to the old sword leaning against the cabinet. "Folks have come a long way in their methods of killing other folks."

She suspected his fatigue was affecting his thinking, but didn't ask him to explain his remark as he limped over to pick up the sword. When sliding it out of the scabbard it made more metal against metal sounds. Anita cringed again, then left for the front room with the ice trays. He leaned the unsheathed sword against the cabinet, wondering how many men it killed or maimed in the fight for a lost cause. *Am I fighting for a lost cause, too?*

Anita was turning down the covers when he joined her. "Never been so glad to see a bed in my life," he said, sitting down on the edge of the mattress. He stretched out on his sore back with a long sigh.

"I seem to remember a time or two that you must have forgotten."

Their eyes met, and for an instant, a surge of emotion made him want to pull her down against him, but his aches and pains wouldn't let him.

She sat the bowl on the floor and put the ice bag against his knees, securing it with a pillow. "This will take care of both knees as long as you hold them together."

"I always thought it was the girl who was supposed to keep her knees clamped shut as tight as a vise," he said, hoping to brighten her mood.

She adjusted the pillow. "Sounds like you're feeling better already."

He watched her straighten the sheet around his feet and wondered why she was so somber. Women's moods had always been hard to read, but he could usually tell when they were holding back their true feelings. When they were, they usually broke the ice by asking a question.

She sat down by the side of the bed and said, "Does what you found tonight help explain what happened to Patti?"

That particular question surprised him, and it must have showed in his expression, because she quickly added, "I hope you don't mind me asking. You have too much to worry about already."

"That's okay. I found a few more pieces of the puzzle. It shows how she was used before they killed her."

She put her hand on his. "I'm sorry you had to find out."

"You already knew?"

"I heard rumors, like everybody else. I figured you'd heard the same things."

"What do you think I found out tonight that used to be rumors?"

She dropped her eyes, not answering him.

"Don't play games with me. Never could stand a woman throwing out little stingers and pretending not to know the answer to her question. If you've got something to say about Patti, out with it."

She folded her hands in her lap. "All right." She searched for the right words. "The truth is, I forgave Patti a long time ago for stealing you away from me. But I still think about you and her, and Becky. I know how much you loved Patti, so please understand I want to avoid saying anything that would dishonor that."

"You couldn't destroy that if you tried. Patti's dead. Talk to me. I'm still alive."

She looked at a faded picture of a water wheel on the wall, obviously dreading what she was about to say. "This is really the first chance I've had to talk to you about Patti. She had so much going for her: beauty, great personality, and her daddy's big plans. But like other teenagers who thought they had to go along with the crowd, she started making bad choices, like smoking pot and taking pills. She knew I hated the stuff. That's why she was so afraid I'd tell you about her meeting Punk and his friends from time to time during her senior year."

Feeling a sudden knot in the pit of his stomach, Raz pushed the ice bag aside to sit up on the side of the bed. "She told you she did that?"

Anita nodded. "I heard about it, and when I confronted her, she admitted it. Patti assured me she stopped goin' to Punk's parties after his friends got too crazy and scared her. They zoned out on grass and pills, and even tried to make her swallow somethin' without tellin' her what it was. She said one of the boys dropped a pill in Francis Kline's beer so they could have sex with her. They made her watch, thinkin' it would turn her on."

"Is all this leading up to something else I didn't know about at the time?"

"Yes. Now, don't get mad, Raz. Please. You said you wanted to hear me out."

"I still do. Just don't drag it out."

"Okay, but don't give me a knuckle sandwich if you don't like the punch line."

"I doubt you'll ever get to it."

"You always were in too big of a hurry. Keep your shirt on and I'll tell you what Patti said happened after she quit goin' to Punk's parties. There was one particular pothead in our class who scared her more than Punk. He kept after her, even threatened to drop a pill in her coke when she wasn't lookin'."

"Who was the creep?"

"Sonny Irby."

He laughed. "That wimp? He wouldn't hurt a fly. Steal from the bank maybe and spend his money on whores, but nothin' worse." Recalling the scene outside the old hotel, he felt his assessment was off track. "I talked to him a couple of times about Patti before I left, and he hadn't changed all that much. Ugly as ever. Acne scars and that big red nose. Only girls he could make out with were Boobs' party girls in the Back Room."

"Well, he sure never lost his feelings for Patti. A mutual friend told me he chased her right up to the time she was killed. It's the shy ones like him that a girl has to watch out for."

"That was the punch line?"

"Don't rush me. I'm gettin' to it. Right after I tell you about Sonny's first wife."

"What in the world does have to do with anything? Besides, I thought he only had one, that weird Pascal girl."

"You hadn't been gone long before he divorced Carol Pascal and married Eldora Snitker."

"You're pullin' my leg. Horton Snitker's ugly daughter? She was so old and homely that ol' Money Bags must've given him a big promotion for takin' her off his hands."

"Nothing less than bank president. But that's not the most interestin' part of my story. I just mentioned that so I could tell you about Carol. She was committed to the Rusk State Mental Hospital around the time your honky-tonk friend, Fran Druman, disappeared."

Thinking back, he said, "Carol? Carol… Seems like I heard somebody else mention a Carol since I got back." He snapped his fingers. "Of course, that thug in your boat shed. He thought I was talkin' about her when I asked him about my wife. If that was your punch line, her being committed doesn't surprise me. She was always a little off."

"There's more. I ran into Carol last summer when I took the kids over to ride that old state train out of Rusk. She asked about Patti."

Raz shrugged. "Why would that surprise you? Patti did her a couple of favors back in high school."

"But Patti was already dead."

"She just forgot. Crazy people do that."

"No, Raz, she didn't know, even though she was still at home when it happened. When I told her Patti was killed, her face turned white and she had to grab hold of a seat to keep from fallin'. Then she asked about Fran. When I told her she'd disappeared, her eyes took on a wild, frightened look. She started screamin', 'They lied to me!' over and over. Then she ran off and I didn't see her again."

He caressed his scars. "Do you think there's a connection between what happened to Carol and Patti gettin' killed?"

She nodded. "Bingo. *That's* the punch line."

"Never heard of a question being a punch line. To bad the answer didn't come with the question." He picked up the ice pack and put it back on his knees. "This adds another wrinkle in my shorts, 'cause I won't know the answer unless I talk to Carol."

"Be gentle with her if you do, Raz. She's like a whipped puppy, and so mixed up. I feel sorry for her, being looked down on by everybody all her life. Sonny's family was poor and uneducated, but even they looked down on her, saying Sonny married beneath him."

"Do you think Patti married beneath her?" The question slipped out, surprising even him. The matter had been a sore issue with him ever since Isham Lawther had such a fit when he and Patti told him they were getting married. What Pop told him had made the issue even more troubling.

"Are you kiddin'?" She slapped his hand lightly. "Raz Jester, the most desired boy in school? Every girl wanted you. So, lay off that guilt stuff. According to what I heard, you did everythin' possible to save Patti and your marriage after she went off the deep end."

Her assurances didn't remove his lingering doubts, but the news about Carol was encouraging. *Maybe that's another critical link in the murder puzzle. If Carol's working, she must be competent enough to give credible information to the narcs.*

"I'm still having trouble believing Sonny Irby was anything other than a harmless bungler even after what I saw tonight." He told her about seeing him at the hotel. "Patti told him she detested him when we were in high school, but I never suspected why."

"Now you know."

"I'll go see Carol first thing in the morning. My knees will be in good enough shape to travel by then. If I hurry, I can get back in time to meet with my narc friend, if he shows."

He laid back down and she adjusted the ice pack on his knees. "I keep tellin' myself the reason I tried so hard to find whoever killed Patti was because I loved her so much. But lately I've been hearin' a nasty little voice tellin' me she wouldn't have been an addict or wound up dead if I hadn't got her pregnant. She might've still been okay if I hadn't insisted on marryin' her to save our baby."

Anita's eyes showed concern, but she didn't respond. So, he added, "So now, that nasty little monster's askin' if I'm still lookin' for her killer 'cause I loved her, or 'cause I'm trying to ease my guilt."

"That must be quite a burden for a man who loves life as much as you used to. I had no idea you felt that way. Let me repeat. Nobody in this town, with the exception of mean ol' Isham Lawther, blames you for what happened to Patti. Promise me you'll stop blamin' yourself for her death." When he didn't respond, she added, "Think of the life you saved. The one you're responsible for now. Becky wouldn't be in this world if it wasn't for you. I know you love her, and I believe you two will be a family again soon."

"I'm not sure about that. She's been brainwashed by the Lawthers for too long."

"You'll get her back, Raz. If there's any way I can help you do it, I will."

"If I'm still alive to go before a judge, my chances would be better if I was married." He continued looking at the ceiling.

"Probably. You have anybody in particular in mind?"

His eyes met hers. "It wouldn't be like jumpin' into strange waters for us. As I recall, we had a lot in common, and we've hit it off pretty good since I got back home."

"Is that a proposal?"

"More like a statement of fact." He smiled. "But if a proposal is required, would you consider it?"

"I'd have to know you cared enough about me to stay married to me after regainin' custody and a few romps between the sheets." Her voice suddenly became tense. "But you haven't even found Fran yet. I wouldn't want that uncertainty hangin' over my head. Best I don't come between you and her if there's somethin' still there."

He recalled what Pop and Snake told him about his former business associate. "How could I be interested in a woman that's done what she did? If I find her tomorrow night, it'll be strictly business between us."

"Tomorrow night?" She withdrew her hand. "What happens then?"

He told her what Snake said, and about their planned trip to Houston. He added, "Why should that surprise you? You knew I was looking for her."

"It may have somethin' to do with your delicate sense of timing."

When she turned away, he decided it was best to change the subject. "What can you tell me about Gerta Hutto?"

"Besides livin' beyond her means? These last few years she's remodeled her house, bought a big car, traveled to Europe and the Bahamas, and she's big in the women's lib movement now. She's always been AC/DC. You know? But here lately she's sticking to this one guy. Don't know his name."

"How come you know all this stuff?"

"Certainly not because I'm a friend of Gerta's, if that's what you're insinuatin'. Why all these questions about a woman you've always despised?"

"Because she's the reason I almost got killed tonight."

"My God, Raz. Are you sure?"

"You saw the shirt, and the hat." He told her what happened.

She remained silent for some time, studying him. "Raz, you can't keep livin' in this town and lettin' crazy people take shots at you. What are you gonna do about this?"

"Keep on keepin' on. See what the narcs can do with Mazurka and the other evidence I dug up. If they chicken out, I might just grab Becky and run, after I talk to Fran."

"And be charged with kidnappin'? That wouldn't be fair to Becky."

"Probably not, but what else can I do if I don't get a break? I'd be so good to her; she'd learn to love me."

"The Lawthers are the only parents she's ever really known, Raz. Her playmates are here, her nursery school. Jerking her away from all that would be scary for a little girl." She returned her hand to his. "I wish there was somethin' I could do to make this easier for you."

"Ever kidnap anybody?"

"Didn't you hear a thing I said?" She jerked back her hand.

"I'm sure Isham Lawther has ordered Olin to keep a man parked in front of his house 24/7. If I go by there again, I'll get busted."

"I'd be happy to check on her and deliver a message. But don't count me in on doing anythin' drastic."

"You'd go to see her for me?"

"Sure. She and my little girl are in daycare together and they're good friends."

"Great. Tell her how much I love her and we'll be together again real soon. Will you do me one more favor? Go by the nursing home and see what would be involved in moving my mother to an out of town rest home for a while. Just make sure you don't let the staff there know what's going on."

"Consider both done. But my guess is, movin' your mother will be impossible on short notice."

"Seems like everything's impossible lately. I'd appreciate if you'd ask anyway." He put his hand on hers. "You've changed, darlin'. You're a regular tiger now."

"I've changed, you've changed, the times have changed. One thing is still the same for me though. I missed catchin' you before, but unless you still want your honky-tonk girlfriend, I don't mean to let that happen again."

"Catching me?"

"Truth is, I did my damnedest to get pregnant when we were together in high school. Wasn't that awful of me?"

"Terrible. You're waking up that little monster in my brain that keeps asking me nasty questions. This time, it's saying Patti might've wanted an abortion when she found out she was pregnant because she *didn't* love me. That ugly thought really does open a whole new can of worms."

"How you figure that?"

"Because you just said you *wanted* to get pregnant because you *did* love me."

She shook her head. "Why don't you stop tryin' to figure out women and get some sleep, cowboy? Rest will quiet that monster in your head."

"Sorry I'm such bad company."

"Am I complainin'? After yesterday, you don't have any idea what it's been like for me, waitin' to be with you again. I couldn't sleep last night 'cause I was too busy thinkin' about us."

His pulse, which apparently worked independently of his brain, beat faster. "You're safe with me tonight — I've got sore knees — but you'd be safer at home. I'll be leavin' early in the mornin' anyway."

"Not without me seein' to ya again."

"You know what? I'm not half as bothered by my sore spots as I am about my reputation. If my friends ever find out I sent a pretty woman home from my bedroom without some hanky-panky, I'd be the laughing stock of the state."

She grunted. "Men and their egos. Your reputation's safe, 'cause I'm spendin' the night here whether you like it or not. No one has to know I stayed to make sure you got patched up and had a good breakfast in the morning."

She stood up and shut off the table lamp. "Now get some rest. I'll be in the back bedroom if you need me."

When she turned, he caught her hand. "Don't I rate a little kiss for bein' good?"

She leaned down and kissed his lips, and when she tried to stand up, he put his arm around her neck to pull her down again. "One more for the road," he said, kissing her longer and harder.

Her face was flushed when she stood up, "My! Guess I'm lucky you've got sore knees." She walked to the south window and opened it some more. "Maybe the breeze from the lake will cool you off." She disappeared into the kitchen, leaving him in the quietness of the darkened room.

His surroundings were made even darker when the kitchen light was shut off. Moments later he heard the sound of running water as Anita filled the tub.

When he closed his eyes, the events of the day raced through his mind, and he couldn't sleep. The new charges filed against him by Tank and Olin made his situation even more precarious, but he still didn't see how he could've avoided doing what he did.

After about half an hour, he tried reassuring himself with a progress report and a pledge to make even more on his third day home. Surely, his efforts would earn him assistance from Lassiter and Schroeder.

He fluffed his pillow several times and rolled slightly to the left, then to the right, finally settling on his sore back. Eventually, he succumbed to the welcoming embrace of sleep, thinking about the lovely Anita in the back bedroom and hoping to still be alive this time tomorrow night.

CHAPTER 26

Raz woke up to the dim light of dawn coming through the open windows. Raising his head, he listened to see if Anita was already up, but heard nothing. He sat up and flexed his arms, finding his back less sensitive than the day before, he swung his feet to the floor. His knees didn't ache as much either, but they were still sore. Even with these lingering discomforts, he felt refreshed and hungry.

All of these good feelings fled when he stood up and the pain in his knees almost felled him. He remained on his feet only by supporting himself by clinging to the bed. Clenching his teeth, he lifted one foot, then the other, walking in place to work out some of the stiffness.

He took short steps on his way to the bathroom, stopping in the kitchen to listen for sounds coming from the back bedroom. He didn't hear any, and figured Anita was still sleeping. *I'll just peek in on her to make sure she's okay on my way back from the bathroom.*

He stopped at the door of her bedroom and pushed it open. Seeing her lying there with her dark hair spilled out on the pillow and her short pink gown worked up high on her shapely thighs made him think thoughts he didn't have the time or mobility to do anything about today.

Limping to the side of the bed, he leaned down and kissed her cheek. She groaned sleepily, turned on her back and straightened her legs, but didn't open her eyes. The gown rode higher on her thighs, and it was all Raz could do to suppress a groan of longing.

Go take a cold shower. You can't do anything about this right now. He leaned down and kissed her lips and she opened her eyes.

"Raz!" Suddenly fully awake, she pushed her nightgown down and covered her chest with her hands. "Well, I guess you're feeling better," she said, chuckling and looking pointedly at the tent in his shorts.

"Too bad my knees aren't as raring to go as the rest of me. If you have a couple of shots of Novocaine in your medicine bag—"

"Calm down, cowboy."

"Calm down, you say? Have you ever tried to stop a two thousand pound bull charging a pretty young heifer?"

"I'm no heifer! Don't push your luck and screw up our second chance."

Crestfallen, he asked, "What's the matter? You turned off by an old man with bad knees?"

"That's not it. I just don't want to rush into anything in the heat of the moment."

"Any other reasons?"

"What I said on the way to the woods with still goes. Even if it didn't, you'd think I was just tryin' to trap you again like I did back when I was young and stupid. Take a cold shower or go jump in the lake." She laughed. "I didn't mean — oh, you know what I meant."

"Guess some ice water might reduce the swelling a bit."

She blushed. "You never give up. Do you?"

"I'm talking about my knees. You have a dirty mind, little girl."

"You're one to talk. I've got plenty of ice water for you to use where it'll do the most good."

He lay down next to her, raising his knees to reduce the pressure. "At least I can lay here beside your for a minute and enjoy the company, even though I can't do anything else right now." He sighed. "This is the life."

"Hearing you sayin' that is a good sign." She squeezed his hand. "I take it you slept well?"

"Yeah, like a log." He caressed her cheek and pulled her against him.

"What a nice way to wake up," she said. "I love ya, Raz. I always have."

"When you say that, it sounds different than it does coming from other girls."

"Now I'm jealous."

He wanted to tell her that not even his wife had said it just like that, but didn't want her to know what a failure his marriage had been. That was a subject he wasn't ready to discuss with anybody.

Feeling stupid for thinking about his dead wife while laying beside his potential new one, he let out a long sigh.

"Did I say something wrong?" she asked.

"No. Just some old ghosts tryin' to jump in the bed with us. Didn't mean to go negative. I'm happy you're here with me."

"I'm glad."

Focusing on the ceiling, he said, "You may not believe this, but with so much of time on my hands the last two years, I did lots of serious thinkin'. I realized a man can love a good woman for lots of reasons other than sex. Patti had her faults, but she gave me Becky. I'll always love her for that. Too bad she turned into a person I didn't know. She made that choice, and now she's dead." He couldn't believe he'd said that out loud. Talking about his dead wife and his child wasn't exactly pillow talk.

She looked at him. "Wow. Talk about old ghosts!" She patted his chest. "I realized you'd changed, but I didn't realize how much. You're soundin' positively deep."

"Life is for the living, and I'm still very much alive." He looked at her. "As much as I'd like to quit all this ugly business, I've got to finish what I set out to do. When I do, maybe I can get back to some real livin' for a change. That make sense?"

"Yeah."

He tweaked her nose and brushed a curl off her face. "Layin' here with you can sure mess up a man's thinkin', no matter how hard he's tryin' to keep his locomotive on the right track. I'd better get up before I try somethin' I shouldn't. If you ever tell any of my friends what didn't happen here, I'll whip your pretty little butt."

He swung his feet off the bed and sat up with a grimace. "And if I find out you're holdin' somethin' back that I ought to know after I just spilled my guts, I'll whup it twice as hard."

"Yeah? If you get too mean, I'll start callin' you by your real first name."

"You don't even know what it is." He gave her a concerned look.

"Wanna bet?" She started to say it, but he put his hand over her lips.

"Nobody calls me that, not even women I've done some heavy breathin' with."

She sat up put her arm around his waist. "Just wanted to rattle you a little, cowboy."

"Consider me rattled. How 'bout some breakfast?"

"How you like your eggs?"

"Like my women, over easy."

She smacked him on the arm for his smart comment and slid to the opposite edge of the bed. "Lay there and rest while I make breakfast. I'll call you when it's ready."

He watched her leave, telling himself, *You're lucky to have someone so good in your life for a change.* The moment she was out of sight, however, his problems came rushing back to spoil his peace of mind. *Wonder what Carol Irby knows about Patti. Maybe she'll pass it on to Lassiter and Schroeder since she might be a little pissed about being committed. Since she wasn't locked up 'til after Fran sold the Hole, she might know what happened there too. She might just be the key to the whole puzzle.*

Still weary from the previous day's antics, he closed his eyes and tried to regain the serenity he'd felt with Anita. It was nice being with a woman who had his best interests at heart and even put him before herself. It was a new, experience for him.

He relaxed and pondered the possibilities for a few minutes, until Tank's fat face suddenly appeared above him, glaring and laughing deliriously. Brandishing his baton, the sheriff yelled, "Guess what, jailbird quarterback? You're under arrest!" That morphed into Boobs' pale, dying face pleading for help, blood streaming from the corner of her mouth and nose. Seconds later Patti's bloody body, cut into chunks of flesh and bones inside a garbage bag, floated through his dreamscape. That was followed by a clear view of the Back Room as the song "See What the Boys in the Back Room Will Have" played on the jukebox. A montage of his friends from high school walked through, including the homely face of the clown-nosed Sonny Irby. He lunged at Sonny, not knowing why. He punched Sonny's ugly face while his friends sang "Rudolph the Red-Nosed Reindeer."

"Raz, wake up," Anita said, standing over him with both hands on his shoulders. "You're havin' a nightmare."

He sat up, shaking his head. "Woah. What the hell?"

"You went back to sleep, and you were yellin' so loud, it scared me half to death."

He tried to reach for a spot on his back where pain suddenly lanced him, but couldn't reach it. "Sorry. Will you check my back? Feels like the devil might've speared me through your mattress."

She slid her hand down to the sensitive area and picked up something off the bed. "It's all right. Just one of my earrings."

"Is that all? For a while there, I thought I'd died and gone to the place reserved for crooked sheriffs and dope dealers. I did learn one thing on that bad trip through dreamville. I figured out who Rudy is."

She frowned. "Rudy?"

"Thought I'd told you about him. He's the one runnin' things for the crooks in Northville. It's the guy who married Horton Snitker's ugly daughter."

"But his name is Sonny."

"Sonny Irby *is* Rudy."

"What led you to that revelation?"

He told her about his dream and the song his friends were singing in it. "Rudy is short for Rudolph. Right?"

"There must be several Rudolphs in this county that go by the nickname Rudy."

He pulled on the blue short-sleeved shirt and khaki trousers he found at the foot of the bed. "Don't bust my bubble. I know I'm right. Is breakfast ready?"

"Oh! I left the eggs on the stove!" She ran out.

After washing his hands and face, he joined Anita in the kitchen. She was waiting with two plates of eggs and bacon. Picking up his coffee, he drank a couple of swallows and sat down across the table from her.

She was wearing a long white T-shirt trimmed in a shade of brown that matched her eyes and barely covered her unmentionables. Her wavy, shoulder-length hair was freshly combed, and she smelled so good he wanted to forget his breakfast and the dream.

He reluctantly turned his mind to getting out of the fix he was in so he could enjoy what was sitting right in front of him. *Those alligators are snappin' at my behind and they're gettin' closer and hungrier all the time. It's time to get rid of 'em for good.*

CHAPTER 27

After Anita left, Raz took more sandwiches and water to Mazurka. He put his hand on the killer's forehead to check for fever. Feeling none, he told him, "I'm feelin' a whole lot like Nancy Nurse, for cryin' out loud. I don't think you'll die on me since you've got no sign of infection, but my luck hasn't been too good the last two days, so I won't be makin' you any guarantees."

Dropping a roll of toilet paper beside the cot, he said, "If what I figured out this mornin' turns the tide in my direction, I'll move you this afternoon. If not, I'll at least bring you fresh supplies and check your wounds again."

Ignoring Mazurka's protests, he left and went back to the cabin to hide the videotapes and camera in a shoebox on a self in the garage. When that was done, he headed for the old motel to leave a note for the agents.

Parking in the weeds across the tracks, he approached the motel room and slid an unsigned note under the door. He'd made sure it was anonymous in case someone other than Schroeder found it.

> Have good stuff. On way to special witness. Update Austin. Inquire as to time of arrival here for prize. Keep local friend advised, try for more help. Meet you here in afternoon.

Rusk was only an hour away, but it took him another twenty minutes after getting there to find the railroad station on the outskirts of town. It was quarter to nine by the time he parked in front of it. Pulling off his boot, he removed his sock and took out two of the twenty-dollar bills Frenchy gave him.

The station was new, but had been built to resemble an old passenger train depot. An iron fence separated the parking lot from the boarding area along the tracks. Several people waited for the ticket office to open, while others sat in their cars.

Just beyond the station, he saw a locomotive near a turn-around. It was fired up and ready for the first run of the day. This was one of the two trains Anita said were making the Rusk-to-Palestine run. She said Carol should be working on the first one out of Rusk.

At nine, the gate opened. Raz bought his ticket and joined those already boarding. The train pulled up, its great weight shaking the earth as it rolled by, pulling three passenger cars.

Raz studied the passengers and attendants, but didn't see Carol Paschal-Irby. He suspected that some attendants were already onboard, so he surrendered his ticket and climbed up the steps of the third car, just as the conductor called out, "All aboard!"

After all the passengers climbed on, the whistle blew and the train jerked forward, moving more smoothly as it gathered speed. As it entered the woods beyond the station, Raz walked toward the front of the coach, studying each person. Still not finding Carol, he walked across the swaying, connecting platforms into the next coach.

He spotted Carol at the end of that car, talking to the conductor. They were in a small cubicle apparently reserved for train attendants.

Carol looked much better than when he'd last seen her, back when they were in high school. She'd been drawn and pale then, but her face had a healthy glow now. Her straight brown hair was neatly trimmed and combed. As he approached, however, he recognized the odd look in her eyes.

When the conductor disappeared into the first coach, Raz moved over beside Carol as she organized a tray of souvenirs. "Hi, Carol," he said softly, not wanting to startle her.

She jumped anyway, and turned toward him. She didn't seem to recognize him.

"I'm Raz Jester," he said, smiling, "from Northville High. Remember?"

She smiled shyly. "You played football."

"Yeah. It's good to see you again. How are you?"

"I can't talk," she said, glancing at the forward car. "I have work to do."

"I'm not here to hurt you, Carol. I came to talk to you about Patti."

A hint of a smile appeared on her thin lips, and her eyes met his. The train was moving faster now, causing her to lean against the wall for balance. "I remember Patti. She..." Her expression changed suddenly, reflecting fear and confusion. "I just remembered. I'm not supposed to talk about her," she said curtly, and left the car.

Following her into the noisy open platform between coaches, Raz found her crying next to the safety door at the top of the steps. Only a short metal door separated her from the trees flashing by.

She whirled when he called her name, her eyes wide.

"I'm sorry, Carol," he said above the rattle of the rails. "I didn't mean to upset you. Forgive me?"

She stared wildly at him, not responding,

Wanting to calm her, he said, "You remember seeing Anita McKnight the other day? She said you asked about Patti. Patti told me you were her friend. She always said nice things about you."

"Patti always smiled at me," she said in a childlike voice. "I wanted to be beautiful like Patti. She gave me things, never forgot me at Christmas. Patti is your wife now."

"She used to be."

"Where is Patti?" She frowned. "Why isn't she with you?"

"Patti was killed over two years ago. I thought you knew."

A shadow swept over her face and she pressed her hands against her cheeks, shaking her head. "Oh, no! Patti's not dead. They told me she wasn't. They told me what I saw that day was my imagination, just like all those other bad things. They said I was crazy. That's why I had to go to the hospital."

He moved closer. "Who told you that, Carol?"

"Sonny. His lawyer, Bryan Fulton. The doctor. Everybody. They told me I didn't see that bad woman with a knife take Patti away."

His pulse quickened. "Woman? What woman?"

"I don't remember," she said, and shook her head, "but she was bad. She said she was going to cut Patti's face so she wouldn't be pretty anymore. She laughed and made Patti leave with her."

"Try to remember, Carol. Tell me exactly what you saw and heard."

She got a faraway expression on her face, and she spoke so quietly he could hardly hear her. "I'm sick. I know I am. They told me so. They said I'd never be able to go home again."

"Carol, please try to remember. What was the woman's name, the one who took Patti away? What did she look like? Where did you see her with Patti?"

Clasping her hands in front of her, she began to tremble. "I promised Sonny I wouldn't repeat what I thought I saw and heard that day, or tell anyone how I thought I saw him with Punk and Olin and the sheriff at our place when I was supposed to be shopping. I also promised never to tell anyone I thought I saw Sonny give Punk all that money, or heard them talk about never letting Patti go home or anywhere else.

"Patti wanted to come home?"

She nodded. "That's when the bad woman brought Patti to the room. Patti was real sick. I heard Sonny and the sheriff tell the bad woman to take her out in the country and see that she didn't come back."

"What was the woman's name, Carol?"

She shook her head. "I don't know. All I know is, she left with Patti. When I saw the knife, that's when I ran into the room to save her. Everybody looked real scared when they saw me."

"What did Sonny say to you?"

"He cursed at me. Told me I didn't see or hear anything. Then he calmed down and promised me Patti wasn't going to be hurt. He *promised*."

He touched her arm. "Carol, think hard. When did all this happen?"

"I don't know. Before I was sent here."

"Did you see Patti after that?"

She shook her head. "When I started asking questions, they took me to a doctor who told me I was sick. Then the judge in Coldwater sent me to the hospital."

"Would you tell some friends of mine what you've told me? They're helping me catch the bad guys in Northville who hurt people like you and Patti."

"Would your friends tell Sonny to let me come home?"

"Possibly."

She nodded, half smiling. "When can I talk to them?"

The coach door swung open and a man in a black uniform stepped out on the platform, stopping abruptly when he saw Carol. He eyed Raz suspiciously, saying, "What's going on out here? Can't you see she's crazy?" He picked up Carol's tray and asked, "What did he do to you?"

"Nothing," she said. "He's just a friend from Northville."

The man turned angry eyes on Raz. "Your name Jester by any chance?"

Raz turned to leave, but the man grabbed his shoulder and jerked him around. "I asked you a question!" Looking at Carol, he asked, "Is this the man your friends told me to be on the lookout for?"

She nodded. "I think so, but he's a good man and he's going to help me. Don't hurt him."

"Get back in the coach, stupid," the attendant ordered. "I'll make sure this guy doesn't bother you again."

Carol gave her co-worker a pleading look. "You won't do anything bad to him, will you, Sonny?"

She left and the man said to Raz, "See? I told you she was nuts. She thought I was her ex." He pulled a pistol from his pocket and pointed it at Raz.

Raz stepped back. "What's that for?"

"For the man I caught fondling a mental patient, who then attacked me when I tried to stop him. He's also the man who stumbled and fell off the train after we had a scuffle."

"Not in your dreams, Rambo. Who's paying you to do this?"

The attendant waved his pistol toward the safety door. "Jump! Jump or I'll shoot you and shove you off."

"How much did Rudy and Tank promise you for getting rid of me?"

"Enough, wise guy. Jump."

"Save your bullets. Carol didn't say anything to incriminate you or your friends."

The man jammed the gun against Raz's side. "Don't matter if she did or didn't, 'cause you're gonna jump."

"No way. That would make it too easy for you. If you want me dead, you'll have to shoot me right here, before God and everybody. How would that look, shooting an unarmed man on a train? Not even your Northville friends could get you off if you do that."

He shoved Raz toward the safety door and reached around him to unlatch it, allowing it to swing open. The *clickity-clack* of the wheels was louder now. The train's speed and the passing rocks below told him he wouldn't survive the jump.

"There's a trestle coming up," the attendant said, backing to the center of the platform. "I'll shove you off into a thirty-foot gorge if you don't jump now!"

"Look, just put the gun in your pocket and we'll forget the whole thing."

"And pass up ten grand? No way. Jump!"

The door to the first car swung open. When the attendant looked at a startled woman passenger standing there, Raz grabbed his wrist, pushing the gun up. It went off, causing the woman to scream and jump back into the coach.

The man began jabbing Raz's stomach, but Raz held onto his gun arm, twisting it until he dropped the pistol. He smashed a left fist into the man's face, and he fell back, but recovered quickly. He lowered his head and grabbed Raz in a bear hug.

Raz felt the man's arms tightening around his middle and heard another coach door open and close as he slammed his fist into the man's kidneys, once, twice, three times. The man grunted and flinched with each blow, but still held on.

Unable to breathe, with his strength ebbing, Raz tried putting his hands around the man's throat, but the gunman raised his shoulders to prevent him from getting a good hold. Raz slammed his right fist into the man's ribs and he finally loosened his grip.

Sucking in fresh air, Raz slammed another right into the same spot, then a right cross to the attendant's chin. He stumbled back and scrambled for his fallen pistol. Raz kicked him in the ribs, scooped up the gun and tossed it out the door of the moving train. He leaned out and saw the trestle ahead.

He grabbed the gunman's hair and jerked his head back. "Why is this train stopping?"

"Ain't stopping," the man gasped. "Just slowing down for the trestle."

Raz pulled the attendant's head back further. "Who paid you to take me out if I talked to Carol?"

The man shook his head. "Don't know. Some guy. Kinda short. Pudgy."

"Who besides you got paid to keep me away from her?"

"Both station managers and the brakeman on the other train. Let me go! You're breakin' my neck!"

Raz dropped him and turned to see frightened faces looking at him through the glass portion of both coach doors. Not wanting to explain his actions or risk facing another assassin, he moved down the steps and, as soon as they left the trestle, he jumped off the train, rolling down a rocky slope into some bushes.

He got up slowly, feeling for broken bones, but found only scratches and more bruises. He brushed himself off and limped into heavier cover as the last coach rolled by. When it was out of sight, he climbed back up the rock-covered embankment and sat down on a rail to consider his options.

I can wait for the other train or walk the rails back, but hoofing in that far with my legs as sore as they are was out of the question. Besides, by the time I make it back, Smeddish or some other thug will be waiting for me.

He thought about what Carol said. He'd never had a high opinion of Sonny Irby, especially after finding out he had a thing for Patti in high school and had even come-on to her. Now that he knew Irby was involved in Patti's death, he was almost desperate to talk to Schroeder and Lassiter.

I never thought Sonny was a risk taker, but drug money does strange things to people. When he married Horton Snitker's daughter and got ahold of even more money, I think that just made him bolder. If Carol told me the truth, that big-nosed banker not only financed Pattie's murder, but also gave Punk the money to buy the Hole. He's probably running the drug money through the bank, too. What a sorry piece of crap!

Who was the woman Carol kept talking about? I've never heard about a woman being involved in this mess. Was it Fran? I don't think she'd do something like that, but then again she'd have to be in deep with Tank and Sonny's operation to be doing business with Punk.

It can't be Fran. Carol knows Fran. That leaves Gerta, but I'm pretty sure Carol knows her, too.

The biggest shocker was when Carol'd told him that Patti had wanted to come home. *Why didn't I try to find her one more time and ask her to come home with me and Becky?*

He heard the whistle of the second train and hid in the bushes. When the last car started to roll passed, he ran to the back of it and jumped on the hitch. Nobody opened the door, so he didn't think anyone had noticed him.

I'll jump off when the train slows down just before Rusk and, with any luck, I can be at the Camino Real Motel in about an hour.

CHAPTER 28

Raz parked in some tall weeds across the tracks from the old motel, cut the motor and studied the back row of cabins. There were a couple of pickups parked up front, but he didn't see Zapata's old Caddy. He didn't know what kind of car Lassiter drove, but was sure it would be unmarked, with a regular license plate. Unless one of them showed, he wouldn't risk another trip across to the cabin. He checked his watch: 2:50.

He really wanted to know if Zapata had carried out the instructions in his note, and if he or Pop had heard from Lassiter. After waiting half an hour, though, he gave up his vigil. Sitting in the van in the Texas heat had left him dehydrated and cranky.

He'd just decided to go get something to drink when he spotted a police car driving down the highway past the Chevron Station. He couldn't tell if Olin was in the car. It reappeared moments later and turned down Market Drive, disappearing behind the buildings along the south end of the Square. Another car with sheriff's markings came into view from the other direction, but the driver wasn't big enough to be Tank. A large silhouette in the back seat might be the injured sheriff, but the car was too far away to tell for sure.

Looks like Tank and his buddies are looking pretty hard for me and Mazurka. Better stay sharp and stay put. He backed the van further into the weeds and opened the back doors for added ventilation. He broke off some small leafy branches and propped them against the grill, hood and top of the windshield, to help camouflage the white van.

Traffic on the highway was unusually light. *Tank's probably ordered road-blocks on both ends of town. Good thing I don't have to cross the highway when I meet Snake at six, or when I drive back to Anita's.*

The disturbing sight of a state trooper's car across the way meant the state was involved now too. *Where are Zapata and Lassiter? I hope Schroeder misjudged how long he'd be gone and is on his way to the right now.*

The police seemed to be concentrating their search on the west side of the tracks, but since both Tank and Olin knew he had friends in The Quarters, they'd soon cover that part of town too. *They've probably already ransacked my house and barn, and they've probably been by Frenchy's place, too. Hope they didn't find my truck. I don't want them knowing I'm in a different vehicle. If Frenchy picked up my truck, surely he had the sense to park it someplace else. He won't let them to search his place without a warrant anyway, so maybe there's no worry there.*

He couldn't see the front of the Hard Rock Club, which was unfortunate. *Knowing Gerta, she's probably already told Punk about my call and is trying to work out a special arrangement with Tank and Rudy that will keep her worthless son out of prison if their house of cards comes falling down.*

Three o'clock came and went, and still no one had arrived. By four o'clock, his thirst was nearly unbearable, but he didn't dare risk driving anywhere before dark.

He was considering walking over to Bull's place when Zapata's green Caddy pulled into the parking space next to the last cabin. It was invisible from the highway and front drive. The heavy Mexican went to the cabin door, unlocked it and stepped inside.

Raz climbed out of the van and flew across the open space between his hiding spot and the tracks. He went over them and down the incline on the other side, stopping behind a bush to take another look around.

Once he was sure the way was clear, he moved into the shadow of the last cabin, breathing hard and sweating. After checking things out one more time, he limped around the corner to the door and stepped inside without knocking.

He shut the door and found Zapata standing at the window, peeking around the shade. He dropped the shade and asked, "You sure no one saw you?"

"Nobody but you. Why so jumpy?"

"Man, you got no idea what a hot item you are! What the hell did you do last night? It sure put ants in Punk's pants. Tank's, too. If the wrong people saw you come in here, I'd be toast for sure. I had to tell all kinds of lies yesterday after my damned car was spotted in The Quarters."

"Welcome to Raz's club of hard knocks." He plopped on the sofa.

Zapata peeked out the window again. "You got the sheriff, that dope head pervert, and the gang's enforcers from Houston all doing a nervous dance. Apparently Alabama has a hotline direct to Tank and Olin ever since Gerta Hutto called him last night. Shag and his dirt-bag friends have been runnin' around at God's Palace like they got hot coals in their ass pockets."

"Music to my ears." He looked for the note on the floor, but didn't see it. "You got my message?"

"I called Lassiter's headquarters on my cell, but he was out—"

"Not good."

"Let me finish before you blow a gasket. I left a message with his secretary. Told him to call your friend, Pop, ASAP with his ETA, 'cause you got something too hot for the two of us to handle. Then I called Pop and filled him in. He said for you to call him in the morning so he can bring you up to date."

"Thanks. Did Schroeder call?"

"Yeah. Be here tomorrow afternoon. Told me to help you find Fran Druman. They're watchin' me like hungry vultures now, so I really got to be careful 'bout who I talk to over at the Hole. I was lucky to make it over here."

"So, I couldn't give you the evidence I got last night even if I had it on me."

Zapata peeked around the shade again and sat down. "At least tell me what has everybody runnin' scared. Make it short; we got to split soon."

"I found pictures and videotapes that you guys can use to get a search warrant. They got a porno operation and a dope den. *And* I got a witness who can give you the lowdown on a local murder and some illegal banking. There should be enough to keep the federal bank examiners busy for a few days." He didn't mention anything about Fran, because he wanted to talk to her first.

"Remember what Schroeder said about not being able to use evidence you got illegally?"

Raz gave the agent a look of mock surprise. "You think I'd do a thing like that to nice, fun-loving scum? A public-spirited citizen who chooses not to remain anonymous gave me those hot little items. I know that line doesn't violate any rules, because reporters and crooked lawyers use it all the time."

"We'll take a look at your evidence as soon as somebody gets here to pick it up. But your line of bullshit won't work on a magistrate. He'll want facts before issuing a warrant."

"Stupid rules. How the hell did we take the country away from the Indians?"

"What?"

"That lawyer stuff makes the lawmen into helpless idiots. No wonder little towns like Northville go bad. I'm surprised things aren't worse all over. Maybe my Aunt Ruth's right — America *is* on the skids."

"Didn't know you were a criminology professor. So where are these hot items you say you got?"

"In a safe place. I'm travelin' fast and light today, and wasn't sure if anybody would be here. Couldn't take a chance of losin' them. Been there, done that!"

Looking around for something to write on, he found an old magazine in a drawer and tore out a page. "Gimme your pen." He wrote down Carol's full name and where she could be found. Handing the paper to him, he said, "I can give you this right now, in case something happens to me before tomorrow. Tell Lassiter and Schroeder to talk to this witness someplace where her co-workers can't see, unless they want a pistol wrapped around their heads. They've been paid off by the bad guys."

Zapata read the name. "Is she any relation to the banker?"

"You just won yourself a big enchilada. I've got reason to believe he's the gang's moneychanger in Northville. That surprise you?"

Zapata folded the scrap of paper and put it in his shirt pocket. "*En el pueblo de diablo donde los gringos quieren dinero mas que vida?* No. "

"Now, wait just a minute there, Montezuma. There are still a lot of good people in this town who love lots of things more than money. With a little luck and some help from you do-right boys, we'll be turning it back over to them real soon."

Zapata raised his eyebrows. "You speak Spanish?"

"I even speak English, contrary to what some high-hat Yankee tourists think."

Zapata scribbled something on another scrap of paper and gave it to Raz. "My cell number. Call me as soon as you find Fran."

"What happens if I call and you're at Punk's place?"

"It's on vibrate, nobody'll know. Might take me a while to answer, 'cause I'll have to go outside. Just in case everything blows up and Lassiter and Schroeder don't show, we'd better agree on a place to meet tomorrow. We can't meet here anymore."

"I'm banking on Lassiter and Schroeder being here by noon so I can get my prize witness to a doctor. I'll call Pop. If he says neither one of 'em has called in more instructions for me, I'll meet you where you want. That is, if I'm still alive and kickin'. Homecoming will be in full swing by then, so you should be able to slip away. Sometime after twelve, drive your green machine north on the highway 'til you cross the county line. Wait there in a place where I can spot you. When I drive by, follow me until I find a safe place to transfer everything I have and Mazurka."

"Will do."

As Raz started toward the door, Zapata grabbed his arm. "*Estás loco?* Don't go out there before I make sure the coast is clear."

"If you're that paranoid, why don't you drive me away in your green machine?"

Zapata nodded. "*Bueno.*"

"*Vamos.*"

Zapata smiled and left the room. Watching him, Raz thought he might learn to like the man after all. He waited just inside the door until Zapata drove to the entrance, then darted outside and jumped into the back of the car and dropped to the floorboard. "Drive across the tracks into The Quarters and turn right on the second street."

Moments later Raz felt the wheels thump over the tracks and the car slowed down. Zapata said, "I see trouble."

"What's wrong?"

"Cop car in front of Bull's place."

"Turn around. Cross the tracks, go south on Fifty-nine. I'll show you another crossover."

"Okay, man, but stay down. Don't even breathe hard, 'cause we'll be going by Punk's place."

"Then turn north. Hurry."

"Take it easy, man. Nobody spotted us." The big car swayed as Zapata made a U-turn. Raz stayed down until they'd cleared the Square, then sat up and said, "There's a crossing about a quarter of a mile ahead. Take it."

His directions brought them back into the bad side of town and across Kennedy Drive. They were out of sight of Bull's place, near where Raz had parked the van. He told Zapata, "Turn right here. Let me out at that vacant lot."

Zapata had almost come to a stop when he sped up again. "Stay down," he warned. "A car's coming. I'll have to go around the block."

Moments later, Zapata slowed down again. "It's clear this time, but I'm going to keep rolling in case somebody's watching. Stay down and jump out on the right side."

Raz unlatched the door and opened it slightly to judge the speed. "Slow down some more. That ground looks as hard as concrete."

As they passed a thicket, Raz rolled out into the weeds. Zapata picked up speed to close the door and drove off.

Grimacing from the jolt to his abused body, Raz climbed slowly to his feet and moved through the weeds to the van. He crawled through its back door and into the driver's seat. It was 5:20, and hotter than hell inside the van.

If I can get to Snake's safe house without being recognized, I can find out about the woman in Houston. Maybe she's the golden prize Schroeder's been looking for.

He was hungry and his lips felt like lizard skin. He wanted to stop at Bull's, but couldn't because a police car was still parked across the street.

The van's makeshift camouflage fell away as he eased onto the dirt road. He slowly wound his way over to the safe house on Sycamore, and stopped at the back steps. Snake's car was nowhere in sight. The back door of the house was shut and the shades were down. *Did Snake sell me out?* Raz hoped the small-time dealer's greed would keep him straight long enough to help find Fran.

He went inside, propped a chair under the doorknob and sat down in the front room where he had a good view of the back door.

After waiting for almost half an hour, he'd decided to leave when he heard someone pushing on the back door. Going to a back window, he peeked around the shade and saw a man standing outside the door, cursing. "Son-of-a-bitch! Who the hell locked this fuckin' door?"

Raz moved the chair and pulled the door open. "You got such a delicate way of expressin' yourself."

"How come you lock me out my own damn house?" Snake growled.

"Had to make sure you hadn't come down with a severe case of cop-itus. You ready to roll?"

Snake peeked outside like he expected somebody to join them. "I'm ready to check out that woman Lobo say *might* be your ol' lady. He say it ain't gonna be easy gettin' to her. If she still alive, she be under heavy cover."

"That why you haven't gone down yourself to see if she's the one that burned your uncle?"

"Gettin' rid of snitches ain't my line o' work."

"It is for some of your friends." Raz watched his reaction to see if he had different feelings about Fran than he'd said, but saw nothing.

Snake fidgeted with his keys then walked into the next room and sat down. Following him, Raz asked, "Where's this place where Fran is supposed to be?"

"Someplace call Kool Mama's in the Houston ghetto. Lobo find out 'bout it a few weeks ago when he start selling to 'em."

"Is Fran the owner, a waitress, or what?"

"What you think I is, a nigga who's-who? All I know is, won't be easy gettin' your white ass in and out o' that place."

"If Fran can get in, so can I. I need to make one quick phone call, then let's get down there."

"No damn calls, man."

"Why not? It has nothin' to do with you or where we're goin'."

"Right. How I know you bein' straight wit me?"

"You can listen if you want. Stop someplace with a payphone."

Snake glanced through the window again as if expecting someone. "Ain't you got a cellphone? Should, this bein' the 21ˢᵗ century and all. I ain't stoppin' nowhere. I get caught wit you one agin an' I likely ta end up roadkill."

"Just think about that pot of gold waitin' for ya when we get back. Don't forget, I'm the only who knows where it is. Didn't I see you with a cellphone the other day? Give it here. It'll only take a second."

Snake threw the phone at him and said, "Here. Make it snappy. Don't mention no names."

They went outside and sat down in the red Porsche. "If I don't like what you sayin', I'm cuttin' you off. No sayin' who you with or where you headin'. Feel me?"

Raz knew Anita's number by heart. He'd called it enough times when they were in high school. He was surprised when a child answered. "McKnight residence."

He'd hardly had time to ask for her mother before hearing Anita's excited voice. "Raz, that you?"

"The one and only, but don't mention names. Okay? I wanted to let you know I'm okay, and I need to ask you another favor."

"Where are you? Wherever it is, you'd better stay put. Tank and his friends are all over lookin' for you. They've even come by here. My dad is pissed."

"I'm on Tank's list of things that need wipin' out. What else is new?"

"You mean you haven't heard?"

"Heard what?"

"Carol Irby is dead."

Raz leaned forward. "*What!* How? When?"

"They announced it on the radio less than an hour ago. The reporter said she either jumped off the train or was pushed. They're not sure yet. You've got to stop fightin' those crooks and leave town before they find you. Just tell me where you are and I'll pick you up and get you away from here."

Too shocked to respond, Raz heard that little voice in his head again. *Another woman dead because of you, Raz Jester.*

Snake leaned toward Raz and said, "Your face *really* white, man. What you mumblin' about?"

Ignoring Snake, Raz moved the phone back to his ear. "I'm so sorry," he said, "but I can't quit now. It wouldn't be fair to Carol or two or three others I could name." When he saw Snake's hand reaching to take the phone away from him, he said, "Gotta go now. I'll call again after runnin' another errand. Bye." He threw the phone back to Snake.

"We out o' here, man," Snake said, pocketing the phone. "That call some kinda signal or somethin'?"

"Cut the commentary and drive."

They took a country road that led to the highway, and Snake said, "Keep that lily white face down an' out o' sight 'til I get clean outta town. Don't want no damn bullet holes in my ride."

Raz leaned down. "You've got a big heart. If you get me to Houston and back in one piece, you might have a bank account to match your fancy car."

Swinging out onto the highway south of town, Snake said, "You really stirred the shit this time."

"It's my charming personality. It'll come in handy gettin' us into Kool Mama's."

"You crazy? You need me 'cause your white ass won't get through the front door."

Raz sat up and looked at the speedometer, which read 85 mph. "Better cool it. We don't want a cop on our tail."

Snake pointed to a small box on the dash. "Fuzz buster. 'Sides, I never stop for nobody."

The speedometer was soon slid up to 100 mph, and Raz hoped Snake was as good at driving as he thought he was.

CHAPTER 29

Raz spotted a Dairy Queen and they were leaving Coldwater." Let's pick up a couple of burgers and a coke. I'm 'bout to keel over."

Snake slowed down, mumbling, "Fuckin' crazy bastard."

"Just think of it as protecting your investment," Raz joked. "I might lose my memory if I don't get somethin' to eat and drink real soon."

"Get down," Snake ordered as he swung off the highway. Pulling up to the drive-thru window, he ordered and waited out of sight of the pickup window. There were no other cars in line.

Raz gave him a ten, and when the food was ready, a nervous Snake drove up to the window and threw the money at the cashier. Not waiting for the change, he dropped the sack in Raz's lap and sped away.

Raz immediately sat up and began eating. Snake drove on, mumbling about having his new car "stinked up" with fast food. Finally, he glanced at Raz and asked, "You sure you ain't lookin' up your ol' lady so you can do a number on her for Cato? I be real happy makin' this trip, that the case."

Wondering about the motive behind the question, Raz replied, "Stop tryin' to figure me out, and don't go screwin' up my plans for finding her."

"*Plans?* That really do sound like you might wanna do a number on her."

Raz swallowed some coke. "Didn't know you were the high authority on human behavior." He took another bite. "Why don't you concentrate on keepin' your wheels on the road and let me worry about the rest. I'll know what to do when I see her. Just make sure *you* don't try doin' somethin' to her."

When he finished eating, Raz leaned back and tried to relax. He decided it was best to keep conversation to a minimum. He tried not to think about

Carol and Boobs, or about what might happen if Lassiter and Schroeder failed to show. He tried to concentrate instead on what he would do if the mystery woman *was* Fran Druman.

He was relieved when the Houston city limits sign swept by them less than two hours later. About that time, Snake slowed down to seventy, which relieved him even more. It was 8:45.

About twenty minutes later, Snake turned onto a feeder lane that veered off the cross-town freeway. They turned onto a street in an older section of the city, and Raz said, "You either had good directions or you've been here before. Care to say which?"

Snake didn't respond as he drove down a one-way street for several blocks before turning left. "This the Third Ward, man. White ain't their favorite color here, so how 'bout slippin' down in the seat so you don't screw wit my rep."

Raz slid down. "I'm beginnin' to feel unwanted."

"Can the cute talk. This risky business here. We talk to somebody, don't make no smartass remarks 'bout nothin'. Feel me?"

Raz sat up far enough to look out at the run-down stores and old frame houses. Some of the buildings looked deserted. The older homes were missing windows and looked like a stiff wind might blow them down.

Snake turned on another north-south street and pointed to a one-story building with a marquee that read: KOOL MAMA'S. He pulled into the parking lot and parked between two cars. He killed the motor and looked around.

Raz sat up and studied the dimly lit lot and surroundings. Unlike other parts of the ward they'd driven through, there were no homes nearby, and the businesses were mostly wooden, one-story deals; a lot of them vacant.

A chain-link fence topped with barbed wire bordered the small lot adjoining the back wall of Kool Mama's. Raz saw two big cars parked under a carport roof extending from two mobile homes sitting side-by-side near the fence. Near one of the cars, he saw a large dog.

Even with the windows up, Raz could hear rap music and the excited voices of patrons inside the club. "Let's go."

Snaked grabbed his arm. "Hol' on, man! You know showin' your face in there be like the devil hisself walkin' into church? Lemme think a minute."

"What about? We can't find that former friend of mind sittin' out here."

Snake shook his head in disbelief. "You might be tough like Zeke say, but you dumb as a post. You cain't beat all them niggas in there. Be cool." He sighed. "I mus' be out my min' bringin' your ass here."

"You're not out of your mind; just greedy. Let's go."

When Raz opened the door, Snake grabbed his arm again. "Shut the damn door! I gotta lay it out or you get us both kilt."

Raz closed the door. "Okay."

Snake pointed at the marquee. "See that? If Lobo right, Kool Mama be your ol' lady. Same one sent Uncle Cato to the pen. You gotta forget she your sweet mama. She ain't yours no more. Got it?"

"Yeah. So?"

Snake waved his hands and mumbled a few curse words. "You act cool an' all, but what you see in there might make you lose it. You can't let yourself get all bent out o' shape you see somethin' in there you don't like. We clear?"

"Like dirty glass. Ready now?"

Snake didn't move. "Lobo say some brothas tol' him the woman he hear 'bout real tight wit ever'body here, but he don't know why. Lobo say he ain't never seen her when he been here. He always do bidness wit Toke and Big Shoulders."

"Then let's go find 'em."

"Not 'til I give you all of it. Big Shoulders an' Toke be mean motherfuckers, Lobo say don't even look crossways at them party gals they got workin' the floor *or* the woman tendin' bar."

"Okay, got it. Now come on, unless you're too scared to go in with me."

"You crazy? You ain't goin' nowhere without me."

"We'll see 'bout that." Raz got out.

Snake jumped out and locked the doors, running to catch up with him. "'Member, be cool."

Loud music blaring out the entrance made more talk impossible. They stepped into a brightly lit room and peeked through the next door into a smoky room filled with people. A live band played in a back corner and people were dancing.

A short black man with wide shoulders and a big neck materialized from the shadows and moved up close to look them over. His short-sleeved, brightly colored shirt hung over his pants, suggesting he was packing something besides big muscles. "You ain't welcome here," he told Raz.

Snake quickly explained the nature of their business, emphasizing that Raz was an old friend of Kool Mama's. The man's expression said he wasn't impressed by Snake's plea, but he motioned for them to walk into the main room ahead of him.

None of the customers noticed them until they were about halfway to the bar at the back. Suddenly they heard, "Hey! What's he doin' in here?"

Ignoring the shout, Raz continued walking toward the bartender. The mirrored wall behind her displayed well-stocked shelves full of booze and celebrity photos. He recognized three of them: Martin Luther King, B.B. King and Hank Aaron.

The band stopped playing, and Raz heard the rumble of anxious voices behind him. He stopped in front of the bar as their escort disappeared through a door near the end of the counter. The bartender had been watching him from beneath her curly red bangs.

Almost choking when he tried to speak, Snake cleared his throat and said, "My friend come to see Kool Mama. He a friend o' hers. You wanna tell her he here?"

The woman's cold eyes looked them over. She said in a coarse voice, "I'm Kool Mama, and I ain't never had no *white* boyfriend."

The men at the bar laughed and slapped the counter. One moved toward Raz, but she raised her hand, stopping him.

Snake brought me on a wild goose chase, Raz thought with a sinking feeling.

Snake smiled nervously. "I thought..." His face lit up suddenly. "Oh, I get it. There *two* Kool Mamas. Mind tellin' the other one my friend here? I know she want to see him, 'cause she from Northville, same as him."

Raz gave Snake a surprised look, impressed by how clever he was under pressure. He heard one of the men at the bar say, "He a cop."

Another said, "Don't make no difference. I gonna whip his ass and throw him out."

Kool Mama shot both of them a warning look.

Snake leaned toward Raz and whispered, "Stay cool, man. Stay cool."

The bouncer reappeared through a curtain behind the bar and moved up beside the bartender. He was calm when he asked, "You want I throw them out?"

She looked at Raz, and said, "His nervous friend say he got a lady friend here called Kool Mama."

"Her real name is Fran Druman," Raz said. "I was in business with her in Northville, a little town up the road a piece."

The man's expression reflected a renewed interest, but he said, "There ain't nobody here name Fran. You need ta leave."

"Lobo say she here," Snake protested.

The man gave Snake a cold look. "Lobo? Who this Lobo?"

"You know, he sell you the good merchandise. Work for my Uncle Cato Hamilton back in the day."

The man's eyes remained on Snake, non-committal. "Cato in the pen. What he got ta do with you?"

"Nothin'," Snake said. "Just droppin' his name." He flashed a big smile. "This man here a friend of Cato's. Done time wit 'im. He ain't no cop or nothin'. He don't see his friend now, he be back tomorrow for sure. Better let 'im see her if she here."

The man hesitated, looking from Snake to Raz. He pointed Raz to the end of the bar and, when they were out of hearing range of the customers, said, "You find this friend, what you want wit her?"

Sensing his trip might be about to pay dividends, Raz said, "It's personal. While I was in the pen, she disappeared. We had a business up in Northville. She sold it while I was locked up, and I want my share. I also want to be sure she's okay. Too many people from Northville been killed lately."

"If she not okay?"

"Then I'll know, won't I."

"Some men quick to blame da ones nearest at hand when they see somethin' wrong with a woman they knowed once upon a time."

Raz asked, "Who are you, anyway? Why do you care how I feel when I find Fran?"

Motioning toward a door, he led Raz into a small room and closed the door. "I'm Shoulders. I'm part owner. You packin'?"

Raz shook his head, raising his arms.

The man quickly patted down his pockets, sides and legs and stepped back. "What you do you don't find your lady friend?"

"Keep lookin'. I'll come back here if I have to. I just got out of the pen and I need my money."

"What you in for?"

"I knocked a crooked cop on his ass"

"Why you do that?"

"He was tryin' to pin a trumped-up murder rap on me, that and for the pleasure of punchin' him in the face."

"'Fore I see if your friend here, I got to check with my partner, Big Toke. Don't leave this room." Shoulders left.

Raz paced the floor, puzzled about Fran's link to this place. *This can't be related to Cato. If it was, she'd be their enemy, considering she turned him in. Maybe they're working for the new gang that took over Cato's territory. With the contacts she had making a case against Cato, she could easily do that. Maybe she went into business for herself with the money she got from the Hole. Or maybe Lobo was wrong and she was never here.*

After about five minutes, Shoulders returned and motioned for to Raz to follow him. "You got to talk to Rachael."

"Why? She know Fran?"

Shoulders didn't reply and Raz followed him to a black door at the end of a narrow hall. "Don't take no liberties with Rachael," he warned. "Big Toke with her and he get mad easy. Rachael want you to leave, you leave. Understood?"

"But you still haven't told me what Rachael has to do with Fran Druman."

"There ain't no Fran Druman here." He knocked and a deep voice responded immediately. "Come in."

His escort pushed the door open and Raz stepped onto a plush white carpet. A tall black man with long hair, a goatee and a diamond in each ear was waiting for him as he entered.

Raz looked around the room. There was a sofa, a refrigerator and a TV. To his right, a blue room divider about six feet high and ten feet long blocked his view of anything beyond. It seemed like a strange setting for an encounter with a woman he'd never heard of who would talk to him about another woman who wasn't here.

The tall man said, "I'm Big Toke. Who're you?"

"Raz Jester."

"Shoulders tell me you lookin' for somebody name Fran Druman. Why you want her?"

Raz told him. "She made me a partner in the Armadillo Hole up in North-ville after my wife left me. When my wife was killed, she was, uh, very nice to me. I want to make sure she's all right and find out if she can afford to pay me my share of what she got for our business."

"Fran Druman dead."

Angered over having been escorted like a prisoner a room only to hear what he could've been told up front, he said, "I didn't come here to play games. I've been truthful with you."

Big Toke's expression remained unmoved. "You leave with a lump on your head you don't stop suggestin' I'm lyin'. You got to forget Fran Druman. She live a while in your town and she your friend, but she dead now as far as your sorry ass's concerned. You 'member that if you ever respect her or call her friend. You half as tough as you pretend, they you have no trouble lookin' at what I got ta show you."

Raz glanced around. "I don't see anything special. Where's Rachael? Maybe she'll tell me what this is all about."

"For sure she will. Come on over here."

Raz followed Big Toke to the room divider, stopping when he raised his hand. He watched Big Toke slowly push the divider aside.

The first thing Raz saw was a hospital bed covered by a white sheet. A woman with a pale, disfigured face framed by long black hair and dark eyes looked back at him.

The woman's face was vaguely familiar, but he didn't recognize her. Her face was drawn and misshapen from horizontal scars across her nose and lips. The sight of her made him want to turn away.

"This is Rachael?"

Without responding, Big Toke slowly pulled down the top sheet, revealing a frail body that was nude except for panties. On her midriff, an ugly scar ran from side to side and another one extended from her naval to a point where it disappeared under the panties. More jagged scars marred her thin thighs. Her nipples had been sliced and her breasts were misshapen and flattened by even more deep scars.

He turned away, angry at being brought to this room and shown such a pitiful person. But then, he suddenly realized this woman was cut up the same way Patti had been. *Did the same sicko do this to her?*

A weak voice behind him said, "Raz, it's me."

His sore knees almost gave way as he turned around and took a closer look at the disfigured face. "My God," he whispered. "It *is* you." He forced himself to look past the grotesque scars and into the large brown eyes that were still as beautiful as ever. Stepping closer, pulse pounding, he asked, "What happened, Fran? Who did this to you?"

She remained still, no doubt seeing the shock he couldn't hide. He dropped his gaze in shame, but realized how that must look. Gathering his courage, he raised his eyes to hers once again. "I hope this didn't happen to you because of me."

When he gave Big Toke an accusing look, she said in a raspy whisper, "Big Toke had nothing to do with it. He's my friend. All these people here are my friends."

Raz shuddered, shaking his head as Big Toke moved forward to gently pull the sheet back over Fran's once-beautiful body.

A skeletal hand extended toward him from beneath the sheet. "Can we still be friends?"

Raz stared at her hand for a second, then held it gently. It was cold and limp, and he found himself at a loss for words.

"If you think *you* were shocked when you saw me, think of how *I* felt when I found out I wasn't going to die."

Why's she being so nice to me? Did Cato tell her something when they had their brief encounter?

"Since you love life so much, you probably don't understand why anybody'd *want* to die. But I did. I tried to kill myself several times. If I hadn't been with friends who cared, I would've succeeded. I'm Rachael Levitt now, so I guess in a way, Fran Druman really did die."

What can I say to her? What could anybody say that would make her feel better? Two things were certain: he couldn't ask her to talk to Schroeder and he couldn't ask her for his share of the money.

Apparently sensing his discomfort, she spoke again. "This is what happens when you get involved in a pissing contest with bad people in high places. Big Toke and his friends found me half dead in an alley and saved my life. Shoulder's wife, the one tending bar, did the most for me while I healed." She touched her head. "They helped me up here, too. I don't think that part of me will ever be completely healed, though."

Raz swallowed the lump in his throat. "Seeing you like this makes my reasons for being here seem unimportant. Who did this to you? You're cut up just like Patti. I heard…" He stopped, not wanting her to relive the experience.

"I assume you've heard I've been a bad girl?" she asked. "It's true, thanks to Tank Zelder, Olin Culpepper, and Punk Hutto." She paused to catch her breath. "I prayed that you'd never find me and see me like this. Not after we'd been so close. I knew if you ever did come back to Northville you'd look me up and get yourself killed. I didn't want that to happen. Didn't Cato ask you to kill me when you found me?"

Her directness left him searching for words again. "Cato always clammed up when I mentioned you. I didn't know why 'til I talked to some people in Coldwater."

She took a long, rasping breath. "You'd be doing me a favor if you killed me. But the way you're lookin' at me, I know you'd never do it. Isn't that ironic? I deserve it, after what I did to you, our business and Cato. To make it even worse, I did it all just to save myself." She threw up her hands. "Look what that got me. Butchered by a maniac and left wanting to die. At least Cato will be glad to hear about that."

"Cato won't know. He's dead."

A look of surprise swept over her distorted face. "I don't understand. I thought he was still in prison."

He told her what happened. "His nephew, Snake, brought me down here. He pulled some strings to help me find you."

She and Big Toke exchanged glances, and then she told Raz, "That's not good. Snake knows what I did to his uncle. That means the wrong people will find me now and my miserable life will truly be over."

"I don't think Snake has the guts."

"His friends do, and you'll understand why they're just as eager to kill me as he is after hearing what happened. But first, I want to say that I'm sorry about Cato. I hated what I did to him, and I know what you must think about me for it. But Cato was good to me until I..."

He waited, hoping she'd explain, but when she didn't, he decided to move on to other things. He didn't know how much longer Big Toke would let him stay. "Remember how all my troubles started after I started lookin' for Patti's killer? Well, I was gettin' nowhere on my own, so I jumped at a chance to do somethin' I thought would get me all the right answers."

He told her about his arrangement with Lassiter and being assigned to Cato's cell. "Even though he knew how much I hated dealers, Cato and I became close friends after I saved him from another convict. He wouldn't tell the cops the time of day, but after I did that, he told me all about the outfit he worked for, the gang that put him out of business and his arrangement with Tank and Olin. Even gave me a tape for the narcs. He didn't know who killed Patti, though, so I got myself locked up for nothin'."

She seemed interested, but said nothing, making him suspect she might be too exhausted to continue. Not wanting to leave yet, he said, "Since I didn't get what I went down there for, I started lookin' again as soon as I got back to Northville. I've found out a lot. Sonny Irby's first wife, Carole, told me just yesterday that it was a *woman* that dragged Patti out of her house. Blackie Mazurka doesn't even know who they mystery woman could've been. So, I figured that since I needed to talk to you about the Hole anyway, I could also talk to you about that missin' pieces of the puzzle. I had no idea—"

"That you'd find me cut up just like Patti?"

Excited to hear who the butcher was, he said, "There couldn't be two sickos with the same knife skills on the loose in such a small town. It had to be the same guy."

She drew a deep, labored breath and pulled the sheet tighter around her neck. "What will you do when you find him?"

It was a question he'd been asked before, and one he had often asked himself. "There was a time when I would've done a number on him without givin' it a second thought. I've done a lot of serious thinkin' since then, and decided it's not somethin' I can handle alone without messin' up my life for good. I've got my little girl to think about. You remember Becky, don't you? Providin' a good life for her takes priority over vengeance. But I'd see to it that he pays for what he did to both of you."

"You *have* done some serious thinking. I'm glad, because I wouldn't tell you if I thought it would get you killed or sent back to prison."

He glanced at the menacing Big Toke looming over him, then turned back to her. "I'm listening."

"Before I tell you who did it, and what I know about those Northville gangsters, you'll have to make me two promises. One, let the authorities handle the butcher if you find him. And two, don't tell anybody I'm still alive. The last condition is one that Big Toke and Shoulders insisted on before bringin' you back here."

"I guess what I said already takes care of the first condition. As for the second, I'll admit I was hoping you'd be willin' to tell your story to some honest cops I met. I was hopin' you'd testify in court. One of the cops is a Fed. The Northville crooks and their friends can't influence what happens in federal court. "

"No!" Big Toke stepped forward. "She suffer enough. She turn to the law for help once, an' almost got kilt again. She with her people now. We take care of her."

Raz looked at Fran. "Your people? "

Fran nodded. "My grandmother..."

Surprised by her statement, he had problems thinking of an appropriate response. "Your grandmother must've been a pretty woman."

"Thank you. If you'd known that two years ago, would it have made a difference to you?"

He hesitated, not knowing why. "I don't think so. I know it won't make me forget those good times we had, and it wouldn't have kept me from finding you."

"Then you agree to my second condition? If it will help you decide, I'll tell you that I did everything I could to have the monster prosecuted. When I recovered enough to sign a complaint, I did. But when the case was presented to a Houston grand jury, the asshole's attorney came up with two witnesses who testified that he was with them in another part of the state at the time. There was no indictment, and I got shot for my troubles." She pointed to her chest. "I should've died then, too, but only lost a lung. After that, I changed my name and moved here. I didn't have much money left after payin' the medical bills, but I gave the rest to Big Toke and Shoulders so they could buy this place."

His first impulse was to agree to anything that would spare her further pain and suffering, but with Cato's tape destroyed and the legality of his other evidence in question, he desperately needed her testimony. "I need you, but I don't want to do anythin' that would make you suffer more than you already have. I don't want to cause your friends any trouble, either." He glanced at Big Toke.

"I appreciate that," Fran said. "They run a legal business for the most part, but cops comin' and goin' would destroy their business. They've been good to me, so I don't want that to happen."

She held out her hand and Big Toke gave her a glass of water and a pill. Settling back on her pillow, obviously exhausted by the conversation, she told Raz, "First, I want to tell you about the events leading up to my thing with Cato so you won't leave hating me." She chose her words carefully. "I'm not sure of the date, but it was around the time when Tank and Olin said they found that bloody knife in your truck. Tank came to me with an arrest warrant. I found out later that one of those transients at God's Palace recognized me and told Punk. Anyway, Tank gave me a choice, go to prison or help the local DA make a case against Cato. They mentioned they had some new friends who wanted to take over Cato's business. Seems those new friends offered them a better deal but they couldn't move in 'til Cato and his outfit got pushed out."

"Pop told me about that warrant."

Her sad eyes studied him again, like she was looking for things unsaid. "I see. Well, I refused, so Tank and Olin put me in jail. They said if I changed my mind, they'd let me go and tear up the warrant. I told them I wanted to talk to you first, but they said you'd already been sent up. So, after staying in jail a while longer, I decided that snitching on Cato was better than being in jail and losing our business. Like you, I had no sympathy for dealers. With you gone and nobody else to turn to, I finally gave in." She shook her head. "Big mistake."

After resting a moment, she continued. "I did what I was told, but as soon as Cato and Mazurka were arrested, Punk told me Cato's boss had men out lookin' for me. I knew then I had to run, but I had no money and no way to get any without sellin' the Hole. Punk said he'd buy it for cash if I'd deed it to him right then. With no one to help me and no time to contact you, I went ahead and signed it over. Right after that, Mazurka and Schmedich kidnapped me."

He gave her a puzzled look. "You mean Smeddish?"

"Who?"

"You know, Mazurka's partner, the short pudgy one. He and Mazurka have had me in their crosshairs ever since I got out."

"Oh, yeah. Cato always mispronounced his name. It's spelled S-c-h-m-e-d-i-c-h. It's German, like medic. We're both talking about the same guy."

Her explanation sent an adrenaline rush through Raz as he recalled an axiom learned in prison: career criminals seldom go by their real names, they take on nicknames or abbreviated versions of their true name. That meant Schmedich was Medic, the one the vagrant at the old hotel told him about over two years ago.

"Why are you so pale all of a sudden?" Fran asked.

"Because for a moment there, I was sure I knew who killed Patti. Then I remembered Carole Irby telling me a *woman* took Patti away."

Fran suddenly began crying. Unable to control the sobs, she bowed her head. Big Toke stepped over and put his hand on her shoulder, giving Raz an angry look.

Raz tried to think of something comforting to say but couldn't. He never could stand to see a woman cry.

When she'd composed herself, Fran raised her head and said, "No woman could've done what that monster did to me. Gerta Hutto is the most vicious woman I know, but to my knowledge she's never hurt anybody physically. She had other women come in, but I didn't know any of them. Maybe Carol was mistaken."

She dabbed her eyes. "Schmedich and Mazurka took me to Houston. Schmedich drove and Mazurka rode in the backseat to shut me up and keep me from jumping out. He got drunk on the way, and when he wasn't pawing me, he talked. Told me I had to be killed because I knew too much. Said his new bosses and their business partners in Northville thought I'd do to them what I did to Cato." She shuddered, near tears again.

Recovering, she continued. "Mazurka said the new boss wouldn't allow another killing in Northville, so they had to take me out of town to do it."

"That new boss would've been Ed Barrow, I guess."

"The only name I heard Mazurka use was Alabama. He talked a lot about him and Punk and Tank. Bragged about Alabama offering Tank and Olin twice the amount they'd been getting if they could get rid of Cato and his backers. Mazurka talked a lot because he knew I was about to die. He even said Alabama told Tank his new boss would triple his take if he'd find a bank to launder the money."

"That made Sonny Irby a big man for the first time in his life, the wimp. I think he's the local boss they call Rudy."

"Could be, but Mazurka didn't mention a Rudy during the two days he held me prisoner in that Houston rat hole."

"Where was Schmedich during that time?"

She began trembling causing Big Toke to put his hand on her shoulder again and say, "That enough. This dude need to leave. You need rest."

She shook her head. "No. I have to tell him everything. I might not get another chance before I die. I owe him this, plus a whole lot more."

Big Toke removed his hand and she told Raz, "I don't know where Schmedich was. With their new boss, Ed, I suppose. They needed approval before offing me."

"Did Schmedich do that to you?"

She began shaking uncontrollably and started to cry again. Sorry for having said something that caused her such pain, Raz waited in silence, hoping she'd recover enough to answer before Big Toke threw him out.

She raised her face to look at him again. "Yes, it was Schmedich."

"Was anybody there besides him and Mazurka?"

"Punk. I know, 'cause I heard him tell Schmedich that Tank had sent him down to make sure the job was done right."

Seething with rage, Raz was having difficulty remaining calm and objective. "I'm surprised he had the nerve to watch, the pervert."

"He was high. I know, because he made me take some of it before they taped my mouth shut. He watched while Mazurka held me down and Schmedich cut me." She wiped her eyes "They tried to make Punk leave, but he cursed them, told them his father was the richest man in East Texas, and he always got his way. After Schmedich stripped me, Punk…"

Her voice broke again, but she took a deep breath and continued. "When Schmedich first started his sick little game, he made small cuts across my breasts and around my privates. After he'd done that, Punk ordered him to stop so he could whack-off."

A grim-faced Big Toke caressed her shoulder. "Don't go through this again. He don't have to know."

She wiped her eyes, telling her friend, "Talking about it is no worse than living with it. Telling Raz might get me the revenge I've been denied up to now."

She fixed her eyes on Raz again. "Laughing like a crazy man, Schmedich kicked my privates repeatedly. The more I screamed against the tape the more he enjoyed himself. I prayed he would stop, but he started cutting deeper and deeper." She shuddered, dropping her head.

"That's enough," Big Toke said, turning to Raz, "You got to go now."

Raz fixed his gaze on Fran and wondered if he should leave or insist on hearing her out. While he was trying to decide, Fran regained her composure and said to Big Toke, "Just a little longer, please."

"I don't think I can ever forgive myself for coming down here and puttin' you through this misery again," Raz said. "But since it's already done, I'd like to ask you one more question before I go. If it's all right." She nodded and he asked, "Did Punk, Schmedich or Mazurka mention Patti at any time when you were with them?"

She shifted on the bed and moaned, "During those times when Mazurka wasn't pawing at me or raping me, he told me his new bosses knew how to take care enemies, even when they were women. He said his previous partners were the same way. He told me how they killed one woman who knew too much. Later, during all that pain and screaming, before I passed out, I heard Schmedich say I was dyin' a lot slower than the Northville whore, but he didn't mention a name. When I regained consciousness the next morning, they were gone. I'm sure they left me for dead."

Raz's pulse raced and his insides were as tight as the scars on his face. He knew he had to go, but something made him stay.

"I'd like to talk to Raz alone, please," Fran said to Big Toke.

Big Toke shook his head and let out a sigh of displeasure. "I be outside the door if you need me." He gave Raz a warning look as he left.

As soon as the door shut, Raz heard Big Toke say, "What you doing here? Get back up front!"

Raz and Fran exchanged glances and Raz said, "Wonder who that was?"

"I had to tell you this in private, Raz. I'm sorry for disappointing you, for sellin' the Hole and spending your share of the money You're the nicest man I ever knew, and the best thing that happened to me."

"Thanks for tellin' me. Like you, I thought for a while that we'd started something good."

"I apologize for not telling you everything then."

His eyes held hers. "It's all water under the bridge now, darlin'."

She attempted a smile, but her face, tight from the scars, made the effort appear painful. She told him, "I was comfortable with you, you know. It would've been good. Nothing's good for me now. You're great with the ladies, though, you'll find somebody else and be happy."

"I think I already have."

"Good for you. I'm sure she'll be better for you than I ever was. Forget about me. Don't worry about your share of the Hole, either. I'll have one of my friends deliver it as soon as my finances allow."

"Consider the debt canceled."

She studied his expression, trying to read his thoughts. "Is there anything else you want to say?"

"Yeah. Cato gave me a cassette tape to use as evidence against the crooks in Northville, but it was lost in a fire. I've got Mazurka on ice, but I don't know if the lawyers will accept his testimony. I have other evidence, too, but I don't know how they'll rule on it either. That's why I need you to give a deposition to that Fed I know. You do that, and it'll be a victory for both of us. Would you do it if he could guarantee your safety and give you complete immunity?"

"I'm willing, but like I said, I'll have to convince my friends."

He glanced at his watch and stood up. "The Fed's name is Schroeder. I'll tell him to arrange to meet you someplace other than here. He's rough lookin', so nobody'll suspect he's DEA if he ends up havin' to come here. I'm gonna go now. I know you're tired." He turned to leave, but stopped, looking into her eyes one last time. "Fran, findin' you has settled lots of things in my mind. Not the least of which is knowin' I've done the right thing lookin' for that butcher all this time."

"Sorry you had to see me like this. I'll be waiting to hear from Schroeder."

"I'll see to it that Schmedich and Mazurka pay for what they did to you, one way or the other. Punk, too. If it turns out Schmedich did the same thing to Patti, I'll make sure he pays double."

She attempted another smile and said, "Thanks for caring enough to look me up. Give my love to Becky and be careful." Tears welled up in her eyes, and he leaned down and delivered a soft kiss to her scared cheek. Then, he turned and left the room without looking back.

He paused outside the closed door, still numb from everything he'd seen and heard. Sensing his mental turmoil, Big Toke didn't speak immediately. After a while, he said, "You satisfied?"

Sensing a note of sarcasm in his voice, Raz replied, "No. And I won't be 'til I get whoever did that to her."

"You say your interest in her strictly business?"

"That was before I saw her. I believe the savage that cut her up also murdered my wife. Who were you talkin' to when you came out while ago?"

"Don't know his name. Say he came wit you and was worried somethin' happen to ya."

"You'll have to take Fran away from this place."

"You crazy? This her home."

"That black dude you found lurkin' in the hall's Snake Hamilton, nephew of the man Fran sent prison. He's in cahoots with the ones who did that number on her. It would make him a big wheel in Northville if he tells them where to find her."

Big Toke gave him a skeptical look. "I don't think he do that to us. You, maybe, but not him."

"You're not gonna move her?"

"I talk to Shoulders and Shug, see what they say. I doubt they want to."

Raz started up the hall. "You may be sorry if you don't."

He didn't see Shoulders in the little room, so Raz returned to the main hall and found a nervous Snake waiting for him at the bar, drinking a beer. Not stopping, Raz said, "Let's go."

Snake jumped up, and followed him close enough to be heard over the loud music. "Man, you look like you seen a ghost. What happen back there?"

Raz kept walking, ignoring the question and the hostile stares of Kool Mama's customers.

When they stepped outside, Snake said, "You find somethin' out, didn't you? Know you did, 'cause you back there so long."

Raz faced him. "Why'd you go back there? Tell me now, so I know if I want to ride back with you."

"Cool down, man. I's jus' tryin' to find a place to take a leak. Why that bother you?"

"'Cause I don't like your choice of friends in Northville. Remember this. If you want to stay healthy and enjoy Cato's money, forget Kool Mama's. As far as you're concerned, you don't even know this place exists. Got it?"

"You *did* find her."

"No, I didn't. Fran Druman is dead. You will be too if you don't forget bringin' me down here. Now, see how quick you can get us back to Northville in one piece."

CHAPTER 30

S-nake pulled into the backyard of his Sycamore Street safe house at 2:10. He turned off the engine and lights, lit a joint and offered Raz a hit. He waved it away, reaching instead for the half-empty six-pack at his feet. Neither the distance nor the beer had eased the shock he felt after seeing Fran.

I need to rest and think about what to do 'til I can get rid of Mazurka. If Schroeder's back by then, I'll tell him Fran wants to give him a statement. I'll probably have to go to Houston for the interview. Hopefully they'll put her in the witness protection program and hide her 'til she can testify.

He hoped for Fran's sake Big Toke and Shoulders had moved her someplace new right after he left. He'd never completely trusted Snake, and now he could potentially ruin everything and get Fran killed in the process.

I'll call Pop early tomorrow to get the latest on Lassiter. He might be able to give Fran some added protection.

Ignoring Snake's attempts to draw him into conversation, he drank his beer in silence. He was exhausted, and had nearly reached his limit, both physically and mentally.

From the time he'd agreed to work for Lassiter, he'd been on a potentially deadly roller coaster ride that never ended. He sighed, realizing he was too tired and angry to make rational decisions. Before he passed out, he needed to go check on Mazurka. Once that was done, he could fall into bed and hope things would look better in the morning.

When they got back to the van, Snake said, "So, Fran Druman's dead. Too bad Uncle Cato ain't alive. He be happy that white bitch got what she deserve.

To show *my* appreciation, I ain't gonna charge you nothin' for them doughnuts you cut in my new leather seat."

"If I weren't so damned tired, I'd punch you."

"Why? That woman ain't nothin' to you no more. That what you tol' me, anyways. Don't forget that little somethin' you promise me for takin' you."

"I can't remember anything when I'm pissed off. Like I told you, I'll have a permanent lapse of memory if I hear you've told anyone 'bout our trip."

"You *promise*, man." He slammed his fist against the steering wheel. "Shoulda knowed not to trust you."

"As soon as I'm rested and if you haven't betrayed me, I'll leave word for you with Bull and we can get together."

He got out as Snake mumbled a few choice words directed at his lineage and manhood. Raz walked stiffly to the van, climbed in and backed out without turning on his headlights. After working his way out of The Quarters and making sure Snake hadn't followed, he headed toward Town Lake Road.

He was still horrified by what he'd seen and learned at Kool Mama's. With each turn in the road, he relived it and felt guilt over his friend's new reality.

Wish I'd captured Schmedich instead of Mazurka, he thought. *Could've avenged her and made him identify that woman who did the same thing to Patti. She's probably one of Greta's friends, or one of the porn stars. Birds of a feather flock together, Daddy always said. The mystery woman probably learned her sick art from Schmedich.*

What am I gonna do to that woman when I find her? Until now, the mere thought of hurting a woman, good or bad, was unthinkable — it was completely un-southern. *I promised Fran I'd let the authorities handle the butcher who murdered Patti, but it's gonna be hard not to kill 'em myself.* The only thing that might stop him was knowing what Anita and Becky would think of him if he became a murderer.

When he got to the lake house, he drove toward the front porch, checking for surprise guests as he went. When he was convinced no one was waiting for him, he drove down the hill and parked in front of the boathouse.

When he went into the boat house, Mazurka was in a deep sleep on the cot, with his back turned toward the boat slip. He didn't move when Raz held the flashlight close to evaluate his condition. He was breathing normally, and there was no sign of fever. He'd also eaten, judging by the empty sandwich wrappers on the floor.

Raz went back outside and locked the door. He got back in the van and drove up the incline to the garage, parking behind it. He got out, flashlight in hand, and walked to the back door. It was a clear night, but the quarter moon didn't give off enough light to see by.

He switched off the flashlight on the back porch and stopped to look and listen. He didn't hear anything, not even a locust or a katydid, which made him uneasy.

He was so tired that he had trouble unlocking the door. He finally managed to get inside, then turned and locked the door behind him. He swung the flashlight around the kitchen and front room to make sure all the shades were down and there were no signs of forced entry. He started limping down the hall toward the bathroom, and had just passed the back bedroom when a rustling sound caused him to freeze and shut off the flashlight. *Somebody's in the house!*

Berating himself for not checking the front door, he waited and listened, wishing he had Shag's pistol, but he'd left it in the kitchen. There were more rustling sounds, this time from a spot near the wall in the back bedroom. Then he heard someone breathing.

He eased back into the kitchen, picked up the pistol and returned to the bedroom door. "Who's in there? Speak up or I'll shoot!"

A trembling female voice replied, "Don't shoot, Raz. It's me!"

He flipped on the light and looked at Anita, who was hiding behind the bed. "Are you nuts? I could've killed you! What're you doing here?"

She stood up, but immediately sat down on the side of the bed. "You scared me half to death. I heard a car drive up and was afraid it was some of Mazurka's friends."

He shoved the pistol into his back pocket and said, "If it had been, you'd be dead by now. You know I didn't want you here by yourself. What if Mazurka got loose and grabbed you? You don't want to be alone with him, believe me."

"Don't be mad, Raz. I left, but was worried and wanted to be here when you got back. Ethan told me Mazurka was harmless."

Raz sat down on the side of the bed with a long sigh. "Don't know if I can make it to the other bed or the bathroom, so I'm not gonna argue with you anymore."

She pulled back the bedspread and top sheet. "Care to tell me about how things went tonight?"

He shook his head and pulled off his boots, then his pants, grunting when he bent his knees. "Too tired. Ache all over. Talk in the morning." He pulled off his shirt and hobbled to the bathroom.

As he walked out of the room, Anita looked at his back, then his knees with concern. When he returned, he found a glass of milk and a sandwich waiting for him by the bed. Sitting down, he ate and drank in silence, not daring to meet her gaze.

When he finally looked at her, he saw both fear and deep concern in her eyes. "Thanks," he said, giving her the glass.

"Would you like something else? Something for your back and knees?"

He responded as if he hadn't heard her. "It was awful, darlin'."

"I'm sorry. Want to talk about it?"

"Fran Druman is dead."

"I'm so sorry." A shocked expression swept over her face. "But how?"

"After this is all over, I'll explain everything. I don't think I can talk about it right now."

Her expression told him she was concerned about more than Fran's welfare. "Okay. I guess I'll just have to wonder if you would've come back to Northville if you'd known she was dead."

He patted her hand. "You don't have any reason to worry about anythin' like that. If I can just keep you safe until I get untangled from this mess, I'll consider myself a lucky man." He stretched out on the bed.

"Get some rest, cowboy. You look nearly dead yourself."

He watched her straighten the pillow and top sheet, and asked, "Were you able to get in to see Becky and my mother?"

"Yes. The first thing Becky said was, 'Where's my daddy?'"

His face lit up. "Really?"

"She wanted to know when you'd be back to see her. She suggested you come when her granddaddy wasn't home, because he's real mad at you."

"I'd feel insulted if he wasn't. What'd you tell her?"

"That you love her and how you two will be together real soon. She's a bright little girl, Raz, but she's confused."

"And my mother? Can I move her without bringin' the law down on me?"

"I'm afraid not. The administrator said government red tape prevents it without doctor's approval. That will take weeks."

"I hate red tape. Guess I'll have to settle for hopin' she and Becky will be all right." He took her hand and pulled her down, kissing her. "Thanks. After I get to feeling better and things settle down, I'll show you some *real* appreciation."

She blushed. "There'll be plenty of time for that after you climb down off your high horse and make a commitment."

"I didn't know an ex-married woman ever blushed."

"Heat rises." With that, she turned abruptly and walked through the door, shutting off the light.

If I wasn't so exhausted and sore, I'd go after her and take advantage of that rising heat. Guess I'll have to settle for sleepin' instead.

As he drifted off, he heard a roll of thunder in the distance. He hoped the storm wouldn't put a kink in his plans. *I'll get up early and call Zapata and Pop. If there isn't encouraging news about Lassiter, I'll call the Houston DEA's office. If they've got an open file on Fran, maybe a supervising agent can contact Schroeder or Lassiter, and then go out and check on Fran. I'll explain how frail she is and warn them about Big Toke and Shoulders. Gotta call Sonny Irby early, too. That'll melt the snow Rudy the Red Nosed Reindeer's sleigh. Gonna be a fun time…*

CHAPTER 31

Raz saw daylight filtering through the shade and heard dishes rattling in the kitchen. He sat up abruptly and raised the shade, disturbed by how late he'd slept. He'd forgotten to tell Anita to wake him early.

Swinging his feet off the bed, he tested his sore knees and found them feeling a bit better. His watch read 10:15. "Damn!" he moaned.

Picking up his shirt off the floor on the way to the bathroom, he called out, "Anita, I'll be leavin' in a few minutes. Go get your car; you've got to leave when I do."

When he came out of the bathroom, she was waiting by the bed. "You're not goin' anywhere 'til you eat, cowboy. It's ready."

"I'm runnin' late."

"Makes no difference. You've got to eat. Nancy Nurse's orders." She said and headed toward the kitchen.

Joining her, he looked down the slope to the boathouse. "Put somethin' in a bag for our hotel guest. He can eat it on the way."

She gave him a puzzled look. "On the way to where? I thought you worked out a deal where the narcs would handle him." She got her own plate of eggs, toast and coffee and sat it down opposite the one she'd put out for him.

"Depends. I'm hopin' Lassiter is already in town, or on his way. I need to meet him as early as possible. Got to call Pop, too, but I've got to call somebody else first." He sat down in front of the food and picked up the coffee.

"I'll make some sandwiches for your boat house friend and put 'em in a sack after I eat."

"Thanks."

He'd slept well and felt refreshed, even though he was still sore. Glancing at his watch between bites, he said, "Drive to the next county and double back. When you leave, I'll follow to make sure you make it."

"Do you have to talk about this while we're eating? I'm scared enough already."

"I'm sorry I've put you through so much. I'll call you at your parents' house around noon to let you know what's goin' on."

Finishing his breakfast, he headed for the telephone. "We'll leave as soon as I make a couple of calls to see if Lassiter is here. I've got to get Mazurka out of here."

Pulling a scrap of paper from his pocket, he dialed Zapata's cell. He waited through ten rings before hearing a cautious, "Hello?"

"Zapata? Raz, if you're where you can talk, I wanna ask a favor."

"I'm clear. How'd the Houston trip go?"

"I found her, but she's in bad shape and would have to be moved to a safe house. If she can get her present business partners to cooperate, she'll cooperate. Schroeder needs to slip in and talk to her before the Northville crooks find her."

"Schroeder called. Won't be here 'til late today. Can she wait 'til tomorrow?"

"Too risky. Call your Houston office. Explain the situation and tell them to send somebody to talk to her." He gave him the name and location of the club, and told him about Big Toke and Shoulders. "They might give your guys some static. Make sure they tell the guys guarding her I sent 'em." He gave him Fran's assumed name and described her physical condition.

"Give me an hour," Zapata said. "Where can I reach you?"

"We don't accept calls here. I'll call you. Haven't talked to Pop yet, so I don't know where Lassiter is. I was hopin' to deliver Mazurka to him or Schroeder this mornin'. If Lassiter doesn't show and I miss you when I call you back, meet me north of town this afternoon as planned. I'll give my prize witness to you then." He hung up.

Using an old directory under the telephone, Raz found and dialed Sonny Irby's home number. Sonny wasn't real sharp when Raz knew him in high school, and he probably hadn't got any brighter since. *I'll rattle his chain just enough to give me a little advantage.*

"Hello? Irby residence," a woman with a Spanish accent answered.

"Let me speak with Sonny Irby," he said in a commanding voice.

"Who calls, please?"

"The FBI."

"Who?"

"Los federales , señorita. Now, put your boss on the phone."

The receiver was dropped and shortly, a cautious male voice said, "Sonny Irby here."

Disguising his voice, Raz said, "Hello there, Rudy. FBI here. I've got some urgent business to talk over with you this morning. What time would be convenient for me to come by your place?"

There was a pause. "You've made a mistake. This is the *Irby* residence. There's no Rudy here."

"Oh, did I say *Rudy?* Sorry. Damn these complicated federal case reports. Just a slip of the tongue, Mr. Irby. Can you meet me at your bank at one this afternoon?"

The long silence at the other end of the line made Raz smile and wonder if Sonny's ugly red nose had suddenly lost some of its glow. Finally, the banker said meekly, "What did you say your name was?"

"I didn't say, but it's Vandiver. Jim Vandiver."

Another pause. Sonny asked cautiously, "Mr. Vandiver, what is the exact nature of your business with my bank?"

"I told you already. We'd also like to check all business transactions your bank has made for the last five years. We've received a complaint about some possible irregularities. I'll have a couple of IRS agents with me. We'll try to finish in time for you to open on schedule on Monday."

"Well, uh, I don't know. Since today's Saturday, the bank's closed. Why don't you call back Monday?"

Raz smiled. "I suppose that'll be all right with the U.S. Attorney, Rudy. I mean Mr. Irby. I'll have to ask you not to discuss this call with anyone between now and then, particularly your sheriff and chief of police. Understand?"

"Well, I—"

"I also want to make it clear that if Raz Jester contacts you, you need to tell him the matter is being taken care of, and not to be worried about anything he and Mr. Mazurka discussed with me."

"Raz Jester? Mazurka? You've talked to them? I, uh, I meant to say I don't know anybody named Mazurka."

"That so? That's strange. Most of our conversations have been with Blackie Mazurka and Raz Jester, and both of them seemed to know you quiet well. Since Mr. Jester is so personally involved in Northville matters, we'd like to keep him out of our investigation from this point forward. See you Monday morning. Have a nice day."

He hung up and smiled. "Sonny, you sorry slimeball, I think maybe you should have a serious talk with your pals, Tank and Olin, before they take a quick trip out of town or come up with a deal that'll make a certain ex-quarterback real happy."

He turned to find Anita watching him, "I think I just hit a hornet's nest with a Hail Mary pass, darlin'. I hope that'll keep Tank and his trigger-happy pals off my back and persuade Beer Gut to give me a killer." He glanced at his watch. "I'll be here a while longer makin' calls, so maybe it's best you don't wait for me. I'll call you later."

He picked up the phone and called Pop. "Pop, it's Raz. You heard from Lassiter yet?"

"I've been worried 'bout you, son. Glad you're okay. Yeah, Lassiter called. Seems Schroeder already filled him in on you lookin' for Fran and about some other evidence you have. I filled him in on what happened here. At this point, he'll still have to operate on the sly, but he said if Schroeder calls back and tells him you found Fran, he'll go straight to the governor's office with a special request. He said findin' Fran'd be too big for any politician to fight."

"I did find Fran and she's ready to cooperate if the agents can get around her bodyguards." He described her condition and those responsible. "It was rough seein' her like that, Pop, but I'm glad she's gonna help us."

"I'm sorry that happened to her, too, son. Her testimony will for sure clean up Northville, maybe all of East Texas."

"Since Lassiter and Schroeder are MIA, I'll have to stick to my plan to deliver Mazurka and the other evidence to Zapata early this afternoon. Hope they're here by then. Tell Lassiter I'll call everybody after makin' the delivery. Wish me luck."

He was encouraged that the Feds in Houston would be talking to Fran, but disappointed that he couldn't deliver Mazurka to Lassiter before noon. *I hope everything ends in a win for the good guys.*

He went into the kitchen to get the sandwiches and a handful of paper towels. Feeling Shag's pistol in his back pocket, he pulled it out to put it away, but hesitated. He didn't plan on shooting anybody, but having it as an insurance policy made him feel better. He shoved it back in his pocket and headed for the kitchen door.

Mazurka was awake, laying on the cot, grumbling about the heat and his poor accommodations. Giving him the sandwiches, Raz said, "Eat up and thank the moccasins you're still alive. I'm takin' you out of here today."

Mazurka began eating. "Where to?"

"We're goin' for a ride to blow the stink off you. This place smells like an outhouse. What'd ya do, crap your pants?" He dropped the towels on the cot.

Mazurka swallowed and took another bite. "I ain't goin' nowhere that Tank and Smeddish can see me."

"You're so good at throwin' lead, you should be real good at dodgin' it by now too. My narc friend'll decide your final destination. I hear the Feds treat criminals like royalty."

Ignoring further protests, Raz left and went back to the cabin. Much to his disappointment, Anita was still there. "You should be halfway home by now."

"I'm not leaving before I look at your back and legs."

He glanced at his watch. "Okay, I won't be leavin' for a while yet. Where do you want me, on the bed?"

"Rein in your stallion, cowboy. Sit." She pointed to a dinette chair.

Taking off his shirt and dropping his pants, he sat down. "I feel ridiculous bein' on my best behavior around you all the time. I feel like a homerun hitter steppin' up to the plate with a broken bat."

"Just keep your eye on the ball. There are more important things to consider right now. Remember?" She touched his back, causing him to jump. "It's still red, but it looks much better." She gently rubbed ointment on it, and then knelt in front of him to examine his knees. "They're still swollen, but they're not as discolored. Want an ice pack?"

He glanced at his watch. "I'll be here 'til I get a report from Zapata, so sure."

After being iced down for half an hour, he looked at his watch and reached for his shirt, anxious to talk to Zapata again and find out if things were under control in Houston. Removing the ice pack, he stood up and pulled up his pants, giving Anita a solemn look.

"Wish there was somethin' else I could do for you," she said. "I can tell you're worried."

"Thanks. You've done plenty already." He dialed and Zapata answered immediately. "Jester?"

"The one and only. Did the guys in Houston talk to Fran yet?"

He paused, "Are you sitting down?"

"What happened?" A sense of urgency swept over him.

"The guys in Houston made a run out to Kool Mama's, but by the time they got there, the place was nothin' but smoke and ashes."

"The hell you say. Is Fran okay?"

"A fireman told our agents that a woman in the back apartment didn't make it out. A big black guy there told them her name was Rachael Levitt. He said he didn't know anybody named Fran Druman."

Feeling weak in the knees, Raz pulled up the chair Anita had brought from the kitchen "Fran was..." He glanced at Anita. "She was the best witness we had. What a low blow. I'm gonna kill Snake Hamilton."

"That small time dope dealer and pimp? What's he got to do with it?"

"Plenty, I think. If he did it, this move made him much more important to the organization." He told him why.

"Proving it will be difficult. A fireman at the scene told our agents the cause of the fire is still under investigation. It could've been started by an oxygen tank exploding. The big guy said Levitt was on oxygen."

"She was, and pain pills of some kind. This makes me wonder if she'd still be alive if I hadn't gone to see her."

"Schroeder'll shit a brick. You still have Mazurka and the other stuff. Right?"

"Yeah. I'll deliver everything to you shortly after noon, unless the sky keeps fallin' on me. Be there." He hung up and turned to Anita. "I guess you heard enough to know what happened."

She nodded. "I'm sorry. Please don't blame yourself for that, too."

He looked through the window at the lake. "How can I not? This is the fourth woman I've been close to who's ended up dead." He looked at her. "See now why I wanted you to leave earlier?"

"There's no hurry. I called mother when I got up and told her where I am so she wouldn't worry. I told her not to call me here, but she must've forgotten, because she called back later. When I answered the phone, she hung up. That was kinda odd."

He felt a sudden knot in his stomach. "You took a call on *that* phone? How could you, Anita? After everything I've told you?"

"I had to call my mother. Besides, I guess I kind of forgot."

"You haven't forgotten how to run have you? Run to your car now and get out of here as fast as you can. Don't even take time grab andything or lock up. I'll be right behind you with my witness."

He took her arm and they stepped out the back door. A shot rang out and a bullet tugged at his hat. Ducking, he jerked Anita back into the kitchen and pulled her down to the floor. He locked the door and said, "Too late to run now. Stay down. Better still, go in the bathroom and get in the tub 'til the shooting's over."

"My God, Raz! Are they tryin' to kill you?"

"Of course not," he said, peeking over the windowsill. "Somebody just hates my hats. Now get into the bathroom. Crawl. Don't you dare stand up."

Raz pulled Shag's pistol from his pocket and peeked over the windowsill. He didn't see anybody. Seconds later, three quick shots came from the boat shed, telling him he'd lost his last witness. The gang was moving fast. Any minute now and they'd shut him up, too.

He shook his head. *I was so close to gettin' this wrapped up.*

He crawled to the other side of the kitchen for a better view of the lake. There was no one in the weeds or bushes, but a bullet zinged by his head just as he ducked.

"Raz? You all right?" Anita called out.

"Yeah. Stay in the tub!"

He moved back to the rear window. Peeking over the sill, he saw a short, pudgy man with a boyish face jump behind a pine tree near the garage. *Schmedich!* He raised the pistol and clicked off the safety. Seconds later, he saw a tall man behind the storage shed near the garage. He didn't recognize him.

"Someone's running to the front, Raz!" Anita screamed.

Sprinting toward the front room, Raz heard footsteps and saw a man run past the front window. *Shag Shammerhorn!* The bearded attacker slammed his weight against the front door, but it held. Anita screamed when Shag began trying to kick the door in.

Raz leveled the pistol at the entrance and waited. When Shag kicked the door open and ran into the room, he spotted Raz and fired first. Then things happened fast. After an eternally long exchange of deafening gunfire, both stopped shooting at the same time and a deathly silence hung in the smoky haze.

Suspecting Shag was moving behind the bed, Raz rushed to a better vantage point and found his adversary on the floor, face down and still. With one killer down, Raz ran to the kitchen to look outside for Schmedich. The door burst open and Smeddish rushed in, firing.

Raz dived behind the dinette table and fired back, but missed. He pulled the trigger again, and heard a click; the gun was empty.

He shoved the table against Schmedich, and tackled him. When the killer's pistol slid out of his reach, Raz grabbed him around the throat.

"This is for butchering Fran Druman, sicko! I might let you breathe a little longer if you give up the name of the woman who cut up my wife two years ago!"

Seeing him struggling to speak, Raz loosened his grip and Smeddish blurted out, "You're gonna die, jailbird, just like your slut wife!"

Raz's fingers tightened again. "Wrong answer, slimeball! Want to try again?"

When Schmedich managed a nod, Raz loosened his grip. Seeing an opening, Schmedich rolled, causing Raz to lose his balance and fall. Smeddish made a dash for his pistol lying near the back door, and Raz tripped him. Raz scrambled for the pistol but was stopped short by a sharp pain in his left thigh.

Schmedich rushed past him for the gun, but Raz grabbed his waistband. *Rip!* The killer crawled out of reach, exposing his lower half.

Stunned, Raz stared. *Schmedich is a woman!*

Recovering, he felt his hand bump his old sword leaning against the cabinet. Grabbing it, he jumped to his feet and whirled to face the half-nude Schmedich, who was raising her pistol to fire.

Raz shoved the sword into the murderer's belly with all his strength. Schmedich cried out and staggered back, white-faced. Teetering on her toes, she looked with disbelief at the sword protruding from her gut. Following a feeble attempt to pull it out, she fell to her knees, then to her side. She convulsed, gasping for air before her body shuddered and became still.

Suddenly remembering the third man, Raz took Schmedich's pistol and knelt by the window. As the tall man ran into the woods beyond the backyard, Raz fired but missed.

Sighing loudly, Raz tried to sit down on the floor. The sharp pain in his leg made him jump back to his feet. Twisting around and looking at the back of this leg, he saw a short hunting knife sticking out of his thigh. He pulled it out with a grunt, and reached for some napkins stop the bleeding.

"Anita?" he called out. "You all right? Talk to me!"

She appeared in the hall and peeked cautiously into the kitchen. Her face was pale, her eyes wide. "My God, Raz! What happened? Are you all right?" She ran toward him, but stopped when she saw Schmedich lying in a pool of blood with the old sword protruding from her belly. "Oh, my God! Is he dead? Where's his pants?"

"*Her* pants. Schmedich is a *woman*. I killed a woman. Can you believe that?"

She looked at Schmedich's bare crotch and turned away with a shudder. "My goodness, he *is* a woman."

"Yeah, I finally got the butcher that killed Patti." He headed toward the door, "Be right back."

"But you're bleeding! Where are you goin'?"

He saw the shoebox on the garage floor near the back wall. When he picked it up, his worse fears were confirmed. The camera, pictures and videotapes were gone. Hoping he might still save his witness, he limped down to the boat shed. The door had been pried off its hinges. He found Mazurka lying beside the boat slip with half his head blown off.

Spent and disgusted with this turn of events, Raz returned to the house. Anita met him at the back door. He told her about his losses and made sure Shag and Schmedich were both dead.

He'd hated his wife's killer and had wanted him dead for more than two years. With the murderer lying at his feet, he wondered where the joy, relief, and satisfaction were. *I thought I'd feel better once the murderer was dead. I just feel numb.*

"Something's wrong with this picture," he said. "I just killed a murderer, but instead of getting me *out* of trouble, it got me in deeper. I can't use you as a witness; that'd just get you killed, too. I have no evidence left for the narcs, which means neither the state nor the Feds can help me now. Plus, there are *three* arrest warrants hanging over my head, two of 'em felonies. Tank can legally take me out if his friends don't kill me first. He and Olin are both home-free now." He shook his head. "All that and I just killed a woman."

"But he …she … was trying to kill you. Doesn't that count for somethin'?"

He righted dinette table and pulled a chair over to it. "Not with Tank and his friends running the show. So far, seems like everythin' I've done has only got me deeper in the stink pit." He sighed. "I really am on my own now."

"You have me."

"I'm sorry." He squeezed her hand, regretting that he'd sounded ungrateful. "Of course I do, and I appreciate you. I wouldn't have got this far without you."

"You've faced tough odds before. You'll get through this, too."

"Not with a gang of cutthroats chasin' me and the law out to get me, too. I'm back to where I started." He looked at her. "Still want to stick by me?"

"Of course," she said, stooping to examine the knife wound in the back of his thigh and his arm where one of Shag's bullets grazed him. He pulled her into the chair next to him and took her hand. Kissing it he put it against the scar on his face. He was about to speak when the telephone rang.

They jumped, and she asked, "Should I answer it?"

"Every crook in town knows where I am now. One more won't matter."

He took the bloody napkins off his thigh wound and tossed them into the wastebasket. He was still bleeding, so he grabbed some more napkins and applied pressure.

From the front room, he heard Anita's anxious, "Hello?" followed by a long pause. She reappeared in the door with a drawn look on her face. "It's for you."

"Who is it?"

"It's Mrs. Lawther, and she's frantic."

"How did *she* know I was at this number?"

"She called mother. I guess Becky told her about me visiting her at school."

"Can't you handle it?"

She shook her head. "She insists on talking to you."

Puzzled, he limped into the front room and picked up the receiver. "This is Raz."

Mrs. Lawther spoke so fast, he understood only two words: "Isham" and "Becky."

"Settle down, Mother Lawther. What's going on? What did you say about Becky?"

"She's gone, Raz. They took her. When Isham tried to stop them, they hurt him real bad. He's on his way to the hospital now. I don't know what to do. You have to do something before they hurt her!"

Absolute terror swept over him. "Who took Becky? When?"

"Two of the most vicious-looking men, not more than ten minutes ago. They didn't say why. Oh, Raz, why'd they do it?"

Numbed by fear and angry enough to kill, Raz sank down in a chair as his legs gave way. He didn't know who took Becky, but he knew who'd sent them. There was no time to talk about that now, or to remind Mrs. Lawther about his frantic call to her over two years ago — the one about *her* daughter and her subsequent refusal to help.

She must've been thinking along the same lines, because she said, "I know I let you down that time you called me about Patti, Raz. I'm so sorry. If I had it to do over again, I'd help you find my daughter, regardless of what my husband said. Please, forgive me."

"I'll get her back. I know who to call and I'll do it right now."

He hung up and looked at Anita's grave expression "Becky was kidnapped."

"Oh, no! Why?"

He reached for the telephone directory. "They want *me*, that's why."

"But you can't surrender to them after what just happened here. They'll kill you for sure."

"That doesn't matter now. I'm getting Becky back safe, no matter what."

He dialed Tank's sub-office and immediately heard a gruff, "Hello?"

"You've done some crappy things, Tank, but I never thought you'd sink this low."

The voice on the other end of the line was loud and confident. "Well, if it ain't our star quarterback. I was sittin' by the phone 'cause I figured you might wanna talk as soon as you heard what them guys did to your little girl. Isham Lawther's wife called me, too."

"What *your* friends did to Becky."

"I had nothin' to do with it. I'm just servin' as the go-between like any respectable public servant would."

"Stop lyin' and tell me what I have to do to get Becky back."

"You can start by surrenderin' to me. 'Sides that simple assault charge Shag filed against you, you're now charged with assaultin' me and Olin at the wreck, plus the murder of them two deputies I sent out to the lake to arrest you."

"Shammerhorn and Schmedich? Don't make me laugh. Even if they were your deputies, they didn't have to shoot their pal Mazurka to arrest him."

"Did Mazurka have an accident? Too bad. With Sonny so shook up that he left town, and two of my deputies bein' murdered, anythin' can happen. That means I've got to work harder to restore law and order, and in the process make sure I win this little contest we got goin' on. It's over, jailbird. Get your butt over here right now and I'll make some phone calls. I've already been told by a confidential source that if you're not here within an hour, they're gonna kill your kid."

Raz's head was spinning, making it nearly impossible to remain calm enough to think clearly. He finally said, "Meet me by the Ferris wheel on the

Square in thirty minutes. Have Becky with you, and she better be unharmed." He hung up.

"Isn't there another way?" Anita asked.

He shook his head, leaned forward and put his face in his hands.

"What can *I* do?" she asked

"Get your girls and leave town. I didn't tell him I had a witness that can back up my version of what happened out here, but it won't be long before they know. I'm sure the one who ran away heard you scream. Leave now, and call Pop. Tell him what happened out here, and ask him to pass it on to Lassiter and Schroeder. Ask him to call a lawyer he can trust, and Ollie Peavy."

"Can't you call somebody to help you? The FBI maybe? Kidnappin's a federal offense."

"I can't put Becky in any more danger than she's already in. The only thing I can do now is surrender to Tank and hope he'll have his friends take her back to the Lawthers."

"But what'll they do to you?"

"Oh, they'll crow to the media about arrestin' another dangerous criminal. Their bought judge will deny me bail, and one of their goons will do me in one night in my cell or they'll shoot me and say I tried to escape like I did before."

She hugged him and said, "Don't give up, Raz. It's all gonna work out. I just know it."

He was thoughtful for a moment. "At least I got Patti's killer, and I got her legal. If I don't survive this, I want you to see to it that Becky is taken care of. She needs a mother."

"Don't talk like that. Givin' up isn't like you. I want to hear the Raz Jester I've always known. Get out there and kick some butts."

He patted her hand and said, as if to himself, "I used to poke fun at prisoners cussing the law and bitchin' about how the legal system only works for people with lots of money and political clout. They always claimed that money controls everything. Looks like those losers were right."

She held him tighter. "Keep fightin' for Becky's sake *and* mine. A miracle will happen. You'll see."

"Never believed in miracles. Luck, maybe, but it looks like mine just ran out."

CHAPTER 32

After putting on another shirt and a clean pair of khakis, Raz followed Anita to her parents' home, then circled back and stopped on the south side of the Square to look at the homecoming crowd. There were the usual carnival rides and concession stands, plus loud country 'n' western music was coming from speakers hung on the utility poles. Cars were parked bumper to bumper along the side streets and out on the highway. It was a festive sight, making him think of past good times. Homecoming had always been the biggest day of the year in Northville.

He heard the rumble and screams coming from the roller coaster. *Becky'd have the time of her if she was here. This just doesn't seem like the proper setting for the end of my life.*

At the center of the crowd stood the giant, slowly turning Ferris wheel. It stopped frequently as people got off and on. Somewhere near it, Tank and his criminal friends would be waiting. *The sooner I give myself up, the sooner Becky will be safe. Best get this over.* He got out and walked to the Square.

He saw the long, sweeping arms of another carnival ride, its crane-like projections sweeping up, out and around. Its passengers screamed inside the revolving metal capsules.

He saw the wooden platform where they'd have the fiddling contest later in the day near the center of the Square. Across from there were a string of concession stands, the Jaycee's dunk tank, the Rotary Club's hamburger and barbecue stand and several other vendors.

He watched intently for Tank and Olin. He knew they'd like to intercept him outside the protecting embrace of the crowd. He saw only the friendly faces of the people he'd grown up with, some of them came up to shake hands while others called out greetings. Apologizing for his hastiness, he kept moving toward the Ferris wheel.

Halfway there, he ran into Frenchy and Lupé. He flinched when his old friend grabbed his arm and said, "Stop and have a hot dog and a shot of cognac with me and Lupé. It'll loosen you up."

"Can't. Gotta go." He cast a worried look at the Ferris wheel.

Frenchy's dark eyes showed his concern. "What you been up to? I been worried 'bout you, and you know we Cajuns hate to worry. You look like shit. What's goin' on? Why you keep lookin' over at that damn wheel?"

"When'd you start comin' to homecoming?"

"When I got rich and respectable. Me and my little woman walk 'round and look down our damn noses at the pricks that used to treat me like trash. I run into that snooty Bryan Fulton a few minutes ago and asked him for a match to light my cigar. When he give me his lighter, I pulled out a hundred dollar bill, set it on fire and lit my damn stogy with it. Thought he was gonna crap his pants, the crooked bastard." He reached for his back pocket. "You sure you don't wanna drink?"

"No, thanks. Gotta move on."

Frenchy grabbed his other arm. "Hell, you just got here. You ain't broke again, are you? I'll give you some more damn money if ya are."

Raz looked around them. "Have you seen Sonny Irby?"

"Hell no. Ain't you heard the rumor runnin' 'round the Square? That ugly little bastard left town all of a sudden. What the hell's wrong with you? You need a woman?" He slapped Raz's shoulder. "That's it, ain't it? You ain't been laid since you got home."

Spotting Tank's big hat near the wheel, Raz patted Frenchy's arm and told him, "Thanks, but we'll talk about it later. There's something I gotta do."

Frenchy called out after him. "You're 'bout as much fun as a man on the way to his funeral!"

Close to the wheel, Raz spotted Olin standing next to the sheriff. Their faces were red, as was the skin between their short-sleeved shirts and bandaged forearms. A bandage below Tank's hat indicated his head was burned, too.

Olin's posture was normal, but Tank was stooped, like he was favoring a burned back or leg. Their expressions were drawn and anxious.

Tank spotted him and nudged Olin. The sheriff started toward him, calling out, "Get yourself over here! You ain't got much time left on that deadline I give you."

Raz stopped in front of Tank, as curious onlookers turned to stare. Raz asked, "Where's Becky?"

Olin moved up behind Tank who lowered his voice and replied, "She ain't here. Them folks I called said she ain't comin' back 'til I tell 'em you're in jail."

"I'm not going anywhere with you 'til I see her."

Tank grabbed Raz's wrist. "Like hell you ain't. Cuff him, Olin."

Spectators moved closer to watch and listen, causing Tank and Olin to hesitate. Uncle Bud's voice boomed over the loudspeaker, "Hold it, folks! I've got a real surprise for you. As all of you know by now, ol' Uncle Bud tries to throw out a few roses with the garlic every now and then to show his appreciation to his listening audience. Well, this is one of them times. You all 'member our recently departed friend, Boobs Noonan. That pretty woman was ever'body's friend, 'specially the menfolk."

Several men laughed as Uncle Bud continued. "Boobs was a friend to all that liked hot chili and scorched burgers, but this song ain't dedicated to her, 'cause that would get me into trouble with my wife and girlfriend. It goes out to all them fine young men in Northville High's class of 2003 who made good use of Boobs' famous Back Room. Here it is!"

A couple of men in the crowd let out a rebel yell, and there was a smattering of applause as a recording of Marlene Dietrich siging began... *See what the boys in the back room will have...* Another rebel yell rang out as the song continued. *And tell them I'm having the same... And when I die, don't send me money or flowers and my picture in a frame...*

Olin pulled out his handcuffs, but hesitated sending a questioning to Tank. Raz heard fellow graduate Duck Campbell say, "What's going on, Tank? How come you pickin' on Raz again?"

Tank threw the crowd a cautious look, telling Duck, "Your jailbird friend is under arrest for committin' a serious crime."

"According to who, Tank?" somebody in the crowd challenged.

"Accordin' to the law," Tank snapped. "Now, ever'body step back. Let us through. This man's dangerous."

His remark caused a titter to run through the crowd, and Duck said loudly, "Dangerous to pretty girls and crooked cops, maybe. He ain't never hurt nobody that wasn't tryin' to hurt him."

The crowd pressed in closer. Made nervous by so many potential witnesses, Tank leaned over and told Olin something Raz couldn't make out. The sheriff looked around like he was searching for someone. He found Lard in the crowd and spoke to him. The fat deputy pushed through the crowd and left running. Tank and Olin tightened their grip on Raz's arms and began pulling him through the crowd toward the highway as the Dietrich song continued to play.

They'd moved about thirty feet through the crowd when the song ended and Uncle Bud announced, "Hold it! Stop the rides. Stop pawin' the girls, guys. Stop everything! Here's something none of you want to miss. It concerns our friend, Boobs, and our star quarterback of 2003. I've been waitin' for a special occasion to play this next little ditty that Boobs loaned me right after Raz came home. Well, I'm gonna lay it on you now, good people. Here's Raz Jester singing 'Trickle Down Love'."

Uncle Bud's stunning announcement sent a rush through Raz, because that song was the first thing on Cato's tape. That meant the tape hadn't burned up, after all. Boobs had done what she told him she wanted to do that first day, she gave it to Uncle Bud so he could play it on one of his programs.

Recovering, he shoved Tank and Olin to the side and made a dash through the crowd, heading for the parked van. He had to get to the radio station before Cato's testimony began playing, otherwise, those who wanted him dead would beat him to it. He knew they'd kill anybody who tried to stop them.

A murmur ran through the crowd as Tank and Olin ordered him to stop. He ran faster, hoping their injuries would prevent them from giving chase. He realized, however, that every thug in town would join the sheriff and the chief in a race to the radio station when they saw him drive away. If any of them got there first, the miracle Anita predicted would be his epitaph.

He'd almost reached the line of trucks beside the highway when the words of the corny song began. "My back is dry, and I'm not high, and I ain't eatin' welfare pie…" When Raz ran past Stretch Loving, his friend yelled, "Come back, Raz. It's not *that* bad."

Raz jumped into the van and sped toward NEHI, located about a mile north of town on Farm Road 2113. He flipped on the radio. The song was still playing. "It's undeniable that my supply is unreliable. My itching love ain't been tickled 'cause my tickle giver's fickle, and won't allow no love to trickle down on me." He grimaced and floored it.

He was relieved to see no police cars blocking the farm road. That gave him hope. Now all he had to do was out-run Tank and the mob's enforcers and get that tape. *That tape'll give me all the ammunition Lassiter and Schroeder needed to blow all them alligators snappin' at my ass right out of the water.*

About halfway to the station, a chill ran up his spine as the sound of the calm, deep voice of his dead friend came through the speakers. *"My name is Cato Hamilton. I'm speakin' to you via this recordin' from the administrative security unit of the Texas prison system on the date printed on this tape's cover. I'm makin' this voluntary statement while of sound mind and body, without promise of reward from anybody, includin' my friend, Raz Jester. I tol' him to give this here statement to the authorities. I swear 'fore God and on my mother's grave that every word I say is true."*

Cato's testimony would put a fire under all the thugs from the Red River to the Rio Grande. It would spell doom for Northville crooks in particular, unless some of them got to the station before him.

The recording continued: *"I hereby give this taped deposition to the U.S. Attorney for the Eastern District of Texas, Raz Jester, the U.S. Drug Enforcement Administration and the Department of Public Safety of Texas, drug enforcement division. Before I go on, I want to say I'm guilty of the offense I was sentenced for and lots of other things, too. All of 'em had something to do with drugs an' payoffs to public officials.*

"I'm makin' this statement now 'cause I don't think I'll make it out of prison alive. This my last chance to get back at them responsible for me bein' here, and them who already try to kill me in prison. I got nothin' ta lose by makin' this statement. I don't got nothin' to gain, neither, 'cept the satisfaction it give me. I givin' this statement to my special friend, Raz Jester, so he can make it right in Northville. So he an' them honest cops can kick everyone of them crooks I pay off out of office.

I hope this tape help Raz get his wife's killer, an' the man that murder his friend, Tim Barton."

Surprised by the weighty details of Cato's remarks, Raz said, "You're talkin' like a courthouse lawyer, Cato. I'm impressed."

The tape continued. *"Durin' the years me and my men distribute drugs in East Texas, I make regular cash payments to deputy, now sheriff, Tank Zelder, an' Chief Olin Culpepper in Northville, Texas, so they let my men an' me sell and distribute drugs in Northville and surrounding areas. I make the same arrangement with other lawmen, too. They named in the last part of this statement."*

Raz slapped the steering wheel and moaned, "Uncle Bud, you idiot. Turn it off and get out of there before you get yourself killed!"

The tape continued as Raz's speedometer bumped ninety. He was surprised by what was on the tape, considering Cato refused to cooperate with Lassiter. As the recording continued, Cato named his local enforcers — Schmedich Mazurka — and detailed how Mazurka had turned state's evidence. He spelled out the organization's methods of operation, and major narcotics transactions in a way that would allow easy verification. He gave the location of his records and permission to search and seize said records at any time Raz considered it appropriate.

He went on to explain how Tank and Olin conspired with the Mexican Mafia's enforcers and others to have the so-called Dixie Mafia take over his employer's drug business.

Raz skidded to a stop in front of the radio station. Making sure Schmedich's pistol was still in his back pocket; he jumped out and ran inside the small frame building. He glanced behind him before he slammed the door shut. So far, he was the only one there.

The front room contained a desk and a couple of chairs and was empty except for the sound of Cato's voice coming from a speaker hanging on the back wall. Calling out theDJ's name, Raz ran down the hall toward a lighted sign over a door that read: QUIET — ON THE AIR. He rushed into the room, but didn't see Uncle Bud.

Looking down the hall, he called out, "Where you at, Bud? Get in here quick and give me that tape!"

Cato's voice stopped and Raz's other song, "The Armadillo Hole," equally as bad as his first, began to play. Running to the console, Raz found the "Eject" button and pressed it, pulling out a full-size cassette. *Uncle Bud must've made his own copy and returned the original to Boobs.*

Raz saw a confused and disheveled Uncle Bud rushing from the restroom down the hall as he was about to leave the station. Swearing as he pulled up his pants over his bulging belly and flowing shirttail, his dark eyes glared through horn-rimmed glasses that were hanging loosely from ears and were barely visible beneath his mass of long gray hair. He yelled, "Why in the hell did you turn it off, Raz? I thought your songs were pretty good. That other fella spillin' his guts on the air was unreal, too, man."

"You'll be getting *your* guts spilled, if you don't leave with me now."

"I've been waitin' twenty years in this hick town for a hot item to come my way. I ain't leavin' now."

Raz shook his head. "Where's the original tape?"

"I gave it back to Boobs. That one's mine. Gimme."

"No way. Where's a phone?"

"In my office." He pointed across the hall. "What's up?"

Raz limped into the office "After I make a couple of calls, I'm leaving with this tape before I get shot. You're gonna have more company soon, and they won't be nearly as friendly as me."

Uncle Bud raced to the turntable. "Damn! I've got to get somethin' goin' here. How 'bout givin' me a statement over the air, Raz? You do, and loan me that tape again, and we'll both be on national TV for sure. We'll make a mint."

Raz called out, "You alone here?"

"Yeah. Ain't it awesome?"

"Lock the door in case we have company before I finish my call. Lay off the pot 'til this is all over, will ya? You need all your brain cells to make it outa this alive."

Raz dialed Pop's number and his old friend answered immediately. "Pop — Raz. I'm in a little bind out at the radio station, so listen close. Cato's statement wasn't lost after all, so see if you can find Lassiter and your Ranger friend and let 'em know I've got it. Tell 'em to get somebody out here pronto, 'cause all hell's about to break loose. If I can get away before Tank and his posse get here,

I'll bring the tape by your place and they can pick it up there. If I don't make it, I hope you'll come to my funeral."

"I was listenin' to the broadcast," Pop said. "I already called Lassiter. He said as soon as the got a call from Schroeder and Zapata about you goin' to Houston, he started up here. Should be here any time now. He'll call in the state troopers."

"Great. Tell him to send one out to Fifty-Nine North and flag down DEA Agent Rick Zapata. He's drivin' an old green Caddy. Tell him Mazurka's dead. Call Schroeder and tell him what's goin' on, too. Did Anita call you?"

"Yeah. I already called Ollie and told him to get a sworn statement from Anita after goin' out to the lake house."

"I don't want her involved in this, Pop. It's too dangerous."

"You've got no choice, son. Besides, she insisted on doin' it when I called her. I also called Harley Ritter's secretary. She said he'd try to get back today."

"Thanks, Pop. Gotta go. Somebody's comin'."

Uncle Bud was staring at him from the studio door; too puzzled or too high to understand the danger he'd put himself in. Putting the tape into his pocket, Raz ran to the room up front and slammed the bolt home.

Uncle Bud called after him, "How 'bout a copy of them songs, man? Gimme a break. You got no right to run off with a hot item like that. We got freedom of speech in this country!"

Raz saw Tank's patrol car swerve off the blacktop out front. He whirled and asked Uncle Bud, "Is there another way outta this place?"

The DJ looked through the front windows at the sheriff's car and shook his head. "What you see is it, man. Ain't that a kick?"

"You got a portable microphone back there?"

"Sure, but—"

"Bring it up here now. Move it!"

Uncle Bud's face lit up. "Man, what a cool idea. We'll make broadcast history."

"Just make sure we're on the air."

Raz looked through the glass panel in the upper half of the door and saw a worried-looking Tank slowly climbing out of his car.

"Hey, Raz, ol' buddy!" Tank yelled. "I come out to tell you not to worry 'bout none of them warrants. Them charges are dismissed. I already sent for your kid, too. I'll tell you where to pick her up soon as you give me that tape."

Raz saw Lard sitting in the backseat beside an unrecognizable passenger. A tall man in the passenger side front seat looked like the guy he'd seen running from the lake house.

Uncle Bud appeared in the hall door and tossed Raz the microphone.

"It on?"

"Yeah, man. I'm tuned in, too. Pretty soon the whole damn county will be tuned in with me. Ain't it awesome?"

Raz slid a chair over by the wall next to the door and put the microphone on it, telling the sheriff, "I'm not interested in more of your lies, Tank. You get nothin' from me 'til you hand over my little girl. She better be unharmed, too. The Feds and the state troopers are on the way. You and all your slimeball buddies'll be in jail this time tomorrow."

Tank motioned to the stranger in the front seat of his car and the tall man climbed out. He had black hair and a neatly trimmed beard. Judging by the bulge under his shirt, he was armed.

The sheriff turned toward the front door and said, "Gimme the tape and I'll sweeten my offer by givin' you the guy that killed your wife and Tim Barton."

"No deal. Patti's killer's already dead. I appreciate your offer, though, 'cause ever'body listenin' to Uncle Bud's broadcast just heard you say you knew who the killer was all along and did nothin' about it."

Uncle Bud giggled. "Cool, man. Keep spurrin' him on."

Tank clenched and unclenched his red, swollen fists, clearly confused about what to do next. "Quit the razzle-dazzle and talk serious, jailbird." That got no response, so he shouted, "Them charges against you ain't dismissed yet, and they won't be without my say-so. I know you don't wanna go back to the pen, so how 'bout givin' me that tape an' clearin' things up once and for all?"

"Where's Olin? You cuttin' him out of the deal or did he skip town with Sonny?"

"Olin ain't here. I'm sheriff of this county. You deal with me."

"No deals 'til I see my daughter. Your friends can take her to Isham Lawther, or bring her out here if that suits you better. She's the only thing that'll get you this tape. Get on your radio and tell Olin, if he hasn't taken off already."

Following another quick exchange with the tall stranger, Tank called out, "You didn't get the one who hooked your whore wife on dope. That makes *him* the one responsible for her gettin' cut up. He set her up with the cutter. Your honky-tonk girlfriend, too."

"You're tellin' me that man beside you did all that? Liar! He's most likely one of Ed's boys, maybe Alabama. I'm not lettin' him in. He'd shoot me and take the tape, no matter what kind of a deal you're offerin' me."

Tank glanced at his sidekick, telling Raz, "I don't mean *him.*" He limped over to the back door of his car, jerked it open and dragged out a half-conscious Punk Hutto. "I mean *him.* Punk not only helped plan Fran's killin'. He even done part of the cuttin'."

Raz saw Tank's willingness to expose Punk as an indication of just how desperate he was. No elected official intent on remaining in office in the county would dare treat the son of the town's richest man that way otherwise.

"If Punk did all those things, make him tell me himself."

Tank shook Punk, but couldn't rouse him from his drug-induced stupor. The sheriff beckoned to Lard, and the fat deputy scrambled out of the car to take hold of Punk's arm and steady him. Tank told his deputy, "Drag him in there so we can get this over with. Olin will be here any minute."

"Lard, stay out of this," Raz warned him. "You got no stake in this mess. Drop Punk and run before it's too late."

"Can't, Raz," Lard replied in his high-pitched voice. "Tank's the only real friend I got. Don't want him goin' to jail."

Lard put his arms around Punk and began dragging him toward the front steps, with Tank limping along behind them. Punk's face was pale, and his eyes were rolled back like he might be dying.

Tank looked back as Olin's patrol car turned into the driveway, skidding to a stop near the front steps. The red-faced chief jumped out. "What the hell you up to, Tank? How come you come out here without me? What the hell's Lard doin' with Punk?"

"Tryin' to save our asses is what," Tank said. "Didn't you hear that damn broadcast?"

"Yeah, me and ever'body else in three counties. The shit's really hittin' the fan. If we can get that tape, the stuff that went out on the air will just be hearsay. We can still keep the Feds from burning our asses. You need to stop tryin' to double-cross me."

"I'm not goin' against you, Olin," Tank said, pointing to Punk. "I'm makin' a swap for that tape. 'Member how Ed blamed Punk for the jailbird's wife gettin' strung out? All this shit's his fault. Can't you see that?"

"Sure," Olin said, "but he's *your* friend. That means *you've* got to face the heat from Ed this time. I told you not to involve him in our businesses."

Tank waved his big hands, raising his voice. "If it weren't for Punk's daddy, I wouldn't be sheriff. I owe the ol' man, an' I figure the best way to pay him back is keepin' his boy out of prison by swappin' 'im for that damn tape. After we get it, Alabama can take care of the quarterback and Punk can leave. Ed sent Alabama up here to make sure the jailbird's taken care of this time."

"Where's the damn tape?"

"Raz has it." He pointed at the station.

"How the hell you gonna get it usin' Punk?" Olin asked, obviously getting more agitated.

"With Medic dead, who else do we have that this crazy bastard wants? Ed's boys won't bring his girl back unless we get that tape."

Still dubious, the chief asked, "That's the way it is, is it?"

The tall gangster nodded. "The rich dope head means nothing to us, so we don't care how you use him. But if Jester won't agree to the swap, we'll have to do it the hard way. Ed says this hassle in Northville is threatening our entire operation."

"You know how the quarterback has always raised hell 'bout not arrestin' the one that got his wife strung out," Tank told Olin. "He'll swap. I know it. That way, we can do it clean like Ed wants and nobody else'll get killed besides the jailbird. You with me?"

Raz heard Uncle Bud moving behind him, and motioned for him to stay down. Raz turned back to see what was going on outside and saw that Lard had pulled Punk across the porch to the front door. Olin and Tank's face-off continued near the steps. He heard Olin tell Tank, "What'd you plan to do with that tape if you got it before I got here? I got just as much at stake as you. Don't think I'll let you out of my sight for a minute once you get it. I'm not takin' a chance on you usin' it to make a deal with the Feds and leavin' me out in the cold."

"Since I have the most to lose and I thought of how to get it back, it's mine," Tank replied. "I sure ain't leavin' it in your hands. Gerta told me how pissed off you was when you found out she called them shooters instead of you after the quarterback called her. *You're* the one wanting to cut deals."

"It weren't me that came roarin' out here alone," Olin replied. "You was gonna get it and bug out, just like Sonny, leaving me to face the music."

Tank put his big hand on the butt of his pistol. "I say it's mine."

Olin stepped back. "Now, hold on, Tank. Use your head. We both need it." He glanced at Alabama. "What if Alabama gets it and keeps it? After all, he works for Ed, not us. He'd take it to Houston to keep his boss out of the pen. That would leave both you and me out in the cold."

Wanting for instructions, Lard turned to look at Tank and Olin. Raz seized the moment and unbolted the door. He jerked Punk inside and re-locked the door. Maybe with no bargaining chip, Tank and Olin would persuade Alabama to send for Becky. At the least, it would delay their attack until help could arrive.

Olin turned in time to see Punk disappear through the front door. Stomping his foot, he shouted at Tank, "Look what you let happen! We'll never get that tape now unless you're willin' to start a firefight that might get Punk killed. Get them three warrants out of your car and serve 'em. That way, everythin' will be legal and we can still get the tape."

To gain some time and cause Olin to be even more suspicious of Tank, Raz shouted, "He can't do that, Olin. He already made a deal with me to dismiss all charges and send for my little girl. Soon as she gets here, I'm giving *him* the tape. I don't care what he does with it."

Glaring at Tank, Olin said. "You *were* gonna cut me out."

"He's lyin', Olin," Tank said, tightening his grip on his pistol

Alabama shook his head. "You badge-totin', money-grubbin' knuckle-heads. You think Ed would let either of you leave with that damn tape? It belongs to us. We took care of Cato Hamilton, and your boys were supposed to take care of his tape and the redneck that has it. Remember? Since you failed to keep your end of the bargain, we're all going inside to finish this while there's still time."

"What if he's got a gun?" Tank said. "I ain't gonna die and miss out on spendin' what I've got stashed."

Alabama pulled a pistol from beneath his shirt. "After I tell Ed about your screwy negotiations, he might decide you're both loose cannons, or worse, canaries ready to sing to the first law man you see."

Tank and Olin exchanged glances, and Tank said, "Now, look here, Alabama. We been doin' business a long time, we never double-crossed you guys."

"You haven't needed to until now," Alabama snapped. "Come on. Let's get that damn tape."

Raz glanced at the clock. *Where is Lassiter with those state troopers?*

When Alabama ran to the window on his left, Raz rolled away from the door to get behind the desk, gaining a clear view of the windows in the front wall and at each end of the room. He saw Olin jump on the porch and disappear behind the front wall next to the door.

"Come on out, Raz!" the chief ordered. "You're under arrest!"

"For doing what you and Tank forced me to do?" Raz called back. "No way. There are too many witnesses in here for you to kill me now."

"You call that ol' pothead DJ a witness?" Olin shouted back. "Give it up."

Behind him, Uncle Bud stirred and mumbled, "Pothead?"

Raz glanced at the window, but couldn't see Alabama. "Pull back, Olin, and let the Feds handle this. If you don't want to face them, leave now. I'll surrender to them when they get here, if that's what they want me to do." He heard glass shatter and saw Alabama jump back. "If you won't leave, at least put on a good show for the folks in Northville, 'cause Uncle Bud's been broadcasting everythin' you and Tank've said since you got here."

Silence on the porch. Olin peeked through the glass portion of the door. "What?"

"Just what I said." Raz pointed to the microphone on the chair. "You're on the air."

Olin jumped back out of sight, and seconds later Tank's face appeared. Ducking back out of sight, he asked Olin, "Reckon that's just more of his razzle-dazzle?"

"Maybe. But we're not leavin' 'til we do what we came to do." He called out to their tall friend at the window, "Ready, Alabama?"

"Yeah," Alabama answered. "But watch it. He's got a gun."

Tank swore. "Oh, shit!"

Hearing footsteps, Raz turned to see Uncle Bud walking into the room in clear view of Alabama. Raz told him, "Get back! Don't you know they've got to kill you, too?"

Uncle Bud gave him a dumbfounded look. "Huh?"

"Did you call the state troopers like I told you?"

"Tried, man, but the operator told me to go through the sheriff's office. The dispatcher there said Tank would handle it. Ain't that a kick in the ass?"

Raz moaned, checking the safety on Schmedich's pistol. He didn't know how many rounds it had in it, and never thought in his wildest dreams that he'd have to shoot a cop.

He heard footsteps outside and peered over the desk in time to see Lard heading for the road. "Come back, you coward!" Olin called out. "You're in this as deep as we are."

"He don't know nothin', Olin," Tank said. "He's too damned dumb to do anythin' 'bout it if he did."

"He can see, stupid,"

A black Continental appeared suddenly, blocking Olin's view of Lard. Lard froze, staring at the two men in the car. The driver jumped out.

Olin shouted, "Stop that man, then get in here! We got Jester bottled up inside. Alabama's at the window down there. One of you take the window at the other end, and the other one can look for a back window to go through. I've got the front door."

Wielding shotguns, Perdue and Lake ran to the studio window to Raz's right, opposite Alabama. Raz heard Tank tell Olin, "Ain't no use in either one of us riskin' our lives for that damned tape. Ed's boys will take care of it *and* Raz. Don't know 'bout you, but I'm pretty well fixed. Since I can't do nothin' here that'll help my cause, I'm buggin' out while I'm still in one piece."

Tank walked off the porch and called out to Lard, "Get in my car, quick."

"You talked me into this business," Olin said accusingly to Tank. "You can't quit an' leave me in this fix."

"Watch me," Tank snapped, not bothering to turn.

"You're weak, Tank!" Olin shouted. "First time the Feds put pressure on you, you'll make a deal with 'em like Alabama said. Just like Mazurka. I won't let you do that. Stop or I'll shoot you and tell the grand jury it was your operation from the start. There'll be nobody around to prove different."

The barrel of Olin's pistol appeared through the glass panel, pointing at Tank. Alabama yelled to the chief, "Do it, so we can get on with this."

Olin fired and Tank staggered and fell as Lake appeared at the end window. Without taking his eyes off him, Raz told Uncle Bud, "Get a gun if you've got one. Defend yourself."

"Gun?" He took off running down the hall.

When the glass in front of Lake shattered, Raz swung the pistol around in time to see the barrel of a shotgun pushing through the window. He ducked and felt a pain in his ears from the sound of the big gun firing. Plaster fell from the back wall. He heard a shot beyond the front door and felt something strike his left leg. He glanced toward the sound and saw a small hole in the lower edge of the glass panel. The chief jumped back out of sight.

Grimacing, he pulled his wounded leg behind the desk and peeked out front again, just in time to see Lake run around to the front porch and peer in through the window. The gunman leveled his shotgun to shoot, but Raz fired first and the man fell back. He heard Olin yell, "Jester's down, Alabama! Lake is down, too. You and Perdue need to finish Jester off."

The sound of breaking glass at the sliding window at the rear of the building told Raz somebody was either entering or leaving the building. He called out, "Uncle Bud, that you?"

No answer. Only running footsteps coming up the hall. He turned and pointed the pistol at the hall's entrance, but realized doing that exposed him to Olin at the front, opposite the approaching Perdue. The footsteps stopped, telling him the gunman was only a few feet away. He'd have to gamble that the chief would miss with his first shot, giving him time to return fire after he eliminated the one with the shotgun, who was a much greater threat.

Out of the corner of his eye, Raz saw Alabama crawling through the window. Raz fired at him and the big man jumped back.

"On the count of three, Perdue!" Alabama shouted at his associate in the hall. "He can't shoot you and me both! One!"

Raz looked back to the hall entrance.

"Two!"

The man in the hall still didn't show himself.

"Three!"

Perdue sprang into sight, shotgun leveled. Raz leaned forward and fired, knocking him back as the shotgun roared, shattering the glass in the front door behind Raz. Raz whirled to fire at Olin, but a pain in his chest meant he'd been hit again.

He rolled over to aim at Alabama and felt another sharp pain in his groin after Alabama fired. He returned fire and the gunman went down.

Clenching his teeth, Raz dropped the pistol as things went out of focus. Fighting to stay consciousness, he frantically searched for his gun but couldn't find it. He heard the roar of an engine outside and saw a helicopter landing on the front lawn. He tried to get to his feet, but was too dizzy and weak to move.

Uncle Bud's pale face appeared above him through the gathering fog. "Stay cool, man. Looks like the cavalry has arrived. I'll call an ambulance." He waved his hands. "This is gonna make me famous!"

Raz said weakly "You wanted a scoop? You got it."

"Yeah. Ain't it cool? We'll both be on national TV for a week, at least."

Uncle Bud's face disappeared... footsteps... excited voices... door opening... "Looks like this weirdo OD'd. No, wait. I feel a pulse."

A blurry face appeared over Raz, but his eyelids were so heavy he couldn't hold them open long enough to tell who it was. It was hard to breath. His mind wandered, and he heard that little voice in his mind say, *"Patti's father was right. You're no good. Not good enough for his daughter or Becky."*

Closing his eyes, he saw Patti's face, then Becky's and Anita's. Boobs smiling face flashed by as he felt his lips moving, and heard himself whisper, "Thanks, ol' gal, for saving the tape."

Then, everything went black.

CHAPTER 33

A dim light pierced the fog in Raz's brain. Then a dark, ugly face appeared. Fierce eyes moved closer, closer. A bright reflection off a shiny object in a hairy hand caused him to grunt and jerk back. The fog cleared a bit more, and he realized the shiny object was the blade of a straight razor. *Patti's killer's about to butcher me!*

He flailed with one arm and jerked his head to the side to avoid the blade. A gruff voice said, "How the hell am I supposed to shave you if you won't be still?"

The fog lifted completely and Raz moved his gaze from the razor to the man's face. Letting his arm fall, he said, "Frenchy, you're the *ugliest* angel I ever seen."

"How you know what a angel look like?" Frenchy snapped, leaning closer. "You ain't never seen one. You ain't likely to neither, goin' where you be goin' some day."

Raz tried to sit up, but Anita appeared and pushed him back. "Careful," she said, "you'll pull out the IV."

He felt a dull pain in his left arm and saw the tiny tube running to it. "Where am I? What's goin' on?"

"You're gettin' some free Cajun blood, Irish," Frenchy said. "Make your nature strong, an' whet your appetite for some good times wit some loose women."

Raz looked from Frenchy to Anita. "You're lots prettier than Frenchy, so move a little closer and tell me what happened." He suddenly remembered the shooting and Becky. Raising his head, he asked, "Is Becky all right? Did they get her back?"

Anita smiled. "She's fine. Question is, how do you feel?"

Relieved, he became aware of something tight circling his body and his aching chest. "Don't know yet." He rolled his head to check out his surroundings. "Where am I?"

"Coldwater Hospital. Your luck didn't run out, after all."

He glanced at the door. "It has if Tank's deputies find me."

"Relax," she said. "There are two state troopers standin' guard outside your door."

He took a deep breath and exhaled slowly. "Maybe I haven't run out of luck after all, thanks to Boobs. Wish she was here so I could give her a kiss. Hope I can make it to her funeral."

"Too late. They buried her yesterday in New Iberia, Louisiana. Knowin' how you'd feel 'bout not bein' there, your old classmates sent a big wreath and put your name on the list of friends that had good times her Back Room."

"I've been out that long?"

"In and out. Welcome back."

"Thanks. Now if I could just see Becky. Where is she?

"Back with the Lawthers. She was scared, but they didn't hurt her. Lawther came by one time when you were unconscious. Said to tell you to come see Becky when you're able. He also said he's willing to give you custody after you straighten some things out."

"Ol' Hatchet Face said that? You're not pullin' my leg, are you?"

"Couldn't find it in all those bandages if I wanted to. No, I'm not kiddin'. Apparently, his little run-in with Tank's friends opened his eyes to what you've been up against all these years. He and his wife both heard what Tank said about what's been goin' on, and how Punk was the one who got Patti hooked."

"Havin' Becky back with me? That'll be one great day."

"Horton Snitker is also willin' to put in a good word for you for savin' Punk's life. That means you're in good with all the town big shots 'cept those you went after. Cecil Cassidy even told me he's organizin' a special Raz Jester Day."

"Shut your mouth. They'd do that for me?" He looked at Frenchy who was folding up the razor. "Thanks for comin' by and tryin' to shave me, ugly. And for everythin' else you done for me since I got hom. Hope you found your van."

"I did." He winked. "Don't forget now. My little flower has a pretty sister waitin' for your battery to recharge." He glanced at Anita. "In case you ain't already made other arrangements."

Raz looked at Anita. "I intend to find out about that real soon. Wow! So much good news. I'm not used to that."

"You been fadin' in and out of the twilight zone like a cheap lantern for two days," Frenchy said. "'Bout time there was some good news."

Raz tried to sit up again, but fell back when sharp pains shot through his chest. "I'm so weak." Then he remembered being shot.

Seeing his expression, Anita asked, "What's the matter? Where does it hurt?"

"Who was in that chopper at the radio station? The Feds? What happened to Tank and Olin? Have I been charged with anything new?"

She held his hand. "You're in the clear on everything, cowboy. I'll let Pop and those officers in the waiting room explain everythin' to ya."

Another wave of fear swept through him when a sharp pain in his groin reminded him he'd been hit there too. Raising his head, he pulled up the sheet to peer down at his crotch, Anita gently pushed him back "I told you not to do that."

"But I have to know what's wrong with me down there."

"You can look later."

"I've got to know now. Tell me."

"Can't. I didn't see that part before they wrapped it up."

Frenchy opened the razor. "Want me to cut off the bandage so you can take a look, Irish?"

"No," Raz said. "Get away from me with that blade!" he said, then laughed weakly.

Touching his face, he said, "Something's wrong here, too."

"That's shavin' lather, dummy," Frenchy told him. "I couldn't shave you dry. Leave it there. It covers up your ugliest part."

Raz looked at the lather between his fingers. "Haven't you ever heard of an electric razor?"

"Beggars can't be choosers, Irish. Next time you get shot, I'll let you shave yourself." He gave the razor to Anita. "Your little woman can finish the job. Maybe you'll keep your mouth shut and lay still for her. I'm goin' down to talk to Pop and smoke a cigar."

Anita picked up a hand towel as Frenchy left the room. "I shaved my grandpa with one of these things," she said. "Be very still and don't talk."

She leaned closer. Her sweet fragrance was refreshing. "Have I ever told you what a snazzy-lookin' chick you are?"

She raised an eyebrow. "Yeah, every time ya want somethin'."

"Wish I felt good enough to want somethin' special right now." He sighed. "I've got to find out if my vital parts are still in workin' order. Tell me the truth. Are they?"

She started to smile, but caught herself and resumed shaving, wearing a solemn expression. "How would I know? All the doctor said was you'd been shot in the chest, leg and groin area."

"That's too general, woman. *Where* in the groin area?"

"I wasn't the attending nurse, so I don't know."

He pushed her hand aside and pulled back the sheet. "Well, I'm gonna find out."

She caught his arm. "Don't you realize you almost died? The doctor said you need to stay calm and not move around too much."

He lay back down. "Then you take a look for me."

"I will not."

"It wouldn't be like you were explorin' new territory."

Her grave expression caused him more concern.

Moments later, she met his gaze and told him, "Like I said already, Raz, you're lucky to be alive. Be happy with what you've got left."

"Maybe I will be, maybe not." He moved his hand under the sheet. "I'll tell you in a couple of seconds." He slid his hand over his crotch. "I'm all bandaged up down there. I can't tell."

"Then you'll just have to wait 'til the bandages come off."

"Like hell I will." He reached for the call button and settled back on the pillow to wait for the nurse. While he was waiting, Anita finished shaving him.

"Aren't you worried just a little about my manly parts possibly bein' out of commission?"

A middle-aged woman in a white uniform burst into the room. "What's the matter?" she asked Raz. "Are you bleedin' again? Havin' trouble breathin'? What's the problem?"

"None of the above." Raz pointed toward his privates. "Did that bullet tear up anything important down there? Are all my parts gonna work like before?"

The nurse gave him a disbelieving look. "How am I supposed to answer that if I don't know how they worked before?"

He smiled. "You should be so lucky, sweet cheeks. Seriously, just tell me if my parts *looked* like they're in working order."

She glanced at Anita. "Hard to tell."

His face fell. "What do you mean?"

A twinkle appeared in her eyes. "The parts I saw looked a little puny and shriveled up."

"Oh. Well, it's been a while since I used 'em, but the last time I did, everythin' worked fine. Can you at least tell me if I've still *got* all my parts?"

"Every inch, honey." She stifled a laugh and left the room.

Raz noticed Anita was also fighting to keep from laughing. Her face sobered quickly, but broke into a wide smile when he let out a long sigh of relief.

The levity left his face as he thought about recent events. He remained silent until Anita finished wiping off his face. "Did anybody ask what happened out at your lake house when those men tried to kill us?"

She put the pan on the table. "I gave a sworn statement. Ollie said you didn't have anythin' to worry about."

"I told you I didn't want you to get involved. Now, those crooks will try to kill you."

"Did you really think I'd stand by and take a chance on the local DA charging you with that, too? Besides, Pop and Mr. Peavey said my statement didn't mention anybody or anythin' that didn't have somethin' to do with that killin' at the lake house. But to make sure, me and the kids've been staying at a safe house out of town."

"I'm glad to hear that. What about all that shootin' at the radio station? I think I hit one or two guys. I hope one of 'em wasn't our chief of police."

She shook her head. "Pop told me Olin was killed by a shotgun blast. Uncle Bud told the Feds you fired in self-defense. Tank's hurt bad, but he'll recover enough to stand trial. He's already offered to turn state's evidence."

"Did they say who shot Tank?"

She nodded. "Olin Culpepper. Pop'll tell you about how they figured that out, and what happened to the others."

He sighed, squeezing her hand. "All this good news'll take me a while to believe. What about Cato's tape? Who's got it?"

She pushed his hair back off his forehead. "Pop said it's in good hands and bein' put to good use. Said somethin' about it being the same as a dyin' man's last will and testament, whatever that means. Believe me, that tape's the talk of the town — that, and your songs. Uncle Bud's so happy he's about to bust."

Hearing a gentle rap on the door, Raz turned to see Pop being rolled into the room by Lassiter. Schroeder and Zapata were close behind. After offering their hands and congratulating him on a job well done, Pop asked, "How you feelin', son?"

"Fine, now. Anita told me I'm not charged with anythin' new, and the nurse said all my important parts are still there."

"The charges filed against you have all been dismissed," Pop said.

"Great!" Looking at Lassiter, he asked, "You guys in on this for real now?"

Lassiter nodded. "Even the governor's man came to town to observe. He's anxious to find out what we've got so he can use it to clean up other parts of the state. Schroeder got some federal warrants. Things are moving fast. Examiners are already at the bank."

"Don't get so busy you forget about Snake Hamilton," Raz said.

"Why fool with minnows when we're after great white sharks?" Zapata asked.

"'Cause he got some explaining to do before I give him what his uncle sent."

"From what I hear, he won't be hard to find," Schroeder said. "Lassiter and I will come back when you're feeling better and give you an update. We'll take your deposition then, too."

"Any final word on Fran?" Raz asked.

"The fire marshal down there said the first explosion was caused by something other than an oxygen tank. Sorry about that, Raz. We could've used her."

Raz saw Anita looking anxious to hear his response. He told Schroeder, "I'm sorry too. I wish she'd been around to see the scumbags that cut her get what they deserved. I could've used my share of the Hole, too. I knew before looking her up that I'd found somebody else to take good care of the really important things," he said and looked at Anita.

"Sorry you had to do so much of this yourself," Lassiter said. "You're not alone now though. Those state troopers will stay outside your door night and day for as long as you're here, so you don't have to worry about Alabama's friends paying you a visit. The state attorney general is sending in a special prosecutor to handle all the criminal cases. We'll be getting a visiting judge, too."

"After this is over, don't be surprised if Horton Snitker recommends you to fill Tank's unexpired term as sheriff," Pop said. "He's already talked to me about it."

"You've got to be kidding. *Me*? I'm afraid bein' sheriff won't fit in with my plans to catch up on some good livin'."

"You'd adjust, like you did with all the stuff you did for Lassiter. Horton still hasn't admitted to bein' Punk's papa, but he's glad you saved him. Punk's in rehab, and his club's closed. Once the drugs wore off, he told the DA he's willin' to turn state's evidence and stay off drugs if they give him a deal that keeps him from goin' to the same prison where Tank and the others end up. Even Islam Lawther is singin' your praises. I expect his missus would've left him if he hadn't agreed to give you custody of Becky."

Raz's face brightened. "If I had a place on me that wasn't sore or covered up, I'd pinch it to make sure I'm not dreamin'. Did anybody talk to you about Rudy?"

"Not yet, but Anita told us what you told her. Regardless of what the examiners find at the bank, we won't be arrestin' Sonny Irby anytime soon. He's departed for parts unknown. Gerta Hutto, too. Now get some rest. We'll visit again tomorrow if you feel up to it."

"See ya," Lassiter said as they left the room.

Buoyed by their news, Raz gently rubbed his facial scar. "I'm glad that sorry, rotten business is finally over. Maybe now we can do some real livin' for a change, darlin'."

"I'm glad it's over too, cowboy. But most of all, I'm glad you're okay."

"Gettin' Becky back with no strings attached will be great."

"Who said there were no strings?"

"What?"

"The Lawthers won't give her back 'til you're married."

"Married?"

"Yep. You're familiar with the term. It's where a man and woman stand in front of a preacher and say 'I do'."

"So what did you tell them?"

"Nothin'. They were talkin' to Pop."

"Smarty pants. If they'd been talki' to you, what would *you* say?"

She puckered her lips and tilted her head like she was giving the matter some deep thought. "Well…"

"You wouldn't play hard to get with a man flat on his back from bullet holes, with his vital parts bound up tighter'n a hat band, would you? Oh, that's the problem. You don't want to make a deal with a man who might turn out to be a dud at the unveilin'. Ain't that just like a woman. When she's got a man at a disadvantage, she plays hardball."

"Now that's the feisty Raz Jester I know. I'd say that's pretty bold talk for somebody who can't even get out of bed."

He gave her hand a gentle pull. "Am I gettin' Becky back or not?"

"That's a pretty poor excuse for a proposal, Chester Jester."

His jaw dropped. "I told you that if you ever called me by my real first name, I'd spank your butt. You're only sayin' it now 'cause you know I can't make good on that promise."

"Prob'ly. What's wrong with bein' called Chester?"

"It sounds dumb, Chester Jester. My daddy must've been out in the sun too long the day he named me. Oh, the bloody noses that name cost me in grammar school!"

"Sorry." She smiled.

He studied her a moment. "Gettin' hitched to me wouldn't be all that bad. Would it?"

"Depends."

"On what?"

"Don't pretend you don't remember how it's always been with you and pretty girls. They're drawn to you like bees to honeysuckle blooms — and you love it."

"Course, I do … did. If I didn't love pretty girls, why would I want to marry you?"

She rolled her eyes

"Okay, Okay," he said. "I'll work on a more romantic proposal. Just say you'll give the idea some serious thought. You already said you love me. Remember?"

"But I've never heard you say you love *me.*"

"Oh, well, ah, this love thing. What is it? If it's carin' more 'bout somebody else's welfare than my own, I think I'm leanin' in that direction. The way I feel about Becky, and the feelin' I get every time you come close, makes me feel good all over. Is that close enough to what you wanted to hear?"

She smiled. "You're crazy, cowboy."

"Yeah, about you and all the good things you can do for me — and that's no razzle-dazzle."

She squeezed his hand. "There might be hope for you yet."

"You sure make me happy. If you marry me, I could be a real daddy again. You'd sure make my bed a mighty fine place to lie down in, too. Can you still dance the Cotton Eyed Joe and stay in step to a good, slow waltz?"

She shrugged. "Don't know. Haven't tried with anyone since I did it with that quarterback, what's-his-name. The one that falls, gets shot at and nearly scares a girl half to death."

"You're kind of feisty all of a sudden. What do you say? Will you be my dance partner for the rest of our lives?"

"If you promise not to step on my toes and ignore all the invites from them other girls."

"It's a deal. Now lean down and plant one on me like you did back in high school."

She did, causing a stirring under his bandages. Beaming, he said, "Yee-ha! I feel some good times coming on, darlin'!"

~ The End ~